Acclaim for the novels of "romance writing superstar"* Jennifer Probst!

SEARCHING FOR PERFECT

"Entertaining and engaging and real. . . . [A] fantastic series."
—*Bookish Bella**

"Wonderfully moving, deeply emotional, steamy, sexy, fantastic!"

—*Sizzling Book Club*

SEARCHING FOR SOMEDAY

"Refreshing."

—*Publishers Weekly*

"Delightfully romantic and fun."

—*Under the Covers*

And the *New York Times* bestselling series
"destined to steal your heart" (Lori Wilde)—
the Marriage to a Billionaire novels!

THE MARRIAGE MERGER   THE MARRIAGE MISTAKE
THE MARRIAGE TRAP   THE MARRIAGE BARGAIN

"Nonstop sexual tension crackles off the page."
—Laura Kaye, *New York Times*
bestselling author of *One Night with a Hero*

"Witty, sweet, and sexy . . . very enjoyable."

—*Bookish Temptations*

ALSO BY JENNIFER PROBST

searching for beautiful

a novel

JENNIFER PROBST

Gallery Books
New York   London   Toronto   Sydney   New Delhi

G

Gallery Books
An Imprint of Simon & Schuster, Inc.
1230 Avenue of the Americas
New York, NY 10020

First Gallery Books trade paperback edition May 2015

GALLERY BOOKS and colophon are registered trademarks of Simon & Schuster, Inc.

For information about special discounts for bulk purchases, please contact Simon & Schuster Special Sales at 1-866-506-1949 or business@simonandschuster.com.

The Simon & Schuster Speakers Bureau can bring authors to your live event. For more information or to book an event, contact the Simon & Schuster Speakers Bureau at 1-866-248-3049 or visit our website at www.simonspeakers.com.

Manufactured in the United States of America

10 9 8 7 6 5 4 3 2 1

Library of Congress Cataloging-in-Publication Data

Probst, Jennifer.
Searching for beautiful / Jennifer Probst.
    pages ; cm. — (Searching for ; 3)
    1. Marriage—Fiction. 2. Mate selection—Fiction. 3. Man-woman relationships—Fiction. I. Title.
    PS3616.R624S415 2015
    813'.6—dc23
                2014037084

ISBN 978-1-4767-8009-2
ISBN 978-1-4767-8014-6 (ebook)

"The world breaks everyone, and afterward,
some are strong at the broken places."
—Ernest Hemingway

"Since love grows within you, so beauty grows.
For love is the beauty of the soul."
—Saint Augustine

This book is dedicated to all my writing friends I
have met along the way and are too many to name.
Thanks for inspiring me with your words, making
me laugh, giving me support, and reminding me
I'm not clinically insane. I'm just a writer.

And for all my readers who have felt broken but
keep moving forward. For all the ones who are
searching for something beautiful in the world.
You already have it within.

one

SHE HAD TO get out of here.

Genevieve MacKenzie bent at the waist and tried to gulp in air. The filmy, delicate veil brushed her face like a dozen fingers bent on tickle torture. Panic clawed at her gut, and she reached up and ripped off the pearl-encrusted lace, placed her hands on her knees, and prayed for sanity.

She was getting married. Right now. In five minutes. Her family stood outside the door, excited and chattering as they waited for her to emerge in all her pristine white glory. David posed at the front of the church in his tux, with the priest and his best man flanking his side. She imagined his beautifully tousled golden hair, killer smile, and sparkling green eyes. Perfect, as usual. While she was getting dressed, a delivery had arrived at the house. Two dozen white roses with just the faintest tinge of pink in the centers. The card read: *I cannot wait until you are finally mine.*

Her bridal party sighed with pleasure. Her twin sister, Isabella, rolled her eyes and clutched her neck in mockery of gagging to death. She'd been quietly shushed by the others while everyone held their breath, hoping she'd remain manageable until at least after the ceremony. It had been a rocky road between the sisters, so that Izzy even bothering to don a bridesmaid dress was a miracle. Gen's best friend,

Kate, hurriedly put the roses in water until they stood straight and proud in the center of the dining room table amid a group of giggling, excited women. Her sister Alexa teased her husband about not receiving a thing on her big day, which brought on a tirade of groaning from Nick and her dad whining about how reality television had given women false expectations of real romance.

Gen kept smiling, murmured the correct responses, and held the card in a death grip. Then she ran to the bathroom, trying desperately not to vomit.

Not the best reaction for a bride-to-be. Of course, she chalked it up to nerves, ignored her nausea, and got her ass into the stretch limo. She nodded and responded to her chattering bridal party. As the limousine gobbled up the miles and sped toward the church, her brain clicked over the final details, worrying if she missed anything. David hated sloppiness of any sort, and with almost three hundred guests, it was an important enough event to guarantee press and some high-society attendees. She'd wanted a wedding planner, but David insisted on keeping it private and personal. Of course she agreed; it would be nice to say they did it all themselves instead of relying on a stranger. Exhaustion beat into her bones, but Gen pushed it back. Yes, she'd done absolutely everything, triple-checking each detail for the past few days nonstop.

From the apricot bridesmaid dresses in silk so light the fabric shimmered, to the exquisite ribbon-wrapped orchids, the bridal party was breathtaking. The venue had been almost impossible to secure without the right contacts on just a year's notice. The castle in Tarrytown boasted stunning gardens, soaring architecture with vaulted ceilings, a banquet hall to rival Buckingham Palace, and French cuisine. Sure, she would've rather been married at Mohonk Mountain House near her parents in a more relaxed, fun atmosphere, but at least David agreed to the church ceremony. And she'd won the argument insisting Izzy stay in the wedding. David may not approve of her, but Gen stood her ground, and now her entire family was by her side.

The limo pulled in. She ducked her head against the flash of photographers, and Kate helped her with the massive pearl-encrusted train spilling onto the sidewalk. The Vera Wang gown was ridiculously pricey and reminded her of someone else, but it was the stuff princesses and brides were made of. Lace, tulle, diamonds, and pearls. Too bad she couldn't breathe.

She kept it together in the back room of the church while her mother cried, straightened her veil, and told her she'd never been more proud. Alexa beamed with joy, and her beautiful niece, Lily, looked like a fairy princess with her basket of petals and mini ballroom dress to match the bride's. Her other niece, Taylor, glowed in her junior bridal dress, a delicate pale pink exactly like the center of the roses. Gina, her sister-in-law, winked and announced the bride needed a moment alone before walking down the aisle. Gen almost sagged with relief, and finally the door shut. Blessed silence filled the room.

Everything was perfect, just like it should be.

Perfect. Like David always wanted it.

Gen panted and tried to get herself together. The murmur of voices and organ music drifted from the door. She stumbled to the gorgeously painted stained-glass window of Madonna and child and yanked on the knob. Stuck. Dizziness threatened. Crapola, she needed air, right now. Her French-manicured fingers wrapped around the old-fashioned handle and pulled frantically. Light exploded off the pristine diamond weighing down her knuckle. Finally, a few inches opened up and she bent her head toward the gap, sucking in hot air. Why, oh why did she have to wait until now to completely freak out? Maybe all the wedding stress had finally gotten to her. She'd open the door, walk down the aisle with her head held high, and say her vows. She loved David. Who wouldn't? He treated her like a queen, told her every day how much she meant to him, and pushed her to be better. Always better. They'd be the envied power couple of their time—surgeons who saved lives, attended charity functions, and changed the world. They were madly in love.

I can't wait until you are finally mine.

A shiver crept down her spine. She looked down at the flawless three-carat diamond ring that shimmered around her finger. A symbol of ownership. Once she committed herself, it would truly be forever. He'd never let her go.

Run.

The inner voice that had been squashed for so long in fear of retaliation rose up from her gut and screamed one last word. Gen clutched at the windowsill. Ridiculous. She couldn't run.

Right? People only did that in the movies. Besides, she couldn't do that to David.

Run.

The past two years with David had taught her to sift through her rioting emotions and connect with the core of rationality that hid in every person's center. Her fiancé despised messiness, impulse, and decisions based on emotion. He cited death and destruction time and again, until she'd finally managed to quiet that crazy voice that had once sung in freedom, slightly off-key but always joyous. Gen figured she'd beaten it back so hard, in fear and determination, that she'd never hear from it again. But of course, with her lousy luck, it had taken this moment of all moments to reassert its independence and general brattiness.

Run before it's too late.

Her brain spun in a mad rush. Not much time left. Once her family came in, it was over. They'd calm her down, term it bridal jitters, and escort her down the aisle. She'd marry David. And she'd never be the same again.

Which would be good, right? She wanted marriage. Forever. Commitment. With David.

Gen looked behind at the closed door. The action she took in the next few seconds would set her on a course that would change the rest of her life. She didn't have time to go over the checks and balances, advantages and disadvantages, and make a neat statistical chart. Instead, she dug deep into her gut that had served her well when faced with a child bleeding on her table: life-and-death decisions that even David couldn't make her stop because it made up the center of her soul. A future surgeon. A woman. A survivor.

Run.

Gen didn't waste another moment.

Breathing hard, heart pounding, she shoved the crank

around and around until it wouldn't budge another inch. The window gaped halfway open. The judging eyes of baby Jesus beamed down at her. She could do this. For the first time it paid to be Hobbit size. Gen stuck her upper body through the window, leaned forward, and wriggled her way to freedom.

two

WOLFE LIT UP the cigarette and looked around guiltily. Damn, this one vice killed him every time. Sawyer would get pissed, and Julietta would do that disappointed stare thing she nailed so well. But they were still in Italy, miles away, and would never know. They might not be his legal stepparents, but they'd saved him, given him a new life, and he loved them like they were his own blood. Just one cigarette and he'd throw away the rest of the pack.

The smoke hit his lungs and immediately calmed his nerves. No one would catch him anyway; the ceremony was about to start. He should be up front and center with the rest of Gen's family, with a big grin on his face as he watched his best friend commit herself to an asshole. And he would. In a few minutes. Right now, he wanted a beat of silence and a smoke before he had to fake his way through the rest of the evening and pretend he was ecstatic.

Guilt nipped at him. He was such a jerk. After all, David Riscetti was perfect for Gen, and just about worthy enough to marry her. Wasn't the guy's fault Wolfe couldn't get rid of that nagging instinct something was off. Wolfe used to catch him looking at Gen with such possessive pride, like he was appraising a racehorse rather than a capable, independent woman. And the way he ordered her around pissed him off, too. But Gen never said she didn't like it, and only had nice things to say about him. Hell, she loved him enough to get hitched, so who was he to judge? Wolfe knew nothing about relationships.

If he delved deep and played therapist, he was probably irritated Gen had replaced him. For almost five years, they'd hung out together at bars, watched movies, and did general best-friend stuff. There wasn't a woman in the world who didn't want money, favors, or sex from him. Except Gen. Hell, the moment they'd met something clicked between them. She was as genuine and real as Julietta and the rest of the women in his adopted family. They had just liked each other from the get-go, and when the hell does that ever happen?

Of course, David frowned upon their relationship from day one, and over the past year, Gen made more excuses not to see him in order to soothe her fiancé.

Whatever. He needed to get over it.

Wolfe held back a whiny sigh. The church bells rang once. Twice. The limos were parked at the curb, and a few reporters lingered on the steps. Guess the surgeon was a big shot in the news, because no one else pulled in such a crowd. He moved backward a few feet, not in the mood to meet and greet any latecomers. The crooked pavement and shaded archways shielded him from any prying observers. He enjoyed the last of his cigarette, pulled at the confines of his tuxedo, and tried not to scrape the polished sole of his dress shoes. Even after working in the corporate and modeling worlds, he always craved his workout clothes and still felt like he was an intruder in his own body in suits. Or designer underwear that cost more than someone's yearly salary. Who would've thought? Scrambling for food and shelter one day. At the top of *Fortune*'s up-and-coming millionaires the next, all at twenty-fucking-six years old.

He beat back the nasty thoughts that threatened to swamp him and got his head back in the game. It was Gen's wedding day and he needed to be there for her. Not smoking like a chump and playing self-pity games. Wolfe crushed the butt under his heel, adjusted his cuffs, and turned.

"Holy shit."

He stared in shock at the sight before him.

The bride lay in a tangle of limbs, sprawled out on the pavement. The white cloud of lace and dozens of pearly jewels floated around her in a swarm of glory. His heart stopped, stuttered, and kicked back into gear. Jesus, she was gorgeous. Gen had always been an attractive female by all standards, but now she looked as delicate as a doll perched on a wedding cake. She must've ripped off her veil because her elaborate twist hairdo lay drunkenly to the side with pins sticking out. The humidity kicked her curls into gear, and already they were springing wild, refusing to be tamed. Snapping blue eyes glared at him, framed in black liner and some sparkly shadow. She never wore makeup. But today, those stunning navy eyes dominated her heart-shaped face with a sultry, sexy air he rarely spotted in her. Four-inch diamond-encrusted stiletto heels stuck out from her balloon hoop gown. Wolfe caught the flash of white lace garters and curved, muscled legs before she flipped the skirt back down and huffed out a breath. "Are you smoking on my damn wedding day? You told me you quit. Julietta's going to kill you."

He fought past his lack of speech and wondered if this was a hallucination. "Not if you don't tell her."

She sniffed. "You wish. I don't want you to die of lung cancer. Don't just stand there gaping. Help me up, I can barely move in this thing."

And then she was just Gen again. His best friend, a general pain in the ass, and the most precious person in the world to him.

Wolfe moved fast and pulled her up. "Are you okay? Did you fall out the window?"

She rebalanced herself on those ridiculous heels and waved her hand in the air. "Yeah, I'm fine. My hips got stuck but I managed."

She dusted off her pristine white dress as if jumping out of church windows were a normal occurrence. Damn, she was a hell of a woman. "Umm, babe? Are you pulling a runaway-bride thing? Or did you just want to confirm the fire exit worked?"

Her ballsy humor faded from her face. She tilted her chin up, and her lower lip trembled. "I'm in trouble. Will you help me?"

He kept his face calm even though his palms sweat. Something bad had happened, but right now she needed his head in the game. "We ditching the groom?"

"Yeah."

Wolfe decided to play it like a big adventure. "Cool. I got you covered. Lose the shoes."

She kicked off the killer stilettos. "Are there reporters out there?"

"No worries, this is a piece of cake. But we gotta move now. Take my hand."

She placed her small hand in his and squeezed. Wolfe swore that even if he had to fight the whole Taliban, he was getting her out of here and to someplace safe. Discussion was for later. "My car is parked down the street, so we're good. Follow me."

He led her down the back steps, behind the rectory, and maneuvered through a perfectly formed line of flowering bushes. She paused in flight, wincing at the chips of mulch and gravel. "Ouch."

"You're such a girl. Here, you're going too slow." Wolfe heaved her up into his arms in a tumble of satin and lace and cut through some weeping willow trees.

"I can't believe you parked so far away. That means you were late. Some best friend you are."

"Be glad I was late. I'm saving your ass now."

She gave a humph. He walked faster, sensing chaos and a complete breakdown not too far behind. If he didn't get her out in time and anyone caught them leaving, it would be a virtual shitstorm. He ducked under a low-hanging branch, tracked through the backyard of a Cape Cod behind the church, and took a hard right. She stayed silent, and Wolfe bet he had two minutes before her crazy impulsive decision hit her and she said she'd go back.

But if something made her run, it was too important to ignore. The hell he'd take her back.

Finally, he spotted his black Mercedes convertible. He fished the keys out of his pocket, hit the alarm, and opened the door. "In."

Another lower lip tremble. "Wolfe, maybe I'm wrong. Maybe I should go back."

"Do you want to marry him, Gen? Deep down, in your gut, where it counts?"

Her teeth sank into her lower lip. Shame and fear and humiliation etched out the lines of her face. Her voice broke on the word "No."

He nodded and calmly pushed her in the seat. "Then you're doing the right thing and we'll work it out. I promise."

She swallowed. Returned his nod. And slid into the car.

Wolfe wasted no time. He revved the engine and did a three-point turn, going out the back way and speeding away from the church like it was a devil's sanctuary and their souls were at risk.

When they hit the open road and no one seemed to be following, he glanced over. She slumped in the seat, her hair hanging halfway down her neck, her graceful profile carved in stone. She stared out the window as if she was watching her life dissipate behind her. And in a way, it was.

Knowing what she needed the most right now, Wolfe hit the speaker system and Guns N' Roses blasted out, hard and loud and raw. He didn't speak.

Just drove.

three

WOLFE PULLED THE car into the Walmart parking lot and cut the engine. The probe of his gaze touched her face, but she was too weary to smile. After all, she never had to hide her real feelings with him. And right now she was about to go full-fledged mental if she didn't get out of her wedding gown.

"Stay here. I'll be right back. Want a soda? Water?"

Gen nodded. "Water would be good."

"Keep the doors locked. The windows are tinted, so no one should see you."

She blinked, trying to focus on the charred embers that now composed her life. "I left my phone. I have to tell them I'm safe."

"We will. Just hang tight for a minute. Okay?"

She nodded again and watched him walk into Walmart. He got a bunch of stares from the teenyboppers milling around in the lot. Wolfe always got stares, but in a tuxedo he was lethal. With that tall, muscled body and wicked tattoo, he had *bad boy wanting to be tamed* stamped all over him. So different from David, with his angelic good looks and smooth charm.

David.

The full horror of what she'd done slammed through

her. She'd run away and left him at the altar. The man she claimed to love. Her boss and chief of the surgical unit where her entire career was carved out. All of her stuff had been moved into his apartment. They held tickets for a Bermuda honeymoon. Her parents were probably sobbing, humiliated, and angry with her. Izzy was the one who brought stress—not her. Gen was the good one. The smart one. The one who never, ever caused any trouble.

What was she going to do? How could she go back to her life?

Thoughts and images swarmed in her head like pissy bees getting ready to attack. She pressed her fingers to her temples and wondered if she'd die by brain explosion.

The door opened. Wolfe thrust two plastic bags at her and a bottle of Poland Spring. "Here. First drink this. You look like you're doing the freak-out thing."

She swallowed a few sips of water. Then looked up at him for his next instructions. He gave a gentle smile and knelt down beside the car. Not speaking, he sifted through the tangled chestnut curls of her hair, and worked out each of the pins. Then he rubbed her scalp, pulling his fingers through the strands until they slid freely of knots. Gen studied his familiar features while he took care of her. Strong square jaw. Facial hair clinging to his upper lip and chin in a sexy goatee. Stinging blue eyes that burned like a laser, cutting through people's bullshit and social veneers with no apology. His head was usually shaved clean, but he'd been growing it in, so dark curls softened his face just a bit. The serpent ink crept up his neck as if choking him.

She was always fascinated by the tattoo. Traced in simple black, the impressive snake started low on his chest, worked its way up his arms and one shoulder, and ended right under his ear. Almost as if the creature was consistently whispering something to him. He was a gym rat, so the muscles under his clothes were hard and unforgiving, from his eight-pack stomach to the meaty biceps. Her gaze traveled to his wrists, where the matching leather bands were revealed by his rolled-up shirtsleeves. She'd never spotted him without them. He'd made the accessories famous by his underwear ads. Many young men followed his example until the wristbands became the hottest new trend.

Funny, from the moment they met, they'd been fated to be friends. Their heart-to-heart conversation set the stage for the future, with none of that crappy sexual tension or flirting. Just a good buddy of the opposite sex who meant the world to her. Kate was her best friend feminine equal, and Wolfe her male.

He reached behind her and pulled open the row of pearl-encrusted buttons down the back. He pointed to the bags. "Put these clothes on."

She took out the denim shorts, T-shirt, and flip-flops. "I look terrible in orange."

His lip quirked. "Not much choice on the bargain table. The rest were extra large."

"Sorry. Being a runaway bride makes me a bit bitchy." Gen transferred to the backseat and tugged off the dress. Sweet, pure air filled her lungs once the tight fabric slid off, and she quickly divested her garters and stockings, scrambling into the comfy clothes and pulling off the price tags.

She dug out a small package of hair bands from the bag and quickly scooped the strands into a short ponytail. Then got out.

Wolfe nodded. "Good. Got us some snacks for the road, so dig in when you want."

Gen peered into the other plastic bag at the contents of a true road trip. Candy bars, Doritos, and a few Slim Jims. "Are those Sno Balls? I didn't think they made them anymore."

"Yeah, me neither. I got lucky."

"Where are we going?"

"Gonna stay at Sawyer's cabin on the lake for a few days. Just until things die down and you get your head together."

Panic reared back up and nipped at her nerves. "I have to call my family."

"Already done. I texted Alexa and Kate. Those were the two you wanted to contact, right?"

She slid her arms around her chest and squeezed, rocking back on her heels. "Yes. What did you tell them?"

"That you were sorry you ran out but you couldn't marry David. That you needed to get yourself together and would be in touch. That you were okay and not to contact you for a bit."

"What about the reception? Where are people going to go? What about the press?"

His voice held a rich command that vibrated with intensity. "Alexa and Kate are a power team together. They'll handle it. Right now, you need to let me take care of things."

Relief loosened her muscles. Yes. For a little while,

Wolfe would take care of things. She'd retreat, make some decisions, and clean up the mess she made. But not now. "Thank you."

"No problem. Let's go."

They got back into the car and drove. The Mercedes gobbled up the miles as they worked their way from Verily, in upstate New York, hit the thruway, and headed north. The music was loud, the wind whipped at her hair, and the scenery whizzed by in a comforting blur. She nibbled at a Hershey's chocolate bar while Wolfe munched on chips and sipped his soda.

Gen closed her eyes and pretended she was off for a weekend getaway. Over the past year, each time she tried to see Wolfe, David gave her a hard time. The pressure and guilt became too much. Her fiancé reminded her how little time they spent together with their crazy work schedules, and her little forays with Wolfe were causing a break in their relationship.

Gen considered herself a strong woman. Gutsy. Opinionated. Yet when David turned his charm and dedication into getting his point across, it was like the South at Gettysburg all over again. Defeat. So, she'd begun making excuses. She hated lying, but David rewarded her by being extra sweet and considerate, telling her over and over how good they were together if only she tried hard. She forgot how nice it was not to worry about saying something stupid, or not being witty or sexy enough. With Wolfe, there was only a comfortable silence and no need to fill the void with intelligent conversation.

The trees grew thicker and the landscape more rural as

they turned off the exit and headed toward Saratoga Springs. They passed through the quaint town with its shops, neat landscaping, and sidewalks, reminding her of Verily, and kept going. Nine Inch Nails boomed from the stereo in direct contradiction to the woody hush as they veered off several side roads. The gravel spun beneath the tires, and wildly colored blooms dragged past the window, sticking out from a variety of brush and trees. Wolfe made a hard right and followed a path up a steep hill, winding in circles higher and higher until he cut the engine.

"This is it."

Gen sucked in her breath. The rustic log cabin held a character and warmth that immediately welcomed her home. Surrounded by brush, its wide porch held two rockers, the carved domes etched into the doorway as if a master wood-cutter had created it. Large windows flanked both sides, and cobbled stones led out toward a lush garden in the back, then shot off in different directions. One led to a fire pit, the other to a small gazebo. The sounds of birds, grasshoppers, and bees swarmed in the air and took over where the music had played. The air hung musky and thick in the summer afternoon heat, and her nostrils filled with the scent of earth and flowers.

Yes. It would be good here. She'd figure everything out and get her life back in order.

"It's beautiful," she said in a hushed tone. "Why doesn't Sawyer rent it out for the summer?"

"He usually does, but this month he kept it open. The cabin's set back for privacy but near Fish Creek. Said if I wanted to get out of town and do some fishing, take some downtime, I'd have it available."

"Who would've thought you'd need to hide a crazy runaway bride?"

He didn't smile. For the first time since their getaway, a worried light gleamed in his eyes. Words hovered on his tongue but she didn't want to hear it, couldn't, so she stumbled out of the car before denial could no longer be her best friend. He paused a few beats but finally followed.

Gen stepped into the cabin. Gorgeous light played upon the pine floors and soaring ceilings with thick beams of support. A stone fireplace took up one main wall with a deep red throw rug in front. She walked around, taking note of the elaborate fishing gear, wildlife photos, and the warm, rustic atmosphere. The kitchen was a chef's dream, all top-of-the-line stainless steel appliances, with double sinks and granite counters in a rich chocolate brown. "I never thought Sawyer was a big fisherman," she commented.

Wolfe snickered. "He's not. He dragged us out here last year, intent on showing Julietta the benefits of country life. Boasted he'd catch her a ton of fish and cook it up that night. Let's just say it's a good thing for pizza delivery."

Gen laughed. "Ouch. Well, he's a billionaire who runs a chain of hotels. Can't be good at everything."

"Tell him that. He's been watching those damn fishing shows on the Discovery Channel now, and thinks he'll redeem himself. Too bad Julietta refuses to come back. She's definitely a city girl."

Gen remembered meeting Julietta and Sawyer when they were in town. They lived in Milan, and had welcomed Wolfe into their family when he was nineteen and homeless. The couple represented everything she'd always wanted. They ran the most successful chain of bakeries and hotels in the world, fit perfectly together, and were madly in love. Exactly what she'd hoped to have with David.

She pushed the thought firmly away.

"Bedrooms are upstairs," Wolfe said. "I'll run into town and stock up on supplies and get you some clothes."

"How long are we going to stay?"

He studied her. Odd, he had such a hard face, all severe lines and carved features. His lips always held a bit of a snarl, as if he'd never outgrown that snarky teen boy he'd once been. But there was a wealth of gentleness underneath that always intrigued her. "When do you need to be back at the hospital?"

The reminder of her real life made her jerk. "A full week. We took a week for our honeymoon." The word made her slightly nauseous.

"Then we have time. We'll take it day by day. Do you want me to pick up anything specific you need?"

She shook her head. "No, I trust you."

The words dove deeper and he took a step forward. "Want to come with me?"

Gen forced a smile. "I'm going to rest. It's been a long day. I'll see you in a bit."

He frowned, and she almost laughed at his papa-bear expression. But then he gave a nod and headed back out the door. Her legs trembled with the sudden fear of being alone. Pathetic. She couldn't remember the last time she had no one surrounding her, or a task to complete, or a deadline to meet. For the past year, the hamster wheel was the only thing that made sense. Even sleep was never for more than a few hours, and always interrupted by dreams of endless lists and tasks. Her mind was no longer her own. Neither was her soul.

She walked down the hallway and into the bathroom. Turned on the light. And stared into the mirror.

The woman who gazed back was hardly recognizable. Brown hair scraped back in a ponytail. Makeup smudged. Shadows etched under her eyes. Full lips, high cheekbones. She'd lost more weight, so the bright orange T-shirt hung a bit loose over her shoulders.

Gen looked harder. Her usual vivid blue eyes were . . . empty. The spark had disappeared, and only a dull light reflected back at her. When had that happened? She'd always been driven but basically happy. Sure, she took on too much responsibility, but the world seemed a big, interesting place and she wanted to fill voids. Maybe egotistical, but surgeons were supposed to have a bit of a God complex. She ached to help, give back, and heal. She craved knowledge and experiences and wonder. But over the past year, all she experienced was crippling fear. The knowledge she wasn't enough for anyone. Not for the world. Not for David. Not even for herself.

Gen turned away from the mirror.

WOLFE DROVE FAST, INTENT on getting back to the cabin quickly. He struggled with leaving her alone, but realized she needed to process. They'd been on the run most of the day, and he bet she was pretending the whole event never happened. Because when the truth struck home, it was going to get messy.

Emotion tore through his chest. Damn, he'd never seen

her like that. When he asked her straight-out if she wanted to marry David, pure fear skittered across her face. What had the asshole done to her? The fallout was going to be epic. Besides her close-knit family loving her fiancé, she had just screwed her career, since he was her boss. Gen disliked bucking the system, especially her family. But Wolfe would get her through it. One lesson always sank home—nothing mattered except protecting your soul. God knows he'd lived through that himself. He'd walked away from everything and dove into the pitfalls of hell. And it was still worth it.

The painful simmers of the past tried to push past his consciousness, but he locked it back down. He needed to focus on Gen and giving her what she needed. Wolfe ripped through his errands, buying a couple of changes of clothes, underwear, a bathing suit, a case of water, and some basic groceries. There wasn't much selection, but the small town was perfect for hiding out for a few days. Most people came here for the recreational activities, to hit the famous racetrack at Saratoga, or to see the Baseball Hall of Fame in nearby Cooperstown.

He threw the bags into the car and reached into his pocket for his phone. Yep, it was bad. Voice mails poured in, from Alexa, Kate, Izzy, and Gen's mom. He pondered the idea of letting Gen know. No, she wasn't up for the consequences yet. Leaving your groom at the altar ended up with a mass of details. He'd buy her time.

Wolfe shot through the variety of messages and quickly dispersed news that gave away nothing. Alexa jumped to support her sister, and he knew he could count on her for calming down the family. Nothing from David yet. What was really going on behind the scenes with them? Was he hurting Gen? Why would she look so afraid of the man she was about to marry? Or was she just scared of hurting him?

He scrolled to the next message and shook his head. Kate was the worst. As Gen's best friend, she was hardcore when it came to protection. He smothered a laugh at the blinking words.

> If u don't tell me where ur hiding her ur ass is grass. She needs me.

Wolfe tapped out his response:

> She needs time, then my ass is all urs. Give her a day. I'm taking care of her.

The phone shrieked. Ah, crap. He stared at it for a while, but best friends were scary. He figured Kate would find a way to GPS them by the middle of the night, so he hit the button. "How is she? I'm coming to get her."

He kept his tone polite but firm. "Not yet. You gotta give me some time. She just ran away from her wedding and needs to get her head on straight. I'm asking you for help, Kate. Help me buy her some space."

A furious silence hummed over the line. "What's really going on? I had no idea she'd pull something like this. I mean, I've been worried about her, and knew she was stressed, but this is not Gen. Has she told you why?"

"No. But I'll find out. Is it bad there?"

A snort filled his ears. "You have no idea. It's chaos and

I'm trying to keep everyone sane. David seems heartbroken and locked himself in the room with Gen's dad and his best man. The press smelled blood and stormed the church. Gen's mom thought she was kidnapped, insisting she'd never run. How the hell did she end up with you?"

Wolfe dragged in a breath. "She escaped through the window and I was there. Listen, Kate, there's something bigger going on, much more than some bridal jitters. I think she's afraid of the son of a bitch."

"What? Oh my God, has he hit her or something?"

"Don't know. Just give me a few days to get the story and get her back on her feet. Please."

He waited her out. He knew Kate was stubborn, loyal, and loved Gen like her own sister. She was also extremely intuitive. "Okay. Keep texting me updates. I'll talk with her family and let them know she's lying low and will explain everything later. And I'll keep an eye on David. Maybe I'll figure out the real issue."

"Thanks.

He stuck his phone back into his pocket and got into the car. Something didn't add up, but he'd find out. Meanwhile, he'd stick close to Gen for the next few days. Purity—the hotel chain he helped run with Sawyer—was doing well, so he'd put in a call to one of his assistants to keep him informed. He couldn't remember the last time he took a day off, let alone a whole weekend. This would be good for both of them. A little fresh air, recharge the batteries, and get back into the real world.

Wolfe headed back to the cabin.

four

GENEVIEVE LOOKED UP as the car pulled into the driveway. A ghostly fog floated around her, almost as if she was stuck halfway on Earth and the other at a higher plane. She hoped much higher, since Catholic guilt from her mother was steeped in her soul. She didn't mind the numbness though. Much better than the panic attack dancing on the edge of her sanity.

No more mirrors. Keep busy. Don't think.

The three new rules of survival.

She jumped up from the porch and helped him haul in the bags. "You okay?" His sharp gaze traveled over every part of her, as if in the hour he'd left her alone she'd grown a few inches. Past her five-foot Hobbit status. He gently pushed her out of the way and scooped up the rest of the bags, allowing her to carry only the bread.

"Fine. You know I can lift a three-hundred-pound patient, right?"

"In that case, take this." He gave her a bag of eggs. "Wouldn't want you to get out of shape."

Their familiar banter soothed her nerves as she followed him inside and set the bags on the counter. "Do you want me to make dinner?" she asked.

He lifted a brow. "You hungry?"

Between the candy diet and her nerves, she doubted any morsel of food would stay down. "No. But I'll make you something."

He chuckled and wrestled out two six-packs of Sam Adams Summer Ale from the bag. "How about we get drunk instead?"

She followed impulse and threw herself into his arms for a hug. David would've insisted on taking care of her health, frowning over alcohol intake, and watching exactly what she ate. She missed having no rules again. She missed Wolfe.

Hard muscle and sheer power closed around her. Her head hit his chest halfway, but his arms held her with a tenderness that made an odd longing clutch at her throat. Treasured, yet not owned. Why had she never noticed the difference? The scent of cotton and soap filled her nostrils, clean and pure. She breathed in to savor the moment, then stepped away.

"Hey." He tugged at her hair. "If I knew you'd be this nice to me, I'd offer you alcohol all the time."

She snorted. "I'm always nice to you."

Wolfe uncapped the bottle and handed it over. The icy brew slid down her throat and warmed her belly. The subtle taste of lemon danced on her tongue.

"Not. You have a sick sense of humor. You enjoy torturing me. What about the time you set me up with your friend Molly?"

A giggle threatened but she tamped it down at his accusing expression. "I was trying to find you a nice girl."

"I guess a dominatrix is considered nice in today's society, huh? She brought her whip. And some scary-ass equipment that made me skip dessert. And I never skip dessert."

Gen bit her tongue and tried for seriousness. "I didn't know it was that bad, I swear. She's a nurse in the NIC unit and complained she couldn't meet a cool guy. She said she enjoyed a bit of kink, not hard-core dungeon stuff."

He blew out a breath, grabbed a beer, and ripped open a bag of pretzels. "Do I look like the submissive type? Or one who'd get off on being tied to a bed with a wrench at my balls? Not fun, Gen."

She took another sip. "You told me you liked edgy sex. I was only trying to help."

"Edgy, not death defying. How would you feel if I hooked you up with some guy who ordered you to drop to your knees and serve?"

The memory hit hard and fast. Another argument. David complaining she didn't put his needs first and had gotten lazy in the bedroom. So he grabbed her hair. Forced her to her knees. Unzipped his pants. And waited.

She'd heard those games were fun and spiced things up. But she'd only felt sick and used. The way he assessed her skill, berating her for not getting it right, until afterward she turned away, trying not to gag as he finally praised her, stroking her head like some prized animal who'd finally gotten a command right. Telling her over and over how he loved her, adored her, and wanted them to be perfect.

Gen turned quickly, shutting her eyes and forcing away the image. No, not now. Had it been that bad? Why hadn't she told him to fuck off and thrown him out of the house? What was wrong with her?

"Gen?"

She shuddered and lightened her tone. "Sorry, as Dug from *Up* would say, 'Squirrel.' Lost my train of thought. Seems to be my new motto lately."

He studied her in silence, then nodded. "I prefer my own motto from *Finding Nemo*."

"What's that?"

His gaze burned into hers with a deeper meaning evident. "Just keep swimming."

Her muscles loosened and she managed a smile. "That's Lily's favorite movie."

"Mine, too. Second is *Avengers*."

She wrinkled her nose. "No way. I always thought you liked the mob movies. You never seemed like a superhero sort of guy."

Massive shoulders lifted. "Nothing wrong with hoping for the good guys to kick a little ass." Something drifted across his face, a light of memory she craved to ask him about, but too soon it disappeared. "Have some pretzels, they'll settle your stomach. I'm gonna get changed real fast. Be right back."

She nibbled on a few and sat in the living room to wait. The gentle whir of the island-type ceiling fan soothed her nerves. She settled on one of the plump couch cushions with her beer. He returned dressed in a simple navy blue bathing suit, T-shirt, and sandals, then took a seat on the opposite chair. The scene reminded her of a casual get-together between good friends. Unfortunately, it was much more. Her fingers tightened on the neck of the bottle. "Did you talk to my family?"

He assessed her under heavily lidded eyes but his tone was casual. "Spoke with Kate. Told her we were going to lie low for a few days. She's going to take care of things on that end until you're ready."

"Has David contacted you?"

"Not yet."

She pondered his answer for a while and chewed on her lip. Still raw, her insides twisted from fear and confusion, as if she'd stepped into Oz and didn't know how to figure things out yet. "You haven't asked why."

"Don't need to."

Gen studied him, trying to dig beneath his calm surface. He must be dying of curiosity, but he'd never questioned her once. "Don't you want to know?"

He surprised her with a half grin. "Hell, yes. You're my best friend and I had no idea you were struggling. But you're not ready. When you want to talk, I'll be here. For now, you need some alcohol and a distraction. Come on, let's get out of here."

He grabbed her hand and pulled her up. "Where? We can't get in a car drinking."

"There's a trail in the back of the cabin that leads to a lake." He scooped up the beers and two towels, and headed out the door. The sun stung her skin, but as they made their way back into the cluster of trees, shadows cloaked them from the burn. The musky scent of earth and rotted wood drifted to her nostrils, and she picked her way over the moss and rocks in her flip-flops until the path opened up.

They walked in silence. The birds sang, the trees watched, and the bugs hovered, occasionally landing for a quick bite. Wood snapped under her feet and a strange lightness flooded her body. How could she feel like this when a few hours ago she was in the church, about to marry David? Why did this moment strike her as more real than the past six months? She needed to figure it out, because the answer was the reason she'd run.

Unfortunately, the truth seemed more dangerous than denial right now.

"Here it is."

The lake was more of a pool that looked as if it emptied at the end of its journey, with a crooked dock that seemed about to fall apart and tall marsh grass surrounding it. Gen stared at it and wondered if the monster alligators would get her like in *Lake Placid* if she put a toe in. She put her hands on her hips. "You want to try to kill me or something? You couldn't pay me to go in there."

He snorted. "Chicken. It's safe. I caught Sawyer and Julietta out here skinny-dipping. I felt blind for a week."

She laughed. "I remember catching Nick and Alexa fooling around in my parents' walk-in closet one visit. I couldn't even look at them, let alone eat Sunday dinner. Ruined my appetite."

Wolfe dropped the beer, kicked off his sandals, and walked onto the crumbling dock. "Saratoga Lake is about eight miles long, but narrows down to Fish Creek. We're at the tail end. Sawyer wanted privacy more than recreation. This is an isolated paradise and you're complaining. Much better than a fancy chlorinated pool."

"Speak for yourself, dude," Gen said.

Wolfe peeled off his T-shirt and revealed perfectly defined pecs and abs of steel. The elaborate serpent tattoo curled like smoke and started at the right side of his belly, moved up his chest, wrapped around the upper arm, and landed just below the ear. She rarely saw him unclothed, unless it was in some designer advertisement, but the breadth and detail of the tat was a living, breathing thing. He kept his wristbands on. Gen knew he never took them off. Ever. She bet he even showered and slept with them, too. At first she'd thought it was some weird fashion thing, but over the years, Gen became used to them, as if they were part of his body. And she still didn't ask questions.

She remembered the first time she met him, when she was twenty years old. A family dinner at Alexa's. Max and Michael—husbands of Alexa's closest friends, Carina and Maggie—had brought Wolfe and introduced him to everyone.

She'd been instantly fascinated. From his ink, to his shaven head, various piercings, and massive muscles, his entire aura sucked out the air in the room and left it silent. He appeared obviously uncomfortable, his mouth turned down in a gorgeous sneer, as if ready to give everyone a big fuck you. But he remained politely still, scanning the crowd, until their gazes met and locked.

A weird connection fired between them. As if they'd met before. Recognized each other. And were being reintroduced.

She had no idea why. Izzy had been the hell-raiser and scoped him out like a hungry she-wolf. Her father frowned and seemed ready for battle. Alexa chattered nonstop and tried to ease the tension, while Maggie,

Alexa's best friend and honorary aunt, spoke proudly of his modeling career and smarts.

Gen walked over, offered her hand, and a smile. "Welcome to the family, Wolfe. I'm Gen."

He paused. For one long, endless second, she wondered if he'd diss her. Instead, his hand clasped hers, warm and strong and safe. "Nice to meet you."

All Gen knew about him was that he'd once been homeless, then lived in Milan with Sawyer and Julietta, and now stayed in New York with Max and Carina. He was also attending NYU for business. Since they were both attending the same college, he'd been seated next to her at dinner.

They fell into an easy camaraderie. Somehow, she understood he held secrets so deep and dark they may never come to light. She didn't care. She sensed on a gut-level instinct he had more honor than most men his age.

After dinner, they'd found themselves alone, talking outside. She'd asked a bunch of questions, wanting to get to know him, but he only gave one-word answers. Tension tightened his frame, and she realized he grew more and more distant. Fragments of the conversation drifted past her memory.

"DON'T YOU LIKE TO talk about yourself?" she asked curiously. This man, who her twin sister pronounced extremely fuckable, seemed so much more than his shaved head, tats, and leather wristbands. Secrets danced in his eyes. She also sensed they were painful. Another reason he didn't like to talk?

"No," he answered. "I don't talk about the past. Just today."

His answer fascinated her. A deep connection flowed between them, as if they'd met in another life and time and were just now picking up where they left off. "So I won't ask you any other questions. We'll just be friends."

The need and suspicion mingled in those gorgeous blue eyes. "Friends? I bet one day you'll ask me stuff. Get mad at me for not sharing. Girls do that."

She smiled. She wasn't like most girls. "Pinky promise, then. We won't discuss either of our pasts unless you want to. No questions." She liked the idea of having a clean slate with this man. Someone who didn't judge her on previous actions or performance, but accepted her for the woman she was at the moment.

He crinkled his brow. "Pinky promise?"

She sighed with impatience. "You know a better way? A swear is a swear."

He reached his hand out tentatively. Their pinkies twisted and locked. Pure energy rushed between them, but it was like a nice, heady buzz that made her feel good in her tummy. "Pinky swear," he said gruffly.

"Pinky swear," she repeated.

And then the best part of all happened. For the first time since they'd met, he smiled at her. Her heart lifted and filled up, and Gen knew she'd be happy around that smile all the time. Finally, she had a guy to tell her secrets to and with whom she could be safe, laugh, and just enjoy the moment.

YEARS LATER, IZZY STILL drove her crazy questioning why she wouldn't fuck him. Even Kate, Kennedy, and Arilyn—

her closest girlfriends—wondered aloud why they'd never hooked up. Gen noticed the general attraction, but she was able to glimpse the big picture. Wolfe couldn't hold on to a relationship. He loved sex and teased her with details of his greatest escapades while she groaned and covered her face, screaming "TMI!" But it was just about the physical. When it came to emotional commitment, he checked out, and Gen realized what they had was so much deeper and more meaningful than a quickie affair.

She studied him in his navy blue board shorts and wondered why their relationship was so easy, even from the start. Maybe because she let him be who he wanted and lifted the threat of painstaking questions. They were able to accept each other on their own terms. Maybe because she allowed him to show her who he was now without expectations of who he had been. And she bet it had been very, very bad.

He poised on the end of the deck in full masculine glory and cocked a brow. Her tummy tumbled, then steadied. She was used to it and never analyzed the sensation. He was an attractive male and she'd have to be dead not to have a physical reaction. The occasional attraction was easily dealt with when she thought of losing their friendship. "Coming in?"

"No."

"Thought you grew up in the country. Come on, Gen. I hate when you act like a girl."

She stuck out her tongue and snagged another beer. Then she plopped her butt onto a fat rock and stretched her legs out. "I am a girl, you idiot. There are bugs and fish and things in there. No way."

"You disappoint me."

He got ready to dive and her inner devil ignited to life after months of being on vacation. "Better watch the spider crawling up your leg."

"What!" He hopped from foot to foot in a clumsy dance, reaching down and swiping his legs in a parody of comedy. Then he toppled into the water.

She laughed so hard she thought she'd crack a rib, especially when he surfaced and spit water out of his mouth. "Oh, that was priceless," she gasped out. His fear of spiders always charmed her. He was big and bad and avoided nothing, except the eight-legged crawly creatures. Reminded her of Indiana Jones and snakes. "I'm sorry, I couldn't help it."

His gaze narrowed. "You know payback is a bitch, right?"

Gen gulped for air. "I left my groom at the altar. Surely that will be enough for the day?"

He grunted. "Maybe. Maybe not." He dove under in one smooth move and did a few laps. She sat back and took pleasure in the view without guilt. Lean muscles cut through the water with grace and speed. A bee circled lazily, hummed, then dove for a bright purple flower. The vivid blue sky reminded her of Wolfe's eyes. "How's the hospital?"

"Good." She took another swig and thought of David. Seemed all detours led to her fiancé. Ex-fiancé. Since he ran the surgical unit and she was under his direction, her career may also be in jeopardy. "Busy."

"You haven't liked your job in a long time, have you?"

She swiveled her head back. A flare of temper hit. "It's more than a job. It's my entire life. College, med school, internship. Days, nights, weekends. I never faltered, never questioned, never lost focus. I stopped asking myself if I liked it a long time ago. I just live it."

He swam back and forth as if he didn't have a care in the world. And he didn't. She was the one who'd blown her life up and took off. "Why?" he asked.

She blinked. "Why? What type of question is that? Because if you want to be a recognized surgeon, you have to work yourself so hard there's only pieces of you left. Then you get to slowly put them back together."

He floated in seemingly utter content. "Just doesn't make sense to me. If I didn't like working at Purity, I'd leave. Do something else. Ever think you've been so obsessed with the prize you never stopped to think if you'd like doing it?"

She choked on her beer and on the bitter taste of outrage. How dare he question her motives. She'd been working to succeed in the medical field since she'd first practiced first aid on her dolls. When her brother, Lance, declared his intention to study medicine, she'd been pissed off he stole her career. Ambition, work, and achievement of goals made sense. Working to save a human life and strive for greatness made her worthy. Yet her best friend treated it like a side job, just casually picked from a litter of careers as if it meant nothing.

"My prize is saving a life. Yours is a nice experience sleeping away from home."

She hated her bitchiness, but he never lost the smoothness of his strokes. "Ouch. We have a spa and a chapel. Surely that makes up for the shallowness."

"Why are you trying to piss me off? This is my life's work. You just don't quit something because it's too hard or you're not enjoying it anymore."

"Have you ever given up on something you didn't like?"

The question threw her off. She guzzled half her beer, took another, and popped off the cap. "Yeah, gymnastics. I had no coordination. Mom had dreams of an Olympic run. I fell off the balance beam once and cried for an hour. So I quit."

"How many lessons did you suffer through?"

Gen frowned. "Well, I finished up the term, of course. Then I never signed back up."

"Ever stop a book halfway if you don't like it?"

She shuddered with horror. "Are you kidding? If I start it, I finish it. I don't know how people sleep not knowing the ending."

"What if you order something at a restaurant and hate it? Do you send it back?"

"If it's cooked properly and I just dislike the flavor? Of course not. I clean the plate; it's my fault for choosing it."

"Hmm, interesting."

She glared at his back as he moved from a float to a steady backstroke. "What's interesting? And what's with the asinine questions?"

"You take your choices seriously."

Gen tilted her chin up. "Of course. Choices mean consequences. Not following through is a type of failure."

"Or maybe it's just a good old-fashioned mistake you need to fix. Not every path in the road needs to be followed. Sometimes it's smarter to quit and go home."

His words burned through her, rising up and swallowing her whole until she shook with pent-up frustration and rage. "That means failure."

"No. Just a wrong turn."

His gentle voice scraped at her like spits of gravel. She practically shook with fury. When her father abandoned them, she'd made the decision to do everything right and never make trouble. She had—and her father came back. Her once-splintered family healed. Being good paid. Following the rules gave rewards. Wolfe didn't know what he was talking about. She jumped up from the rock, put her beer down, and walked to the edge of the dock. Her finger jabbed in the air. "Who are you to dump all this psychobabble on me? You're just as driven in work as I am. You detest failure, laziness, and mediocrity."

His laugh splintered the wooded silence. The sun began to sink slowly over the hill. Shadows danced from the swaying trees. "Yeah, I do. You look mad."

"I am mad!"

He swam over and stood. "How mad?" he drawled.

She growled. "Really mad."

"That's what I thought. Better cool you off."

She didn't have a chance. With a graceful motion, he loomed up from the water like some type of monstrous sea creature, grabbed her, and pulled her in. Her shrieks got cut off by the slap of warm water closing in. She hit the bottom, and her feet scraped against soft moss before she kicked herself to the surface. The huge grin on his face pushed one vow to the forefront of her mind.

Revenge.

Oh, it would be sweet.

"Proud of yourself?" she drawled, shaking her head like a wet dog to get the hair out of her face.

"Kind of. Things were getting way too serious."

His outrageous statement made her laugh. Damned if he'd be the one to let her sulk, even on her failed wedding day. Wolfe sensed when she needed to stew, be depressed, or push through. Right now, there were so many emotions churning like choppy waters she didn't know where to focus. The water helped clear her head.

Gen kicked her feet, treading water. "Ewww, it's all soft and gooey on the bottom. God knows what's down there."

"Scared of a few fish?"

She pursed her lips. "Don't come running into my room tonight."

One dark brow shot up. He swam around her like a shark circling his prey. "A proposition? I had no idea you lusted after my body."

She snorted and almost choked. "Oh yeah, it'll be romantic. Me, you, and the big hairy spider I'm putting in your bed."

The humor drained from his face. "Don't fuck with me."

She laughed and stuck out her tongue. "Bet there's a lot around here. Ever seen one of the wood spiders?" She gave a shudder. "Furry, with fat legs and superfast, so you can't catch them."

He tried to laugh it off but she caught the paleness to his features. Damn, this was too much fun.

"You know what comes with spiders?" he said.

"What?"

"Frogs. Lots and lots of green frogs. Like Kermit."

The horror washed through her. "I told you that in secret," she whispered. A creepy shiver raced down her spine at the image. "You're a horrible, evil human being."

"I find a spider in my bed, and you'll wake up to a portrait of Kermit."

"Asshole. I was drunk when I confessed. Drunk info should be sacred—you broke the cardinal rule." She'd had a dream once that haunted her to this day, and was stupid enough to confide in Wolfe after too many beers. She'd woken up from a wicked nightmare of Kermit the Frog faces attacking her. Instead of sweet smiles, they had bloody teeth, and had gone after her like a herd of piranhas. She hadn't been able to watch a Muppets movie since.

"An eye for an eye and all that," he said. Then dove beneath the water.

Gen watched him swim, appreciating the raw power and grace of his body and flexing muscles. Awareness trickled through her, but she was an expert at ignoring it.

Wolfe needed so much more than a quick lay or another affair. He needed a friend. Gen knew him better than anyone, and was gifted with the trueness of his soul. Sex was the surefire pathway to disaster, heartbreak, and the loss of one of her most important relationships.

No thanks.

What he offered was enough. No expectations, only acceptance, respect, and love.

Very different from David.

The thought was like an uppercut, and for a moment she fought for breath. She'd done a terrible thing, and she was going to pay. Wolfe was wrong. Mistakes ruined lives, and by not following through, she'd let everyone down.

No. You protected yourself. You know why.

The inner voice whispered slyly, as if she knew much more and couldn't wait to spill. But Gen didn't want to hear it.

She swam to the dock and jumped back up, reaching for her beer. Her goal of drunken forgetfulness was the only thing keeping her together right now. Thank goodness for Mr. Samuel Adams.

Wolfe surfaced, pulled himself out of the water, and grabbed a beer for himself. Quickly arranging the towels over the battered dock, he lay on his back, bottle propped up on his belly, and stared up at the sky. With a sigh, she did the same, shoulders touching, drying off in the hot breeze, watching the first stars poke out from the clouds. The alcohol gave the scene a nice blur that dulled all the sharp edges.

"I should be on a plane to Bermuda," she said.

"This is better. Pink sand is overrated."

"The cake was coconut with chocolate icing. Five tiers."

"I got you Sno Balls. They have coconut on them."

A smile touched her lips. "True. My negligee was five hundred dollars of pure silk. Maggie got it for me in Europe."

"Well, that's just stupidity. Gonna be on for two minutes and ripped off you. Never understood the expensive underwear crap."

"You modeled them and made a million dollars." Maggie had turned Wolfe into a superstar of designer boxers, which he wore in billboard and magazine ads in place of formfitting tightie whities. Wolfe posed at a delicious side angle wearing simple black boxers, arms crossed in front of his chest, and a moody expression on his face. He was the rebel hottie incarnate. The tagline read *F— Briefs: Wear What Feels Good*.

The United States bucked the curse word. Europe loved it. He became a legend, a millionaire, and the biggest model in the industry.

He quit after a year to go to college for his business degree and to run Purity. Women still chased him, but he never threw his fame around, and since he was growing his hair and usually covered up his tat with long shirts, many never knew.

"It was a pisser for a while, but I'd never buy expensive boxers. Who's gonna see them?"

A genuine laugh escaped her lips. He was so different. David adored anything with the right label, and he sniped about her boring wardrobe and lingerie constantly. "Agreed. But what about sex? Honeymoons are known for endless sun, drinks, and sex. I probably won't have sex again for a year. Maybe more."

"You got beer, the sun was just out, we're by a lake, and I'm here. If you're hard up, I'll have sex with you."

That earned him a punch that hurt her more than him. "Gee, thanks. You're a real buddy."

"They call them fuck buddies. You know, great friends who don't want to mess up the dynamic so they just agree to occasional sex."

"I hate that term, it's so crude. I've seen every one of those movies and they all end up the same. One of them falls in love, the relationship explodes, then someone confesses their undying love and they get together in a romantic way."

"Hence the word *movie*, Gen. Fiction."

"Some movies are based on reality. Maybe those are, too."

She felt rather than saw him roll his eyes. "Other than the occasional war film, no romance movies are based on reality."

She turned over, propped up on her elbow, and stared at him. His challenge sung to her sense of competition. They both had a strange need to win, and could spend hours debating ridiculous points of inane information. "*Marley & Me.*"

"Oh, for God's sake. I'm removing war, animals, and historical movies from the pool."

"How many do I have to name?"

"Two is good."

"What do I get?"

"I'll protect you from Kermit."

"Hardy-har-har. You have to tell me one secret you've told no one else. I don't care what it is."

She had no idea why that request popped out of her mouth. Gen waited for him to blow her off, and almost retracted her words. But something kept her silent. Probably since her life had exploded around her, she had nothing to cling to. A secret for a secret. Something to make her feel not so alone. Not so . . . broken.

Arilyn would have been proud of her ability to self-diagnose her issues. As the counselor of the matchmaking agency Kinnections, she counseled clients on awareness in relationships and helped break down barriers that would block their journey to happiness. Of course, knowing she had emotional problems because she'd run away on her wedding day still didn't make her feel like snagging a gold star.

"Wolfe, forget it, I—"

"Agreed."

Wow. She didn't see that coming. Of course, now she had to find two movies based on real life that had some type of romantic relationship in them. No wonder he'd agreed. "Give me a minute to think."

He rested his arms behind his head and gave her a cocky grin. "Take all the time you need."

The lightbulb went on. "*Titanic!*" She beamed with pride.

"Buzz. Based on history. Disqualified."

Her mouth fell open. "Oh come on! The love story is separate from the ship sinking!"

"You agreed to the rules. No history. Try again."

Grumbling under her breath, she polished off her beer, grabbed another, and wracked her brain. Crap, there went *Shakespeare in Love*. Was there anything not based on history? "*A Beautiful Mind*! And don't try to argue a historical event. That counts."

He didn't answer for a while. She knew he was checking loopholes, so Gen prepared for a big fight. "Okay, I'll give you that one. Not a bad movie."

Yes! One more to go. "Oh, oh, *The Sound of Music*!"

"Buzz."

"It's true and it's a love story!"

"Hmm, let's think about this. World War II. German invasion. Trek into the mountains to escape Hitler's regime. History, baby. Disqualifier."

"I knew you saw that movie and lied about it."

"Julietta forced me to watch it and I gagged the whole time."

She pouted, drank some more, and realized she didn't know too many happy endings. No wonder. They were all fake.

"Give up?"

"No."

He laughed. "Depressing, ain't it?"

A few minutes later, she realized she won. "Get ready to spill."

"What do you got?"

"*The Vow*." Gen did a little victory floor dance, feeling more triumphant and capable than she had in a while. "I win, I win, I win."

He frowned. "What the hell is *The Vow*?"

"You never heard it? Channing Tatum, baby. Rachel McAdams gets amnesia in an accident, doesn't remember her husband, and he has to get her to fall in love with him all over again like a stranger. It's so good."

"No way is that based on reality. Buzz."

She shot up. "No buzz. Look it up on your phone—did you bring it?"

He reached over the towel, snagged his phone, and began the search. His disgusted look told her he found it. "This is the most asshat thing I've ever read. Amnesia into a love story?"

She sniffed. "It was very romantic and believable."

"Tatum is so overrated."

"Jealous?" He flopped back down and took a long swallow. If she was honest, she'd say Wolfe beat out Tatum any day, but she'd die rather than admit it. No need to give him a bigger head than he had. Damn, he smelled good though. Clean. Like pine, water, and cotton, with just a tang of male sweat to grab a woman's attention. Thank goodness she didn't think of him in *that* way. He'd always reminded her more of Adam Levine anyway. Tats, bad-boy angst, and a beautiful soul was a yummy combination.

"The boy can barely act so he takes off his clothes to compensate."

She hooted with laughter. "Says you." His image blurred into two. The crickets chirped music and everything around her softened and became more vivid. Oh yeah. Beer number four and she'd be good to go. No, it was five, right? Her nerves calmed, and suddenly, she wasn't as scared anymore. So she was a runaway bride? So she dumped the best thing that ever happened to her at the altar? So she broke his heart and made him endure endless humiliation?

Big deal.

"Feeling better?" He watched her as she opened her next beer and collapsed back on the ground. The sky spun.

"Yeah. Snooze you lose on the beer."

"I think you deserve them. Just don't want you to get sick."

She giggled. "Remember that time at Mugs they tried introducing karaoke and after too many drinks we got on the bar and sang 'I Got You Babe'?"

His laugh was infections and stroked her ears like a caress. "That was bad news. If anyone put it on YouTube it would've gone viral. Good-bye, respectable hotel career. Good-bye, doctor in training."

"David hated me drinking. Said it reflected on him and the hospital. Said I'd become an alcoholic like my father."

His body stiffened next to her, then slowly relaxed. "You're not a hard drinker, Gen. Believe me, I've seen them firsthand. You had some harmless fun before you became a resident. We were younger then. You'd never do anything to jeopardize your reputation or career."

"Maybe. But sometimes . . ." She trailed off, too horrified to finish. Putting the thought out in the world might make it real.

"Sometimes what?"

She meant to shrug it off. But the world floated above her, beneath her, and she was safe. "Sometimes I wanted to get caught. I fantasized about David breaking up with me and getting kicked out of med school. I craved a huge scandal that would yank my choices from me." Emotion choked her throat. "I got my wish. And I hate myself for it." The shame of not being as strong and fierce as she always believed nauseated her. David was right. He'd called her weak, disgusted at her inability to communicate and do what needed to be done. Every day, he'd urged her to be better, but she'd failed over and over, until she ran like a coward on her wedding day.

"My mother was a drug addict."

Gen sucked in her breath. He spoke softly to the sky, as if by releasing the words into the night they'd be carried off to a magical place that couldn't hurt anymore. She remained silent, waiting for more.

"She'd do anything to get high. Usually it involved starving us both to shoot up, or prostituting her body for a quick blow. I remember once when I was about seven, I got home from school and heard her screwing in the back room. I was used to it by then, so I started looking for something to eat and found some old Cheerios left in the cupboard. When I went to get a bowl, I found her stash. A small bag of white powder tied with a twisty thing. I was entranced. I mean, I was used to seeing her high, but she always hid the stuff well. It looked just like powdered sugar, something I'd put on waffles if I had any."

Her heart pounded so loud she barely heard his words.

"I took it down, opened it up, and realized I could be a user, too. I'd be happier that way. I'd be closer to her—like partners. She was happy when she was high, and would hug me, sometimes sing and dance, and I imagined it could always be like that. I swiped my fingers inside, rubbed it around, and brought it up to my nose. I wanted that coke so bad I shook with it. I wanted to go far away like her and stop being so scared and needy all the time."

He let out a sigh. She didn't say anything, just waited.

"I didn't get the chance. They came out of the bedroom,

and when they saw me with the bag, her client beat the crap out of me. I never found her stash again. Guess she was afraid she'd have less if I got hooked."

Her insides hurt. Shame washed over her. Even with her past, her parents loved her, and rallied together. Her family was the most important part of her life. What type of person would she have become if there had been no safety net in her world? No one to trust or depend on or love her unconditionally?

Gen knew pity would make him vomit. He didn't deserve pity anyway; he was too strong for that. She made sure her voice never wobbled. "Motherfucker. Sorry, Wolfe, but I hate your mother."

A surprised chuckle escaped his lips. "Yeah, me, too."

"At least you didn't take the drugs."

"I think I would've. And that's something I never forget. It wasn't strength of will that saved me. Just coincidence."

She wanted to tell him he was full of shit, but sensed an argument. Gen let his words float back up to the sky with the rest of the stuff. He wasn't ready for a deep heart-to-heart, but this was the first time he'd ever shared information about his past. If that was a tiny piece, she wondered if she'd be able to handle the whole story.

"Too bad. I was hoping for some awesome sex secret. Like telling me you really are into dominatrix stuff."

"Sex again, huh?"

"Must be the alcohol." She finished up the fifth or sixth beer, and enjoyed the heat coursing through her veins. The fake happiness would soon turn to depression, but she didn't care for now. It had been so long she let go of control and did something reckless. "David said I sucked at sex."

This time, he rolled over. Those stinging blue eyes pierced into hers and his jaw tightened. "David was an asshole and that's why you left. You don't suck at sex."

The giggles overtook her. "How do you know? We never had sex. I probably do. I'm too in my head, always waiting to see if I'm good enough until faking orgasms became my art."

Fury laced his words. "Let me repeat. He was an asshole, and lousy in bed if he had you faking orgasms. He messed with your head, babe. Don't let him get in."

She waved a hand in the air and tried not to giggle again. Oh yeah, she was drunk. It wasn't so funny before, but now it seemed kind of lame not to be able to rock the bedroom with your fiancé. "S'okay. I'm not the sexy type, you know? I'm vanilla. Boring. He even said my kissing was like missionary sex every night. But I know he didn't mean to hurt my feelings. He was just saying it to make me better, so I got some books, but it still didn't really work."

His teeth clenched. She was fascinated by the naked rage flickering over his face, the way he held his body tight as if he was about to explode like some badass superhero. "I'm going to kill him."

She almost laughed, but then he looked a bit too serious. Gen frowned and reached out. She got lucky and hit vision number one, which was real and not the duplicate dancing in front of her. Her fingers stroked his stubbled jaw in an effort to soothe his temper. Damn, she used to be able to knock back five beers in a night. Maybe because shc had nothing in hcr stomach and it had been a hell of a day. Why did he look so mad again? Oh yeah, because she sucked at kissing and he was gonna kill David. "Not his fault. He never wanted to hurt mc, told mc that all the time. I kinda made him do it by not listening."

"You really believe this shit, Gen?"

"It'll be okay. I'll get a vibrator or something, or maybe take lessons. Kate's mom is a sex therapist, you know. Maybe she can help."

He grabbed her hand and squeezed tight. "I'm gonna rip him apart piccc by piccc. You *are* good at sex. You *are* good at kissing. Are you listening?"

She nodded hard. Ooooh, cool. Three faccs now. He was so nice to look at, she could stare at him all day. So much better than evil Kermits. "Uh-huh. You're a good friend. My fault though. You don't know how bad I am at it."

"Fuck." The vicious curse erupted from his sexy mouth. His warm breath hit her chcck. Shc hatcd when he got pissy. "You better remember this tomorrow."

"Huh?"

Suddenly, he loomed over her, pressing her back into the ground, his hips cradling hers. Oh wow. His body heat scorched through her wet clothes and her bare legs automatically opened in a primeval urge to surrender. He planted both hands on either side of her head and lowered his mouth. What was hc doing? His delicious scent rose to her nostrils, and her hands found their way to grip his hips, his damp skin sleek and muscled beneath her touch.

Another curse escaped. He seemed grumpy and torn as

he stared at her, inches away from her mouth, and Gen blinked a few times because his head kind of floated around, and her body screamed for more contact, please, just a bit more, and then he muttered, "I'm gonna prove you're good at this kissing thing, okay?" and his mouth took hers.

She whimpered, literally whimpered, at the amazing feel of those ultrasoft, smooth lips coasting over hers with an expert grace and blistering heat that made her toes curl. Oh, alcoholic visions were so yummy! Wolfe, her best friend and confidant, was kissing her, and it was too good to be real, so it had to be some sort of psychedelic mirage from too much Sam Adams.

Her mind spun, tried to make sense of it, and gave up.

Her body roared forward and seized control.

Hips arched, nails digging into his lower back, she surrendered to the sensations rocketing in her core and spreading like fire through her veins. He kissed her for a while, until she was a soft, gooey mess beneath him, and then his tongue parted her lips and surged in.

She opened her mouth and met him halfway, crazed for the full taste and essence of him. His tongue pushed, stroked, and explored, taking her deep. She moaned and reached for more. God, she wanted more, the taste of citrusy lemon and male hunger pulling her under. He grew hard between her thighs and she nipped at his bottom lip, sucking gently, and he muttered something foul, deflowering her mouth like she was a virgin asking to be ravished and taken and fucked.

Time stood still. It was too short, it was endless, it was

everything. Her head spun, her breasts grew achy and tight, and she was so wet he could've slipped between her thighs and slid home without a protest. She made a sound deep in her throat when he slowly pulled away, the wet slide of his tongue over hers bestowing one final taste.

She blinked. Blistering heat and fury and lust mingled in those blue eyes. She felt eaten alive, scoured raw, and Gen shook as the solid foundation underneath her shifted and broke open.

"Are you listening, Gen?"

She couldn't speak, so she managed a nod.

"You're an amazing kisser. I could've fucked you right here and now and been the happiest guy in the world. A guy has to be dead not to want you. David is a piece of shit. Understood?"

She swallowed. Nodded again.

"Good." He slid off her and she almost cried out at the loss of his heat and pressure. The sky opened and swallowed her up as utter exhaustion suddenly hit her. Turned on, spent, emotions ripped and bleeding, she grabbed for his hand so as not to lose physical contact, and he interwove his fingers with hers and lay back on the dock. Slowly, she relaxed, his presence a bone-deep comfort and something else, something she refused to examine.

Gen gave up and let the blackness take her. But first she said the words.

"I love you, Wolfe."

She slid toward sleep. His response drifted in the sultry air among the chirp of crickets.

"I love you, too, babe."

five

HE'D MADE A huge mistake.

Wolfe kept his hand firmly within hers while she slept. Her words crawled under his skin and embedded into his muscles, veins, heart. He knew, of course, what she meant. She loved him as a friend, a protector, and the one who had rescued her from making a lifetime mistake. Still, he'd only said the words back twice in his life. Once to Sawyer. Once to Julietta.

Never to a woman outside of family.

But he meant it. He did love her. She was more precious than any of his other relationships, and he hoped he hadn't screwed them up by introducing a sexual want that still rattled his dick. The love was deeper and purer than any crap in his past. How many women had uttered those words, when he knew it was only the sex and power and excitement of the encounter? They knew nothing about him. Not their fault. He rarely opened up and was content to keep it on the surface of the physical, with companionship and a few laughs the extra bonus.

Wolfe dragged in a lungful of air. Cleared his mind. When was the last time he'd reacted on impulse? Never. Impulse had no place in the business world or his personal life. Sure, it may be an illusion of control, but it worked for him. He'd been in and out of enough shrinks' offices to know his way around the mental blocks and issues a screwed-up individual created for survival. He hated therapy, but he'd gone for Sawyer because he never wanted his honorary stepfather to wonder if he could've done more. Sawyer had saved him—both literally and figuratively. He had a life he wanted to live because the man he pickpocketed cared enough about him to try and make a difference.

Wolfe shook his head as the past reared up. He'd been living on the streets, and began staking out big luxury hotels like the Waldorf for patsies. Stealing uniforms and pretending to fit in was easy, but he'd picked the wrong mark. Sawyer was street-smart and superrich, and had dragged his ass to the management.

Wolfe remembered the sick fear when he realized he was going to jail. Instead, Sawyer offered him a bargain. Work for him, and he'd stay out of jail. The judge had agreed. The night before Sawyer was about to pick him up, Wolfe realized he was terrified. He didn't want a chance at a life he'd only screw up. He refused to trust anyone anymore, so he'd hurriedly gotten his tat, styled his hair in a bizarre mockery of Johnny Depp, and pierced his face in every way possible.

When Sawyer picked him up, Wolfe waited for him to call off the whole deal.

Sawyer didn't. The man took him to Italy and gave him the opportunity to learn the hotel business. Sawyer built Purity, the luxury hotel chain, beginning in Milan, and Wolfe had learned everything from the ground up. But the man had given him much more than a job and some security. He took him into his life and his heart. When Sawyer finally met and fell in love with Julietta, they both welcomed him and created a family together.

When Sawyer asked him to get a college education so he could eventually run the Purity location in New York City, he'd agreed. The rest of the Conte family took good care of him during his school years, like an adopted family. Who would've known he'd meet the third most important person in his life at a family dinner? Gen treated him like an equal from the first. She cared about the man he was becoming, not the dark, twisted creature he'd lived as in his past. Their friendship bloomed through college and just kept getting stronger.

Gen let out a throaty groan and his thoughts got dragged back to the kiss. He'd only meant to prove a point before he took off to batter the hell out of her ex-fiancé. Instead, he got sucked in, forgetting it was a lesson, forgetting they were more than the physical. His instincts kicked in, along with the testosterone, and all he'd been able to concentrate on was the softness of her body underneath his, and her delicious scent that always made him half-drunk. Who else smelled like fresh wild-flowers and Ivory soap? He was used to exotic perfumes meant to seduce. Instead, her simplicity beat through her kiss, an honest reaction from her gut that intoxicated him more than any Playboy bunny or supermodel could. The hitch in her breath, the fullness of her breasts, the easy way she'd spread her legs in greeting as if he belonged inside her.

Wolfe gritted his teeth and fought for control. This

could never happen again. He'd play it as if they were both drunk, emotionally wrung out, and impulsive. Hell, he'd never even bring it up again. Maybe she wouldn't remember. He'd never forgive himself if any part of their relationship changed or got weird from the kiss.

His tongue dragged over his lower lip and caught her taste. He squeezed his eyes shut and burned the memory into his brain for safekeeping. For those lonely, horrific nights when he craved something beautiful to help him get through the hours in the dark.

When his breathing was regulated, Wolfe slipped his hand from hers and stood up. She frowned in her sleep and rolled a bit, as if reaching for him. He left the bottles outside, figuring he'd clean up in the morning, and easily scooped her up into his arms. She was a perfect bundle of feminine softness, and her head buried against his chest in complete trust.

His stomach lurched but he managed to carry her to the cabin, get her inside, tuck her carefully into bed, and pull the covers up to her chin. He placed a chaste kiss on her forehead. Those pale pink lips quirked upward in a sleepy half smile.

How anyone would want to hurt her was beyond him. Wolfe swore to get to the bottom of that mess and find out what really happened. Definitely some type of abuse. She'd kept her secrets well. Almost as well as he did.

He shut the door, stripped off his clothes, and lay on the mattress. His body twitched with leftover energy and sexual arousal, but eventually the events of the day took their toll.

Sleep settled over him, an uneasy and fickle companion he didn't trust.

VINCENT SOLDANO HATED HIS mother.

Unfortunately, he also loved her, feared her, and would do pretty much anything for a smile or a kind word. He'd learned early when to bother her and when to stay far away. The white powder was king, father, and all things holy. He could deal with the sugarlike substance. The needles. Even the occasional backhanded slaps or screaming sessions.

What scared him was the men.

He shuffled toward the front door, his palm already sweaty against the broken knob. The house was barely a shelter, just a few walls, leaky roof, and endless weeds choking the broken pavement outside. Two windows were taped up. They lived on Happy Street, on a dead end. When he was first learning to read, he thought it was good luck. He figured out quickly it was one of God's bad jokes played just on him.

Vincent stepped into the house. The room was empty. Relief buckled his muscles, so he moved fast. Who knew how long he had before the strangers would troop in and the noises would start? He placed his one book on the folding table and began scouring the refrigerator and cabinets for something to eat. Mama's bedroom door remained tightly shut.

He flicked off the band of cockroaches scuttling in the sink, chugged a glass of water, and found an old granola bar with chocolate chips. Score. He ate it slowly at the table, savoring every bite, and flipped through his math book. He missed school a lot, but when he was able to go he found it easy. Especially anything with numbers. He'd just look at a page, shut his eyes, and then be able to recall the entire thing from memory. He swung his skinny legs, making a note to try and wash up tonight, and then heard the squeak.

He froze. Looked up.

The man stared back at him with a funny grin on his face. "Hey, little dude. Didn't hear you come in."

Fear choked him. He didn't know why. Just realized a few years back that the men were bad, and they wanted to do things that made his stomach hurt. He tried hard to look mean, but he figured it didn't go over well when the man grinned wider and took a few steps closer.

"Where's Mama?"

The man's hair was straight, slicked back, and looked greasy in the few rays of sunlight that poured through the broken window. He was tall, wore jeans and a T-shirt, and had eyes that reminded him of a shark. Like Jaws. Grayish, flat, and kinda cruel.

"Ran to the store. She'll be back soon. You like school?"

Vincent stiffened but pretended he was unafraid. "'S okay."

"Bet you're a smart boy. But there's a better way to make yourself some money. Bet you'd like that."

Warning bells clanged. He peered up and gauged the distance from the table to the door. "Don't need no money."

The man laughed. It held no humor. "Gonna depend on your poor mama to provide for you, huh? Not very manlike.

Maybe it's time to step up and help out." He licked his lips and took another step. "I can help."

He got ready to run. He'd been here before and thank God he was fast. He knew when and where to hide. Outside in the woods he stashed an old blanket and some water to hole up with if needed. His closet door locked and most didn't want to bother bashing in the door.

He clenched his fists, rose to his feet, and got ready.

The door opened. His mama stumbled through, a cheery smile on her face. Her nose was bruised and pink from her last nosebleed. She had on a short strawberry skirt and a tank, and her bones stuck out in odd places when she moved. He remembered how much he had loved her hair when he was little. It was long, dark, and silky, and he'd bury his face in it and take a sniff, and she'd giggle and call him her shining star. Now the strands were cut uneven and choppy around her head.

"Hey, baby."

Vincent relaxed. She was normal today. For a while. "Hi, Mama."

"Getting to know Johnny?"

He nodded. The man named Johnny forced a fake laugh and grabbed the grocery bag she held, walking over to the small linoleum counter. "Yeah, we're having a man-to-man talk."

"That's nice. I got some chicken on sale, baby. Gonna cook it just like you like it."

Vincent stood up. "Thanks. I'm gonna go study for a while."

"'Kay, don't go far, it'll be ready soon."

He made his way to the large closet that served as his bedroom, and not for the first time wished to hell he was Harry fucking Potter and was really a wizard. Wished he could escape the hell of his life and feel safe. Just for a little while.

Instead, Vincent tried not to think of the man's face and ignore the feeling that his luck was starting to run out.

He was ten years old.

six

GENEVIEVE OPENED HER eyes.

Ugh. Blinking through crusty lashes, she groaned and rolled over tentatively. Her stomach gurgled with an emptiness that craved carbs, and her head felt like a bowling ball that had knocked out hundreds of pins. What happened? Where was David?

The memory made her head jerk painfully. Not a nightmare. It had really happened. She'd left David on the day of her wedding, at the altar, in front of hundreds of people. She was ruined. Her life was over. She was going to die.

The emotions wracked her body like the flu, causing tiny shivers and convulsions to break out. Why get up? She'd lie here under the covers until they discovered her rotting skeleton. Then everyone would cluck that she'd been mentally unstable anyway, and David had been saved a lifetime of pain. No one would ever remember her again. Except her sisters. And parents. Oh, and her friends. But that was it.

The door creaked. Gen refused to look up. No reason when she intended to commit suicide by not leaving the bed. Also, it hurt her head.

"Sweetheart? It's almost eleven. You need to eat something."

She mumbled into her pillow. "Gsh rway."

Footsteps. His scent hit her nose, a clean twist of soap, coffee, and sunshine. "I'm not going away. And I'm not letting you sleep all day either. Come on, I have something planned, but first you need actual food and not Sno Balls. And a shower is mandatory."

"Lrve me rawlone."

The mattress dipped. She opened one eye.

His face was serious and determined. She knew then he wasn't like her girlfriends and refused to let her languish in bed with a box of tissues, lamenting over her mental state and how her life was ruined. Men sucked. They were so action oriented, as if actually doing something productive helped. Which it wouldn't. Was that coffee?

He spoke as if he heard her thoughts. "Yes, here's your mug, and two aspirin for your head. I know you're freaking, but this is my vacation, too, and I don't want to spend it cooped up, sharing heart-to-hearts about our broken love lives."

She sniffed. Managed to sit up an inch. "You don't have a love life."

"Right. Well, it's my job to distract you for at least another twenty-four hours and then we'll deal with the shitstorm at home. Deal?"

Every time she tried to think about what to do next, splitting pain like sharpened knives stabbed her brain. The tempting idea of playing the denial game for one more day was heaven. Tomorrow she'd have no choice but to contact everyone and begin putting back the pieces. Problem was, she had no clue what to do. If she spent the day with Wolfe, maybe she'd get an aha moment and be able to figure out what her next step was.

"I'm glad you agree. Now sit up, take your pills, and come eat."

She took a sip of the strong, hot brew. "What's for breakfast? Pancakes? Omelet? French toast?"

He rolled his eyes. "Cereal, Gen."

"But you bought eggs!"

"For hard-boiled. Maybe. You know I suck at cooking."

"You lived with Julietta, who made homemade pasta and sauce and those delicious sausages and meatballs. You told me you were focusing on learning her trade secrets."

"I lied. I'm rich enough to get takeout."

She gave a long sigh. "I'm disappointed in you. And I swear, if I see you smoke again, I'm calling her."

He glowered at her. "Some friend you are. I quit, okay? It was just one slipup."

Gen popped the aspirin into her mouth and swallowed. "Fine. You know how many cases we get at the hospital for lung cancer? Throat cancer? How about living without a tongue or a voice box and having to speak with a machine?"

He turned a shade pale. "You know I hate hearing stuff like that—cut it out."

She puffed up with importance. "It's my job to make you aware of the consequences of bad choices."

"You're a real Debbie Downer."

She jumped in and imitated the old *Saturday Night Live* skit. "Whaa, whaa, whaa."

They both cracked up. "I'll meet you in the kitchen. Rice Krispies or Frosted Flakes?"

"Tony the Tiger, please."

"You got it. Don't be too long, I have a full day planned."

He left. Gen grumbled under her breath, but as she sipped her coffee, she realized that when she was arguing with Wolfe, she wasn't thinking about anything bad. He had this amazing ability to be real with her, yet not let her wallow. He listened, but he didn't judge. He pushed, but never insulted. And damn, he was the best kisser she ever—

The thought broke off. Oh no. She had kissed her best friend last night. Or, he'd kissed her. The memory was a bit misty, but her body remembered the touch of those lips resting on hers, the writhing sexual heat that claimed her, the gorgeous press of his hips and erection against her core.

Horror washed over her. Gen dropped her face into her hands. This was bad. Very bad. What had she said afterward? Had she passed out before uttering something stupid? Would it make things weird for them? How could she have been so slutty, when she'd just left her fiancée at the altar?

The door opened. Wolfe stuck his head in.

"Oh, BTW, don't worry about the kiss thing. You're probably freaking out, but let's not ruin the day. Deal?"

Her mouth dropped open. "R-r-right. I'm sorry, Wolfe. So sorry. I don't know what I was thinking." She paused. "Umm, it was good though?"

A wicked grin tugged those lush lips. Once again, she was struck by his bad-boy hotness, the leather wristbands, tattoo, eyebrow ring, and those piercing blue eyes blazing in his face like he knew all the bad things to do to women and enjoyed every last one.

"Hell, yeah, it was good. But we were kinda drunk and sad and we needed it. No need for any weirdness between us. And I kissed you first, so don't feel guilty."

"Umm, okay."

"Gen?"

"Yeah?"

He winked. "You're an amazing kisser. If you weren't my best friend, I would've tumbled you right there and you wouldn't have had a shot."

Her heart leaped and sudden hot need hit her gut. Her lips curved in a smile. "Thanks. I think."

He laughed and shut the door. Damn the man. He had a talent for playing Jedi mind tricks on her, always sensing the right thing to say or do. Fine. If he wasn't going to think about the kiss, neither was she. After a few moments, Gen managed to shower and pull on denim shorts, a yellow tank, and flip-flops. Face bare of makeup—she'd left that behind when she crawled out the window—she scooped her hair into a ponytail and made her way to the kitchen.

She slid onto the stool and dove into her cereal. She spooned up a banana slice and shot him a look. "Fruit, too? You're getting to be a real gourmet."

"Wait till you see what's on the pizza for dinner."

"What are we doing today?"

"Think Hemingway."

She raised a brow. Damn, she'd forgotten how good Frosted Flakes could be in the morning. All that bran and granola was seriously sucking the fun out of her life. "Are you kidding? I'm still recovering from alcohol. And why do you look so chipper? That Sam Adams kicked my ass last night."

He sipped his coffee and leaned against the counter. "You lost your edge, woman. Used to be able to keep up."

"I got soft. Also switched to Michelob Ultra. I wasn't prepared."

Wolfe grinned. He looked just as casual as she did, with cutoff denim shorts, a navy blue T-shirt, and leather sandals. His hair was freshly washed and fell in damp waves over his forehead. The ring in his brow winked merrily, and the ink of his tattoo peeked through the collar of his shirt and climbed up sensuously over his neck. She always wondered why he'd picked a serpent. She'd never asked.

"You gonna tell me or are you going to torture me with more trivia?"

"Me, you, and the fish, baby."

She blinked. "Are you kidding? That's not fun! Sitting on some leaky, rotted dock catching smelly, wiggly fish so you can butcher them? I'm going back to bed."

"Not on my vacay. We're not sitting on the dock. This is much more exciting."

"How so?"

"We're renting a boat."

She got up, put her bowl and spoon in the sink, and headed to the bedroom. "Good luck with that. Night."

He caught her around the waist and swung her around. "You don't have a choice. It's gonna be epic. We'll sail the seas, catch fresh fish, fry them up tonight for dinner, and bond with nature."

"I'm not cooking fish."

"No problem. I can handle that."

She laughed. The image almost made the whole thing worth it. Almost. "I'm gonna be bored," she whined.

"Not with me. Get your sweet ass in gear, our poles are outside."

She grumbled but did what he told her. Unfortunately, she wasn't capable of making decisions for herself right now, so she depended on his direction. He picked up some type of tackle box, the poles, a case of water, and various snacks, then headed into the woods.

Gen dragged her feet, muttered zingy one-liners, and tried to keep up. He whistled and ignored all her barbed statements, not letting up the pace even though his legs were four times longer than hers. After a good twenty minutes of walking through brush, getting bitten by mosquitoes, and huffing and puffing, she opened her mouth to say she was quitting, but he stopped short.

"About time! Why didn't we drive? I hate walking in the woods. I'm tired. Can I have water? Where's the boat?"

"Should be back here." He dropped the stuff and began searching through overgrown brush and pussy willows long enough to be someone's weapon. "Ah, here it is." He disappeared in the vegetation for a few moments, then rose up with a boat by his side.

Gen stared.

She'd expected some elaborate power motor thing with music and air. Something to jet around the lake on while she sunbathed.

This thing would barely keep them alive.

The rowboat was wooden, with old-fashioned oars, and creaked dangerously. Narrow and definitely unbalanced, it bounced back and forth as if just waiting to dump them. The water was greenish, and big globs of seaweed floated in it. She shivered with fear at the idea of being in there. What the hell? He dumped the stuff into the boat and held out a hand to her.

"No. Way."

The man had the nerve to look like he was holding on to his patience. "Now what's the problem, princess?"

She practically spit in fury. "Are you nuts? Where's the life jackets? The boat that doesn't sink? The man that makes you sign contracts about liability and gives you lessons on boating before allowing you out in the water?"

"That's the beauty of this whole thing. It's natural, not forced. We're heading to a great hidden place where the fish live. No rules, no contracts, no people. Just me, you, and the fish."

"This is worse than not getting married!"

"Will you just trust me? It's gonna be great. You'll love it."

She glared. Stamped her feet. Dammit, did she have a choice? She didn't want to be stuck in the cabin all day, thinking about David and her mistakes and the mess her life was. Maybe it would be helpful. She'd read Hemingway and that boring book about the man and the sea, trying to catch a fish. She had seen that old movie *On Golden Pond* with the Fondas. When had she gotten so structured that she didn't do anything impulsive any longer?

Since she got engaged.

David disliked veering off course where things could get sticky. He'd book a fishing trip at a nice marina, with a full-service concierge, a professional fisherman, and a compass. A rowboat in the middle of a mossy lake with no constructed plan for hours would never happen in his world.

In the beginning, she thought it was charming. She actually preferred a man who took things seriously and was ruthlessly organized. Until she realized he'd left no room to breathe. When she tried to embrace a more open viewpoint, his disdain and subtle punishments slowly eked away any enthusiasm she had until it became easier to give in.

Was it really his fault? Or hers for not fighting for what she wanted?

Gen pushed the thought away and set her jaw. "Fine. Let's do it." With careful movements, she climbed into the boat and gingerly sat on the rear seat, clutching the sides. Wolfe undid the ropes and pushed off, taking the main position by the oars. After a few minutes of sheer terror, she relaxed when the boat held and Wolfe actually seemed to know how to steer. Okay, this could be cool. It was a beautiful, warm day, the birds sang, the woods hugged the lake with gorgeous views, and she didn't have to worry about anyone finding them.

"Feel better?"

She nodded. "Yeah. You seem to know what you're doing."

"It's not rocket science, just rowing."

Gen stuck out her tongue.

They floated in silence. Her mind quieted a bit, just taking in the moment. Little plops and ripples on the surface promised a wide variety of animals. She fought a shiver and hoped to God it was only little fish and not some type of disgusting sea creature ready to take down the boat.

"Why are you looking down like you think Jason is gonna pop out of the water with a hockey mask?"

"Don't say that! Ugh, this lake is gross. I can't believe I swam in it last night."

"You only think that because we're used to chlorinated pools. People need more germs. They'd be healthier."

She shook her head. "Thank you, Dr. Wolfe."

"Has a nice ring to it."

"Remember when my father learned you went by only one name?"

He rolled his eyes. "Your father hated me from the first moment."

She giggled at the memory. "He said, 'Wolfe, like Prince?' And you said, 'Not really.'"

"Then he just stared at me like I was a bug on his shoe he wanted to scrape off."

"He doesn't hate you, I keep telling you that. He's just wary. Izzy was always staring at you like she was hungry, and he's old-fashioned. Used to tell us if we got any piercings or tats we'd be in big trouble."

"Hmm, the threat didn't work well with Izzy."

"Not much did." She'd been dying to ask a question for a long time. In the boat, alone with her thoughts, the words popped out. "Did you ever sleep with Izzy?"

He stumbled with one of the oars and the boat did a shaky jerk. She grabbed onto the sides until they smoothed back out. "Are you kidding me? Of course not! Why would you ask?"

Relief coursed through her. Gen shrugged. "She always wanted you. I think she's jealous of our friendship and it would've been a good way to get back at me. Said I was the good one. The one Mom and Dad loved. I always felt bad she was branded the troublemaker from when we were young. And then we tried to do exactly what everyone expected of us. I followed the right path and she raised hell."

He seemed to choose his words carefully. "She tried a few times, but I always knew she didn't want me. She was confused. In pain. Not sure what she was dealing with."

"Me neither. When she got hooked on drugs, everything blew up. Dad couldn't reach her, felt like a failure, and barely spoke to her. She was isolated. I wouldn't blame you if you did sleep with her, Wolfe. Promise."

Her tummy slid to her toes when he met her gaze. Those piercing blue eyes held a fierce intent that spoke volumes. "We didn't sleep together. I never wanted Izzy. Understood?" Her breath strangled in her throat, so she managed a nod. "Good. We're here. Let's catch some fish."

The isolated inlet didn't seem to be the fish-catching capital of Saratoga, but Gen didn't care. He taught her to hook the bait, educated her on tackle, and gave her a quick lesson on throwing the rod. Gen sat back and watched the line, waiting for a wiggle or a jump. Now that she was here, she wanted to catch a fish. A bigger one than Wolfe, so she could always lord it over him.

"I don't even want to know what you're thinking with that grin on your face," he commented.

"Good, 'cause I'm not telling. Can I ask another question? One that may be out of line?"

"Sure."

"Why do you have only one name?"

His shoulders tightened, and she regretted asking. Since she'd escaped the altar, her curiosity about his past was growing stronger. She waited for him to call on their pinky promise, but he surprised her once again.

"I was someone else a long time ago. Shit happened. When Sawyer took me in, I was so mixed-up I thought if I changed my name I'd be someone else."

"That makes perfect sense. A new slate. Why did you pick Wolfe? How come it wasn't Snake or Serpent like your tat?"

His lip kicked up in a half grin. "That would just be stupid."

She grinned with him. "Guess so."

He was quiet, staring down at his fishing rod. "I picked Wolfe because it's a symbol of a great hunter. I wanted to feel that type of power for a change. The hunter and predator. Not the hunted. Not prey."

His words blasted through and connected to her on a deep level. Somehow, he was giving her the piece to the puzzle that had made him, but it was too fast and too big to decipher. The snap of the line interrupted them, and suddenly he was jerking the rod, reeling in his prize, while Gen got caught in the excitement and started yelling.

"Pull harder, to the left, you're gonna lose him, you got one!"

"Shush, you're scaring them away. Think it's a big one."

The rod bent and the fish appeared, flopping madly and spraying water everywhere as Wolfe dragged the fish into the boat. Wolfe unhooked the line, staring with sheer pride at his catch.

Gen stared at the fish. Medium sized. Silvery. Its gills working, its eyes seemed to bug out as it realized its life was officially over. It'd be asphyxiated and suffer a slow, painful death.

"Son of a bitch, I got one! Now, I think Sawyer said to knock him out with one of those hammer things. I brought one right here, I think, and I— Gen, what are you doing? Gen? Hey!"

She dove across the boat, grabbed the slimy, slippery fish, and, barely managing to hold on to it, tossed it back into the water.

Ripples vibrated on the surface, then stilled. Relief loosened her shoulders. Thank goodness. She never thought she was squeamish, but no way was she going to be a part of hurting and torturing a poor animal. It'd swim back to its fishy family and hopefully avoid such tricks in the future.

She was probably more like her sister Alexa than she thought.

Smiling, she turned and stopped dead.

Uh-oh.

"Did you just throw away the fish I caught?" His voice hit a high-pitched note she rarely heard. Like he was really pissed. So pissed he couldn't control his voice.

She winced. "I'm sorry. I couldn't do it. I couldn't be a part of a murder."

His brows lowered in a fierce frown. "Are you kidding me? It's a fish. You eat fish all the time and never had a problem. Now you're comparing it to a homicide?"

She tilted her chin. "Because it is. You were going to smash his head. It'll hurt. Let's just catch them for fun and toss them back."

He growled, took a step toward her, then gripped the fishing rod like he imagined it was her neck. "Fish have no nerve endings. And forgive me, but I don't find it fun to toss back a catch that I earned. It's lame."

She glared back at him. "How do you know fish have no nerves? Were you reincarnated? And it's not lame, it's humane."

"Touch my fish again, sweetheart, and you're gonna be in trouble."

She opened her mouth to yell back at him, then saw a black object moving quickly along the floor toward Wolfe's foot. When she realized what it was, she snapped back her words and shrugged. He wanted to act like a murderer without conscience? Fine. He'd be punished in own way. It was karmic.

"I'm glad you finally agree." He gave a half-assed swat at his lower leg, but she watched the fuzzy body avoid the swish of his fingers and travel higher. Yeah. This was gonna be good. "Now stay quiet while I try and catch another one."

"Not a word?" she asked sweetly.

"Not one." He swiped again, but the bug reached the edge of his shorts and hovered. What if it went underneath? She nibbled at her lower lip, suddenly worried. Could a young, healthy male have a heart attack if his phobia came to life? Should she mention it even though he was being mean?

"Umm, Wolfe, I should tell you one thing."

"You've done enough. I want fish for dinner tonight and I'm gonna get it."

"Maybe instead of trying to kill fish you should try and murder something more important."

"Yeah? Like what?"

She pointed to the spider on his bare thigh. "Like that spider."

"Holy shit!"

It happened so fast the scene was a blur.

Wolfe hopped on one leg, swiping furiously at his shorts, and began to fall over. The boat tilted to the right, paused, and dumped the two of them over the side.

They both tumbled into the water. Gasping and trying to close her mouth, Gen felt cold liquid seep through her clothes and hit her like a shock wave. Her hair stuck to her face, and she spit frantically, afraid she'd gotten a mouthful of seaweed. The idea of being in the same realm as an alligator or sea monster made her go nuts.

"Get me out of here!" she yelled. "Don't let me die here!"

Strong arms wrapped around her waist, holding her up. His legs scissored between hers as he kept her on the surface. "Why are you yelling like a crazy person? You know how to swim."

Gen screeched and wrapped her arms and legs around him tight. "There are things in here! Creepy, crawly, swimmy things. Get me back in the boat now!"

His low laugh vibrated in her ear. Goose bumps broke

out on her skin, and a melty sensation throbbed between her thighs. His hair-roughened leg slid back and forth, hitting a sweet spot. "There was a spider on me. A giant spider. Did you know about this?"

She shook her head hard and whimpered. "No, I swear, please get us back in the boat."

"Okay. But no more interfering with my fishing. I'll just grab the boat and—what the hell was that?"

"What? What?"

"I don't know, something touched my leg. It seems to have fingers, almost like a hand."

Gen opened her mouth and screamed.

His laughter barely processed as she began wiggling and trying to claw her way back to the boat. She finally reached the side, and felt strong hands cup her bottom, lifting her higher and higher until she fell in a tangle of limbs back to safety. Gen jumped up and began slapping at her legs, pulling off pieces of seaweed. Wolfe climbed back in, sat down on the seat, and chuckled.

"Oh man, you should have seen your face. Priceless."

"You are an asshole! There was no hand, you liar."

"Sorry, sweetheart, I couldn't help it."

"I hate fishing. This entire episode sucks. I'm wet and tired and icky."

"It's been a challenge, but I'm sure it'll get better. Not much else can happen. It's a nice day. Maybe we can go back to the dock and go for a hike."

God spoke again.

The sun disappeared and a few raindrops fell from the sky. She blinked and looked up. Not possible. Was it?

"Is it raining?" she screeched.

Wolfe looked up. The drops began to fall faster. "Yeah, we better get back. Where's the oar?"

"What are you talking about? They're bolted to the thingy there, aren't they?"

They both looked at the boat, which held empty rings and no oars. She glanced to the right and saw them floating off in the distance. Her heart began to pound. They were pretty far from the cabin and the shore. "Wolfe? What are we going to do?"

He rubbed his head like disasters commonly occurred in his world. "Huh. This could be a problem. I guess we swim."

Her mouth fell open. "I'm not going in the water with bad things out to hurt me! I saw *Scooby-Doo! Curse of the Lake Monster* with Lily! No way in hell!"

"Fine, then get on my back. I'll swim and protect you."

Thick, cold droplets began to strike her in a random, peppering pattern. She moaned in misery and stared down into the water. "I can't do it."

"You're doing it." He jumped back into the water and treaded water while he waited.

"What about our supplies?"

"I think bottles of water and fishing gear can be sacrificed for the greater good. Come on, Gen. Jump."

"I can't."

She shivered, getting colder by the minute. His voice came out like a whiplash.

"I'm gonna say it for the last time. Get your ass in the water. I promise I'll never let anything happen to you."

She gulped. "Promise."

His face softened, and suddenly Gen realized she'd go anywhere with him without hesitation.

"Promise."

She jumped.

THE FIRE ROARED. THE rain pounded nonstop against the windows, while logs crackled and filled the air with the scents of burned wood and pizza. Wrapped in a toasty blanket, Gen stretched out a piece of melty cheese and sighed with delight. "Sooo good."

Wolfe munched, eating from the crust downward as he preferred, and mumbled in agreement. "Better than fish."

"Told ya so." She licked her fingers and settled back on the couch with a groan of contentment. She glanced outside, where the wind roared and an old-fashioned summer thunderstorm raged onward. "That boat is long gone. Hope it wasn't too pricey."

He laughed and wiped his hands. "I just found the sucker in the woods during my morning hike."

She paused. "What? You didn't even know if that thing was safe? You could've killed us."

He snorted, leaning back and stretching his legs on the coffee table. "I protected you from the creature from the black lagoon, didn't I? You almost killed me. Strangling my neck so hard I couldn't breathe."

She tried to be mad, but a smile tugged at her lips. He was pretty lucky. She had never loosened her grip and the swim back had been brutal. "Fine. We're even."

A comfortable silence settled. She sipped a glass of

Chardonnay and let the warmth of the evening wash over her. So nice. She used to crave sitting like this with David, just basking in his company. Enjoying his sharp intellect. But as they continued dating, the moments got further apart. He was always busy doing something, or telling her to do something. Idle hands and such. Until she'd forgotten what it was like to just sit in silence with a man, talking, being in the moment. Was this so sinful? Did every waking second of life need to be productive, with a target for output?

She remembered the way she'd try and fight back, give her opinions, and how he'd crumble in front of her, an emotional wreck. David struggled with receiving love. His parents divorced early in his childhood, and his mother was an absentee, not seeming to care about her only son. He'd devoted himself to the medical field, to achievement, to prove his worth. And he had. But Gen saw the cold glimmer of intent in his eyes, as if he only wanted to cut out his past with a surgeon's scalpel. When she disappointed him, he reverted. At first she was amazed at his willingness to share his past. His openness regarding his limitations and weaknesses. He told her over and over she was the one to save him.

She'd tried. Hadn't she?

But she wasn't strong enough. The constant back and forth between cold disdain, teacherlike discipline, and loving, needy partner began to destroy her. So many times she'd chosen to forgive the way he hurt her because he loved her. But what was real love anyway?

She didn't know anymore.

Darkness began stealing her peace inch by inch. She blinked back useless tears, caught between the misery of the past and her guilt over trying to save herself. The lives she had ruined by being selfish enough to run away. Coward. Coward . . .

"Sweetheart? Are you ready?"

She shook her head and tried to focus. Wolfe knelt beside the table with a battered maroon box in front of him. "What?"

"Scrabble. Here, help me set it up." He handed her the bag of letters and she automatically began laying out the wooden tile holders.

"Wolfe, I'm tired. Maybe I should just go to bed." Exhaustion overtook her mind and body. The idea of having to think of words was overwhelming. She waited for him to agree, patting her gently on the head and allowing her to escape.

"Tough. I'm bored and you're playing. Don't forget the rules. You can't use all medical terms or it's not fair."

She bristled, shaking the bag of letters. "You're so mean and selfish. I'm tired and you're making me play."

"It'll be good for you." He left to refill her wineglass and returned with a notepad and pen. "What are we playing for?"

She let out a breath. "Geez, I don't know. I'm a resident and you're a millionaire. How about money?"

"You're such a smart-ass. We'll play for secrets."

She froze. Studied his face. He seemed serious, intent on fishing out his first letter from the bag. "What type of secrets?"

Wolfe shrugged. "If you win, you get to ask me any-thing and I'll tell you. Vice versa. Deal?"

She had nothing to lose. Her spirits spiked and she picked the letter *S*. Nice. He got an *A*. Sucker. "You go first."

Gen forgot how much fun Scrabble was. She used to play tournaments with her family, yelling, challenging each other at every turn. The dictionary was a well-worn friend. The simple complexity calmed and focused her mind, and suddenly she found herself locked in a stiff competition with one of the smartest men she knew. Best of all, he never showed it. Someone looking at him would never know from his casual dress and rough speech how highly intelligent and educated he was. But on the Scrabble board he was frickin' deadly.

She was ahead a good twenty points and still held a magic *Z*. It was her game to lose, and she didn't intend to do it. Her turn. The open square sung to her in a symphony. Ah, the beauty of having an *S*.

Zips.

He whistled. "Nice job."

She preened. A surge of adrenaline made her jump a bit on the couch. "Triple word score!" She grabbed the letters for replacement and turned the bag over. "No more letters!"

She was so gonna win.

He chewed on the edge of the pencil, gaze focused on the board. "Hmm, space is getting tight. This is going to be tough." She drank her wine, waiting happily for the little word she expected, and swore she wouldn't be a bad winner. Well, at least she'd try. All he had to work with was an open *A*, and it wouldn't give him much.

"Got it." He began laying letters down one by one across the board.

Anestrus.

Huh? Gen leaned over and tried to focus. Wait, had he gotten rid of all his letters? She blinked in astonishment at the empty tile holder. He just scored an extra fifty points for the bonus.

"Hold off. What the heck is *anestrus*? That's not a word. And how did you manage to keep two *S*'s hidden from me?"

He shrugged as if it meant nothing. "Don't know. Wanted to save them for a good one. You don't know what that means? It's a word."

"I challenge!"

He cocked his head. "You're a doctor and know biology. You're telling me you never heard of it?"

"Of course I haven't, because it's not a word. What does it mean, smarty pants?"

"Anestrus is the period of sexual inactivity in mammals."

She blinked. "You're kidding me, dude."

"Nope. Look it up. You challenge and lose, it's my game."

"Fine. I still challenge." She grumbled in irritation as she flipped through the dictionary and came across . . . *anestrus*. The period of sexual inactivity in mammals.

Bastard.

She shut the book with a snap. His delighted grin stole all her thunder. "Believe me now, Doc?"

Oh, she so wanted to scream "Cheater," but she couldn't. He was just smarter than her right now, and it burned her bad. Another trait she had gained from her sister. A penchant to win all board games.

She studied him, relaxed, a tiny grin still on his face while he cleaned up the board and allowed her to pout. He'd changed into running shorts and a tank top that showed off his carved arms and cut shoulders. His skin was a lovely golden brown from the sun. Funny, any woman would be going nuts right now to be alone with him, in front of a roaring fire, in a deserted cabin. He was a walking, talking sex god, and here she was, playing Scrabble in her Walmart clothes, with no makeup and crazy hair.

It was pretty awesome.

Sleepiness began to claim her again. She leaned her head against the side of the couch and yawned. "I hate losing."

"I know."

"You won fair and square. I'm yours for the taking." His brow shot up. "For a secret, I mean. Mind out of the gutter, please."

"Was just concerned you wanted to end your anestrous state."

She couldn't help it. Gen threw her head back and laughed. "One day. Not tonight."

"Good to know." She waited for his question, knowing it would be about David. How sad it was that she'd begun shutting Wolfe out under her fiancé's demands. Soon she'd need to admit her wrong and hope Wolfe could forgive her. Now, at least, she could offer the truth for anything he wanted. "What was the thought that crossed your mind right before you decided to jump out the window?"

The question threw her off. Wringing her hands, she thought back to the one critical moment before she ran. Before she blew up her controlled, perfect, orderly life. And told the truth.

"I used to have this inner voice that would talk to me. Tell me things. Either my subconscious or gut, not sure. I got used to trusting it. But after a few months with David, it started to become quiet. At first I thought it was because I didn't need it anymore. I had the man I loved. But then I realized the loss was dangerous, because I was just afraid to listen to it anymore. The voice died." She sucked in a breath, trembling. "Right before the wedding, I heard it again. The voice kept telling me one thing over and over."

"What?"

"Run," she said simply. "So I ran."

The emotion hit her hard. Wrung out, sad, confused, she slumped on the couch, not able to keep up her defenses any longer. Quietly, Wolfe got up and disappeared. Came back with a pillow. He laid it gently under her head, tucked the covers around her, and smoothed her hair back. The tenderness of his touch made a purr sound deep in her throat. She closed her eyes and welcomed the darkness, where nothing else mattered and no thoughts were needed.

"The voice was right, sweetheart. It always is. And thank God you listened."

He pressed a kiss to her forehead, but she was already sinking into sleep.

seven

"WHERE ARE WE going?"

After she'd moped around a bit, Wolfe declared they were going on a road trip to keep her mind occupied. After more cereal, and some grumbling, she agreed and climbed into the car.

"A place where dreams come true."

"In a tiny hidden upstate town? Wait—is it the spa? I'd love that! We can do dual massages and mud body baths to release toxins. Arilyn has been begging me to do one but I haven't had the time."

"Not the spa. You couldn't pay me enough to put mud on my body and release anything. I happen to like my toxins."

"Oh." She buckled her seat belt and thought hard. "Shopping? Women love shopping when they're depressed. Not that I'm a big shopper, but I'd be willing to try it. I do love shoes."

"I don't. I want to have fun, too, not be slowly tortured by girly shit. This place will cover both of our needs."

"Fine. You gonna tell me?"

"Nope. First rule of the road—keep on going and don't look back." The shadow over his face told her he'd experienced pain she couldn't imagine. Gen didn't want to. Right now, she trusted him to do what was right. The security of such trust humbled her, but if she tried to express it he'd only shrug the whole dialogue off and get embarrassed. Instead, she accepted his direction for the second day and nodded. "Then I'm ready to find out."

"Let's drive."

The rain had stopped in the middle of the night. The day was hot, the top was down, and Gen let the wind tear at her hair, whip her face, and bathe her in sensation. Blue sky whizzed by streaked with cotton-ball clouds. Once again, there wasn't a lot of talking. Wolfe pumped up the radio as Imagine Dragons sung about demons and they headed into town.

The memory hit hard. David driving toward Newport for a getaway weekend. The excitement that curled in her belly, knowing they'd finally be alone without hospital beepers or prying eyes. She'd stared at his godlike profile and wondered again how she'd gotten so lucky to have him notice her.

The car had hit something in the road and the tire blew out. They'd spent hours on the side of the road, on Memorial Day weekend, waiting for Triple A. Gen was used to mini disasters and approached life with a sense of humor. But as she watched David get more and more surly, the knot in her stomach began to tighten. When the car was finally fixed, he'd accused her of flirting with the mechanic. Told her if she hadn't been distracting him, he would've seen the debris in the road. The attack was finely launched, with cutting sarcasm but delivered with an angelic grace that confused her. By the time they got to the bed-and-breakfast, she was apologizing and not really understanding what it was for.

It was only the beginning.

Gen rubbed her arms, suddenly peppered with goose-flesh. Why hadn't she seen the manipulation before? Had it always been lurking? Their relationship unfolded so fast it was hard to keep up, but he consistently told her how much he loved her. Wanted to protect her. Wanted her to do well in her career and as his mate. How could that have been bad?

Bad enough you escaped through the church window, her inner voice snapped. *Bad enough every night he came home you were a nervous wreck, making sure you did everything perfectly.*

Not now, she answered. *I'm not ready for this now.*

Fine. But when you are, I'll give you some hard truths.

"Are you cold? I can put the top up."

Gen turned. He stared at her with assessing eyes. "No, I like it. Just the crazy voices in my head screwing with me again. I'll be fine."

He nodded. "Get them all the time."

"What do you do to make them stop?" she asked.

Wolfe concentrated on the road, but she knew he saw much more. "Make the music louder."

Gen smiled. And cranked up the volume.

When they finally reached their destination, Wolfe slowed to a crawl, inching toward the racetrack. Horse racing? Ugh. Why hadn't she guessed? She hated gambling; she always lost.

"Really, dude? First my groom, now all my money? This isn't fun," she said glumly.

He sent her a sharp glare. "Has anyone ever showed you the true beauty in horse racing? The adrenaline rush? The pounding of horses' hooves as they break away from the gate? The screaming of the crowds? Saratoga Racetrack is one of the most famous, and the home of the great Travers Stakes. Champions have raced here, and people travel from all over to be a part of it . . . Are you yawning?"

She delicately patted her mouth. "I went horseback riding once and didn't like it."

He rolled his eyes. "You won't be riding these horses. Just betting on a winner. Though you're probably the right size to be a jockey."

Gen huffed out a breath. "That was low. I thought you liked making money, not losing it."

"I never lose at the track."

"I'm gonna be bored. This is gonna be just as bad as the fishing disaster."

"Get moving, Gen."

She did, sighing and whining a bit and dragging her feet like a cranky toddler. The crowds were lined up and streamed from the sidewalk, chattering with enthusiasm. Rolled-up books were tucked under their arms, and they pointed tiny pencils at the pages, talking odds and breeding and trainers. The tangy scent of earth and horse manure rose to her nostrils as she and Wolfe paid and walked through the elaborate wrought iron gates.

The scene surprised her. Instead of a bunch of men smoking and huddled around a small track, it was like a slice of old-town America burst around her. Concession stands selling homemade lemonade, hot pretzels, and various snacks were set up along the twisting sidewalks. A festive band played at the entrance, with children dancing and laughing to the beat. Large trees shaded areas of picnic benches where television monitors were scattered about. The air practically sizzled with energy while the broadcaster spoke about scratches and listed the horses in the race with both advantages and disadvantages. Women dressed in gorgeous dresses and elaborate hats strolled past her in elegant glory. Funny, it felt more like a picnic event than a dirty track.

"How could hard-core gambling attract so many wholesome family members?" she asked, trotting after him. He bought two racing forms, some pencils, and a large cup of lemonade. Then headed toward a bench.

"Because horse racing is a respected sport. August is the only month the track is open, so many families stop here on vacation on the way to Lake George. It's one of the only tracks you can see the jockeys and horses up front and stand right near the gate to see the race."

She sat next to him and took a large gulp of lemonade. It was tart and sweet at the same time, and she licked her lips with enthusiasm. At least she'd eat good here. "Okay, so what do we do?"

He studied the book for a few minutes, tapping the pencil. She kept quiet and waited for the elaborate plan. "We bet. Did you bring money?"

Gen blinked. "I left in my wedding dress, remember?"

He winced. "Oops, sorry. I'll front you for today."

"Oh gee, what a great friend."

"But that means I get ten percent of any money you make."

She released the straw from her lips and gasped. "That's not fair! That's robbery! What type of person are you, taking advantage of the weak and uneducated?"

He kept his gaze trained on the book, muttering under his breath as his pencil made scratches and notes in the margin. "You're the strongest woman I know and wicked smart. You'll be taking advantage of me by the end of this day."

She sniffed haughtily, even though the compliment was nice. She batted her lashes coquettishly. "I don't know nothin' 'bout betting on no horses, Mr. Wolfe."

He looked up as if annoyed she'd broken his concentration. "We can do this the hard way or the easy way."

"What's the hard way?"

"I educate you on narrowing down the field until you decide what horse is best for you. We calculate speed ratings. Check breeding, trainers, jockeys. Look at their past performance. See if they dropped in class. Glance at the odds. Then make an overall pick using all that information."

She shuddered. A root canal sounded more fun than that. "What's the easy way?"

"You look at the names and numbers and bet on your favorite."

"Sold. The easy way it is. Give me the form." His suffering sigh told her he was disappointed in her choice but she didn't care. She certainly didn't have to worry about her weight anymore, so while he took his time gathering all the useless information, she'd make her way through the food carts.

Gen glanced down at the list of horses. Disappointed

Dreamer. The inner bell rang and she stabbed her finger at lucky number four. "That's the one."

"Umm, yeah. Not a great choice. Let me show you how to read the stats. This column shows his past races, and he hasn't won a race since April. Looked promising, but something must have happened and he's been dropping ever since. These are the speed numbers. None of the handicappers picked him even to show."

"I don't care. What type of bet do I do?"

"I would highly suggest a few bucks on show. You can do win, place, or show. Win is first, place is first or second, and show means he can come in first, second, or third. Odds are twenty to one, so it's a long shot. The morning line favorite is going off at three to one."

He spread open the page and showed her the numbers. "See, number one is the favorite because he won his last three races. This is the one to beat. Want to throw a few bucks on him so you get the feel of the win?"

A dark cloud settled over her. Winning was always so important to David. Be the best. Be graceful with the ones you defeat, but make sure you come out ahead. She was so sick and tired of trying to be that person, just like poor Disappointed Dreamer probably was trying to keep up with the stupid number one horse. Maybe his trainer wouldn't let him run his own race. Maybe he wouldn't be first all the time, but at least he'd keep his head high because he tried his best. Well, forget number one and his victories. She was done with betting on favorites.

Gen practically spit out the words. "Screw number one. I want the four horse. Give me money."

Wolfe cocked his head and studied her. His lips tugged in a grin, but he just nodded and reached into his pocket to slide a twenty at her. "Here you go." She scooped up the bill and kept her hand out. "What?"

"I want more."

"More? Sweetheart, twenty bucks on a long shot is plenty—you're just gonna lose it. I'll give you more later." He reached over for the lemonade and took a sip.

She shook her head hard. "I want to bet one hundred dollars on him to win."

Wolfe choked. Gen waited patiently. "Are you nuts?"

"Are you a multimillionaire, Wolfe?" He lapsed into silence. "Just what I thought. I'll give you your ten percent bookie fee, but right now I want a hundred. Oh, and an extra twenty for snacks."

He reached back into his wallet, peeled off the bills, and handed them over to her. Damn, he was grumpy when he didn't get his way. "Thanks. I'll be back."

"I need to show you how to place a bet!"

"I see a line up over there. You finish tracking your statistics, I'll figure it out. See ya."

She walked away, feeling an odd buzz in her veins. Like she had an instinct something big was going to happen. Gen waited her turn and eavesdropped on a bunch of different conversations, finally narrowing in on a group of three guys arguing over the race.

"The only reason you're betting the four is because you got dumped, man. Don't let her take your money, too."

"Yeah, there's plenty of hot women around you can

sleep with this weekend. Just forget about her. Pick number one and get a win."

The dumpee looked generally miserable. Shaggy blond hair, ruddy cheeks, stubble, and clothes a bit wrinkled told her he was indulging in the breakup blues. Poor guy. His friends flanked him on either side, beer in hand, trying to do the manly thing by insulting him enough so he was happy. Men were an odd gender she didn't think she'd ever figure out. They were young, probably college age, and seemed more intent on looking around for hot women than horses.

The dumpee sighed. "Who cares if I win if I really lost?"

His friends groaned in horror at the emotion. "Ah shit, I can't hear this all weekend. We're here to have fun, dude. Make some money. Drink. Get lucky."

Gen couldn't help it. She tapped one of them on the shoulder. "Excuse me, but I think the four is gonna win."

All three of them checked her out, and it seemed she passed the test. The dumpee's companions gave her broad, welcoming grins. "Hey, that's great. This is Ed, I'm Tom, and this here is Steve."

"Hi, I'm Gen." She focused on Ed. "I'm sorry about your girlfriend."

The other two winced, but Ed nodded. "Thanks. It sucks. We've been together for two years but she fell in love with some actor in her class. He's got bad teeth but she didn't care. Said he was exciting and artistic."

She clucked in sympathy. "If she didn't appreciate you, it's better this happened now. But I know that won't make you feel better. You're lucky to have awesome friends to try and help."

Tom and Steve puffed up. "Why don't you hang with us and watch the race? We're going up to the rail. Did you come with your girlfriends?" They looked around hopefully.

"No, sorry. Can you help me though? What do I say to put a hundred bucks on number four to win?"

"Whoa, you really like four, huh?" Tom asked.

"Yeah. I'm tired of the cool horses winning all the time. I think he has a shot."

Ed gave a small grin. "Me, too. I'm sticking with my bet."

Steve shrugged. "Your money. I'm taking the one. Gen, when you get to the booth, say you want race one, a hundred dollars to win on the four horse. Got it?"

"Thanks. I got a feeling."

The Black Eyed Peas song played in her brain as she got her ticket. Wolfe wasn't at the picnic table so she decided to go to the rail with the guys. They were really nice to her, joking around and flirty in an innocent type of way. Had she ever felt that young? Lately, at only twenty-six years old, she felt as if she'd aged a hundred years. It was nice to relax in the hot sun and pretend she had no other cares in the world except winning on a horse.

She clutched her ticket and peered over the gate, cursing her wimpy five feet. Before she realized, Steve hauled her up and onto his shoulders. A squeal escaped her mouth. "I'm too heavy for you. Ah!" She frantically gripped at his shoulders for balance while the guys broke into laughter. The people surrounding them gave a cheer.

"Are you kidding? You're light as a feather. See, now you can see the horses."

Gen relaxed a bit. He was right. It was actually kind of cool; she'd never been on a guy's shoulders before. The stream of horses pranced in front, bodies gleaming, heads tossing, and then were guided into their separate gates. All of a sudden, there was a buzz and the announcer screamed over the speakers, "And they're off!"

She never knew a race could be so long. She never knew a race could be so short. The horses flew around the track at a rapid pace, dirt flying up from their hooves, jockeys leaning over, the pace punishing and brutal as they fought each other for space.

Disappointed Dreamer was dead last. The number one horse—Rapid Rose—held the lead, keeping tight to the rail. The crowd screamed different names out loud, gazes pinned to the field of ten, and slowly, ever so slowly, the number four began to inch his way toward the middle.

The scarlet uniform stood out boldly among the jockeys. Head tucked, legs a blur, the rider made up ground in rapid time, and they neared the finish line. Other horses dropped one by one, with Rapid Rose still holding the lead, but Disappointed Dreamer hit his stride and closed in so fast Gen couldn't believe it was possible.

She yelled so loud her throat hurt, and Steve bounced up and down, so she grasped his head to make sure she didn't topple. And then number four was neck and neck with number one, and they battled for two long, long seconds.

Disappointed Dreamer crossed the finish line a few noses ahead.

Steve reached up and easily plucked her from his shoulders. The moment her feet hit the ground she danced like a crazy person. Her heart raced and her palms sweat and raw adrenaline pumped through her system. The photo finish was quickly resolved. It was official.

"Holy crap, you made over two grand!" Tom said, shaking his head. "What a race."

"We won, we won," she screeched, hugging Ed. "I told you I had a feeling."

Suddenly, a cold voice broke through the revelry, making her stop and freeze.

"What the hell is going on?"

She jerked around and stared into a pair of icy blue eyes.

Uh-oh. Now she had another feeling.

She was in trouble.

eight

*I*F THERE WAS one thing he lived as his motto, it was "Be cool."

Not much rattled him anymore. After a brutal past and hard journey to get where he was, Wolfe decided he was pretty much done with all those highs and lows of emotion. That's why he did better with women for the short term. He didn't have a jealous bone in his body. And he might get a bit irritated at work, but nothing really moved him to show actual anger.

Until now.

He was about to pound on Pretty Boy's face and he had no idea why.

She'd been on his fucking shoulders. With her crotch jammed in his neck. The tight threesome seemed quite enchanted with her win—not to mention he was a bit amazed at the four horse himself—but it was the expression on her face that made him want to go apeshit.

Happy. For the first time in a long time, she looked happy.

And it wasn't because of him.

Now, where had that weird stuff come from? Wolfe narrowed his gaze as the college dudes looked at each other nervously and took a step back. Before David, Wolfe had been known to double-date with Gen and speak briefly about their other relationships. They'd agreed on the rules beforehand. No crazy sex stories. Sure, he liked to tease her, but they were usually made up to get a rise out of her. They stuck with minor details, some emotion, and a lot of humor. After David, she began to clam up fast, and he'd lost her within the year. It hurt, and he was pissed, but he kept telling himself if she was happy, it was his duty to swallow the disappointment. He just usually . . . missed her. But not in an unkempt, raw type of way.

Right now? Yeah, not so much.

He had no time to ponder or question the strange mess bubbling up inside. Gen rolled her eyes. "Wolfe, you're scaring them." She jerked her head toward him and spoke to her crew. "Wolfe's not my boyfriend, just a friend. You're not gonna get body slammed. This is Ed, Tom, and Steve."

The dudes relaxed and tried to do that friendly bonding ritual, but he remained cold. Gen was vulnerable, and he wasn't about to have her played by some guys on a weekend to get laid. One of the guys raised a hand but didn't come forward. "Hey. Nice to meet you."

Gen's navy blue eyes actually sparkled. Damn, she was pretty. He'd forgotten the old Gen and her bubbly personality. She loved practical jokes, bawdy humor, and having fun. A pang pierced him deep. He'd really lost her these past two years. Only now he was beginning to realize she had just been a ghost of her former self.

"Got nervous when I couldn't find you. Thanks for keeping an eye on her." He nodded at the guys and motioned her forward. "Let's cash that ticket of yours."

She bounced toward him, grabbed his hand, and spoke to her admirers. "Ed also won, so we should go together. Hey, why don't you join us? Wolfe got a picnic table, and you can help me with the next race."

Irritation flowed freely, but their enthusiastic reply cut him off.

"Thanks, that sounds great!" Ed announced.

Steve and Tom heartily agreed. "Maybe some of your beginner's luck will rub off on us."

Wolfe remained silent as they headed to the ticket counter and collected their winnings. Seemed like Ed and Gen had bonded, since they both did a little dance with their money in hand. How sweet.

Suddenly she pressed two bills into his palm. "Here you go. Two hundred dollars, ten percent for the loan. I don't think I'll need any more money from you today, so thanks."

Uh-oh.

In seconds, the mood chilled. Three guys gazed at him as if he was the scum of the earth.

"You made her pay interest?" Ed asked. "I thought you guys were friends."

He refused to shift his feet. "Just a joke."

Gen laughed. "Yeah, right! You never joke about money—you probably would've sicced a loan shark on me."

Shit. Tom fisted his hands, and Steve practically spit in disgust. "That's lame, man," Tom said. "Ed was short this week so I lent him money. No interest though. But I guess friendship means different things to different people."

Gen shrugged it off, completely clueless to the pissing

contest currently going on in her honor. "Nah, it's okay. Millionaires are kinda tight with their money anyway."

Steve choked. "You're a millionaire?"

Double shit. This was going nowhere. Wolfe glared, giving Steve the intimidating look he saved for his business meetings. "Forget it, I'm not explaining. Gen and I go way back."

"I bet." Ed glared, not the least bit intimidated, and hooked his arm through Gen's. "Come on, I'll buy you a hot dog."

"But I won more money than you."

"Score another race and you buy the beer."

"Deal. Coming, Wolfe?"

"Yeah. Coming." He trailed behind the chattering group and wondered how the day could get worse.

THREE HOURS LATER, WOLFE realized he shouldn't have asked such a question to the universe.

He sat alone, racing form in his lap, and watched the growing crowd at the picnic table. Mostly men. Surrounding Gen. Not sure how it had happened.

She'd won race two with another long shot on Magic Dude. He'd followed her to the rail, watched another of his horses lose, but managed to keep her off Ed's shoulders. Or Tom's. Or whoever the hell they were.

Somehow, in all her excitement, she had managed to recruit two new followers. One with a military cut and roving eyes, the other his skinny sidekick, who looked harmless. Wolfe already knew it was impossible to win three races in a row on raw luck, so he stuck to his original plan. He picked Hammering Halo at three to one, since they were racing on turf and the horse had the best grass trainer in history.

Gen scored again on a ten-to-one shot.

After that, time blurred. The men pegged her to have a magic touch, and every time she stood on line to place a bet, more people followed her back to the table. The latest recruits had some girls in it, but they seemed more interested in Gen's ability to attract all the single men at the racetrack.

He tried to control his temper and be happy she was finally eating again. Seemed Ed and she had become close foodie buddies, plowing their way through fish tacos, hot dogs, beer, and pretzels.

He'd never been good at speaking with strangers or making friends. Wolfe fought off the urge to grab her and go home, where it was just them and they could settle back into a quiet conversation and general teasing. But he also realized she was distracted, and the moment she left the track she'd remember the shitstorm she'd left behind. He couldn't stand the idea of the sadness leaking back into her eyes, or the disappearance of her smile, which always squeezed his heart and made him happy. No. He'd just keep an eye on her and try to enjoy her excitement.

Ed whispered something in her ear. Gen tilted her head up, laughing. His arm came around her shoulders and he pulled her in for a fast, hard hug, strangely more intimate than a full mouth-to-mouth kiss. *WTF?*

Wolfe jumped up. "Time to go!" he declared loudly.

All gazes turned toward him.

Gen blinked. "We're only on race four. What's up?"

Everyone kept staring. He hadn't been this off-kilter in years. "Figured you'd be tired and we'd head home early?"

Ed piped up. "She can't leave when she's on a roll! Doesn't that mess with juju or something?"

"I think that's baseball, dude," Steve said. "If you wanna head out, we'll make sure she gets home safe."

Wolfe's voice iced. "Don't think so. Gen doesn't leave my sight. Get it?"

Gen gave a sigh. "You're losing, aren't you? Are you getting cranky?"

For God's sake, he suddenly felt like a toddler. "No, I'm not losing. Listen, if you want to stay, that's fine. Just didn't want you to lose all your money."

She gave a blinding grin with perfect white teeth. The woman could do a Trident commercial. "Not gonna happen. I'm rich today!"

The crowd closed back in on her, getting her take on the fourth race, and he went back to his picnic table. Alone. Just the way he liked it. No interruptions or distractions.

Cool.

He lost the next two. Gen won. So did everyone else, since half of the park realized she was on a blessed run and wanted a piece of the action. He left to get a beer, and when he came back, she'd officially lost race six. Sad faces surrounded her, so he went to check if they were packing up for the day. About time. He'd never heard of anyone with such a long winning streak.

"Sorry, sweetheart. Happens to all of us eventually."

Ed patted her shoulder. "We'll get the next one."

Gen was already studying the form in front of her, leafing to the next race. "I had a bad feeling about the last one. Should've held back. My skin is tickling again, so I think we can do this."

Wolfe put up his hands in surrender. "Your call. Let me know. I'm here if you have any questions."

She was already back to ignoring him, seemingly entranced by the field of six running in the next race. Wolfe went back to his table, caught between amusement and irritation at how quickly he'd been replaced at the track. Seemed to be a pattern. She was finally out of David's clutches, and had now recruited a whole new batch of men to be her *friends*. Seemed she gave them a hell of a lot more attention than she had given him these past two years.

The spiteful thought made his temper even darker.

He watched as she lost the next three races in a row and he picked up a couple of wins. Finally. Her crowd began to disperse as the magic disappeared and she was left with her original crew.

His phone convulsed like it was possessed. Wolfe scrolled through the text messages and voice mails, which were getting more frantic, and knew he didn't have much more time to hide her. Kate would get into the car and track them down. Alexa would call Sawyer, who'd tell Julietta, and then he'd be in trouble. His gut said she needed one more day to process before he took her back. So he bought the precious time by texting to a dozen people that she was fine and they'd be returning tomorrow. Then turned off his phone.

Screw it.

Wolfe glanced at the field for race nine. What a mess. A dozen horses, most of which hadn't raced before, and the odds were all over the place. He wouldn't even trust the Clocker Lawton tip sheet on this one, so Wolfe decided to scrap it. He tossed his form and his empty bottle, then headed toward Gen.

"One last bet, or are you ready? You did great today."

Gen looked up. There was an odd light in her eyes he recognized well. Sheer determination, fierce will, and stubborn pride.

It was pure nightmare.

Suddenly his heart began to thump. "Gen, what are you thinking?"

She smiled. Even Steve and Tom looked a little cowed by her. "Last race. Last shot. Number six."

He glanced at the monitor: fifteen to one. Not good in this mix-up, but at this point she couldn't lose much, right? "What's the name?"

"Phoenix Rising."

He swallowed. Yeah, this could be bad. Especially if she took it as some kind of sign. Wolfe forced a laugh. "Sweetheart, these horses have never run before. You had some beginner's luck, but placing a bet on a name is fun, not practical. Let's take your winnings, get a steak dinner, and call it a day."

"I have three words for you, Wolfe."

He tried not to panic, but he already recognized the craziness. She had a stubborn streak that rivaled no other. If you told Gen no, she only got more determined to prove herself. He remembered when he joked and said she'd never be able to pull an A on her Italian final back at NYU. She was a science wiz, but sucked at languages, so he'd had a field day teasing her while almost flunking her family's second language. What did she do?

Immersed herself in Italian for a week and refused to speak English in the house. Then scored an A on the exam.

She was scary.

"What three words?"

Gen smiled. "Let it ride."

Ed looked worried but slowly nodded. "It's the only thing left to do. The only move left. If this horse wins, it'll be a sign."

Wolfe stared. "What sign?"

"A sign I wasn't meant for my girlfriend. Ex-girlfriend. If Phoenix wins, it means I'll rise from the ashes and find a new love."

Steve groaned. "That's the stupidest thing I ever heard, bro. It's a horse. Not some kind of screwed-up analogy of your love life!"

Wolfe almost lost it, but Gen nodded as if she agreed and believed he was sane. "Ed, I completely agree. But we need to make a statement to the universe. Let's bet it all."

Ed clasped her hand as if they were married and had just asked the bank for a mortgage. "Yes. Let's do it."

"Are you nuts?" Tom yelled. "People only do that in the movies. We need the money for gas and food and stuff!"

Ed shook his head. "This is bigger than that, man. You're gonna have to back me on this."

Wolfe came out of his trance and shook his head. "Hell, no, you've both lost it. Names of the horses mean nothing when it comes to winning a race. You'll only be disappointed and more depressed. Walk away on a high note. I mean it, let's go."

She clucked her tongue in sympathy. "I'm sorry you don't understand, but I need to do this. If I take the risk and believe, something wonderful will happen. It's time to watch the Phoenix rise from the ashes. Come on, Ed."

Wolfe watched her walk away with his mouth half-open. What had just happened? When had he lost control of her and this whole nutty day?

Steve cleared his throat. "Damn. We'll be fronting him all weekend."

"What the hell does a phoenix have to do with a horse?" Tom asked.

"It's an analogy of rebirth," Wolfe said. "The phoenix is destroyed and rises above the ashes."

"Did Gen break up with someone, too?" Tom asked.

Wolfe didn't answer. Ah crap, it had nothing to do with losing the money. He was afraid if the horse lost she would spiral back into a deep depression. She was putting way too much into a horse that had no clue it meant more to her than a race. She was looking for forgiveness. Hope.

"Do you guys believe in religion or anything?" he asked.

They both shared a look. "Umm, we went to church when we were younger. We believe in God."

"Good. Pray hard we win. 'Cause if we don't, it's gonna be a disaster."

GEN CLUTCHED THE TICKET in her hand and trained her gaze on the field of twelve. Number six was dark brown, with a beautiful silky mane and stocking legs. His jockey wore navy blue. When he trotted past her on the way to the gate, she noticed the spring in his step, and thought it was a good sign.

Until he slammed his head against the gate and refused to go in.

Wolfe's expression made her palms sweat. He looked a bit worried. He never looked like that. She was so used to him being in control of every situation, the idea he could be nervous about her losing a silly race made her wonder why she was making such a big deal of it.

Because.

David didn't believe in chance, or luck, or God. Once she had. After two years of being with him, she didn't know anymore. He had consistently showed her how science was a tool, how odds were calculated and coincidence was just a blip on the monitor screen that really meant nothing.

Slowly, she'd begun to lose her sense of magic. Rationally, she realized the six horse was nothing but a target of her current heartache, an attempt to regain a mysterious emotion she believed may have died.

Simply put, she didn't care.

Gen needed Phoenix Rising to win.

They finally got him loaded into the gate. A few precious seconds ticked by. The doors exploded open and they were off.

The field was a mass of pounding legs clustered together in a tight herd. Phoenix was in the middle of the pack, holding his own but not doing spectacularly. She chewed on her lip while the guys yelled encouragement at the horse and the field rounded the first bend. Dirt flew. Ears pinned, the navy flag streamed in the air, slowly inching forward.

From the back of the pack, the eight horse flew past the mishmash and took the lead. Damn. He was gray. She'd heard about gray horses being lucky.

Phoenix held his own, and as they neared the second turn, the space between them closed. Ten inches. Six. Four. Three.

Ed screamed, "Go, you motherfucker! Go!"

Neck and neck, they neared the finish, the jockeys' whips nipping their flanks, hooves digging in, eyes fierce with the lure of victory.

They flew over the finish line together.

"Did he win?" Steve screamed. "Did he win?"

"I don't know! Fuck! I don't know!" Tom moaned, pacing back and forth. The crowd muttered in excitement, all trained on the board in front, waiting for the results. Ed didn't speak, just stared at the field.

Heart beating madly, Gen choked for breath, and then a warm, firm grip surrounded her. She looked down, and Wolfe's fingers clasped hers, as if they had always belonged there.

Wolfe smiled. "He won."

"How do you know?"

Those beautiful blue eyes darkened with a whisper of something deep. "I just know."

The word *photo* disappeared from the screen.

Number six, Phoenix Rising, was posted in the first slot.

Number eight was listed in the second.

"We won." Ed turned toward her, pure joy skating over his face. "We won, Gen!"

He grabbed her and spun her around, breaking the hold of Wolfe's grip. The guys whooped and shouted, spilling beer and pounding backs in a whirlwind of activity. When they showed the magic tickets, she came out with thirty thousand dollars and an IRS form. Ed pocketed two grand.

She walked in a daze as the boys celebrated, talking about champagne and dinners and bar hopping. Wolfe walked beside her and stopped at the front gate. "You're coming with us, right?" Ed asked. "You're my lucky charm. Let's get some dinner and relax. Get to know one another."

Steve and Tom stood behind, trying to be cool. Wolfe took a step back and said nothing.

Uh-oh. She caught the interested gleam in Ed's eye and wondered how she'd once again trapped herself into hurting another man. Still, it had been an incredible day and she'd never forget him. Gen raised herself on tiptoe and kissed his cheek.

"I just broke off an engagement, Ed," she told him. "I'm a wreck. But today, for a few hours, I forgot. I had a blast and I'll never forget you, but I have to go home now."

She waited for puppy dog eyes and a crestfallen expression. Instead, he nodded, brought her hand to his lips, and kissed her palm. "You're a hell of a woman. Thanks for today. It was a sign for me, too. Tracey wasn't for me."

"And you're a hell of a man. You deserve more." Gen smiled, said good-bye to the other guys, and made her way back to the car with Wolfe. A strange lightness poured through her, as if the universe had just told her things would work out. Maybe not right away, or next week. But Phoenix Rising had won, against all the odds, and maybe there was magic in the world after all.

"You okay?"

She glanced toward him. He leaned back in the driver's seat, hands wrapped around the wheel. Ready to take her away from any demons following them. What would she do without him?

"Yeah. I won more than you today."

"You did." He started the ignition and pulled out.

"Where are we going now?"

"Prime rib, baby. On you. Up for it?"

She settled back in the leather seat and grinned. "Hell, yeah."

nine

WOLFE KNEW EXACTLY when the guilt hit.

They'd just ordered their meal at Mouzon House. Offering fresh farm-to-table food in an intimate setting, the place was perfect for conversation, quiet, and culinary genius. Wolfe's background in Italian dining taught him one thing. Simple didn't mean average. A five-star dish was based on quality ingredients used to showcase the flavors without a lot of fancy stuff getting in the way.

Too bad he still couldn't cook.

She'd been upbeat and chatty on the drive, but now a shadow passed over her features. Her shoulders slumped and she stared at her plate, lost in another world. Somewhere not as safe.

"You missed the bread." He pushed the basket over and breathed in the scent of steamy dough and rosemary. "Rip away, I can get more."

Gen shook her head. "No thanks. Carbs aren't smart. I shouldn't have had that pizza either last night."

He raised a brow. "You used to plow through the whole basket, leave me with the crumbs, and have never once been overweight. Where'd you come up with that crap?"

"David."

The name shot like a bullet and shredded through denial. He fought the blistering anger again at the asshole's ability to make her question everything about herself—from her career, to her sex life, to her damn weight.

He sharpened his voice. "You work out regularly. I'd also bet you're underweight now and could use some bread. Try a piece."

A ghost of a smile passed her lips. "You're bossy."

"That a surprise?"

She tore off a piece and nibbled. Then closed her eyes in delight. "Oh, this is good. It's got garlic, too. Better not breathe on you later."

He snatched up a slice and munched. "Now we'll both reek. Did he make you doubt yourself?"

She jerked. Wolfe knew well the best way to grab a secret is the art of the surprise attack. Sawyer had taught him the move well, trying to pull information from him he'd tried to lock down inside. "No," she said softly.

Lie.

He didn't challenge her. Just nodded. "Good. Because if he did, that would be a major reason not to get married. Not that I'm an expert, but I think you're supposed to inspire confidence in your partner. Right?"

"Right."

The waiter interrupted them with the appetizer. The crawfish beignets were the specialty and had the delicious crunch and flavor as if they had been plucked straight from the lake. Damn good.

"He's a perfectionist. Part of his talent, I guess. He's one of the most sought-after surgeons in New York. You can't blame him for wanting to be better and pushing others to do the same. Look at you and Purity. You've dedicated everything you have to making the Manhattan site a success. You even learned golf."

"Thanks to Nate." He'd met Nate Dunkle on the course when he'd been desperate to learn the game in order to sign an important client. Though they didn't know each other, Nate gave him private lessons and taught him enough to play decently in record time and score the deal. He was now hooked up with Gen's friend Kennedy. "Who would've thought I'd enjoy hitting a little ball across a field to put it in a hole? I used to make fun of golfers and now I am one. And you're right, I'm a bit of a perfectionist in wanting to succeed and not accepting failure. Nothing wrong with it as long as you don't break the cardinal rule."

"What rule?"

He kept his attention on his plate to give her space. "Don't hurt people while you're doing it."

"I don't think he meant to."

"Intentions are noble, but if you still hurt someone, does that make it acceptable?"

The waiter took their plates, refilled the water glasses, and disappeared. The tension between them tightened. If he ripped David apart, she'd defend him. The guilt was eating her up alive, so he'd play the game and maybe she'd come to the true realization on her own.

"I'm a selfish bitch, Wolfe."

"Why? Because you went with your gut rather than make the biggest mistake of your life?"

"No. Because I had fun today."

His gaze locked with hers. A mixture of emotion beat from her body, gleamed in her eyes. Anger. Sadness. Shame. Frustration. She held herself stiffly, as if afraid once she let go, she'd never be able to go back.

She was right to feel that way. He knew too well you couldn't go back.

"When was the last time you did have fun, sweetheart?"

The desolation on her face broke his heart. "I don't remember. But that's not a reason to dump your fiancé at the altar."

"Probably not. Which means there's a bigger reason you haven't gotten to yet."

The waiter slid new plates in front of them. The impressive piece of Angus beef was rare, crusted with a peppercorn brandy, and placed over fried oysters. They forgot their serious conversation for a moment.

"This is sick," she said in awe.

"Agreed. Just a heads-up: you'll need to roll me out of here."

"I have no problem with that."

"Good."

They feasted in silence. She was the only woman, besides his family, he felt comfortable eating around. Still didn't know why. When he took dates to dinner, he was never settled enough to really dig in, as if he needed to play a certain role and it might slip if he revealed too much. Probably those years in Italy around Julietta's mother, Mama Conte. Food was an analogy for emotion and the soul, she used to cite repeatedly. Both were nourishment if received with the proper respect. A pang shot through him. It'd been months since he'd visited and he missed them. But Gen was able to manage heavy conversations in between bouts of quiet that no one else had mastered. Another bond they shared.

"I laughed today."

Her self-disgust made him want to comfort her, but she needed tough love. "Humor is a good way to deal with heavy stuff."

"I wasn't dealing with anything. You're not understanding or you're playing dumb, which just pisses me off. I forgot about David. Forgot I destroyed his life, left him at the altar, and ran away from my family. I was having fun. What type of person am I?"

He clenched his fork and leveled his gaze. "Normal. You did the best you could at the time to deal with the situation. Doesn't that tell you something was off? Ever stop to think you were so miserable in his presence that just getting away from him made you happy? How'd he get you so twisted up?"

"Maybe it's me. Not him. Maybe I'm screwed up."

"Nah, I'm the one who's really messed up. You've always been the stable one in this relationship. And as for David? I think he loved the idea of who he could make you be. Not who you are. Not the woman I see sitting across the table from me."

Her eyes widened. "Better is good. He wanted to make me better."

"By whose standards? His?" He leaned over and stabbed his fork in the air. "There is no better when you decide to marry someone. There's just you and all your is-

sues and bad qualities and crap. If he wanted some princess, he should've gone to fucking Disney World. Finish
your steak."

She stared at him for a while. Wolfe waited for her famous temper, or sarcastic wit, or even a torrent of tears.

Instead, she picked up her fork and resumed eating.

GEN FINISHED HER MEAL, trying not to lick the plate in
the process, and wondered how Wolfe was able to hone in
on the real issues in record time.

Practice, maybe. Lack of social niceties. His name fit
him well. Though he was civilized and the perfect business-
man, there was something quite primitive lurking beneath
the suit. As if rules did not apply behind the façade.

A shiver skated down her spine.

Was that why he hadn't found anyone to settle down
with? Because there was no one who would accept his so-
called baggage? Though he proudly held his man-whore
card with style, the way he spoke about his family confirmed he'd flourish in a steady, loving relationship. Kate
had been begging him for a while to sign up with Kinnections, but he just laughed her off. Maybe Gen should push.
He deserved happiness.

The thought of him never belonging to her again stole
her breath, but she figured it was a normal emotion. There
was no way his woman would feel comfortable having him
hang out with his best female friend. Women didn't like
that stuff. Of course, she'd experience some natural jealousy at being replaced.

Had Wolfe felt like that with David?

The thought startled her. Sifting back through the last year, she realized how slowly the most important people in her life had begun to fade away. When she'd try to visit her sisters, David would calmly suggest they do something as a couple and spend time alone. She tried many times to hit Mugs after her shift, but suddenly he'd call her to cover another shift, or suggest nicely that she'd been a bit slow on rounds and probably needed extra sleep. Lately, the only outings she went on revolved around him and the hospital, until a slight distance began to grow around her and the people she loved.

Even Wolfe's texts were ignored more and more. David would regularly check her phone to make sure no one was bothering her from the hospital. Sure, she tried explaining that her phone was personal, but when he got upset and subtly suggested she was trying to hide something, she gave in. The consistent texts from Wolfe made David question the whole basis of their relationship. After all, if her best male friend wasn't her future husband, what chance did they have at making a marriage work?

It had made sense at the time. Right? Yet she never really told Wolfe what was going on. She just stopped responding until their communication slowed to a dribble.

Confusion swamped her. She didn't know what was right or wrong anymore. Today had been amazing. She'd forgotten how much fun it was to let the day guide you. Meeting new people without worrying if she was flirting or giving off mistaken vibes. Being silly and impulsive without being gently scolded. It was almost as if she'd escaped from prison.

Was that what she equated David with? Prison? He'd never done anything to hurt her. Never, ever hit her. He'd been patient, and told her every day how much he loved her, lived for her, and dedicated his time to making sure they had a perfect relationship.

"Gen?"

She shivered again. Funny, Wolfe had said her name a million times over the years, but lately it sounded more intimate. A low, sexy growl. Is that how he acted with the women he took to bed? She knew he liked a bit of domination. Did he grip her wrists and whisper in her ear while he pounded inside her, taking her on a wild ride where nothing else mattered but orgasm?

"You're blushing."

Gen grasped her water glass and chugged. She was officially losing her mind. She'd never fantasized about Wolfe in bed before. Not like . . . that. Then again, her emotions were so raw and strange, she shouldn't be surprised. She pulled herself together and forced herself to meet his gaze.

"Just got warm. Wolfe?"

"Yeah?"

"I'm sorry."

He lifted a brow. "For what?"

"Letting you go." The shock in his blue eyes startled her. So vivid and naked, delving deep inside and plumbing every secret she had. Her thighs tightened as sudden lust struck her right between her legs. "I—I didn't realize what

I was really doing. David was angry over our closeness, so I stopped texting you and following through. It seemed easier that way. I started to pull away from the girls, too, but he got focused on you and used to ask if—if we were fooling around. He got mad when you called. I didn't know what to do so I began ignoring you."

He leveled her with his gaze, taking in her halfhearted apology. How awful would she feel if Wolfe suddenly replaced her because his new girlfriend was jealous? She'd be hurt. Angry. Resentful. Not once had he ever spoken badly about David, or gotten pissy with her. All those dates she broke at Mugs, and calls never returned.

The loss of her friend washed over her.

"I understand, sweetheart. I do. Gonna have to be honest here and admit it stung. I felt like I was losing you, but didn't know what to do. What the hell did I know? I never had a serious relationship."

She swallowed past her shame, but once again, with his truth came acceptance. "Can you forgive me?"

"If you promise not to dump me again for the next best thing. Especially Ed."

He smiled, and her heart exploded. She loved his smile. The stark features in his face softened, and she never felt so cherished as when she was receiving such affection. "Never," she whispered.

"Deal."

They finished their food and she pushed her plate away. Time to dive into the only subject left undiscussed. She gathered her courage. "How bad is it?"

Wolfe didn't pretend to misunderstand. "The calls? I

told Kate and Alexa we need some time. I turned my phone off this morning."

She winced. "I left everyone with a mess. I'm such a coward."

"If you were a coward, you would've walked down the aisle and married him. Say that again about yourself and I'll have to teach you a lesson."

She choked out a laugh. "Yeah, you're real scary."

"I can be." Their gazes locked and she swallowed. There was another side of her friend leaking out, one she'd never really seen before. It made her a bit uneasy.

And hot.

"I have to go back."

"Of course you're going back. But you needed space so you could figure out why you really left. Let me be clear. You're walking back into a clusterfuck. Questions, accusations, family chaos, and David trying to manipulate you. If you don't have your head clear, you may do something you regret. Go back on your own terms."

She pushed trembling hands through her hair. "I know. I've never done anything like this before. I do the right thing. I don't screw up."

"Life is messy. Get over it."

Her mouth dropped open. Then she laughed. "You so don't have the friendly female touch. I need Kate."

"You need truth. Dig deeper, Gen. I'll be next to you when we get back, but if you need more time, take it. Hell, we can get in the car and head to Lake George. Leave everything behind us."

The thought was so deliciously tempting. A road trip of

extremes, like *Thelma and Louise*. Kind of. No running from the law, of course, but still a buddy movie. "If I did that, I'd probably go to hell. Everybody will hate me."

"Not the ones who matter."

Her mind raced. Could she? Just disappear from the world a few more days, hitting the road in an endless twist of empty highways and the next adventure? Her soul leaped with joy. Yes, she may go to hell. Yes, she was the most horrible person on the planet. But she could do this, buy more time, get her head straight before diving into the mess. She'd call Kate and Alexa tonight and explain. To be anonymous and part of the world without worrying about being beautiful and charming and intelligent. Just to *be*.

Hope exploded. "You're right," she said, trembling with excitement. "Let's do it. Just a few more days."

He grinned. "That's my girl."

"I'll call home when we get back to the cabin so no one panics."

The waiter placed the bill down, leaned forward to collect the plates, and froze. His gaze roved over her features as if trying to commit them to memory. "You look so familiar. Do we know each other?"

She studied him with a frown. Light hair. Dark eyes. Beautiful olive skin. A bit younger than her, but Gen didn't recognize him. "No, I'm sorry, I don't think so." Wolfe handed him a credit card, which he snapped into place inside the folder.

"Sorry, it's the strangest thing, almost as if I saw you before. I apologize for the intrusion."

"No need." She smiled as he left to ring them up. Wolfe looked amused. "What?"

"Another admirer like the one at the track?"

She rolled her eyes. "Cut it out. Ed was sweet."

"And after you big-time. You know what line his buddies were coaching him with."

"What?"

"Quickest way over a woman is under the next one."

She laughed. "Sounds like something Kennedy would say."

The waiter glided back, set the bill down for Wolfe's signature, and beamed. "Now I know! You're in the paper!"

An icy foreboding slunk into her veins. Her mouth grew dry. "What paper?"

"The *Saratoga Herald*. You're the runaway bride!"

Wolfe jumped up from the table, threw the signed receipt down, and grabbed her hand. "Keep your mouth shut, buddy, or I'll do more than yank your tip. Understood?"

The waiter gulped, realizing his error, and nodded. "Sorry, sir. So sorry."

Wolfe didn't answer. Her body felt like glue, stuck to the ground and so stiff she couldn't move. Not that she needed to. He wrapped his fingers around her elbow and guided her out, until the hot air rushed over her and she suddenly gulped for oxygen.

"Bend over. Hands on your knees."

She did, gasping for more air, trying to calm her racing heart while the waiter's words burned in her brain. *Runaway bride. Newspaper.*

Oh, God.

She tried to speak, failed, and finally got out the words. "Need to see it."

"Gen—"

"Need to see it. Now."

His fingers tightened around her flesh in punishment. The slight pain cut through the panic and centered her, until she was brave enough to unfold and stand at full posture.

"Stay here."

She waited on the darkened sidewalk. The moon shimmered amid the mountain peaks, the blue-black sky a gorgeous streak of art. A couple walked past her, laughing softly, and went inside. Gen wrapped her arms around her chest until he came back out with the paper. He didn't speak, and the worried light in his eyes told her it was bad.

She unfolded it and read the headline:

"Surgeon Scalped at Altar."

Her engagement photo mocked her. Glowing in a white linen suit, hair curled and twisted up in a sophisticated knot, she clasped hands with David, who gazed adoringly into her face.

The picture next to it showed the packed church, endless roses bursting from spaces, glittering candelabras, and her father patting David on the shoulder, who grinned broadly in excitement.

The final photo sealed her fate.

David's broken face reflected back on the page as he exited the church to a blinding array of flashing bulbs, surrounded by reporters thrusting microphones in his face.

His eyes looked dazed, as if she'd ripped his heart out and stomped on it.

The world spun. Gen forced herself to skim the article. Phrases leaped out at her in mocking glee.

Renowned surgeon left at altar by his own resident.

Brokenhearted and abandoned, family rallies, refusing to speak to reporters.

Bride climbed through the window and escaped via a guest and her supposed friend. Another lover?

Her body shut down. Hope for the future shriveled like ashes, leaving dark stains and a bitter taste that choked. She'd done the unthinkable, and now it was time to pay.

Gen lifted her gaze. Her voice sounded wooden to her own ears. "Take me home."

He clenched his jaw. "Are you sure? We can still stick to the plan. Get in the car and go."

"Not anymore. It's over, Wolfe. Take me home."

He muttered a vicious curse. Then finally nodded.

She climbed into the car and they sped into the night, her fingers still clutching the paper.

ten

HE'D LOST HER.

Wolfe glanced over. She stared out the window, expressionless, completely removed from the present. He knew where she was, too—an in-between void of numbness and dark space that emptied the soul and left only a husk for earth.

He mourned more than the loss of her presence. In only three days, he'd remembered the joy of being with her, sharing her friendship and laughter, and the person he became around Genevieve MacKenzie.

He didn't try to bring her back. Plenty of time for that later. Instead, he let the music play loud, and closed in on home.

She'd made the necessary calls with his phone, agreeing to meet at her parents' house first thing in the morning. If it had been earlier, they would've waited up, so he was glad she'd be able to have a few more hours alone. Thank goodness David hadn't answered. Her awkward voice mail message made Wolfe wince. He had a gut instinct the man was playing some game with Gen beyond that of a heartbroken dumpee. The only thing Wolfe could do was keep an eye on Gen and make sure she was protected. He drove past the Welcome to Verily sign and crawled down Main Street toward the bungalow. Kennedy and Nate had rented it for a while before deciding to move to a bigger place, so thankfully it was empty. Wolfe wouldn't be surprised if Kate was waiting at the door though. That woman was hard-core mean when it came to protecting her best friend.

The streetlamp flickered as he pulled up to her cheerful yellow house, which looked as happy as she used to be.

"Ready, sweetheart?"

She nodded and climbed out. Grabbing their bags from the trunk, he walked up the curved pavement.

She froze in the doorway. He peered over to study the scene.

The place looked empty. Sure, it was still fully furnished, with the aqua blue sofa and throw cushions, bright watercolors on the walls, braided rugs, and the sturdy pine table that reminded him of Mama Conte's. The curvy metal spiral staircase leading to the tiny loft/attic gave the place a quaint charm. But the space pulsed with a hollow gloom, and a fine sheen of dust covered the surfaces. It had been empty only for a few months, but damned if he didn't get the impression of sadness, as if the place needed human inhabitants in order to be happy.

"I never thought I'd be back here," she said faintly. "I have nothing. No clothes. No laptop. Not even my toothbrush."

He gently pushed her through and shut the door behind them. "That's easily fixed in the morning. Besides, I'm not minty fresh myself. I'll run into town early and get what you need."

"David wanted me to put it on the market. I refused. Not sure why."

He didn't say the truth because they both knew it. She'd sensed something wasn't right between them, and selling her home gave her no exit plan. Wolfe checked the closets and found a set of sheets and blankets. He quickly made the bed while she stood and watched, so exhausted she seemed to sway on her feet. He took her hand, pushed her gently onto the edge of the mattress, and knelt before her. Untying her sneakers, he removed them, giving each foot a quick squeeze, then urged her under the quilt. Her face reflected a childlike trust that made his gut clench and a fierce sense of possession rush through him. Damned if he wouldn't battle anyone in order to protect her. He'd let her go once to another and her heart got trashed.

From now on, any guy would have to get through him first.

Wolfe refused to analyze the emotions beneath the thought. He pulled the tie from her hair so it was loose, and pushed the unruly waves back from her forehead. "Sleep, sweetheart."

He turned to leave but her whisper stopped him.

"Will you stay with me? I'm sorry—I'm such a baby, and a mess, but I'm just—scared."

She blinked furiously, her lower lip trembling. Hell. He didn't like sleeping with anyone because of the nightmares, but he wouldn't leave her alone. Not like this.

Wolfe nodded. Toed off his shoes. Then settled himself on top of the quilt and drew her against him. Her scent swamped him, the sweet scent of daisies, and the pureness of soap. Fresh. Clean.

So unlike him.

She wiggled her butt, settled in, and slowly, her muscles relaxed. He tightened his grip around her waist, soaking in the closeness and body heat that simmered like a campfire. Cursing under his breath, he concentrated on his breathing and tried not to get aroused. He'd kissed many women. Slept with even more. Yet the honest passion she gave him during that one kiss would haunt him forever.

But Gen was his friend. His confidant. His everything.

He'd never ruin it with sex.

Sleep came slowly.

THE NOISES WERE BAD tonight.

Vincent increased the volume and wished he had one of those awesome headsets that canceled out noise. The cheap earbuds and used iPod usually did the trick, but the thin door leaked a constant groaning, thrashing, and creaking of furniture. He knew there was more than one out there tonight. The sound of two males, grunting and yelling phrases at his mother like "Suck it, whore" and "Take it this way" rattled his eardrums and made him sick.

But he'd learned his lesson the last time not to show his face. Even if it was for hours.

He should've escaped into the woods, but it was damn cold and he hadn't been prepared. Usually the men came later, but right after school one had been munching on his cereal, checking him out in that familiar way.

His mother had been getting worse. The powder was now replaced with needles. Her eyes turned mad when she craved her fix, and the men seemed to know they could push her harder. He wasn't sure how long before he might need to run. He had only been able to hide a little over a hundred dollars so far. That wouldn't get him far. He'd heard terrible stories about foster care from his mother, who always warned him to hide their secret or he'd never see her again.

She had no one else to watch over her. He had to stay. When he got bigger, he'd get them both out, but right now he needed to bide his time.

His skin crawled from the screams. Finally, footsteps came out to the kitchen.

"You said I could get some if I did that," his mother whined. "I did what you wanted. Give it to me."

"Greedy bitch. I'll say when."

Something crashed against the wall. "The night's young. We got more to do."

"Just a little hit. Please."

Low laughter. "Be a good girl and you'll get what you need. Where's that boy of yours?"

"At a friend's."

"Is he in that fucking closet again? Let's get him out to party."

Vincent's heart beat wildly but he remained completely still. Fists pounded on the door. The lock rattled but held. "Hey, boy, come out and play. I got some stuff for you."

"Told you he's not here. Leave him alone, you have me."

A few more minutes of harassing, pounding, and threats. Then a clatter of needles hitting the table. "Ticktock, little boy. One day you're gonna be a man and get your ass out here to help your mother. You hear me, boy?"

His mother said something he couldn't make out. Then

there was blessed quiet as they shot up and went back into the bedroom. The noises started up again.

Vincent concentrated on the music, rocked back and forth, and wished he was dead.

He was eleven years old.

eleven

GEN SHOT OUT of bed.

The door banged repeatedly in a nonstop rhythm, getting more and more demanding. What if they were reporters? She glanced over at the empty bed. Where was Wolfe? Had he left for the store? What should she do?

Gen hunkered down, crawled to the living room, and peeked out the side window.

Kate, Kennedy, and Arilyn peered back at her.

"Babe, it's us, let us in!"

She fumbled with the latch, flung open the door, and was engulfed in a tight circle of hugs.

Unfortunately, the numbness and walls she'd built up over the past few days crashed down with a tumble.

She burst into tears.

Gen let herself go, crying and shaking as they moved her to the couch. Kate held her tight, Arilyn patted her knee and whispered soothing words, and Kennedy crashed around the kitchen, cursing like a banshee.

"Asshole prickface! Putting on some type of wimpy show for the reporters to look good! I knew something was up, Gen. I never trusted him. Anyone with teeth that white is trouble." The bang of a kettle and the rushing of water echoed in the air. "Jumping out the church window was the best damn move you've ever made."

Gen dragged in a tearful breath. "But I left him at the altar. He loved me, and I'm so messed up, I panicked and now everybody hates me and I don't know what's going to happen next."

Kate gripped her shoulders. Her voice was strong and calmed the rising panic. "Yes, you do. You just didn't want to face it. It's time to look at the truth, honey. You didn't want to marry David. I think you wanted to leave for a long time."

"You've changed over the past six months," Arilyn said. "We all saw it but didn't know what to do. You avoided your friends, you looked stressed all the time, and you lost your joy."

Kennedy slammed down a mug on the counter. "Bastard asshat. I had a feeling he was working you behind the scenes. Every time we had plans, you'd call with an excuse regarding David. You started to disappear. And you were so jumpy, I'm so pissed I didn't talk to you sooner. I should've known he was an abuser."

The past year drifted before her, and the inner voice she kept tamped down rose to a shrill scream. *Yes. Remember how he'd tell you what to wear. How to act. How to please him. Remember the cold look in his eye when he was displeased? The temper just barely kept under control if something didn't go his way?*

"He never hit me." Her voice came out weak. Gen realized it was her last defense. At night, when she thought of leaving, when she thought of how her life was so entangled with his, and her fear of him grew, she'd tell herself that. As if it was a prize. He never hit her. Wasn't that a good thing? Didn't that prove that she was crazy to believe he was slowly taking over her soul, piece by piece, until there was nothing left but a shell of who she used to be?

Arilyn smiled. Her strawberry-red hair glowed around her face, giving her the look of an angel. "Of course he didn't. That would have given you a reason to leave. Rarely do abusers start with the physical. It's a slow build of control, a subtle shift of power as they isolate you from your support system, until there's no one left."

The truth slammed through her. A gasp wrenched her lips. My God, how many times had she wished he would just hit her? Arilyn was right. She would've left without a glance back. Clean. Instead, he cloaked manipulation with love until she didn't know what was real anymore.

Kennedy brought her the mug of tea. She clasped her fingers around the heat and took a sip of the scalding liquid. Blessed warmth coated her belly. "Did he make you nervous? Make you question your decisions? Check your phone and messages and all communications? If you did something wrong, did he have ways to punish you?"

Kennedy knelt on the floor in front of her, gazing up at her with knowing amber eyes. Again, the flashbacks hit her like stinging pebbles. The time she'd burned dinner when his friend was over. He'd laughed and chided her gently at the time, but when they were alone, he refused to speak to her for two nights. She never screwed up cooking again.

The time she refused him sex. His complete disappointment and subtle jibes about her selfishness, the flirting with other women at the hospital while he warned her not to push him into another's arms by denying his needs. She always said yes to sex after that.

"Yes. He did. All of it. I don't know who I am anymore without him."

Kate squeezed her shoulder. "You. But a different you. We're never the same after a relationship, or a tragedy. We're not supposed to be. You'll figure it out on your own terms."

Disgust curdled her blood. Her entire life she'd been independent and strong. At least she thought so. "I never knew I could be this weak," she whispered. "I used to read these novels with some dumbass women who kept being abused by the hero and it was supposed to be okay because they had good sex. How did I get here? Why couldn't I just have said no, or leave before I made everything into a disaster? Am I that needy?"

Kennedy snorted. "Hell, no. Listen, most of the books I read are romance, and they mostly show women saving the men's dumb asses and sell more copies. We're not perfect, sweetie. We do the best we can. You were strong enough to run before you got married. Strong enough to listen to your gut. Now you just have to move forward."

The words reached deep and clicked into place. Yes. They were right. Punishing herself for mistakes wouldn't make them go away. But she'd have to retake charge of her life and figure out what she wanted. The real Genevieve. Not David's creation.

"I love you guys." She sniffed. "Seriously."

"We love you, too," Kate said, pulling her in for another hug. "I was so worried. I threatened Wolfe if he didn't take care of you, I'd kick his ass."

Gen gave a half laugh and wiped her eyes. "No, he saved me. Gave me the time I need to realize how different I was away from David. We came back after we saw the headlines in the paper. Have reporters been bothering you?"

Kate waved the question off. "We took care of them. Most of them are trying to find you in Nashville."

"Huh?"

"Kate led them on a false trail. Alexa backed us up. Said you had a dream to be a country star and you had texted us you were on the road toward Tennessee. They're probably still waiting for you to show up."

A laugh escaped her lips. "Thanks. It'll buy me more time."

"Where'd you and Wolfe stay?" Arilyn asked.

"Sawyer has a cabin in Saratoga. It was good. I forgot what it felt like to have fun without worrying I'd do something wrong. He took me to the racetrack. I won a lot of money."

Kennedy gave her a high five. "Nice. I think Wolfe's missed you."

"Yeah, David gave me a hard time about our friendship. I realized I began avoiding him, so we talked a lot this weekend."

Kennedy and Kate shared a look. "Just talked?" Ken asked.

The memory of their kiss seared into her brain. The heat of his mouth, the softness of his lips, the decadence of his tongue. "Of course. I just ran away from my wedding. I'm not the type to jump into bed with my best friend. There's nothing like that between us."

"So you've said for a long time," Kate commented.

"Because it's the truth."

Arilyn tapped her finger against her lips. "Hmm."

"Guys! There is nothing going on with Wolfe and me. Never has. Never will. Got it?"

The door opened. "I got breakfast, sweetheart. Time to get up. Oh. Shit."

He stared at the group of females for a moment. Then shrugged and dropped the bags on the table. "Hello, ladies. Kate, I'm surprised you waited till morning. Figure you'd be guarding the door when we got here last night."

Kate crossed her arms and glared. "You turned off your phone. I'm pissed you didn't give me full disclosure."

Wolfe grinned and began unpacking. The scent of eggs and bacon drifted through the room. "You're scary when you're being protective. I took good care of her. Right, Gen?"

When she woke in the middle of the night, her head rested on his chest and his thigh lay heavily over hers. His breathing and heartbeat soothed her. The delicious scent of washed cotton and male skin surrounded her. She knew she should untangle herself but he felt so good, so solid, she went right back to sleep.

"Right."

"You just come over now, Wolfe?" Kate asked.

Uh-oh. "Umm, he—"

"Nah, we slept together last night."

Crap.

Arilyn cocked her head. "Hmmm."

Kennedy grinned. "About time. You know what I say about getting over a guy?"

Wolfe rolled his eyes. "Yeah, I heard, get under another. You share that theory with Nate?"

Kennedy flushed. "I plan on being under Nate for a damn long time."

"Still no wedding date yet?"

Her friend gave a long-suffering sigh. "Soon. Why mess with perfection? Now, stay out of my love life or I won't let him play with you on the golf course again."

Wolfe laughed. "Trust me, Ken, you're the one whipped in this relationship."

"Screw you."

Gen burst out laughing. God, she'd missed this. Missed them. The back-and-forth banter, insults, and love shining underneath. How had she made it this long without her friends?

Arilyn, always the peacemaker, spoke up. "What can we do to help? Are you talking to David today?"

"I left him a message, he wouldn't pick up. I'm heading over to my mom's house to talk. I asked for everyone to be there. They deserve an explanation."

"We'll go with you," Kate stated.

"No. I think it's time I'm honest with them and myself about what type of relationship I was in. I need to do this on my own."

Arilyn nodded. "We understand. Listen, we'll be at Kinnections all day. Why don't you come by and we'll have a girl's night? You can come to my place."

Gen smiled. "Thanks, but I don't know if I'm up to it

right now. I need some time to think. Deal with David. How about I let you know?"

Kate looked worried, but finally agreed. Wolfe broke off pieces of the breakfast sandwiches and handed out coffee, and her friends finally left. Odd, she felt different already. As if a piece of her had flared to life, reminding her there were plenty of people who loved her for who she was and never asked for changes. Isn't that love, like Wolfe had said? Had David ever really loved her? Had she ever loved him?

"What time are you heading out?"

She shook off her thoughts and put the dishes in the sink. "Now."

He washed his hands, dried them, and grabbed his keys. "I'll drive."

Gen stared at him. "You don't have to come with me. It's my family. I'll be fine."

"I know. I haven't seen your parents in a while, and I'd like to hang with you today."

She narrowed her gaze. "You and my father don't get along. Izzy will probably be there. I don't need a babysitter."

"I know. I'm still going."

She glared at him. He stood in her kitchen, relaxed, the black ink of his tattoo crawling up his meaty shoulder and caressing his ear. The diamond in his ear gleamed, along with his eyebrow ring, and his hair was a delicious mess of dark curls. Gen knew he wasn't budging. She'd seen that look before, and it was all pretend casual. Inside, he was a rock, and if he wanted to go with her, he was going.

She huffed out a breath. "Fine. Come on."

When they pulled up to her mother's house, Gen was grateful for his presence. A mass of cars filled the driveway, and her stomach fluttered. Had she always been afraid of disappointing her family? Funny, they'd never pressured her with career, or their expectations of what type of person she should be. Had it all been her own aspirations and drive for success? Maybe it was time to be brave enough to admit her mistakes. That she didn't know all the answers, and maybe wasn't the person they always thought she was.

"Ready?"

He grabbed her hand.

"Ready."

They walked together up the steps to the big porch, where white wicker rocking chairs and tables spread out. Their family had called her home Tara because it was the core of who they were. She remembered when her father had abandoned them for the lure of the bottle, and how her mother struggled to keep the house on her meager salary. Remembered the endless crying at night from her mother's room, and the anger burning in Izzy directed at her father. Her brother, Lance, was in medical school at the time and had gotten his girlfriend pregnant. The house welcomed all of them in, along with the new baby, who became her first beloved niece. Lance married Gina and raised Taylor there for the first few years as he struggled through medical school.

One day her father returned, sober, determined to get his family back. It was a long, hard road to forgiveness, but never forgetfulness. Eventually her mom took him back and they healed, but scars were left behind. She knew something had changed in Izzy during that time. Her twin had always been physically the same, but so very different under the surface. Where Gen longed to fit within the rules and be the best, Izzy flouted those same rules and embraced rebellion. It was almost as if she felt too much, and her emotions had gotten too big to contain. The long spiral into trouble almost broke the family apart again.

She remembered the day she discovered marijuana hidden in the closet, deep inside an old gym bag. Izzy begged her to keep the secret, promising she was holding it for someone else, and that Gen needed to trust her.

Gen wondered if things would've been different if she'd listened to her sister. Instead, she told, and after that everything changed. Izzy never trusted her and shut her out, and the closeness they'd once shared dissolved. A coldness seeped between them, a wall so high it couldn't be scaled. Gen mourned the loss of her twin every day.

Gen took a deep breath and opened the door.

The house enfolded her in a tight embrace and memories of comfort. The scent of lemon polish floated around her. The gorgeous staircase with the elaborate Southern charm emphasized high ceilings, bay windows, and an innate coziness that welcomed visitors.

"Genevieve!"

Her mother rushed toward her, holding her tight with a mother's strength. Maria MacKenzie was of Italian blood that bred a foundation of family, food, and iron willpower. Alone, she held all the fragments together and was always loving to strangers, opening her home and herself to anyone who needed her. Petite, with curly dark hair and strong, animated features, she took control in moments.

"Wolfe, thank you for taking care of my own. I knew you'd bring her back."

Wolfe nodded, kissed her cheek, and stepped back.

The rest of the crowd bum-rushed her.

Alexa reached her first, gripping her fiercely like a mama bear bent on protecting her cub. "I was so worried," she whispered. "I'm glad you're okay."

"I'm sorry," she said. "So sorry I did this to everyone."

"Shush, we just want you to be safe."

Gina and Lance came next. Lance gave her the older brother worried stare, while Gina fussed, explaining Taylor was at a friend's house so she didn't have to deal with her thousand questions about why her aunt ran out on her wedding.

As they made their way into the hallway, her gaze fell upon the last two members of her family standing back. Izzy wore her usual badass outfit. Leather shorts. Tight black tank. The red ink of the thorny rose peeked over the curve of her breast. She used to have the same crazy curls Gen sported, but she had had her hair straightened. Long choppy strands entwined with purple framed her face. They were twins, but had never looked so different. Again, the distance between them panged. Gen opened her arms. Her sister responded but remained stiff, as if not used to physical affection. "You sure know how to make an exit," Izzy said. "You okay?"

Gen choked out a laugh. "About time I caused the excitement around here. I'm hanging in." The comment brought a tentative smile to her twin's face. Gen looked over her sister and met her father's gaze. "Hi, Dad."

Jim MacKenzie blinked, his blue eyes filled with raw emotion. "Genevieve. We were worried."

"I know. Sorry, Daddy."

He swallowed, then closed the distance to give her a hug. Even though he'd broken her heart when she was young, he was her knight in shining armor. A tarnished knight, yes. But he'd come back for his family, fought for redemption, and never allowed her to doubt him again. She hated disappointing him, but he also allowed her to see the possibility of making mistakes and recovering.

When he turned his head, his eyes iced. "Wolfe. What are you doing here?"

"Jim! He's welcome in our house," her mother said.

"I didn't say he wasn't. Just wanted to know why he's here. In fact, I'd like to know how my daughter ended up in your car in the first place. Did you plant this seed in her head?"

Gen gasped. "Dad, cut it out! Wolfe took care of me— it isn't his fault. This was my decision. I'm the one who ran out of the church, and he happened to be outside. I asked him to get me away."

"Convenient."

"Jim. Enough," Maria snapped.

He fell silent. Wolfe didn't say a word. Gen didn't know why her father was always suspicious of Wolfe. From the early days of their friendship, a scowl would come over her father's face when she spoke about Wolfe, and he'd urged her many times to be careful of him, even though he was family to Alexa and Maggie.

"Let's go into the living room and talk," Maria said.

Jim grumbled something but followed. Her mom had set up an array of pastries, coffee, and tea. Everyone grabbed something to eat and sat down. How weird. Usually they had family meetings regarding a crisis, which usually involved Izzy. It had never been about her.

Wolfe perched in the chair farthest away, but his presence pulsed around her in an almost physical manner. She relaxed, reminding herself they were here to support her decision. She just needed to tell them the truth.

"First off, I can't say how sorry I am for doing what I did. I know I left everyone without an explanation. I stuck you with a mess and I never meant for it to happen. I just . . . panicked."

Alexa spoke up. "We don't care about the fallout. We're more worried about why you ran."

Jim cut in. "You heard what she said. She panicked. She had a bad case of bridal jitters and didn't handle it well. We can fix this."

Lance nodded. "I loved Gina, but getting ready to say your vows is a big deal." He grinned when she punched him in the shoulder. "Look, I know how the hospital can get when you're a resident. Crazy hours, little sleep, and planning a wedding. David explained he's been worried about you for a long time."

Her inner voice woke up from sleep and bellowed in protest. *David was talking to her family about her? What was going on?*

Gen shook her head. "Wait. What did David say about me? This was more than a regular panic attack, Dad.

There's been a problem between us for a while but I haven't wanted to deal with it."

Her parents shared a pointed look. Alexa looked sympathetic. Izzy frowned. But there was something strange going on, an aura of anticipation as they were listening to her story. Jim cleared his throat. "Honey, I just wish you would've shared things with us. We could've helped you. David said you've been having some panic attacks. He said you're constantly questioning if you're good enough at the hospital, and started to feel you didn't deserve him as a husband. He's been honest with me and your mother about the issues, but he loves you. Why won't you take the medicine?"

Her breath got trapped in her chest. Warning bells clanged madly in her brain. "What medicine? I don't know what you're talking about."

"There's nothing shameful about taking meds," Alexa said. "Many people are on them for depression or anxiety. You took on too much. David said he wanted to cut back your schedule but you refused. He wanted to hire a wedding planner but you insisted on handling every detail yourself. Sometimes you have to ask for help."

The blood rushed to her head and exploded. "Wait a minute. I don't know what he's been telling you but that's not true. He kept asking me to pick up extra shifts at the hospital, not the other way around. And he told me over and over we didn't need anyone else running our wedding, that we should do it ourselves."

Alexa stared at her. "Honey, David called me for the name of a wedding planner. He tried to hire her but you said no. Don't you remember the conversation we had at lunch? I told you to call her and you refused?"

She remembered. Except that morning, David told her he'd be disappointed if she gave over the wedding to a stranger. Asked if she was comfortable giving over her children to a nanny to raise—if that was the type of mother and wife she wanted to be. How had he manipulated the conversation so easily? By the time Alexa brought it up, she'd been determined to show him she could do it all on her own. Had he been spinning stories and lies about their relationship from the beginning? And if so, why?

She had to fix this and make them understand. "I don't need meds. And he twists things. I started noticing a pattern of manipulation and a need for control in every part of my life. He began checking my phone, trying to keep me away from my friends. Do you know how many times I wanted to see Alexa, or come over for dinner, and he'd give me an excuse for why I couldn't go?"

Her mother frowned. "Really? I always found the opposite. He called me once a week to check in with us, tell us about you and what you were both doing. He confided in your father about a month ago that he was trying to get you to leave the house more but you were having bouts of depression. Remember when I called you? Kept asking if you needed me to come over but you said you needed sleep?"

She'd asked David to have her parents over for dinner. It had been a rough night at the hospital so he'd lost his temper, asking why he wasn't enough for her. Asking why they couldn't enjoy a quiet dinner together instead of dragging everyone else into their relationship. By the time her mom had called, she'd been so upset she'd lied and said she needed sleep for an excuse. She'd always been protecting her dark secret with David, trying to keep people from learning the truth about their relationship.

Including herself.

The tangled web she'd gotten herself into was all her fault. Gen dragged in a breath. "Mom, I didn't want you to know that David gave me a hard time when I asked if I could have you over for dinner. When you called, I was embarrassed at having to say no so I told you I was tired."

"I see."

No, she didn't. In fact, Gen realized in a blinding light-bulb moment, her entire family didn't believe her. Somehow David had convinced them he was the good guy and she needed help.

"If you were having these problems, why did you move forward? You had a big engagement party. Plenty of time to tell any of us your concerns with David," her father said.

"I knew something was wrong, but I didn't want to admit it. I was scared. We were living together, he's my boss, and I felt trapped."

"Trapped? Did he ever threaten you?" Jim asked.

"No. But I think he's an abuser, Dad."

Lance leaned forward. "Did he hit you? I'll kill the son of a bitch."

"No, he never hit me."

Silence fell. Gina ducked her head. Alexa frowned, as if trying to figure out the puzzle. Izzy remained quiet, concentrating on her nails, as if afraid to give her opinion. Her parents looked confused.

Gen's gaze connected with Wolfe's.

Strength. He believed her. He *knew*. But this was her fight, her family, her truth. She needed to make them see the whole picture.

Gen opened her mouth.

The doorbell rang.

Jim stood up. "Good. We need to get to the bottom of this."

"Dad, who's at the door?"

His jaw tightened. "David. You have to understand how desperate he is to see you, Gen. He's been a mess. Here every day since you left, going over everything he could have done wrong. The man loves you and you owe him an explanation."

Panic bubbled up. She didn't have time to gather her thoughts or prepare for the confrontation. Suddenly, David was in front of her, staring into her face, and she froze, unable to tear her gaze from his.

She'd fallen for him the moment she looked into his face. He was a god of male beauty and skill, and she'd loved him from afar for almost two years before he finally noticed her. Long lunches led to dinners, and when they fell into bed with one another, she felt as if she'd met her match.

How long had it lasted? That short period of bliss, diving into the physical state of arousal, hours spent under the covers, making love and sharing thoughts and ideas and dreams. He was everything she'd ever wanted. It had been so easy to ignore the signs, the quiet disappointment when she did something he didn't approve of, the slow ordering of his expectations and wants to come before hers.

His emerald eyes shone in his tanned face. His thick golden blond hair reminded her of a halo, highlighting the laugh lines bracketing his mouth, the sense of power and presence he radiated by just walking into a room. Her mouth worked to form some type of words, but he moved too fast.

He pulled her into his arms and kissed her. Wrapped his hands around her waist, stroked her hair, murmured loving phrases into her ear. Such tenderness and care. Oh, how she'd adored this side of him, the gentle lover who made her feel whole by just obtaining his approval. She also knew how fast he could turn, how deep he could punish and make her hurt by a few cutting words or cold looks.

Gen tried to step back but he held her tight. "I'm so sorry, baby," he said over and over. "This is my fault. I pushed too fast, I didn't listen to your concerns before the wedding. Forgive me, my love."

Nausea hit. Desperate to get away, she pushed against his chest and stumbled back. The devastation on his face, the raising of his arms into empty air, sliced her deep. She heard her mother's quiet gasp at the complete rejection of his emotions, and she wondered again if she was crazy, if David really was a good man. If she needed to give him another chance.

"I'm sorry. I never meant to do this to you, leave you in this way. I have no excuse." Her voice broke. "I'll never forgive myself for forcing you to deal with the mess I left behind."

"I forgive you, Genevieve. I just don't want to lose you. I want you back."

In that moment, the noises died down and her heart took a step forward. She'd loved him once. Believed he was the one. Somehow, along the way, that love had turned to fear, doubt, and sadness. There was no other chance for them, because she didn't like who she was with David.

She didn't even know who she was with him.

A quick glance around the room showed hope. A happy ever after. But she couldn't give it to them.

"David, I—I can't. I can't."

Jim cleared his throat. "I think you two need to talk in private."

She nodded. They walked silently up the stairs and closed the door to the spare room behind them. Since the house had emptied, her father had turned it into an office, with a small futon, computer, desk, and television. The walls were pale peach. She fingered the slight dent by the window, remembering when she and Izzy had played *Dance-Off* and Izzy banged her head in an attempt to do a handstand gone horribly wrong.

"Why? Why did you leave me, Genevieve?"

He always used her full name. She used to find it intimate. Now he only sounded like a teacher figure rather than a lover.

"I should've realized the truth of my feelings before. I've been unhappy for a long time. I don't think we're good together."

His brow arched. "How could you say that? We've been perfect together from the beginning. I love you. I want to protect you and be with you forever. What's not working?"

She shifted her feet. She needed to be strong and focus. "I don't feel like I'm me anymore," she said softly. "I feel like I'm turning myself inside out to please you but it's never enough. I'm not happy. I don't think you are either. You're constantly telling me how to fix myself to make you happy. People who love one another are supposed to accept who you are."

"Did you get that line from Wolfe?" She flinched. "Do you even realize the humiliation you put me through? Everyone knew you were with him. Believed you'd run off for some wild affair and left me holding the bag. The hospital is full of gossip; it's been impossible to work. Strangers stare. Reporters have staked out our house and harass my parents and your family. And did you even give me the courtesy of a phone call? No. Just disappeared with that lowlife."

The charm began to disappear. He took a few steps in, forcing her to back up against the wall. Anger pulsed from his frame, but he held still, caging her in with his body. He was an expert at aggressive maneuvers without saying a word. Gen tried to keep calm, but already the panic leaked through, urging her to run. Why was she so intimidated by him?

"Nothing happened between us. Nothing ever has or will. He was outside when I came through the window and I asked him to take me away. It's all my fault. I didn't call because I was trying to get my head together. I've been afraid to face the truth about us."

She remembered when Wolfe tempted her with more time away. The empty road ahead. If it hadn't been for that newspaper article, she would've run even farther with him, maybe never stopped or looked back. The guilt crippled her, but she needed to push through.

"I can't make you happy," she whispered. "I'm not enough."

The intimidation faded away. His body sagged. His eyes held a naked sadness and longing that she'd first fallen in love with. Not only the brilliant doctor, but the broken man who craved love and promised to give her everything. "No," he said softly. "I'm not enough for you. I've never been." He pushed his fingers through his hair, tilting his head back as if searching for answers from the heavens. "I didn't mean what I said about Wolfe. I know it wasn't like that between you, I just don't know what I'm saying. I haven't slept since you left. I go over every detail to see what I did to make you scared of me or doubt my feelings for you. And then my greatest fear came true. You left me." His voice broke. "Just like my mother did. Just like I was always afraid you would."

Gen squeezed her eyes shut. She didn't want to hurt him. She might not want to marry him, but her love for him had been real at one point. His past haunted him, and her actions only emphasized his weakness. Shame flared. "I'm sorry," she said again. "I hate what I did, I have no excuse except I panicked and had to get away. I was afraid to face you."

"Have I ever hit you, Genevieve? Physically hurt you in any way?"

She shuddered but managed to shake her head. "No. But your words did."

He tilted his head, confusion evident. "I always said I loved you. Praised you. The only reason I would ever ask for more is because you are a brilliant doctor and I want you to succeed. I see your potential and didn't want you to settle. If that hurt you, I'll fix it. I'll be different."

The panic leaked in, the same fear he'd talk her back into this relationship. Somehow, with this man, her determination and strength disappeared in a puff of smoke. She fought to stand her ground and be honest. "I don't want to fix it anymore, David. We need to end this."

The tears that glinted in his eyes broke her heart. A tortured moan caught in her chest.

"Please," he whispered. "Give me some time. Give us some time. I pushed too hard with the wedding and the details, and your schedule. To think that I hurt you, or gave you the impression I didn't love you with everything I am, makes me sick. I'm begging you for some time."

"I don't know." She trembled. "I don't think it's a good idea. We don't work."

"We can work." He reached out halfway, then dropped his hand. "You need space. I won't push for anything right now when you're not ready. Spend some time with your family. Think. I'll see you next week at the hospital and we'll take it from there."

"No. David, I don't want . . ." Her words trailed off when he left her standing alone in the middle of the room.

Her body began to shake, so she crossed her arms in front of her chest and squeezed for warmth. Why wouldn't he listen? Why was she so weak around him? He played on her guilt like a master, until she found herself giving in without realizing how it had happened. She was never going back to him again. Space and time wouldn't fix their relationship, yet his stubborn refusal to accept her words as truth only made the pain drag on.

Gen sucked in a breath and slid to the floor. No more. She'd give him the few days he insisted on, and when she returned to the hospital, she'd talk to him. Be clear about their relationship being over. Maybe at work she'd have a better handle on things and be able to project a competent, confident woman who knew her own mind and heart. She never wanted to hurt him, but there was no way to avoid the final outcome.

They were over.

"Sweetheart?" Wolfe stood above her, a looming shadow. He hunkered down in front of her and tipped her chin up. "Was it bad?"

"He's not ready to let me go."

His finger caressed her cheek. "He doesn't have a choice."

She nodded. "You're right. I hate hurting him, but I have no choice. He said to take a few days to think and we'd talk when I get back to the hospital."

"Did he threaten you?"

"No. I think he's still in shock. I'll talk to him again at work and repeat everything I said. Maybe he'll be ready to accept it when he sees I won't change my mind."

Wolfe's face hardened, contradicting the gentleness of his touch. "And if he doesn't?"

"He will. I just don't understand why he would say such things to my family."

"For control. To keep you with him. Wrecking your support system leaves you dependent on him." He helped her stand and studied her face. "Your family will understand, just give them some time. He worked on them for a while behind the scenes. Don't feel too guilty about hurting him, Gen. He knows what buttons to push with you. Trust me, he's a bigger son of a bitch than I thought."

Maybe Wolfe was right. David was not going to make her afraid or doubt herself again. It was time she took control of her life. "I'll talk to him on Monday. Get my stuff. Make some decisions about my future."

A smile touched his lips. "Sounds like a plan. How about we go downstairs and show a united front to your family?"

He reached out his hand. When she took it, his warmth and strength gave her the boost she needed.

Gen followed him out.

"MACKENZIE! WHY AREN'T YOU on rounds?"

She looked up from shuffling stacks of clipboards and papers threatening to smother her alive. "I was assigned to the desk today. Sheila is overwhelmed so I was told to skip rounds."

Dale sneered at her, peering over his glasses like she was pond scum. "Maybe if you'd get your head out of your ass you'd know how to handle instructions better. You're needed on rounds."

Gen held tight to her temper. "Got it." As she hurried down the hall, his hateful gaze bored into her back. She used the time to toughen herself back up, swearing she wouldn't break no matter how bad it got.

And boy, things were bad.

She'd prepared for the worst, but reality hit her harder than expected. Gen had no idea how much David had told the staff, but it was evident she was the new rotavirus. She'd made many casual friends at the hospital during her years, but once her relationship with David went public, most of her so-called friends drifted away. Doctor/student relationships were tacitly frowned upon, but because of David's status and reputation, they'd been able to slide past most difficulties.

Not now though. No one spoke to her. If they were forced to give instructions, they related them in a cold, bitter tone, as if she'd run out on them instead of David. Whispers and accusations flew about her having an affair. Her charts were misplaced, her schedules consisted of night and double shifts, and when she tried to grab coffee at the cafeteria, she was told they'd have to brew a new pot. Fifteen minutes later, she'd been forced to leave, and had caught the new nurse with a steaming cup right after she left.

"How you holding up?"

Gen didn't slow her pace but relaxed slightly at the feminine voice beside her. Sally Winters was the only other resident who was still polite to her. She was pretty in a natural sort of way, with honey-colored hair pulled back and sparkly brown eyes filled with mischief. She'd always enjoyed practical jokes, and was the most supportive in her group, helping out with extra shifts or duties with a cheerful disposition.

"Be careful, you may catch the virus."

She frowned and kept up. "What virus?"

"The one you get when you talk to me."

Sally laughed. "Give it some time to blow over, hon. David is like a god around here, and people are picking sides."

Gen hit the elevator button and glanced at her watch. "I think I'm on the losing one. Tell me the truth, Sally. Is the gossip brutal?"

Her expression was all Gen needed. Her heart sank. It was humiliating to have her personal life picked apart and analyzed, especially when no one really knew what happened behind closed doors. Still, she would not break, no matter how hard it got here.

"Look, as soon as the Kardashians do something, everyone will be so over you."

Gen grinned and stepped into the elevator. "Thanks. It's nice to have one person left to talk to."

"I'm tough. I'll catch you later for coffee."

She wrinkled her nose. "They don't make it for me anymore."

Sally shook her head. "Jerks. I'll straighten them out. Meet you downstairs after your shift."

"If I ever get out."

The doors swished shut and Gen prepped to take her medicine.

Hours later, beaten up emotionally and physically, she managed to slip into the break room and found it blessedly empty. She grabbed a paper cup and slugged down some water, trying hard to keep it together.

"Genevieve?"

She stiffened. There'd been no time over the past few days to talk, and she didn't know if she had the strength right now. Who would've thought being hated by the entire hospital would take so much out of her? He moved beside her and she struggled to straighten up and meet his gaze. "David."

He studied her face. "You look tired."

A humorless laugh escaped. "I am."

Her refusal to elaborate made him tighten his lips. "I'm sorry you're having a hard time. Things will blow over and get back to normal soon. I've been thinking about us."

"So have I."

"I'm glad." Determination carved out his features. "I'm going to do better. *We're* going to be better. I figured out how I was expressing myself and intend to change. I also think the wedding was too much pressure. This time, we'll elope. My parents will be disappointed, but this way it'll be more subtle and stamp out some of the negative press. When things settle down, we can throw a tasteful party when we can both enjoy it."

Nausea clawed at her stomach, and her heart thundered in her ears. Why didn't he get it? She shook her head hard, frantic to make him see they couldn't keep going on like this. "You're not listening. I spent my time thinking about us, and what I want. We're not good together. This is not something we can change. I'm ending it."

The shock emanating from him was almost palpable. "No. We love each other."

"Not anymore." She forced herself to hold his gaze.

"This type of love is wrong. It's not healthy, and I'm unhappy. We can't do this to each other anymore. You have to let me go."

He stared at her hard, assessing, then shook his head. "You're mine, Genevieve. Always will be. I picked you when I could have had anyone because I see you in me. Our drive. Our purpose. Our need to be better. You're wrong about love. Love is pushing the limits, not accepting."

"David—"

"I will not allow you to push me away anymore because of your fear. You need me."

Dread slithered in her veins. "I don't want to marry you. It's over."

"No. It's not."

He moved so fast she never saw it coming. Grabbing her around the waist, he dragged her against his body and kissed her. Forceful, brutal, a stamp of ownership and not an ounce of care. By the time she tried to fight him off, it was over.

She panted, clenching her fists. "Don't ever do that again."

"Don't tell me what I can and can't do." The ugliness was back, turning him into a man she didn't recognize. "You've humiliated both of us enough. Are you willing to throw away your entire career on a whim?"

"This has nothing to do with my career!"

"Your mental state has everything to do with your career. Everyone knows about your consistent panic attacks. Your own family backs me up. Do you know I documented your breakdowns with the hospital?"

She pressed a shaking hand to her mouth. "You know I don't have panic attacks. You're a liar."

He shrugged. "You've been a wreck since the engagement. Everyone saw it. I told HR you were having some episodes but I believed you were still safe on the floor. Told them I urged you to look at some medication, but that the wedding had been adding to your stress. It's too late to back out of this. We're meant to be together. If I have to, I'll prove it to you."

"You're insane. You'll never get away with this. You can't force me to have feelings I don't have!"

David shook his head. "You're still not understanding me. I will do everything in my power to show you we're meant to be together. I've fought for what I wanted in my life without fail. You are no different." He turned from her. "Think, Genevieve. You're under my direction. Your career is in my hands. We can have the life we dreamed of if you would just give me another chance."

"I will never get back with you." Her body trembled with rage. "I will not let you bully me anymore. I'm getting my stuff today and reporting you."

"Go ahead. I've already told key people at the hospital about your mental state. I have witnesses to back me up. As for your stuff, I already changed the locks in my apartment. You'll be moving back in with me eventually. This will just give you the proper motivation."

"Fuck you."

He frowned and glanced back. "You know I dislike gutter language, Genevieve. You've been hanging out with trash for too long. Wolfe is a problem between us. Get rid of him." He paused. "Or I will."

He left.

Her knees shook. And for the first time, she was truly scared.

What was she going to do?

Her first instinct was to call Wolfe, but she battled back the urge. He'd been so sweet and supportive, sacrificing his own work schedule to babysit her. They'd been growing closer since they returned and she was tired of him consistently rescuing her. He was prepping for a business trip and didn't need the distraction. No, she'd handle it. David was probably in a temper and would back down in a few days. He'd never follow through with his blackmail threats to HR. Right? They'd shared too many things together for such ugliness.

No need to blow it out of proportion yet. She'd dig in, focus on her work, and avoid him as much as possible. Another week and things might be completely different.

Genevieve prayed she was right.

twelve

WOLFE PUSHED AWAY from his desk and paced his lush inner sanctum. He'd learned young to follow instincts. Civility and society did a good job trying to cover up the truth of gut instinct, but he'd take the primitive anytime. It had always served him well, told him of danger, a bad deal, or the way to survive.

Now it was telling him Gen could be in trouble.

He had to work late tonight and prepare for a three-day conference he couldn't get out of. He'd be locked up nonstop in a train of meetings focused on growing their clientele and sifting through all their investors. The time away with Gen had given him a fresh perspective on Purity, and a few things needed to change. Usually he'd pick a good business deal over a person's character. After the episode with David, Wolfe decided he didn't want any weak links in his chain. Odd, he'd always had a unique ability to be ruthless in the pursuit of profit. It made sense. It was cut-and-dried and clean. But lately, he decided Sawyer's heart and soul were in the hotel empire of Purity, and it ran deeper than money. Both deserved more. Maybe it was time to clean house.

He grabbed his cell and hit her number. The hell with it. Her first week back at the hospital had been brutal. Fortunately, he'd cleared his schedule and been able to spend plenty of time in the evenings with her. Things should be a bit better this week, if he could get over this strange feeling something was going to happen. Of course, Kate and her crew would watch out for her, but he'd gotten used to being the one she depended on.

Wolfe wondered why the fact satisfied him. Maybe because he'd never been needed? Gen was the strongest woman he knew, and her faltering only made him respect her more. There weren't too many people in the world who dug deep, tried hard, and didn't make excuses. Everyone lately was full of whiny crap. Poor me with my dead mother or alcoholic father or crappy sibling. Poor me for not getting a job and not having money and getting bullied. Poor me period.

He had no patience for the climate lately. It was much easier to blame your junk and issues on someone else. Gen owned it and wanted to do the work.

He got connected to her voice mail. "Hey, it's Wolfe. Call me when you get a minute." He clicked off.

When was the last time he worried about a female other than family? The only thing he ever worried about was if she orgasmed fast enough so he could get home. He didn't mean to be cold or cruel, it was just how he was built. He had stopped trying to be someone else a long time ago.

The voice taunted. *Then why do you want to be more for her?*

Shut up.

The voice grew quiet.

He didn't trust David. This was bigger than wanting

Gen back—this was about retribution for trying to leave and humiliating him. He knew how abusers worked, and how easily it could escalate behind closed doors. Better be safe than sorry. Another clichéd motto he believed in.

After this conference, he'd keep a close eye on things. For now, he needed to focus. Gen could take care of herself. They were friends, not lovers. No reason to blur the lines and make things complicated.

Complicated for who? Her? Or you?

This time he didn't snap at the inner voice. Just got back to work.

GENEVIEVE WEAVED HER WAY through the chaos of the ER and headed toward the next patient. ER rotation was sometimes a bitch, and today was one of the worst. They were short beds and staff, and since she'd gotten back there'd been no time to pause.

The whole thing was a nightmare, but she figured she would hunker down like it was the Alamo and battle through.

Gen pulled the curtain back and read the chart for bed three. Susan Avery. Age forty-two. Symptoms of abdominal pains. No allergies. She smiled and met the gaze of a pretty blonde with big brown eyes and a thin face. "Hi, Susan, my name is Genevieve. Are we having some stomach issues today?"

Susan looked slightly flushed. "Yes. I really didn't want to come to the ER but the pains aren't going away and I got a bit nervous."

"Of course. Any other symptoms?"

"Not really. I took some antacids last night but nothing worked."

"And when did this start?"

"Late last night."

"Okay, let's check a few things out first." She retook Susan's blood pressure, which seemed slightly elevated. "Any past history of high blood pressure?"

"No."

She noted the chart, but numbers were sometimes a bit high due to anxiety. "I'm going to do an ultrasound on you, Susan. We want to rule out acute abdomen so we'll set that up. Just relax and I'll have a tech here in a few minutes."

Susan shifted position. "I don't have any insurance." She lifted her chin as she uttered the statement, as if trying to protect her pride. "Is that a problem?"

Gen hated the massive inflow of patients who needed certain tests but couldn't afford it. The hospital did its best, but there were too many gaps in the system and no way to stave off the leaks. She shook her head. "Not a problem. Let's take it a step at a time, okay?"

"Thank you."

Gen ordered the test, noting the glare the tech gave her as if he hated being the one to help her. She hurried to the next bed, finishing up two more patients, and her phone buzzed insistently in her pocket. She glanced at the screen and saw Wolfe's number. Juggling charts, she listened to his brief voice mail, and couldn't help the smile on her face. She'd kept the confrontation with David to herself, and things seemed to have settled a bit in the past few days. Though she was still treated like a leper, David kept his distance. She quickly sent a text saying she was fine and would be working late.

"Dr. Mackenzie, it seems you still think you're on vacation rather than in an overcrowded ER. If you have time to chat on your phone, maybe you're not doing your job."

She stiffened and thrust the phone back in her pocket. Dr. Tyler Ward was head of the ER, a real son of a bitch, and friends with David. "Sorry." Giving any excuses would just make the situation worse. His bushy brows lowered in a disgusted frown, and his gaze swept over her. "We need bed three for incoming. What's the status?"

"Waiting on the ultrasound report, sir."

"Get it faster."

"Yes, sir." She already knew the tech probably buried her request in the back of others, so she hunted him down again. Gen glanced through the report, which came back clean for acute abdomen. Good sign. But something niggled at her that didn't sit right. She went back to talk to Susan.

"Did you get the results yet?" Susan asked.

"Yes, the ultrasound came back fine."

"That's good, then, right? Maybe I should just switch antacids and sleep it off?" The joke fell flat as her hand settled on her stomach, obviously uncomfortable.

"I want to check a few more things."

"Sure."

Gen rechecked the blood pressure. Hmm. Still elevated, and she didn't think it was nerves. She touched the woman's skin, which felt clammy and sweaty. As she pressed over her muscles and examined her, she noticed her ankles were definitely swollen. How many times had a cardiac problem in women been misdiagnosed as indigestion?

"Anything big going on at home?" Gen asked casually, listening to her heartbeat again.

"Just the normal stress. I'm planning a bridal shower for my daughter and it's been taking a lot of time. And my promotion at work is good news, but I've been working late a lot."

"Congratulations on both. I'd like to run one more test to rule out any other possibilities before sending you home. Excuse me for a moment."

Gen grabbed the chart. With no insurance and the ultrasound coming back negative, she'd need approval to run the cardiac enzymes test. She fell in step with Dr. Ward, who was barking at a nurse for existing on the same planet.

"I need bed three."

"I know. Dr. Ward, I want to run one final test on her for cardiac enzymes."

"Why?"

"She's having abdomen issues and the ultrasound came back clean."

"Then why the hell would you run another test? Send her home."

"I think it's her heart."

"Oh, for God's sake, give me the chart." He stopped, glancing through. "She has no insurance. Send her home."

Stubbornness hit her. "I'm asking you to look at her."

The gleam of hatred that sprung from his eyes made her take a step back. "Seeing things that aren't there, Doctor? We don't have time for babysitting in the ER. You better not be wasting my time."

He followed her, pulling back the curtain and turning into Dr. Charm. "Hello, Susan, I'm Dr. Ward. Your ultrasound came back fine. Did you eat anything strange last night that could have contributed to your stomach problems?"

"Chinese."

"Hmm, lots of salt intake." He shot Gen a glare and knew he'd just ruled out her swollen ankles. "How about stress? Anything going on that's unusual?"

Susan laughed. "I was just telling Genevieve my daughter's getting married and we were on the phone for an hour last night, arguing over the guest list. My goodness, by the time the wedding comes I don't know how I'll survive."

"Weddings are wonderful but stressful events. Did you take antacids?"

"Yes, just Tums though."

"Hmm. Well, the good news is you're fine. We'll set you up with Prilosec and make sure you eat bland for a while. No Chinese."

"Thanks, Doctor."

"Welcome."

Gen followed him out. "Dr. Ward, I think—"

He whipped around and jabbed a finger at her. "I don't care what you think. Do your damn job and stop wasting hospital resources on ridiculous tests for patients with no insurance. Another incident like that and I'll throw you out of my ER. Understood?"

He marched off. Frustration shot through her. Dammit,

in a way she didn't blame him. In another way, her gut was screaming that there was something bigger going on, and if she sent Susan away she'd regret it.

In medical school, there was so much information to absorb her brain was constantly on overload. But she'd always felt she had good instincts. If she listened and looked beyond the surface facts, letting the individual and the body guide her, she discovered things that routine exams or logic didn't. She used to pride herself on such an ability until David. Over the past two years, he had showed her to trust the evidence only. The tests were God; the facts were survival. Gut instincts in a surgeon only led to chaos, and death.

So she'd changed. Smothered the voices and primitive instincts that she used to respect.

Today she made a different choice.

She swallowed hard and went back to her patient. "Susan, if you don't mind, there's just one test I'd like to run before we release you. I think it's important."

"Oh, okay. It's probably more restful here than at home anyway."

"Thanks. I'll have a nurse come by shortly."

Her hands barely shook as she ordered the cardiac enzymes test from the lab. "I need a signature on this one," Ted said gruffly.

She didn't miss a beat. "David—er, Dr. Riscetti approved." Ted let out an annoyed huff and punched out the number. He spoke briefly, then looked up. "He wants to know if you asked Dr. Ward."

The lie fell easily from her lips. "Of course, but he's

busy right now." Ted repeated her words, nodded, and clicked off. "We'll run it."

"Thanks. Can you put a rush on it? We need the space."

Her heart pounded, but for the first time in a long while, she felt like she'd done the right thing. Gen ran back to her other patients, checking the time and hoping she'd get the results back before things blew up. But maybe she'd get lucky. Maybe Ward was so crazed he'd miss the extra test she ordered and things would work out. Maybe—

"Why the hell is bed three still not empty?"

She ducked her head and pretended to be busy doing something vitally important so she couldn't respond. "She's almost ready, sir."

"She was ready twenty minutes ago. What's going on?"

Sweat dampened her brow. Crap, this was bad. "Umm, I'm just running one more test, which should be done shortly."

He blocked her path. Fury rumbled from him. "What test?"

"The cardiac enzymes, sir."

His voice dropped. "I told you to release her. Who signed off on the test?"

She paused and wished she could lie. "Dr. Riscetti."

Ward gritted his teeth. "I don't care if you're screwing him on your personal time, but don't think you can run my show here." He grabbed his phone and pounded out numbers. "David, why the hell did you give approval on the troponins when I specifically denied it?"

Gen closed her eyes. It was over.

"I see. Yes. You better get down here now."

Ward narrowed his gaze. "Go wait in the conference area for your boss. And get out of my ER."

She didn't respond. Why did she suddenly feel like she was living out an episode of *Grey's Anatomy*? Except on the show the residents got to do crazy-ass things and never got kicked out or in real trouble. She knew she'd stepped over the line, but she'd do it again no matter what the results. Did that make her a bad doctor? Or a good one?

David walked through. His burnished hair was mussed, and his eyes looked tired. She'd heard he was doing double shifts, trying to drown his sorrows in work, while the bitch that she was looked healthier than she'd been in a while. No wonder everyone hated her. In only one week, she'd eaten, slept better, and laughed more than she had in the past year.

"What are you trying to prove, Genevieve?"

She tried not to be defensive, but old habits die hard. She kept her voice smooth and professional. "I'm sorry. Dr. Ward wasn't listening to my concerns regarding a patient I believe is having cardiac difficulties. Women are misdiagnosed many times for indigestion and I wanted to run this last test. He refused."

"He refused for a reason. Because it's indigestion and Dr. Ward said she's uninsured. You gonna pay for it?"

She tightened her lips. "If I have to."

"How superior you are. Think you're smarter than Ward?"

"No."

"Think you're smarter than me?"

She glared. "No. I went with my instincts. Something's

wrong and I couldn't live with myself if it was my fault and I sent her out of here. She's still my patient."

"Instincts, huh? The same one that told you to escape from me outside a church window?"

Gen flinched. "This has nothing to do with us."

"It has everything to do with us." He pushed his hand through his hair and closed the distance. "I miss you, Genevieve."

"Please, don't."

"I want you back and it's been enough time. Marry me."

"I can't. It's over. I'm sorry it happened this way, that I hurt you. But I can't be with you anymore. Ever."

The beauty faded to ugliness. Those lush lips turned in a sneer. "I don't think you understand. I refuse to be humiliated and mocked. I also refuse to lose you. We can make this work between us and be happy, but if you still deny me I have one option left. I will make you pay." Her breath strangled in her throat. He loomed over her, cheeks red. "Starting with a formal disciplinary mark in your file. You disobeyed two doctors—your bosses—and ordered unnecessary tests we refused."

"I was trying to do the best thing for my patient. How many times have you told me that was key to the job?"

"I also said look at the facts. Making random choices based on an odd feeling puts everyone at risk. And I don't want a surgeon like that on my team."

"You're doing this to get back at me," she whispered.

"I want you back because we belong together. I can forget the whole incident and get you back on the floor with Ward."

"If I marry you."

"If you come back to the man who loves you."

Her chest felt hollow. Grief and anger swirled together in a mess that rose up and exploded. "Never. Just stay away from me and let me do my job. Your love is an illusion to control and manipulate me. I know what you've been doing behind my back with my family, trying to set yourself up as the good guy. I'm done."

"Yes. You are done." He reached out to touch her hair but she jerked away. "We'll start with the write-up in your file. I'll have Ward lodge a formal complaint about your instability. Many of your peers have noticed your erratic behavior, so that could become a problem. You can continue working here, Genevieve, but this is my world you live in. I promise to make every day hell and eventually get you kicked out of the hospital. I will destroy your career piece by piece. Do we understand each other?"

Tears threatened, but she'd die rather than release them. "Is this how you show your love for someone? By hurting and abusing them?"

"It didn't have to be this way. You chose this. Remember that."

Her future flashed before her. She could take the whispers and taunts. She could handle the coldness and manipulation. But the slow eroding of her skill and growth as a doctor would destroy her. By the time he was done, she'd lose every shred of confidence in her abilities and the love for medicine that was in her core. He'd leave her with nothing. And he could do it.

Gen knew she had options. She could go to HR. Fight

him and go on record. But with his support, prestige, and position, especially with their previous love relationship, it would look like she wanted him back and he'd refused her. David could spin it any way and people would believe it. She'd never be welcomed into another residency program.

A piece of her heart slowly broke off and crumbled. In that moment, everything was crushed. Her hope and love for a man she once believed in, and the career she'd dreamed of since she was young.

All gone.

"I understand."

"Good. And your decision?"

She stepped back, numb. Maybe it was better this way. The pain would come later as she said the final words to destroy the final fragile thread between them.

"I resign from my residency. Good-bye, David."

She walked out the door. Everyone stared at her, greedily watching for a medical soap opera to unfold. Gen refused to give them anything else of her.

The tech touched her on the shoulder. "Doctor, the results came in for the cardiac enzymes."

"What are they?"

"Positive."

She enjoyed the quick rush of satisfaction before she turned to David, who stood in the doorway watching her leave. "Give the results to Ward and tell him I was right. She's got blockage and we need to stave off a heart attack."

Those were the last words she spoke before she left everything behind.

G EN, GET UP."

"Ugh, what's that smell?"

"I think it's her. I told you we should've busted in yesterday."

"I know. I couldn't find my spare key. Why won't she wake up? What if she overdosed?"

"Don't be so dramatic, there's no wine or pill bottles. But the empty ice cream cartons and candy wrappers means she's on a sugar crash. Gen, sweetie, open your eyes."

The voices swirled together in a beautiful musical harmony. Her eyelids felt heavy and she had a bad feeling that if she opened them she'd remember something terrible. She tried to ignore them, but the nice voices came with hands that were poking her and trying to turn her over. Gen growled. "Go away. I'm tired."

Her body was shaken harder than a James Bond martini. "Wake up, I mean it. You're freaking us out."

She opened one eye. Three female faces peered down at her. "How come you're not at work?" Gen mumbled.

"It's Sunday," Kate said. "We've been trying to reach you since yesterday. Thought you were with Wolfe, but he's at some kind of convention thing, so he told us to break in. How long have you been in bed?"

Huh. When did her life splinter into tiny pieces so she had no job, no possessions, and no future? Oh yeah, Thursday. "Few days."

Kennedy pulled back. "Woman, you need to brush your teeth."

"Tomorrow." She tried to roll back over but they forced her to sit up, climbing on top of the bed so they all surrounded her.

"Did something happen with David or the hospital?" Arilyn asked.

Gen realized they didn't know. After her exit, she'd gone directly to the grocery store and bought everything that looked like it would kill her. Saturated fats and sugar galore. Trying to avoid a big pity party on top of her wedding fiasco, she'd texted everyone that she'd be working nonstop and would catch up later. Knowing Wolfe would be checking on her anyway, she'd told him she was staying at Kate's and she'd contact him next week.

Then she'd gone to bed and stayed there.

"Honey, what happened? Wolfe was frantic. You lied and said you were with me," Kate said.

"Didn't want him to worry. He's been babysitting me and it's getting embarrassing. I'll be fine."

Kennedy lifted two empty bags of Funions. "If you ate these you're not fine."

Gen took a breath. "I quit the hospital. My residency is over. I had a huge showdown with David and he threatened to make my life hell, and I realized I can't continue there."

Kate stood up and smoothed back her hair. "Okay, I'm

going to go kill him now. Remember, you're my witnesses, so I was never there."

Gen grabbed her hand. "I know you're serious, so sit back down. I need you here, not in jail."

Kennedy fumed. "He can't get away with that. You need to report him."

She lifted her hands. "Guys, he's covered his tracks well. In fact, he planted seeds of depression and anxiety. Wrote up a report for HR. He runs the unit, and I'm just the silly runaway bride. I'm not going back, and I don't want to get involved in a lawsuit or investigation I'll lose. It'll actually be worse for me."

"I'm sorry, Gen. But I am going to kill him for you."

She smiled at Kate. "I know you would. You're such a good friend."

"Let's avoid talk of murder, please, and figure this out," Arilyn piped up. "Can we hook you up with a tape recorder where you can get him to confess his evil plans on record?"

They stared at her. For such a sweet, gentle soul, Arilyn had a vicious streak that always fascinated Gen. "Good idea," Ken jumped in. "Nate can help us set it up."

Gen laughed. Only her friends could introduce humor into every situation. "Thanks for the suggestion, A, but I think I'll pass. I just want to move on. Nothing else matters right now."

"What are you going to do?" Kate asked. "Transfer to another hospital and residency program?"

She shook her head. "I'm taking a break. I need to figure out if this is what I really want, or if it's just been a goal

I've set for myself. I'd still need to commit to years more of training to do surgery. Maybe this is a sign I'm not meant for it." They jumped in together to protest, but she held up one hand. "No, I'm not saying I'm not good enough. I just don't think I ever gave myself any other options. I need time." A small smile touched her lips. "I have nothing left. Maybe it's a good thing, since I can start fresh. Find out who I really am again. Make sense?"

Arilyn nodded. "Perfect sense."

"Is David pressuring you? Are you afraid of him? I still think we should call the cops," Kennedy said.

"No. Now that I left the hospital, he has no more need to torture me. He can keep my stuff, I couldn't care less. I just want to be free and start over."

"Okay, but you're not going to spend endless days in bed eating bad food in an attempt to figure things out," Kate announced. "You're getting a job."

"Where?"

"At Kinnections, of course."

Kennedy and Arilyn high-fived. "Yes, that's perfect," Kennedy squealed. "We're growing so fast we're getting behind and need to hire another assistant. You start tomorrow."

"What? I can't work for Kinnections! I know nothing about matchmaking."

"You don't need to," Kate said briskly. "We'll teach you what you need, but you already have half the battle won. You've always had an amazing instinct about people. You just need to rediscover that part again."

The idea was so ridiculous she almost believed it could

work. She'd learn about her friends' business, keep busy, and help out. She'd get paid. And what better environment than around the people she loved best?

"I'm not letting you say no, so just get over it," Kate said.

Gen grinned. "You're always so bossy."

"Yeah, Slade loves it."

Ken rolled her eyes. "Oh please, he's so the dom in your relationship. You get all gooey when he commands you to do all sorts of nasty things."

Kate sniffed. "What's Nate studying now, Ken? Anal play?"

Gen laughed at the red flush on Kennedy's cheeks. Priceless. Her geeky rocket scientist had a passion for studying academics and new subjects that included the best ways to have sex. His inventiveness had kept their sex life quite active. Many times Kate said she'd found Ken asleep at her desk in a desperate effort for some actual sleep.

A pang of longing hit. That should've been her and David. She wondered if there'd ever be someone who'd understand and love her for who she was, warts and issues included. As much as she didn't want to admit it, her confidence was badly shaken. Would a man ever want her with such a raw passion and longing? Was it even possible for her?

The memory of Wolfe's kiss flashed before her. The solid press of his erection against her thigh. The blistering heat of his skin. The thrust of his tongue claiming her mouth. Yes. With David there was a physical connection, especially in the beginning, but it faded to technique and never cut deep. Just that one kiss from Wolfe gave her a taste of what he'd bring to his partners in bed. Was that wrong to crave such passion for herself?

She pushed the thoughts out of her mind and tried to focus on the present. "If you think I can be helpful, I'll do it."

Kate smiled with satisfaction. "Good. Nine o'clock. This is going to be epic."

"But first you have to shower," Ken piped up.

Arilyn patted her shoulder. "Why don't you clean up and we'll order some takeout from Mugs? We can have a movie night."

"Oh, how about *The Heat* with Sandra Bullock? That was hysterical," Kate said.

Ken sighed. "You and your comedies. How about *Magic Mike*?"

Arilyn shook her head. "We've seen that together three times. There's no plot."

Ken lifted a brow. "And your point is?"

Gen got up from the bed and headed for the shower. A glimmer of hope flared. She'd get to the other side eventually, and things would work out. And if she was a surgical dropout and future spinster, so what? She had great friends, family, and a working brain and body.

Today, that was enough.

"HI, WELCOME TO KINNECTIONS—Wolfe? What are you doing here?"

Oh, he wanted to strangle her.

He strode over to the receptionist's desk, where those wide navy blue eyes looked innocent. He was used to seeing her in scrubs or jeans, so the sexy black lace top and flash of bare leg from her skirt threw him off for a moment. Her usual ponytail had been replaced by curls flying free over her shoulders. Chestnut waves flopped over one eye, which looked annoying but damn seductive. Flirty. Definitely not like the Gen he knew.

He laid both palms flat on the desk and leaned over. "I think the better question is, what are *you* doing here?"

She gave a pout. Was she wearing lipstick? He wouldn't have pegged her to wear a bold color, but the rich, coffee-colored lipstick clung to her mouth and tempted a man to try a sip.

What the hell was he thinking?

"You're in a mood. I work here now."

His temper rose another notch. "You're a doctor. Why aren't you at the hospital?"

She shifted in the chair. "I quit."

He turned. "I'm going to kill the son of a bitch. Wait here."

Wolfe took a few steps before she scrambled and skid ahead of him, blocking his exit. "Kate already tried twice. Listen, I'm sorry I didn't tell you, but it's for the best. There was an incident and I realized I won't be able to work there."

"Why didn't you tell me? I get a text saying you're working late, then staying at Kate's. You refuse to answer my calls, and when I finally get in touch with Kate, she says you're not with her. Crap, Gen, you gave me a heart attack!

I'm stuck at the convention with a bunch of suits and couldn't get to you. What incident?"

"A patient thing. I needed some time alone and didn't want to bother anyone."

Wolfe gritted his teeth and prayed for calm. "You're not a bother. You're my friend."

Her face softened and she grabbed his arms. Her fingers lay directly over the thin leather that covered his wrists, but the heat from her touch still burned. "I know. You have to understand how I've been feeling lately. Like a whiny, pitying, weak female. Suddenly I'm doing all these crazy things and I broke. I'm better now, but thank you."

Her patronizing words made him more enraged. He still wasn't sure why. Her self-imposed isolation drove him nuts, but the thought of her turning to someone else was much worse. He wanted to shake her until she understood how important she was. "You're not better. I refuse to let that asshole push you out when you were born to be a surgeon. You can't work at a matchmaking agency. It's totally beneath you."

The softness disappeared and turned to fire. She practically growled like a she-cat. "Who the heck are you to judge me or Kinnections! Did you suddenly turn into a snob, O playboy turned millionaire hotel magnate?"

Wolfe fought not to flush. "Don't be ridiculous. I'm just saying you were meant to save lives, not make matches!"

She sniffed like it was a reasonable argument. "I disagree. This may be my true calling after all. I'm tired of stress and medicine and decisions that are life-and-death. I'm going to have fun. Who knows? Maybe I'll even find real love."

Irritation scraped him like a Brillo pad. "You'll get bored of this place in a week."

She stuck out her tongue. Was she serious? "No, I won't. And I'm not quitting till I help make a great match for someone. I need to be around magic and hope. Hey, want to sign up? Kate says if I get clients on my own I get a recruitment bonus."

He stared at her. "Are you kidding me? No, I'm not signing up for Kinnections. Listen, I'll help you get transferred to another hospital. I can make some calls—I know some guy in Albany who's high up the ladder. You can't leave your residency when you worked so hard. We'll fix this."

"There's nothing to fix. This is my job now and you'll have to get used to it." The phone rang and she brightened. "Gotta get that."

Wolfe watched her run to the phone and lean over the desk. The skirt stretched over her full rear, rode up her thighs, and left her indecent. She wobbled a bit on three-inch stilettos till she found her balance. For God's sake, she never wore heels. Had Kennedy gotten ahold of her? Why was it so hot in here?

He dragged his fingers through his hair and listened to her chirp about some upcoming mixer at the Purple Haze. She gave a low little laugh that sounded suspiciously like a giggle. Oh yeah. Kennedy had definitely done something horrible to her. She hung up, wiggled back around, and

tugged down the indecent minuscule fabric that consti-
tuted office wear. Even her perfume was different. The lingering sweet scent of peach mixed with a sharp citrus and
musk that tantalized. Was she working here to find dates
for herself? No, that wouldn't be like her at all. She used to
say she needed months to get over a relationship. A broken
engagement would take at least a year.

"Sure you don't want to help me earn some more
money?" She gave him a wink. "You'd be a hot commodity
with the women."

Ugh, he refused to be embarrassed. "No. I can get my
own dates."

"Fine. At least I'll get something for signing myself up."

He opened his mouth, then shut it. Opened it again.
"What are you talking about?"

Gen grinned. "I'm going to be a new client of Kinnections!"

"You just broke up with David. You're always bitching
about people needing months in between serious relationships in order to heal. Remember that time I broke up with
Allie, and you made me cancel my date the next weekend?
You forced me to be celibate for two whole weeks!"

She rolled her eyes and cocked a hip out. The black top
shifted and he caught a fragment of lace peeking from her
shoulder. Huh? He had it on authority she only wore cotton
underwear. "You needed to suffer. You broke her heart."

"I did not. She knew up front what the deal was."

"It's still wrong. Claiming there's no strings doesn't
mean things can't change. She fell for you, and you walked
away without trying."

This time he did flush. "I explain to every woman I'm not interested in long-term—you know that. You always praised me for being honest and up-front."

"Well, I'm changing my mind. I think it's crappy. You need to begin looking at the future. Why don't we be clients together? We can double-date!"

Wolfe wondered if he had had something bad for breakfast or if he really wanted to vomit. The image of them at a dinner table with two strangers was painful. She was giving him a headache.

"I'm happy the way things are. And I think the last thing you need is another emotional upheaval with some guy. Take a break from dating. Maybe you can learn a hobby. Knitting?"

She glared. "Am I eighty years old? No, I need to get my feet wet again. David almost broke something in me, and I want it back."

Crap. When she put it like that, he'd do anything to help her. "Sweetheart, don't you want to find healing within yourself rather than from outside sources?"

Her eyes widened. "Wow. You're getting really deep. Usually, I'd agree with you, but I'm tired of feeling afraid and unsure. I want to be brave and take a leap into the unknown. Does that make sense?"

Yeah, it did. He didn't understand why the thought of her diving back into dating bothered him so much. Usually they'd trade war stories and he'd help her get fixed up. What suddenly changed? Crankiness stirred so he changed the subject. "Why are you wearing that?"

"Huh? A skirt?"

"You hate fancy clothes. Did Kennedy try to do something to you?"

She stared at him like he'd sprouted horns. "You're acting really weird, dude. Did you work too hard at the seminar? How was it?"

"Fine." He didn't want to talk about work, or endless meetings, or sales figures. "I think we should talk more about this. How about we go to dinner tonight? I'll pick you up at seven."

She crossed her arms in front of her chest. "As long as you promise not to try and change my mind."

"I can't promise you that. But I'll buy you a burger."

Gen shook her head. "Fine. I'm easy. See you tonight."

He watched her walk back to the desk and slide into the chair, crossing her legs. The smooth expanse of white skin blinded him for a moment. She always joked about not having a drop of her Italian blood heritage, since she burned so easily and never tanned. But there was something about all that gorgeous naked flesh, soft and pure, that made his fingers curl to touch her.

Wolfe turned his back on her and his startling thoughts. He needed a cold shower and a nap. Lately he was beginning to wonder if the past three months of celibacy had been such a smart move. The break seemed like a good idea. He'd been tired of the delicate game of seduction lately, and how fast his partners seemed to get attached. Almost like they looked at him as a challenge to break down.

If only they'd realize there was nothing inside that hadn't already been broken.

Still, sex might take the edge off. The last thing he needed was lustful thoughts involving his best friend. She was the only healthy relationship with a female he'd ever been able to maintain. He refused to screw up the best thing that had ever happened to him due to a surge of testosterone.

Wolfe made the drive back to his place in Manhattan. His penthouse apartment had tons of security, luxury, and every amenity he could think of. The parquet floors and high ceilings were elegant, but his furnishings were spartan and masculine. Dark wood, glass, extensive computers and media, and bare walls. He barely slept there, finding it more convenient to stay at Purity, where he kept a tight rein on things.

Wolfe took a quick shower, changed, and put on a pot of coffee. Maybe he'd relax, watch a baseball game on television, then get some more work done. All in all, it had been a tough couple of days and he needed a break. Dinner with Gen would put him in a better mood. They'd get back to their usual buddy routine, and he'd begin working on finding a new sex companion who had nothing to do with Kinnections.

When the doorman buzzed and said a uniformed officer needed to see him, Wolfe got a bad feeling.

He was handed the temporary restraining order on behalf of a Dr. David Riscetti, who accused him of harassment and a host of other sins.

His bad feeling was right on. As usual.

He glanced through the papers. Wolfe had to give the son of a bitch credit. He was playing a chess game, and he was a great player. Wolfe couldn't care less about himself, as long as David stayed away from Gen. Unfortunately, his spidey senses were tingling again, as if he was missing a piece in an elaborate puzzle being put together.

Yeah. All in all, it was a shitty day.

GEN FINISHED INPUTTING INFORMATION into the specialized system Arilyn had created and wondered what was up with Wolfe.

She figured he'd be overjoyed to see her ready to ease back in the dating world. Instead, he looked grumpy and generally miserable. Probably the convention. He got so involved with his work he'd go nonstop for days without taking a break in the drive for success and to consistently show Sawyer he was worthy.

Her heart twanged. He was so guarded, but when he loved someone he'd put his life on the line. Was it wrong to want him to experience real love with a worthy woman? She needed to work on him. If he signed with Kinnections, he'd have a better chance at finding the right one.

Maybe it would cut off the weird sexual thoughts she'd been having about him lately.

Gen held back a sigh and went to refill her water bottle. He'd always been attractive. He made millions in underwear ads, flaunting tats, rock-hard abs, and lean muscles that elicited lust. But she'd always been able to separate the physical, and it never interfered with their friendship.

Until lately. She almost fell off her chair when he stormed in. The European suit was bold blue to match his eyes, and cut tight to mold to his body. With those chocolate curls, sensual mouth, and powerful aura, he sucked all the air from the room. No man should look that good dressed. It wasn't fair.

And he'd looked at her differently today. His gaze had stroked her bare legs and lasered under her lace T-shirt as if he was . . . hungry. The worst part? For one horrific moment, she'd yearned to be the one to strip for him, have him look at her with raw desire like he wanted to eat her alive.

A shiver bumped through her. Silly. Probably a combination of her broken relationship, quarter-life crisis, and a touch of horniness.

Had to be.

Her cell phone chirped. Gen glanced at the number but didn't recognize it. She clicked the button anyway. "Hello?"

"Genevieve! It's Sally. How are you?"

She smiled. She missed so many parts of the hospital, but no one had reached out to her after she left except Sally. Even though Gen hadn't given her too many details, she'd been pretty vocal about the crappy way Gen had been treated. It was kind of nice having someone in her corner. "Hey, Sally. I'm good. I didn't recognize this number."

"I'm on one of the volunteer's phones. Sorry I haven't called in a bit."

"Are you kidding? You'll be lucky if they allow you to breathe. Anything going on?"

"Wanted to see if we can schedule dinner sometime. I miss you around here."

"Thanks. That means a lot. How about you text me

when you're free? We'll work around your shifts. Mine are more reasonable."

"Sounds good. Umm, there's one other thing, but it's a bit awkward."

Her skin prickled. "You okay?"

"Yeah, but it's David. I don't want to get in the middle of this, Gen, so I hope you're not mad. He asked me if I was in contact with you. I told him we'd spoken briefly, and he begged me to ask you to call him on his cell phone today. Something about your stuff?"

Gen frowned. "He asked you to contact me?"

Sally gave a strained laugh. "Yeah. But he's been working double shifts so he probably didn't get time to call you himself. I'm sorry, I didn't know what to do."

Anger simmered. Poor Sally was getting dragged into the middle. Of course, she didn't want to make David mad when he was her boss. "No worries. I'll give him a ring. Don't forget to text me about dinner."

"Thanks for understanding. Promise, no more messages back and forth. Oops, gotta go, I'll text you!"

The phone clicked.

Gen tapped her finger against her lips, uneasy about the request. Should she call him? What if he wanted to give her stuff back and move on? If he was busy with work, she wasn't surprised he'd get someone to call her—David refused to let distractions get in the way of his patients. Such a good doctor. How could he be so cruel and manipulative?

Gen didn't want to think about it too long. Heart pounding, she dialed the familiar number and listened to it ring. Once. Twice.

"Hello."

His rich voice poured in her ear. She used to love listening to him, especially when he taught. Until such a beautiful voice began whispering subtle barbs in the dark, drawing blood and never understanding why she got upset. Gen fought a shudder. "It's me. Sally told me to call."

"Ah, yes. We're getting slammed here today with a bus accident. I haven't had a moment."

"What do you want?"

He paused. "I don't want to keep anything from you, Genevieve," he said. "If we've decided for a clean break, of course you can have your belongings. Let's be adult and not make things worse."

She relaxed a bit. He didn't seem in a rush to try and get her back. Maybe now that she'd quit the hospital he realized it was truly over. "I agree."

"I'll drop by tonight with your computer and some other things. You can make arrangements to get the rest when I'm out of the apartment."

"Oh, no need, I can wait."

His tone held disapproval. "Your computer has personal files. Since you've left the hospital, you need to make arrangements, and I don't want to be responsible. I'll be there around seven."

"I have a dinner appointment."

"Then six. I won't stay. I'm not in the mood to drag this on any more than you are. Agreed?"

There was no reason not to. He was being reasonable and wanted to return her items. "Yes."

"Very well. I'll see you tonight."

Gen tried to get back to work but depression settled in. She was so . . . sad. To be in love and think you knew a man, only to find you had fallen in love with a stranger. Her upswing began to slide. Maybe she didn't need to get back out there. It might be better to lie low for a while.

Arilyn came through the office dressed in black yoga pants, a long skinny shirt, and comfortable clogs. Her hair hung loose and rich, and a tote bag was thrown over her shoulder. "Hey. How's it going today?"

Gen smiled. "Pretty good. I'm acquainting myself with the files on some clients, getting a feel for the computer program, and answering the phone."

"You're doing great. I have a manual I created that I think can help. I'll grab it at home."

"I can wait—no need to get it now."

Arilyn sighed. "I have to meet the plumber anyway. Not sure how much more I can take of my rental. Besides leaky ceilings, burst pipes, and barely any heat last winter, now my electric is on the fritz."

Gen raised a brow. "What about your landlord? That's illegal."

"He's useless. I leave messages, but he's out of state, so he rarely gets back to me. He's desperate to sell. I may have to move, but it needs to be a place that takes dogs."

"I'm sorry. I'll start asking around."

"Thanks. I'll drop the manual by after my yoga class."

"Umm, how is yoga going, A? With . . . him."

A shadow crossed her features. "We're having some growth spurts. But he's committed to me this time, and I'm sure we'll work it out. It's difficult when so many students develop a crush and he feels he needs to give them part of himself as a teacher. Lines get blurred. He's truly an amazement."

The affair with her yoga teacher had been going off and on for a while. Gen didn't know the full story, but from her friend's expression, endless defensiveness, and refusal to use her lover's first name because of the need to hide their relationship, Gen didn't have a warm, fuzzy feeling. The last time Arilyn caught him cheating, she changed. Her calm center scattered, and she couldn't focus. Kate had threatened to show him the true meaning of yoga by beating the hell out of him, but after a week they'd gotten back together and Arilyn defended him wholeheartedly.

Not a good scenario.

But since Gen had run out on her wedding, she had no judgment. "I'm glad," she said. "You deserve happiness."

Arilyn smiled. "And so do you. How are you holding up?"

Gen sighed. "David's coming over with some of my stuff tonight. I was in a good mood today, but it suddenly hit me that I really screwed things up. I can't believe I spent two years in a relationship with a man I loved and I didn't see what was really going on. I wonder if I can trust my instincts after all."

"Your instinct told you not to marry him. Strong, independent women are the most vulnerable to abuse. We like giving up control once in a while, and we want to be protected and cherished in certain ways. Many times the lines are blurred, and love clouds our vision. Don't be hard on yourself. We're all here to make mistakes, but you'll find your way."

"Maybe I shouldn't use Kinnections after all. I'm not ready."

Arilyn raised a brow. "Usually I'd recommend space to heal, but I think dating would be a good thing. You need some confidence. It takes a few weeks to get matched properly anyway. Sometimes the promise of something new and fresh gives you a whole new outlook."

"Maybe."

Arilyn floated toward the door. "Think about it. Kate and Kennedy are in their offices if you need anything. See you later."

"Bye."

Gen slumped back in her chair and picked at a nail. Lots of ups and downs lately, like she was trapped on an emotional roller coaster. A part of her missed the organized chaos of the hospital, the meaning behind every motion and every thought. The other part was relieved she didn't have to think for anyone else anymore.

Gen turned back to her computer and threw herself into the search for love for other people.

fourteen

"COMING!"

The second knock owned the impatient tone of a man not used to waiting. Gen hopped on one foot, pulling on a pair of silver ballet flats, then stumbled to the door.

David's gaze flicked over her outfit, subtly assessing. She fought the urge to squirm and wait for verbal approval. How many times had she come out of the bedroom and been greeted by a shake of his head, asking her to change? His consistent opinions on the type of clothes a successful surgeon's wife wore made her self-conscious, until she got in the habit of having him lay out the items he wanted to see on her.

She tugged nervously at the dandelion silk jersey, swallowed, and stepped back. "Come in."

He strode inside with an aura of entitlement. "You're looking extremely . . . bright." She stiffened but refused to answer. "Back to the cottage, huh? I'd hoped the time we spent together would have benefited your taste a bit."

"I like my place. Where's my computer?"

"In the car." He was still dressed in his scrubs, cutting a suave picture of the ultimate professional. Slight stubble darkened his jaw. He kept a razor handy wherever he went, so she was a bit surprised he hadn't stopped to clean up. David despised being seen as unprepared. Said it was a surgeon's job to instill trust at first glance.

A pang hit her. He was so beautiful, yet cold. Like a statue to admire, dream about, but never truly own. Gen turned, trying to blink away the sudden tears over the loss of someone she'd never really had.

"I can get it. I'll be happy to come over Sunday during your normal shift to get the rest of my things."

"In a hurry?" he drawled, walking in front of her.

Gen drew herself to full height, which was pathetic, and tried to look composed. "I have dinner plans."

"So you've said. Not till seven though."

"I'd rather we be done with this episode."

He lifted a brow. "You're acting like a sulky child. Don't act entitled to anything. You walked away and humiliated me on my wedding day. The woman I held in my arms and made plans with for a future would've never hurt me so deeply."

She winced. "I'm sorry," she said softly. "I can keep telling you that forever, but you're not understanding the real problem. I panicked. I felt as if you never heard me, no matter what I did. You told me what to wear, eat, and say. How to act. Who to see. It was smothering."

He twisted his lips in a bitter sneer. "Is that the problem? 'Independent woman, hear me roar'? I tried to care for you, give you what you need. And you repay me by acting like a slut and throwing it in my face?"

Her heart pounded. She hated this part of him, the one who scared her in a gut-level way she never understood.

Starting to step around him, Gen tried to keep her calm. "Let's not redo this scene. I'll just get my computer and we'll call it a night."

He shoved her back so fast and so hard she toppled onto the couch. Shock held her immobile for a moment. "We're not done. Not by a long shot. I listened to you talk and bitch when I gave you everything. You think you can run off for some dirty affair without consequences? I think you've been playing both of us for a long time."

She jumped up and glanced toward the phone. The ugliness in his gaze caused sweat to collect under her arms. She tried to keep breathing, not sure what to do. Once, she'd swear David would never have laid a finger on her or try to hurt her. But right now, she saw a stranger who'd never shared her bed or her life. And it scared the hell out of her.

"I'm listening."

Once again he moved like a bullet, locking his grip around her arm and throwing her against the wall. She hit her back hard, tried to scramble for balance, but he'd already pressed his body and grasped her wrists in a cruel grip. His breath struck her face. Rage glittered in his bright green eyes.

"Don't patronize me, Genevieve. Do you give it better to Wolfe than you did to me? Because I'll tell you, after the first few weeks you became a true disappointment."

She tried to jerk up her knee and twist out of his grip, but he held her with an iron strength. The words got stuck in her throat as she gasped for oxygen and sanity. "Don't. Just leave, please."

"When I'm done." He thrust his hips against hers. His growing erection made her moan in agony, the sick feeling in her stomach rising and expanding. "Did he teach you the right way to do a blow job? Did you act like a bitch in heat when he fucked you? 'Cause you never did with me. Oh, you had the technique right, but you were like a blow-up doll. A pretty moan here, a fake orgasm there. Think I didn't know? Bet if I put my hand under those jeans you'd be dry as a bone."

The assault on her ears was almost as bad as the one on her body. A deep trembling shook her, until her teeth began to rattle in fear and shame. She'd dreaded making love with him, knowing something was lacking and desperately trying to please him, please herself, always hoping for more. He criticized and suggested so much there was no feeling left, just a yawning emptiness that could never be filled.

"Please leave me alone," she whispered.

He grinned. "Just pretend like you always did, baby." The snap on her jeans rang like a bullet in the air.

She lost it.

Half near hysteria, she shoved and pushed like a demon, ready to use her teeth and nails and anything else to get him off her.

Suddenly he was flying through the air backward and she was blessedly free.

Gen watched Wolfe stand over the sprawled man. Like an avenging demon, fists clenched, blue eyes shooting sparks of fury, he hovered between civilized man and primate. "Are you okay?" His calm tone was in complete contradiction to the fury pulsing in waves around his figure.

"Yes."

"Good."

David rolled to his feet and straightened his scrubs. "How convenient. The knight in armor to the rescue. No worries, Wolfe. She'll always be my sloppy seconds." He sneered. "Maybe I'll try again after you get done with her. See if she got any better."

Wolfe gave an easy grin. "I'm gonna enjoy this." His fist snapped. David staggered, holding his jaw in disbelief at the direct hit. "You come near her, think about her, or even say her name, I swear to God I'll kill you."

Gen gasped as Wolfe moved again. Wicked fast, he punched David in the stomach, then followed with a brutal uppercut. Blood spurted, and David slumped back down to the floor. Something dark flickered in Wolfe's gaze, as if he had neared a precipice and could easily snap. Gen knew if she didn't try and stop him, he'd go over the edge and she might never get him back.

She stumbled over and threw herself into his arms, clinging tight as the mad sheen of rage slowly cleared. "Wolfe! Don't!"

David coughed and held his stomach. "You're done. I'm going to sue you!"

Wolfe took another step forward. Gen grabbed his face, half sobbing, and forced him to meet his gaze. "No more, please, Wolfe, he's not worth it, he's not worth it." He blinked, as if coming back from another world. With frantic urgency, he touched her all over, caressing her hair, cheeks, arms, hips.

His voice shook. "Did he hurt you? Did he touch you?"

"No, you came in time, it's over. He didn't do anything to me."

Wolfe cupped her cheeks, staring down into her face. Then yanked her into his arms.

His body heat leaked into hers and stopped the shaking. Gen hung on, her arms wrapped around his shoulders, her head against his chest.

"Stop! Police!"

The blur of flashing lights lit up the window. Two police officers stepped through the half-open door. "Let her go. Now."

Gen gulped for breath. "He didn't do anything wrong, Officer."

"No one move. Ma'am, please step away from him. Slowly." Gen obeyed, allowing a few inches of separation. David groaned and rolled over in a half-bent posture. "Everyone stay where they are. Sir, do you need an ambulance?"

"I don't think so. This son of a bitch hit me. I want him arrested."

"That's not true!" Gen turned toward the cops. They wore the Verily blue uniform, pistols on hips, taking in the scene. She got a quick impression of opposites. One had dark hair cropped close to the scalp, which only emphasized his rough goatee and staggering height. Damn, his head almost hit the doorway. Lean, sharp features took on an almost brutal look. His lips curled in a bit of a natural sneer. She'd never want to meet this man in a deserted alley. The other looked as if he'd stepped out of Hollywood, with tousled caramel hair, hazel eyes, and a face meant for the movies. Finely sculpted features, full lips, with a boy-next-door aura. He was half the height of his partner. "Officer, he was assaulting me. Wolfe broke it up in time before anything happened."

David got to his feet, cradling his jaw with his palm. His eyes filled with hurt. "Are you playing this game again with me, Genevieve? You called me to come over. Begged me. Now this asshole catches us and you throw me to the cops? Jesus, don't I mean anything to you?"

"This man is a liar!"

They all turned as the female voice rang out in the room with pure authority. Arilyn raced past the cops as if she had every right and hugged Gen tight. Gen slumped in her arms, feeling as if she were in a weird combination of mixed-up television dramas. Did this ever happen on *NCIS*? Oh, that was military. Government. Something like that, oh, God, she was losing her mind.

The scary officer narrowed his gaze. "Who are you?" he cracked out.

"Arilyn Meadows. I'm the one who called."

"How?" Gen whispered. "How did you know?"

"I came by to drop off the manual since I never got back into the office today. When I saw his car out front, I sensed trouble. I didn't want to do anything by myself so I called the cops. But Wolfe beat them to it." She stuck her nose in the air and sniffed like she smelled something bad. "I called in with an emergency and it took you forever to get here." She glared at the cops. "I thought Verily would be better prepared. You've been quite disappointing."

The beautiful one grinned. His partner grunted and

looked annoyed. "You got a set of balls on you, lady. How about we get past the tea-and-cookies part of this and I get some answers?" He motioned toward Wolfe. "Don't move, Rambo, got it?" Wolfe lifted his hands so they were in plain sight. "Let's keep our distance and go one at a time. You. Tell me what happened."

David spoke. "Genevieve and I went through a breakup, but we discussed getting back together. She called me this afternoon while I was at the hospital and asked me to come over. Wanted to talk. Said she was sorry about cheating with Wolfe—that guy." He motioned to him. "Things were going well, got heated in a good way, and we were against the wall, kissing. Then this psycho roars in, grabs me, and starts beating the shit out of me."

Gen grabbed Arilyn's hand for strength. "Not true," she said raggedly. "It's a lie."

Both officers studied David, then nodded. Beauty spoke. "Ma'am? What's your side of it?"

She began shaking again. "David and I broke up. We were never getting back together. He called and said he'd bring some of my stuff over from his apartment. When he got here, I asked him where it was and he said it was in the car. Then he started getting verbally abusive, pushed me against the wall, and intended to . . . intended to . . . to—"

"Hurt her!" Arilyn finished. "Rape her. For goodness' sake, Officers, do your job and arrest this man."

Brute gave her a sharp look. Arilyn fell silent.

Beauty strolled forward and guided them toward the kitchen. "Ladies, why don't you come over here. I can get more specific details on your story."

Brute turned toward Wolfe. "And you? What's your side in this?"

"Gen and I had plans for dinner at seven. I got here early. Saw his car. Heard her yelling when I was at the door, so I busted in and found him trying to assault her. I pulled him off and hit him."

David shook his head. "You son of a bitch! You set me up! You have Gen so scared over your temper she's afraid to tell you we're back together. Why do you think I got a restraining order?"

Gen froze. "What?"

Brute gave Wolfe a look. "Is that true? Is there an order of protection out on your behalf?"

Wolfe's jaw tightened. "I just found out about that today. He's been manipulating this whole scene from the beginning."

The cop muttered something under his breath. "I need to check this out. Let me call it in."

Beauty looked at her with concern. "Ma'am, do you need to go to the hospital? Were you assaulted?"

Gen rubbed her hands up and down her arms for warmth. The room began to blur. "David threatened me. I'm not sure what would've happened if Wolfe hadn't come in."

David stabbed a finger through the air. "Do you realize my whole medical career can be destroyed by your lies? Hell, I can prove it. She called me on my private number. She's the one who set up the whole encounter. Check her cell phone for proof."

"No, no, you called me! Well, I mean, Sally called me

and asked if I would . . ." She trailed off, the whole scenario suddenly making sick sense. "You told her to do it." She pressed a trembling hand against her mouth. "You made me call you so it would be on record."

"I've had enough. I want to press charges against him. I'm calling my lawyer right now. He'll prove there's a restraining order that he failed to obey. I want him in jail."

"No!"

"I'm her witness!" Arilyn shouted. "We're pressing our own charges."

Brute raised his voice. "Everyone calm down now. No more speaking and stay separated." He muttered something foul under his breath, communicated with his partner via psychic silent communication, and grabbed his radio. Beauty took some notes on her story in his pad, nodding as Arilyn faltered from her usual calm center and began babbling on her behalf.

Finally, Brute turned toward Wolfe. "I'll have to ask you to come with me down to the station. There is a legal restriction against you being in the same vicinity, and proof of physical abuse."

Wolfe nodded. The cop took out the cuffs.

"Oh my God, no. This is ridiculous—I'm coming with you," Gen said shakily.

"That's probably a good idea. I'd like all of you to come. We'll take official statements there."

David glared, his face full of dried blood. "I'll drive myself. My lawyer will meet you downtown."

Brute rolled his eyes. "We're not downtown, sir. You'll find us on Main Street. It's actually uptown."

Beauty looked amused. "I'll take him in my car."

Wolfe took a few steps toward Gen, but Brute grabbed his arms. "Not yet. I'd rather you not talk to her until we get everyone's story."

Uh-oh. She watched Wolfe struggle with his temper, grinding his teeth with vicious purpose. "I'm fine," she said strongly. "Go with him and I'll meet you at the station."

"What's wrong with you?" Wolfe ground out to the officer. "She's just been attacked. Get her a blanket and some water."

Brute narrowed his gaze. "Get him out of here," he directed his partner, motioning toward the door. She watched helplessly as Beauty guided him out. Arilyn growled something undignified under her breath while Brute settled them in his police car. He shut the door, disappeared, and returned with a blanket and two bottles of water from the trunk. "Here." He thrust them into Arilyn's hands and took his place in the driver's seat.

Arilyn covered Gen up, tucking the blanket carefully around her legs and opening the bottle. Gen took a few sips. The blessed warmth of the scratchy material relaxed her a bit. She was so stupid. It was all her fault for calling David. Believing his story. How had their relationship disintegrated to such violence and hate?

And a restraining order? Had David bribed a judge or falsified evidence? Wolfe had never threatened or touched him before. She had to fix this somehow, but now that David had shown his true colors, she was afraid of making things worse for Wolfe. David had so many connections in the community, he'd be able to make Wolfe's life a living hell. Her thoughts spun and she lapsed into silence as they drove to the station.

Arilyn patted her knee and launched an attack.

"I hope you're not one of these cops in the good old boys' club," she said, voice dripping icicles. "Officer — ?"

"Petty. Stone Petty."

Stone? Huh, the name fit perfectly. Even his tone was stone-cold, challenging Arilyn's tit for tat.

"Why don't you tell me what the good old boys' club is, Mrs. — "

"Ms. Arilyn Meadows. I told you my name on the phone."

"I didn't take the call, Ms. Meadows." He placed emphasis on the *Ms*. "I only respond to Dispatch."

"Verily isn't that big. Were you on break when you received the call? I imagine you were doing something else, since it took fifteen minutes to get here."

Half-fascinated, Gen watched her kind, calm friend turn into a bitch.

"Yeah. I was getting a donut and talking to my good old boys."

Arilyn tightened her lips. "I'm just concerned about appearances. Police seem to judge by first impressions, and David is a liar. He's abused my friend and manipulated the situation, and I also suspect he set up the whole thing to get caught by Wolfe. I would hate justice not to be served because of some surface charm and connections."

The temperature in the cop car dropped like a ghost had just visited. "I see. I'll try not to be blinded by a charming smile and give the rocks in my brain a workout. Amazing how lucky I got passing all those tests and physicals and training. Hell, at least I get my daily jelly donuts and get to ride in a cool car."

Arilyn huffed out a breath. "You're being ridiculous and mocking me. I'm just warning you to examine the entire situation and look at the facts."

"Yes, ma'am. You're the taxpayer. And you are correct about wrong judgments. Why, my initial impressions of you were completely wrong."

Her friend's brows snapped together. "What do you mean?"

Stone Petty's voice held true innocence. "I originally thought you were a sweet, calm, hippie do-gooder."

"Oh. And now?"

Gen held her breath. Some strange kind of tension squeezed between them, and she was caught in the middle. It was so unlike Arilyn to go on the offensive, especially with someone in authority. She usually respected teachers or anyone in a uniform a bit too much.

"Now I don't."

The unspoken insult hit the target. Arilyn gasped, but he'd already pulled up to the small station and parked by the curb. He opened the door, escorted them out, and brought them inside.

Gen had never been in the police station before. It looked like the typical small-town, Main Street facility like the firehouse and ambulance volunteer corps. The lobby held a high counter, a few chairs, and the stale scent of coffee, sweat, and guilt. Officer Petty guided them through a long hallway, which opened up on a room with a few battered desks, filing cabinets, a makeshift kitchen, and a few doors she imagined led to private offices. Definitely nothing to regale Kate and Kennedy about. She bet they would ask her a million questions regarding the inside.

Petty settled them at a corner desk by the wall. She sat down on the metal chair, noting various photos and mishmash pinned to the wall behind each desk, but nothing personal lay on Officer Petty's. Files. Computer. Desk calendar. Clock. Seemed he liked his sweets, judging from the multiple crumbled cookie bags. Half a pack of Marlboro cigarettes lay open. Oh no. Maybe Arilyn wouldn't see. Maybe she'd realize they were in a dicey situation and not go on a rant. Maybe—

"You smoke?"

The high pitch of her friend's voice made Gen wince. Too late. Petty cocked an eyebrow, slid the pack into the top drawer of his desk, and stared at her.

"You got a problem with that?"

Arilyn leaned her elbows on the chipped wood. "Yes. I have a huge problem. Besides polluting the environment and killing others with secondhand smoke, you're a time bomb of health issues. Cancer. Pain. Death. Still worth it?"

Gen kept still. The tension between them tightened another notch like a noose, and the stare-off was too intense for breathing. Finally, Petty grinned real slow and deliberate.

"Yeah. It is. Now, why don't you tell me your side of the story before you piss me off enough to put you in jail for something."

She gasped. "You can't talk to me that way."

"Yeah, I can. You're on my turf, little one. Better get used to it."

Gen almost closed her eyes but it was too fascinating to miss. Her usually centered friend glowered, muttered something violent under her breath, and slammed her butt down on the uncomfortable chair.

"Where's Wolfe?" Gen asked.

"With Officer Devine. Ms. Meadows, you can start. What did you see or hear before you called us?"

Arilyn recounted her side of story with just a bit of a sulk. Gen took it slow when it was her turn, trying not to leave anything out. She gave Petty her cell phone so he could see the initial call from the hospital and her subsequent one to David. Petty kept focus, interrupting with an occasional question. Finally he closed the folder and looked up.

"We'll go over the facts and be in touch."

Arilyn leaped to her feet. "That's it? That's all? Aren't you going to arrest David?"

"Are you pressing charges?"

"Yes."

"No," Gen said. Arilyn jerked her head around. "I can't right now. I just want to get Wolfe out of here and go home."

Her friend grasped her hand. "He assaulted you," she said quietly. "I know you're scared, but we'll all help you. Report it."

"Not now. Please, A, don't push this. This is so much bigger. I have to think of the hospital, legal issues, publicity, Wolfe. I'll apply for a restraining order against him so he'll stay away from me. I never want to see him again."

Arilyn bit her lip, obviously frustrated but not wanting to push. "Fine. Let's get Wolfe and go home."

"Sorry, ladies, we'll have to hold your friend overnight." Officer Devine, aka Beauty, strolled over and looked at them with a bit of sympathy. "He violated the restraining order and assaulted Dr. Riscetti. We'll have to wait for bail in the morning when the courts open."

Gen battled tears, then realized Wolfe would hate her crying. She swallowed them back, tilted her chin, and swore she'd be practical. She'd been the one to drag him into this mess, and she was going to get him out. "Did he call for a lawyer?"

Devine shook his head. "Not yet."

"We have some work to do, then. A, let's get Kate on the phone and talk to Slade. Then we'll call Max. He always knows what to do."

"Got it."

"Can I take you ladies home?" Petty asked.

Arilyn treated him to a glowering look. "I think you've done enough." She paused. "Or not."

The man actually sputtered out a laugh. "I'll be in touch, Dr. MacKenzie." Suddenly he turned his head and gave Arilyn a blistering look. "And you, Ms. Meadows. I will see you soon."

It was more of a threat than a promise. Arilyn tried to keep her cold dignity, but stumbled once on her way out. His chuckle told her he'd caught it.

Gen decided not to bring up the odd dialogue between them and got to work.

fifteen

"NOW, THIS IS something I hope to avoid when my son is of age."

Wolfe looked up. Maximus Gray, his stepfather's close friend, general badass, and partner in La Dolce Maggie bakery—a local New York chain born from the Contes' original bakery in Italy, La Dolce Famiglia—stared at him through the bars of the jail. Dressed in jeans and a T-shirt dribbled with baby saliva and an array of interesting stains, he still looked more intimidating than most men Wolfe knew. A touch of humor twisted his lips.

Wolfe got up from the bench and walked over. "You will. First thing I'll tell Max Jr. is to call his old friend Wolfe to bail him out. You've always been cranky about losing sleep. Hey, who contacted you? I didn't get a chance to make my one phone call."

"Gen. What happened?"

"A clusterfuck."

"Sounds familiar. Give me the story."

His muscles relaxed. He related the whole story, sparing nothing. Usually he was stubborn enough to get himself out of his own messes, but there was one goal in his mind that left all others to the side.

Get back to Gen as quickly as possible.

He couldn't do that in jail.

Max scribbled a few notes. "First thing to do is get you out. I'll make some calls. Riscetti's restraining order sounds fishy. No prior evidence, so maybe strings were pulled. Is Gen okay?"

"Think so, she's strong. But I need to get out of here, Max. I need to be with her."

Max nodded, looking thoughtful. "You guys together now?"

Wolfe let out a half laugh. "No. Just friends. Why has the whole family been intent on hooking us up since day one?"

He waited for Max to laugh with him, but he was strangely silent, probing his face as if he suspected something Wolfe didn't even know. Wolfe tried to keep calm, hoping no one ever found out about that one stolen, perfect kiss between them.

"Because you both fit," Max said simply. "Not that I didn't want to see her happily married. Glad she ran from the asshole before it was too late. She's always been wicked smart."

"Yeah. This guy's good, Max. He set the whole thing up, got her to quit the hospital, and likes to control her. I'm worried. I don't want him near Gen."

"Got it. Let me take care of some things. Want me to call Sawyer and Julietta?"

Wolfe winced. He didn't need them worried when they couldn't do anything for him. "No, I'll tell them when it's all over. Knowing Sawyer, he'd fly here and start kicking ass and taking names. Let's get this done first." Max nodded.

Wolfe was so used to Max being able to do anything, he remembered he wasn't a lawyer. "Hey, how are you gonna get me out?"

A vicious smile curved his lips. "Let's just say I know people. I'll be back."

Wolfe shook his head. Thank God Max was on his side. He wouldn't want to be the other guy.

Wolfe paced back and forth in his cell and waited.

"YOU'RE OUT!"

Genevieve flung herself into his arms. He lifted her easily, kicking the door closed with his foot, and let her cling as tightly as she wanted. Usually he laughed and called her a girl when she was overcome with emotion. Right now, he seemed content to allow the well of messiness to overflow on his behalf. Good, because she didn't know if she could let go if she tried.

His lips pressed against her scalp and he whispered low nonsense to her. The ugly events of the night unfolded and caused a deep trembling. She expected him to smell like stale sweat and musk. Instead, she caught the soothing scent of cotton, water, and soap. His familiar warmth wrapped her in a cocoon, and his soft shirt cushioned her cheek.

"I'm so sorry," she whispered.

He tilted her chin up. "That's stupid. You gonna apologize for serial killers and natural disasters, too?"

She gulped in a breath and ended up snorting. "Yes. I'm sorry for those. I'm sorry for anything that's hurt you."

His face softened and something hot flared in his blue eyes. He stroked her messy hair back, which he'd done hundreds of times, but this felt different. More intimate. Like she was a lover rather than friend.

Uh-oh.

He seemed to reach the same conclusion simultaneously. Wolfe cleared his throat, released her, and stepped back. "You were smart to call Max. He straightened everything out, but I still have to appear in court. I've got a few things to do first and then I'll be back. Are you okay?"

She nodded. "Yes. Arilyn stayed with me last night. Slade's taking care of the restraining order against David. I'm sure he'll never come near me again when his reputation is at stake. Slade said he'll make arrangements to get my stuff back without me having to see him."

His lips tightened. "There's only one way to guarantee he never comes back. I'm moving in with you."

His words slammed through her. A crazed laugh escaped her lips. "Are you nuts? You can't move in with me."

"Do you feel safe here, Gen?"

She fought a shiver. "No. But I'm getting a locksmith to install a dead bolt and get an alarm system. Everyone will be on the lookout for his car. I have legal protection. I'm covered."

Wolfe narrowed his gaze. "Not good enough. You insulted him by leaving, and he wants revenge. I don't trust him, and I'm too far away from you in Manhattan. We'll both feel safer if I'm sleeping here at night."

Gen paced the room. She couldn't let him disrupt his life. Once again, he was rescuing her, and he must be getting sick of it. "No, I appreciate the offer, but I can handle this. You can't live in Verily when your apartment is close to Purity. The commute is an hour. My home has only one bedroom. We'd be ready to kill each other by the second week."

"You're being ridiculous—we get along great. I'll sleep fine on the couch. It'll be fun, like a monthlong slumber party. Girls like that, right?"

She rubbed her forehead at the craziness of his suggestion. "We gonna braid each other's hair, too?"

"If you want."

"No! I can take care of myself. My friends live local, and I can always have Arilyn stay over if I get spooked. You are not moving in with me."

"Fine, then I guess I'll be bunking in my car. Because I'm packing up my stuff and keeping watch every night. If you want to ban me from the house, that's on you. Personally, I'd prefer the couch."

He'd do it. He was stubborn and frustrating when he decided on a course of action. She'd watch him sleep by the curb every night until she broke down. Gen fisted her hands. Dammit. When had she become a damsel in distress? She hated those stupid Disney princesses— they sucked.

But the truth was his presence would make her feel safer. She was spooked. Afraid she'd see David's face around a dark corner, at her window at night, telling her to relax and fake it like she always did. The ugliness ran too deep to forget overnight.

Maybe a week or two. Tops. She'd prove David had lost

interest, and soothe Wolfe's protective instincts. They'd look back on the episode with a few laughs, their friendship stronger, and she'd be able to finally move on.

Besides, she had no choice. Better to save her strength for a battle she could win.

"Fine. You win."

"Good choice." He ruffled her hair and grinned. "I'll pack, check in with Purity, and head back. How about I cook dinner for our first official night together?"

She rolled her eyes. "I'd like to actually eat, so I'll cook."

"Even better."

Gen crossed her arms in front of her. "Don't think I'm gonna spoil you like Julietta does. I swear, if you begin leaving dirty underwear around the house you're out of here."

He actually looked wounded. "I'm the perfect roommate."

"Because you've never had one."

"It's been on my bucket list. Now I can cross it off."

He left. She looked around the small bungalow, noting some of the cobwebs she hadn't gotten to clean yet, and decided it would be a good time to restructure. There were a bunch of repairs to make, and already her neighbor Mrs. Blackfire, aka the Wicked Witch of Verily, had begun leaving more nasty notes telling her to cut down her favorite tree. The large, old pine was beautiful, overgrown, and leaned slightly to the right of the front yard. The Witch insisted it was dead and would fall on her roof. Gen disagreed. One lawyer, insurance inspection, and town hall meeting later, she'd won. Kind of. Moving out finally silenced the feud, but now that she was back, Gen realized round two was coming.

Still, she loved her place, and refused to let David steal her sense of safety.

Or the Witch steal her right to have a healthy tree in her yard.

Gen pulled her hair into a ponytail and got out the buckets, sponges, and cleaners. Later she'd hit the store for pillows and bedding. At least he'd be comfortable. She needed some groceries, too, so she could cook a nice dinner. Maybe pork chops with an apricot glaze.

Gen hit the music on her iPod and set to work.

"YOU'RE MOVING IN TOGETHER?"

Kate squeaked out the words and fell down onto the purple chair. They were in the counseling room, going over some of the most important characteristics in order to match up a couple. After cleaning and shopping, she'd gone in for her shift, needing work as a distraction. Funny, she'd gone from endless hours on her feet at the hospital to trying to fill her time so she didn't implode. But she was determined to look at the change as an opportunity. Work had become her crutch and a distraction from the real truth.

"Not together like a couple," she quickly corrected. "As friends. Just until I convince him I'm safe from David."

Her friend studied her, blue eyes thoughtful. "Do you think he'll try and hurt you again?"

Gen shrugged. "No, but Wolfe isn't convinced. It was

easier to let him do the 'I am man, let me protect the little woman' thing rather than fight him. Besides, I was a little freaked out. It'll only be a short time."

"Actually, I think it's a great idea. You know you could've moved in with me, Slade, and Robert though, right?"

Gen laughed. Robert was a paraplegic pit bull Kate had rescued from death, and the sweetest dog on earth. Slade had fallen in love with both Kate and Robert in a two-for-one deal. "Two doors down? Thanks, but I'll pass. Besides still being stuck next to our nightmare neighbor, I'd rather be living with someone not having sex."

"Is she bothering you again? I swear that woman has a telescope to spy. Do you know what she did to me last week? Left a paper bag of doggie doo on my porch. The note said, 'If you leave it on my lawn, I give it back.' As if Robert would ever stoop to poop on her property!"

A strangled laugh rose to her lips. "Poor Robert. Verily would be so much better without her. Think she'll ever move?"

"Who knows? The senior citizen center wouldn't take her. Not after the Jell-O incident. Does she still want your tree cut down?"

Gen nodded. "I now term it the Tree of Spite."

Kate laughed. "I love it. At least it blocks her view. She's gonna freak when she gets a look at Wolfe."

"It'll be so worth it."

"Back to the sex." Kate pointed to the files on her desk. "The faster you fill out the questionnaire and sign on as a client, the faster we'll get you hooked up."

Gen hesitated. "Wolfe said I'm not ready. Suggested I lie low for a while."

"Is he jealous?"

"No! He's just a worrywart. Kind of an older brother thing. But not."

Kate seemed to analyze her words but remained silent. "You've been in an abusive relationship for two years. I don't think it's a bad thing to experiment with the dating world. It's been over a month since the wedding, and I think dating will be good for you."

"That's what Arilyn said. As long as it's safe and I take it slow, I'm willing to try." Gen examined her nails, bitten short again, and gathered the courage to ask the question haunting her. "Did you ever feel the touch with me and David?"

Gen knew she crossed a line. They had all made a pact no one would ever use Kate to test a connection with the men they chose. Kate expressed fear in giving her opinion and not allowing them free will. She'd broken the rule only once, confessing to Kennedy that she was meant to be with Nate. Of course, the circumstances were different. Kennedy had believed she wasn't meant for love, and almost lost Nate forever. But Gen knew her question was different.

Kate sighed. Sadness glowed in her eyes. "No. But I only had one opportunity to touch both of you at the twins' birthday party. That was when I realized I had lost the touch. I never tried again, so I really don't know."

Her shoulders slumped with relief. She was glad. If Kate had experienced the touch between them, it would've made her even more confused about why they couldn't work. "I remember that day," Gen murmured. "He took me by surprise when he asked me to marry him. I never expected him to do it in front of my family."

"I think it was another control move. To make sure you didn't say no." Kate shifted in the chair, her teeth worrying her bottom lip. "In fact, I noticed you glanced at Wolfe before you said yes."

"I did?"

"Yeah, you did. Why?"

Gen turned away from her friend's probing gaze. God, she'd wanted to forget. The man she loved and wanted for so long finally proposed, and before she gave her answer, she'd needed to look into Wolfe's eyes. He'd been standing on the edge of the crowd, face hard and frozen. What had she wanted from him? Approval? A smile? Or something else?

Their gazes locked, and raw heat licked at her nerve endings—a promise and threat in those aqua depths that scared her. It had all happened so fast. For one crazy instant, she opened her mouth to tell David no. But something passed, and Wolfe turned away, and her family was staring, with David on bended knee, and she said the only word she could, and thought she wanted to.

Yes.

"I don't remember." Kate's silence was almost worse than the lie. Guilt struck, but she didn't want to think about that day ever again. "Can I ask one more question? And then I promise to never say another word."

"Sure."

"Did you ever feel the touch with me and Wolfe?" Kate jerked. Shock radiated from her in waves. Why had she asked such a stupid thing? She didn't want to know. They were friends, not soul mates. "Forget it, you don't have to answer. My brain is mush from lack of sleep last night."

"No."

Gen held her breath. "No, you haven't?"

"I sense a connection with you both, but never had the touch. I'm sorry."

Gen forced a laugh. "Don't be silly, I never expected you to. I'm still not sure why I asked."

"I think you do, sweetie."

She refused to analyze her comment. Gen smiled brightly and grabbed the files. "I'm going to input this into the computer, and then Kennedy is taking me to a make-over session so I can see what goes on behind the scenes."

Kate nodded, allowing the retreat. "Let me know if you need anything. We're trying to plan a girls' night out this weekend. You in?"

"Absolutely. Cocktails and gossip is exactly what I need."

She went back to work, trying to ignore the rush of disappointment. Maybe in some screwed-up way she was dealing with her breakup by spinning odd fantasies about her and Wolfe. Sure, the kiss had been wonderful, but they'd never repeat it. They treasured their relationship too much to cross the line into sex, especially if there was no future for them to fight for. Kate had never felt the touch. Therefore, they were never meant to be more than friends. And this was good.

Very good.

sixteen

"I DON'T LIKE BRUSSELS sprouts."

Gen glanced over and noticed the toddler's sulk. With his tattoos, piercings, and massive muscles, it fell a bit flat. "Tough. They're good for you. You'll like the way I make them." She pulled the pan out and tested them with a fork. Deliciously crispy on the edges, they tasted like heaven with the olive oil and seasonings. She'd learned early that roasting anything makes it tasty. "Can you double-check the biscuits? I tend to burn them."

He popped open the toaster oven and peered inside like it was a *Scooby-Doo!* mystery. "They're kinda brown."

"Shoot. Turn off the oven, please, and put them on that plate over there."

His large hands fumbled a bit and she held in a laugh. Wolfe dominated the small kitchen by his looming presence, but seemed a bit intimidated by each task. She swore he'd learn to cook a few things while he stayed there. He needed some survival techniques in the domestic zone. He figured out they needed butter, fished around, and put it on the table. The mismatched china and uneven glasses would've given David a heart attack. When they first got together, she was a disaster in the kitchen, preferring takeout or a bowl of cereal for dinner. He'd quickly divested her of that attitude, insisting she needed to cook a homemade meal in preparation for their family and up-coming dinner parties. Soon she was able to set a stunning table, with silverware in its right place and the napkin neatly rolled up. She'd stopped burning most things, learned to follow a recipe, and resented every moment when David ate the first bite, waiting to proclaim his opinion.

Gen smiled at the messy place settings, chipped dinner-ware, and cramped pine table covered with the assortment of pans lined up. It was . . . perfect. Even the burned bis-cuits yelled a big fuck you to her ex-fiancé. How many times had he clucked his tongue in disappointment at her inability to serve a decent biscuit?

Personally, she liked them crispy. But she still burned them. "Sorry about the biscuits."

He snorted. "You kidding me? The last time I had bis-cuits was back in Italy. I always liked them burned a bit anyway."

Gen laughed, her heart a bit lighter. "Me, too." She poured two glasses of Chianti and sat down to eat. Wolfe bent his head and closed his eyes. She watched in fascina-tion at the humble act of honoring his food. When he grabbed a biscuit and slathered butter on it, he caught her staring.

"What?"

"I never noticed you saying grace before."

A tinge of red flushed his cheeks. Another thing she loved about him. Big and bad, playboy millionaire, with a tendency to blush. Did it get any better than that? "Mama

Conte always said every meal is a gift. There was a time in my life I had to scramble for food on a daily basis. I ate from the garbage a lot. After eating home-cooked meals awhile, it didn't take much to give thanks for getting out of the shit that was my life."

Her heart tugged, but she concentrated on her food, knowing this was a delicate line. Gen knew little about his past, and the pinky promise they had shared solidified his intent to keep it that way. There was a darkness he carried with him she was always aware of. She regularly let him know she was willing to listen and be a friend if he ever wanted to talk. He'd nod, thank her, and remain silent.

Gen took a leap and asked for more. "How long did you have to live like that?"

He scraped his fork across the plate. "Five years. I left home when I was fourteen."

Yes, he'd been about nineteen when Sawyer took him in. Twenty when he and Gen had met. "Was it because of your mother? And the drugs? Is that why you had to run?"

He took a sip of his wine and avoided her gaze. "Partly."

She pushed a bit more. "No foster care? I can't imagine how you survived on the streets at that age. How brave you must have been."

His hand clenched around his glass. Self-disgust and a deep loathing suddenly flashed in his beautiful blue eyes. Shocked, Gen held still, afraid to speak or say anything further.

"Never think I was brave, Gen. Never. I did what had to be done."

Her heart cracked open and bled. Her voice caught. "Wolfe—"

"When did you learn to cook like this?" He grabbed a handful of brussels sprouts and popped one into his mouth. "These aren't half-bad."

The wall slammed down. Question-and-answer time was officially over. Gen struggled to get back on firm ground. "Umm, David insisted I know how to cook well. Said it was important for a wife and mother to know."

"You're gonna be a surgeon with enough money to hire someone to cook for you. Bet asshole never put the same standards on himself."

Her lips twitched. "No, he didn't. I was resentful for a while, but then a strange thing happened. I began to like it. Cooking is creative, but also scientific. Following a recipe to gain a particular product was soothing."

"Feel free to continue having fun on my account."

She arched a brow. "Oh, not just me. You're going to learn a few things while you're here. It'll be good for you."

He groaned. "Should've known you'd try to torture me. Listen, we'll have to go over the schedule. Make sure we mesh."

Confusion made her frown. "My work schedule is simple enough. I'll post my shifts, and I already know you work around the clock. You can just text me when you'll be home for dinner and stuff. Won't be too hard."

He rolled his eyes. "I couldn't care less about work. I'm talking TV. The remote. Who gets what and when. And don't think I'll be tortured with those crappy reality shows you try and sneak in. *The Bachelor*? *Hell's Kitchen*? You should be embarrassed."

She threw a brussels sprout at him. He yelped as it bounced off his rock-hard chest. "Screw you. Anyway, *Bachelor* doesn't start a new season for two more weeks. They're finishing up *Dancing with the Stars*."

"You can DVR it."

"I don't think so! I'm not getting tortured with your stupid *Searching for Bigfoot* or *Paranormal* whatever. They never find a beast or a ghost. You need help."

He scowled. "They find plenty of evidence. You gotta stop watching junk food for television. Broaden your horizons."

"I have. I checked out *Scandal* and love it. It's all about Washington, D.C., and politics."

He rubbed his face with disgust. "I just died and went to hell. Seriously."

"Hope they have good programming in hell," she chirped, scooping up a sprout and popping it into her mouth. "Or at least DVR."

They continued the argument over cleanup, hanging his wardrobe in the closet and fussing over cabinet space in the bathroom. She gave him the new comforter set she'd purchased with a brand-new pillow and helped him make up the couch. Damn, it was short. Those long legs of his might get uncomfortable. A twinge of guilt caught her.

"You got memory foam."

She tucked in the top sheet and glanced over. He was holding the pillow with a look of wonderment. "Huh? Oh yeah, didn't you tell me you got addicted to memory foam? I wanted you to be comfortable."

A smile curved his lips. His face softened, and Gen tried very hard not to let a girly sigh of pleasure escape. She'd do anything to keep that smile on him.

Anything.

"We can watch *Dancing with the Stars* if you really want."

Gen laughed. "You're such a nut job. You get a jump on the television, I have to get in the shower. Are you sure you're going to be able to sleep out here?"

He waved a hand in the air. "You wouldn't believe the places I've slept. This is the Taj Mahal, baby."

Her gaze flicked to his leather wristbands, wondering again what he hid beneath them. She couldn't imagine him sleeping in alleys and hunting for food at fourteen years old. What types of horrors did he hide at night? Gen pushed away the nest of emotions, knowing she needed to leave it for the lucky female who'd be the one to completely earn his trust. Sure, she was his best friend, but Wolfe would only share his innermost secrets with the woman he'd love.

Gen hated her already.

She trudged to her room, grabbed her pj's, and hit the shower. No more thinking in those terms. Especially when they were sharing space. She needed some type of distraction. Some type of antidote to Love Potion Number Nine.

Gen twisted the knob and made the shower a bit colder. Just for extra insurance.

WOLFE HAD TO ADMIT he was having fun.

Since he left Italy, he'd gotten used to being on his own.

Calling the shots. But there was something about being with Gen in her home, hanging out, cooking dinner, sniping at each other. A sense of rightness and intimacy he usually only experienced around Sawyer and Julietta.

He adjusted his pillow, stretched his legs out, and channel surfed. He might not have the convenience of a short commute to Purity, but maybe it was a good thing. While Gen was resetting her priorities, he might do the same. The past five years had been a whirlwind, mostly good, but work was his driving force. Since meeting Nate and making another true friend, he added a weekly golf outing to his schedule, which he protected at all costs. Should he try getting back into the dating world? Maybe look for a woman with a bit more depth? Usually it scared the crap out of him, but Gen made him realize he might need more than his body scratched.

The quick flare of hope sputtered out as if he had dumped a bucket of water on it.

He wasn't up to real emotion or truth. Never would be. Eventually, a woman would need to see the core, dig too deep for comfort, and he'd bolt. Textbook.

Even Gen didn't know the whole truth.

His finger paused briefly on some singing reality show but he continued clicking. Anyone else would've tortured him to death by endless questioning. Not her. She respected their youthful pinky promise and never probed, but her eyes told him the facts. She hungered for him to share, to allow her to know the real him and trust her with his past. Wolfe hated seeing the naked emotions on her face. The disappointment when he changed the subject, and the cheerful way she always pretended it was okay.

It wasn't though.

But that wouldn't change.

He fingered his leather cuffs and remembered that night. Fought a shudder. And wondered what the hell he'd do if the nightmares came when he was here. He was in the living room, so maybe she wouldn't hear. He had a full gym at his place and Purity, but there was no room to work out his demons in the bungalow. He made a mental note to check out the local gym and see if they stayed open twenty-four hours. If not, he'd have to rely on running, which wasn't as effective.

"Is *American Idol* on?"

Her lilting voice caressed his ears. Wolfe figured it was that singing show so he shook his head. "Nope, went through the whole list. How about we call a truce and watch a comedy? I'm always good for . . ."

He trailed off as his gaze took in her figure.

Holy. Shit.

The blood roared in his head and beyond. He was used to leather bustiers, garters, and four-inch heels on naked bodies. Musky perfume. Red lips.

Her skin was still damp, and the cotton nightgown was simple, stopping at the knee, with a scoop neck. White, with pink flowers. Pink socks on her feet. Her hair hung loose, the wild curls springing around her head in joyous abandon. Her face was free of makeup. Her lips a pale pink, with a tiny smattering of freckles over the bridge of her nose.

She was fucking gorgeous.

He tried to breathe and almost let out a moan. There

were a few scents in his life he wished he could steep himself in. Fresh-mown grass. Clothing just pulled from the dryer. An orange just cut open. She smelled like all of his favorite things combined. Was that possible? He couldn't gulp air fast enough, and his mind spun, wondering how she'd taste. Her breasts were unrestricted, and strained against the soft fabric in an effort to burst free. Was there anything in the world sexier than soft cotton clinging to damp skin? He always knew Gen's body held amazing curves, but he hadn't seen them on such stunning display before. Her hips were the perfect hourglass, with enough flesh to grab onto and hold tight. And her ass? It was a gift from the gods. Better than JLo's. Better than Kim Kardashian's. Better than anything.

His saliva dried up and his body went into a full aching attack. Ah shit. Was she going to sit next to him? His dick strained against his jeans and wept for release. His fingers curled into the pillow and he frantically searched for something to think about to let the tension ease. It was their first damn night. If Gen thought he was hot for her, she'd kick him out and never let him back in. And as much as it was torture, he wasn't going to let her be alone until he knew she was safe from David.

"I think you're lying to me." She crossed her arms in front of her. The shadows of her nipples were clearly outlined under the innocent white. He stiffened and tried to drop his gaze.

Really, really tried.

"Uh, lying?"

"*Idol*. I bet it's on and you lied."

Wolfe shifted painfully and threw the remote across the couch to the farthest side. "You're right. Here. You can have it tonight." *Please just sit down under the covers. Quickly. Please.*

She cocked her hip and looked suspicious. The hemline crept up an inch. Her skin looked smooth, soft, and pale. He wondered what his hand would look like against her. Dark against light. She'd probably cushion his hardness, just like that night on the dock. No, don't think about that. Not now.

"Take it!" he barked. "Here, get comfy." He lifted the blanket and urged her underneath. Finally, she rolled her eyes, took a seat, and snuggled. The breath left his body in a relieved rush, but his dick remained hard enough to cut stone.

"You're acting weird, but I'm not gonna fight you." She happily clicked on to the end of the singing show, where contestants belted out on the stage for the judges' and audience's approval. Wolfe focused on some nerdy guy and tried to imagine him naked. His erection slowly softened. He'd reached a new low. Next he'd be imagining nuns. Yuck.

"I miss Simon on the show," she chattered, moving a leg so it thrust out of the blanket. "He was rude but honest. Oh, it's the end anyway." She tapped the buttons, crossed her feet, and propped them up on the table. A long line of naked skin peeked out, running all the way up to the hip where the gown twisted.

His second head sprung back to life.

Shit.

"Hey, how about HGTV? *House Hunters* is on. They show three houses and the person has to pick one. I like to make a game out of it. My stats are impressive. Wanna check it out?"

He grunted. His gaze got stuck on the delicious curve of her hip. Where was her panty line? How come he couldn't see it. Unless . . .

His eyes popped out of his head at the thought and he dove across the couch, yanking the covers up and over her.

"Hey! What's your problem?"

Her hair flopped over one eye and those pink lips pursed. He remembered how she tasted. Sweet and clean, with just a hint of sin he ached to dive deeper into. Nuns. Nuns in bikinis. Yeah. Gross.

"Your—your nightgown was tangled." His voice sounded mangled. "Didn't want you to think I was sneaking a peek."

Perfect. That sounded like a friend.

"Oh, sorry." She wriggled again, adjusting her position. "Didn't mean to scare you. Hey, you know what I was thinking about doing?"

"What?"

"Getting a tattoo."

Heat punched him. Innocent, good-girl Gen with a tattoo. It might kill him. "They hurt."

She rolled her eyes. "I'm a surgeon, I can take it. I thought it would be kinda sexy, right? Maybe a rose with a thorn and drop of blood. Your ink is gorgeous, and it gives you that bad-boy aura. Helps with women, right?"

He never wanted so badly to watch a couple hunt for a house in Austin, Texas. "Sometimes. I don't think you need one. You may regret it later if it's on an impulse."

"I wouldn't get it in a place people could see. Maybe my lower back?"

No. He'd never be able to look at her again without imagining peeling down her jeans to reveal the secret right above the sweet swell of her ass. No. Way.

"Ah, people call them tramp stamps, Gen." He wished he were in Alaska right now, buried in a snowbank.

She wrinkled her nose. "So? Or maybe here?"

No. She wouldn't. She wouldn't.

She did.

She threw the covers off her, hiked up her nightgown, and revealed the naked curve of her left hip. "What do you think? You could see it in a bikini but it would be more for me. Right?"

Okay, she was wearing panties. The delicate line at her waist showed through the cotton. Definitely white to match. So innocent. What would it be like to order her to strip off her panties and be bare and ready for him underneath? He'd play with her, torture her with a bit of orgasm denial, then finally let her fly. Her nails would bite into his shoulders and her pussy would clench around his dick and his tongue would dive deep into her mouth—

He jumped up from the couch like his ass was on fire. "I'm gonna take a shower. Watch whatever you want."

Her eyes widened in surprise but he didn't wait for her answer. Wolfe bolted for the bathroom, cranked the water to Arctic freeze, and went back to the nuns.

He needed to get his shit together.

* * *

VINCENT SOLDANO PUSHED THE lump of cash deeper into the hole of his mattress. Soon. A bit more and he'd take his chances.

He didn't have much time left.

Carefully folding the stained sheet over, he lay back down and turned his iPod on high. Spaces between the highs were getting shorter. His mom used to occasionally make dinner, do some shopping, and once in a while be sober. Those moments were better than anything he could imagine. Brown eyes soft, sometimes she'd stroke his hair, call him her baby boy, and put her arms around him. Even though he knew he wasn't a baby anymore and didn't need his mommy like some kind of pussy, his heart still kinda ached. For a little while, his mind was quiet, and his body relaxed. He'd pretend she was clean, and they'd be together as a team against the world.

But that never happened.

Instead, he watched her staring sightlessly at the wall. She rarely bathed. Her hair hung limply and greasy around her face, and her clothes, if she was wearing any, were mostly stained and hanging off her bony body. The welfare checks used to buy a few groceries to keep them afloat. Now he didn't see a dime. The men got them first, and used the money for more drugs.

He was worried she was going to die. If he left, she probably would. At least he made sure she ate, and he'd clean up her bruises and bloody lips when the men went away.

But he had no choice. She couldn't protect him any longer, and many of her drug pushers stared at him like a commodity, a sick lust glittering in bloodshot eyes. He wasn't going to let that happen. Mostly he slept in the woods if the house was full, but winter was nearing again and he needed a plan.

He was so fucking tired.

How many times had he been ready to call a cop or social worker? Just press 911 and he'd be out of the hellhole. But his gut said he'd be trading one nightmare for another, and then his mother would go to jail and die from not getting the drugs. He was trapped, so he needed to run.

"You in there, boy? Open up! Your mama needs you."

He closed his eyes and tried to bury himself in the music, but the door began to shake so hard he knew the lock would break. Vincent grabbed the makeshift knife and slipped it into his back pocket. Just in case.

Then opened the door.

It was the man he feared the most. He worked his mother the hardest, liking to slap her around for a sick appetizer before he gave her the drugs. He liked to watch, too. He was short but strong, with huge biceps and tattoos covering both arms like sleeves. A bulldog face with lots of facial hair, dark eyes, and thinning hair. Scars crisscrossed his right cheek.

Vincent scowled at him. He knew showing fear was the worst. Bulldog liked it, and tried to get him to cry or beg when he threatened him, but Vincent hadn't broken yet and never intended to. "What do you want?"

A quick backhand whipped across his jaw. Stars exploded in his head, but he fought through the pain and kept glaring. "Your mama needs something and you better give it to her."

She stood behind him, wringing her fingers, a desperate tentative smile on her lips. His stomach twisted hot and acidy and he casually glanced at the front door. He might have to run. She was far gone and wouldn't be much help.

"I need money," she said. Her voice was thin and wheezy. Her left eye was still swollen from yesterday's events. "Bad, baby, real bad. You gotta get some for me."

He remained calm even though his heart pounded like crazy. "Got no money. You used the last of it for smokes and beer."

Bulldog sneered. "I think you're lyin', boy. Been noticing a few bills missing here and there, and I think you're stealin' from me."

Vincent shrugged. "Think what you want, I never touch your stuff."

Bulldog peered into his face for a long time, trying to probe for the truth. Then he smiled real slow. "Guess you won't mind if I look for it, then, huh?"

Vincent blocked his door. "Not my room. You keep your shitty hands off my stuff."

The blow caught him in the head this time and bashed him against the wall. He heard his mother cry out, but Bulldog was already tearing through his room, which he liked to keep neat and tidy. Tears pricked the backs of his lids from the ache in his temple and the way Bulldog trashed his precious stuff, little knickknacks collected, a book or two, his iPod, a photo of him and his mom when she wasn't high.

Fuck this.

With a roar, he charged Bulldog, swinging his fists like madman. The rush of adrenaline helped him get in a few good punches, but the asshole's biceps were like bricks. Soon he had him under the arms and lifted him like a lightweight, tossing him across the room like a fly caught by a swatter. He crashed to the floor and twisted his ankle. Red-hot fire ripped up his leg, but he tried to scramble toward his screaming mother, desperate to gain some space.

Too late.

Bulldog flipped the mattress. The gaping hole mocked them both, and sick dread coursed through his body, shaking his limbs. No. No no no no.

"Whatta we got here?" Bulldog stuck his fingers through the rip and pulled out a stack of cash. "Your precious boy is a fucking liar, whore. Keeping it for himself and letting you go sick without your hit. Is this gratitude for giving him a roof over his head?"

His mother's eyes lit up at the money. Her tongue shot out to wet her lips, and suddenly Vincent knew it was truly over. He would never win over the coke or meth.

Never.

The man loomed over him. Vincent tried to pull himself to his feet, but a rough kick in the gut tossed him back down. He reached for the knife, tried to palm it and make a quick jab, but Bulldog caught the movement and twisted his hand hard until the knife dropped uselessly to the floor. Vincent stared at it. Bulldog laughed, cracked his knuckles, and leaned over.

"I'm gonna teach you a lesson, boy. And it's gonna hurt."

It was a long, long time before consciousness blessedly left him.

He was thirteen years old.

seventeen

"LET'S GO FOR ice cream."

Wolfe groaned from his prone position on the couch. "I'm exhausted. We had a theft in our office, I lost a potential client, and the vending machines ran out of Reese's Peanut Butter Cups. I had to settle for crappy Skittles."

"Oooh, I love Skittles. Hey, don't you have gourmet five-star chefs you stole from the Food Network? Why are you hitting vending machines?"

He snorted. "I like them. Besides, snobby chefs don't do Peanut Butter Cups. I asked. Michael said he'd reexamine the offerings at La Dolce Maggie, but I think he's humoring me."

"We'll get ice cream and cappuccino. Come on, don't be a grump. It's a beautiful summer night. You need fresh air."

"I need sleep."

She walked over and shook his shoulders. He was so rock solid he didn't budge but managed to let out a grumble. "Why are you so frisky tonight? Hard day matching up happy couples?"

"Brat. No, I had a great day. There's a new recruit that Kate thinks will be perfect for me, so we're setting up a date. I'm just feeling a little restless."

Gen refused to tell him the real truth. She was going a

bit stir-crazy. She loved working at Kinnections, and adored seeing her friends behind the scenes. They were a trio of powerhouse females who blew her away. But she still felt lost. Her fingers itched for a scalpel, for her scrubs, and for the junkie rush that shot through her system when she had a new patient. When Kate got a paper cut today, Gen actually got excited and tried to double wrap it.

A sad state of affairs.

Guilt twanged her. "You win. I know you're tired. I'll go myself. Want me to bring you back something?"

Those laser-blue eyes lifted and probed deep. He rolled to his feet in one graceful motion. "I'll go. Sugar and caffeine sound pretty damn good, and you never get my order right."

He was lying. He wanted to veg out on the couch, but he sensed she needed company, and once again donned his knight-in-shining-armor outfit. The thing would be completely tarnished after he was done with her.

"You don't have to."

"Nah, I need to get out more. When golf dates with Nate become the hottest thing on my schedule, there's a problem."

They walked outside. The muggy air slammed into them, wrapped around, and stayed. The sun burned through the trees lining the sidewalk. Verily exploded with activity, from children on bikes to dog walkers and couples linking hands. The shops stayed open late through the fall, and Main Street screamed for customers to spend money in the quaint river town. Local artists sat outside painting canvases, carts filled with bright, fun knickknacks tempted passersby, and both humans and canines lined up outside the Barking Dog Bakery for goodies. Gen relaxed under the heat and familiar hum of chatter and laughter of her home.

"How come you stopped dating?" she asked. "I mean, Nate's good looking and all, but a millionaire underwear model turned hotel magnate should rate someone a bit more feminine."

Wolfe shrugged. He'd changed from his work clothes to a simple pair of frayed denim shorts, flip-flops, and a black T-shirt with the Purity logo on it. So why did he look like he'd just stepped out of *Esquire*? He wore clothes with a casual neglect most men couldn't pull off. Fabric bent to his will, hugged lean muscles, and surrendered. It made total sense why he'd become such a hot rage in the fashion world. He gave away nothing in his face, in his eyes. Just a big fuck you, which drove women mad with the urge to tame him.

Crap, even his feet were sexy, and she was so not a foot person.

Gen glanced over, appreciating the tanned muscles and flex of his calves, the bunched biceps and gorgeous scrawling tattoo. In a way, he was a work of art, but better appreciated from afar. She wondered if there was a woman out there who could claim him.

"I'm lining up a date for Friday night."

She flinched, then quickly covered it up. "Oh, that's great! Umm, we didn't talk about our arrangements. I'm not too good with socks on the door, but if you text me I can head over to Kate's for the evening. I'm sure she wouldn't mind."

"Why the hell would I need you to leave?"

She let out a desperate laugh. Damn. This was lame. And embarrassing. Did he have sex at his apartment? In his car? The image burst through her brain and almost gave her a concussion.

Leather squeaking under his naked ass. Slamming her against the steering wheel as he moved her up and down over his cock. Pulling her hair and watching her come hard and scream his name.

"Agghhgh." She let out a little shriek and drove the image back with a mental cattle prod.

"What happened?" He grabbed her arm and fiery shocks burst over her flesh. This was getting worse.

She yanked herself away. "Nothing! Ugh, I got a bug bite. Mosquito. Sorry."

Two kids on scooters whizzed between them. The newly gained distance helped her calm down.

"Make sure you put that pink stuff on it when we get home."

"Yes, Dad."

"Let's get back to our chat. You wanna talk about sex, right?"

Sweat trickled down her back. She pulled her tank away from her chest and pulled in a breath. "Yes. Sex. I certainly don't want to keep you from your normal activities just because you're doing me a favor. Unless you intend on staying at your apartment afterward."

"Seems fair. If the date docs go well, I'll text you so you don't worry. Deal?"

She nodded her head enthusiastically. "Great. Sounds perfect. And I'll do the same for you."

He stopped walking. Scowled. Damn, he was sexy.

Dark stubble highlighted the full arc of his bottom lip. His nostrils flared. Kind of like a pissed-off stallion whose mare had been stolen. "You? You're not ready for sex." He resumed his pace with longer strides.

Gen trotted faster to keep up. "Hey, aren't you being a little chauvinistic? Just because I had a breakup doesn't mean I want to be celibate. I think sex will be good for me. Especially great sex."

"You're not the type of woman for a one-night stand," he said firmly. "You'd only be happy having sex in a committed relationship."

Gen rolled her eyes. "Did that. Failed. Maybe doing something different will be good. Step out of my comfort zone. Have crazy orgasms. The walk of shame. Like you."

His scowl deepened. "I'm different. I don't do relationships."

"Maybe we should switch. I'll have sex with a hot guy with no strings. You try having a real relationship without the sex. Sound good?"

"No."

They reached Xpressions, a small café with gourmet ice cream and various coffees, organic teas, and chocolates. The scent hit immediately, giving her a sugar and cocoa high on contact. Perfect.

They stood at the back of the line. "Why not?" she demanded.

Wolfe let out a disgusted breath. "Because I'm not ready for long-term."

"You never tried it," she pointed out.

"And it's been working great for me."

"Where did you meet this upcoming date of yours?" she asked, trying to be cool.

"She's the sister of one of my clients. We had lunch before, but now we're ready to step up to dinner."

"Does dinner equate with sex? I need to learn this stuff."

The guy ahead of them turned his head and looked a bit interested. "Straight ahead, buddy," Wolfe warned. The guy flushed and swiveled back.

Gen laughed. "You're so uptight. I'll ask Kennedy."

"Why do you make me have these conversations? Any guy who expects to have sex with you because he bought dinner is scum. Walk on."

"What if I want to have sex with him?"

The guy in front choked on a sip of water. Wolfe glowered. "If a woman wants to have sex, most men will take you up on the offer. But most women do not sleep around on the first date. I think. It's about the third or fourth when they make their decision. And it's best to mix up the first few dates to test out all social arenas. Lunch, dinner, a movie, a cocktail, et cetera. You need to see the other person in different backgrounds to make sure you're compatible."

"Got it." The stranger nodded as if he agreed with Wolfe. Gen smothered a laugh. "Is that what you do?"

"Sometimes."

His obvious discomfort told the truth. "You just sleep with them, don't you?"

He pushed her gently forward as if ending their conversation. "Order your ice cream, Gen."

She spent a long time considering all options and or-

dered her usual—mint chocolate chip. It used to drive
David batty when she took so much time and always
picked the same thing, but Wolfe didn't seem to care. Wolfe
chose cake batter, which should be illegal for anyone over
the age of twelve, but still looked ridiculously good. When
they walked out, the sun was caught in mid-descent. The
sky shimmered with gorgeous pinks, and the faint strains of
music drifted in the air.

"It's music in the park!" she screeched. "Let's go."

He seemed more interested in his cone. "I'm not into
polka."

Gen grabbed his hand and led him past the gated dog
park and onto the main lawn where community events were
held. The Hudson River was the perfect backdrop for the
makeshift stage to the right of the white gazebo. Tables
lined the area from local shops selling their products. Families squeezed onto blankets, sipping soda and snacking.
"You're such a snob. Local bands play once a week but I haven't had any time to indulge. Most of them are pretty good,
too. Oh, there's the Barking Dog Bakery table. Let's go buy
Robert a treat."

Fingers entwined, they melted into the crowd. She
stopped to chat with various neighbors, who all stared curiously at Wolfe, studying his tats and piercings with evident
curiosity. No one mentioned her broken engagement or
runaway-bride scenario. Gen didn't know if it was better or
worse. Lately, every person who approached her acted as if
she was breakable, afraid to raise their voices or mention
anything in the way of romance.

She bought a few gluten-free peanut butter biscuits for

Robert, then tried on a few handmade beaded bracelets with power words on them such as *hope* and *love* and *heal*. The band was called Safe Word, reminding her of some BDSM novel, but they looked pretty cool and the lead singer had pink streaks in her hair.

"Genevieve MacKenzie."

She turned at the sound of her name, looked way down, and froze. Oh no. Not tonight when she was finally having fun.

The elderly woman before her was small, petite, and meaner than Cruella De Vil. She held a walker in her iron grip, and wore a faded red paisley housedress with white orthopedic shoes. Her stockings bagged around her calves. She squinted her eyes behind thick lenses, and her face was a map of wrinkles.

Gen knew those wrinkles weren't from laughter. She doubted Mrs. Blackfire ever cracked a grin. Ever. She was the scourge of Verily, known to be bad tempered in every shop she patronized. She hated animals, and had once called the local shelter to pick up one of Arilyn's dogs, claiming the beagle had peed in her rose bed. Her acid words, inability to experience humor, and general misery were well-known. Everyone avoided her.

"Hi, Mrs. Blackfire." Gen tried not to tremble. "How are you?"

The woman curled her upper lip. "Terrible. Your house is ruining my ability to sell. It needs a paint job, and your front step has bricks missing."

Hope bloomed. "Are you moving?"

Steely eyes that matched her gray hair glared. "No. But

that doesn't matter. Between that awful dog of Kate's ruining my rosebushes and your tree ready to destroy my house, I'll never sell at full value when I do. Who's this?"

Gen swallowed. "This is my friend Wolfe."

"Nice to meet you," he said politely, wiping his sticky hands on the napkin.

"That's a ridiculous name. You're a human being, not an animal. Whatever happened to James or William? Something normal. Not good enough for you?"

Gen held her breath, but Wolfe actually had a twinkle of laughter in his eyes. "At least my name isn't Jackass."

Mrs. Blackfire leaned forward with pure suspicion. "You making fun of me, boy?"

"No, ma'am."

"Hope not." She studied his various piercings and tattoo. "Are you in a gang? You look like a Jet. We don't tolerate shenanigans in Verily."

"I don't plan to bring any, ma'am. If there's anything you need help with around your property, let me know. I'll be glad to help."

"I take care of my own business. Are you living with her at the cottage now?"

"For a little while."

Mrs. Blackfire snorted. "This is a quiet neighborhood. I don't want to hear disgusting sex noises keeping me up at night."

Holy crap. She almost threw up in her mouth. "Umm, the band is starting, we should go."

Her neighbor turned her attention back to Gen. "While you were gone, I had a tree service analyze that pine and they agreed it was rotten. I'll be sending you the report."

She tamped down on her impatience. "The tree is healthy, and on my property. I'm sorry, but I won't be cutting it down."

Mrs. Blackfire pointed one bony finger toward her and shook with mad glee. "You've brought scandal on our town, you know. Reporters crawling around, asking a bunch of questions. You running out on that nice doctor. Heard you quit the hospital, too, and are working at that ridiculous matchmaking agency. In my day, we did what needed to be done. Lived with our choices. You're weak, girl. You quit on everything that mattered."

The words sliced and shredded tender flesh. Deep down, wasn't that what she was afraid of? She'd tried so hard to do everything right, but instead made a mess of things. She destroyed everything she touched and turned her back on her careful choices. "Maybe you're right," she whispered.

"I disagree."

The woman's head whipped around at Wolfe's voice. "What did you say?"

Wolfe stepped between them. "I said I disagree. People who don't make a change in their life, who are too afraid of the unknown, are cowards. They watch life pass them by, getting meaner by the day because everyone seems to be happier than they are. You think it's easy to walk away on your wedding day when you know you're making a huge mistake? How about going to medical school for years and having the balls to take a break in order to be sure it's what you want?"

Mrs. Blackfire's mouth gaped.

Wolfe leaned in real close.

"I bet you would've stayed and been miserable. Does that make you strong? Smart? Or just unhappy?"

The elderly woman made a low squeak of rage. Her cheeks were mottled a dull red. "How dare you? You're a guttersnipe. I'll be watching every move you make, young man."

Wolfe grinned and stepped back. "I'll be looking forward to it. Have a pleasant evening, Mrs. Blackfire."

He turned and led Gen across the lawn. Shadows fell, and the lead singer stepped up to the microphone to introduce their first song. Wolfe kept walking until he was at the back of the field near the fence, away from the crowd. Leaning against a gnarled pine tree, he crossed his ankles and snagged her fingers within his. She propped her back against the rough bark next to him, enjoying the warm strength of his grip.

"You didn't have to say those things," she finally said. Man, he smelled good. Like freshly washed laundry and sunshine. "She's just a cranky, mean old lady."

"I kinda liked her."

"What? No one likes her! She's evil. Wicked-witch evil. She'd probably steal Toto and take him to be destroyed. Probably right about me though."

"She's been hurt badly and never recovered."

"How do you know?"

He shrugged. "I can tell. But she's wrong about you. And I meant every word I said." He turned his head and snagged her gaze. "Every. Damn. Word. You are the bravest woman I know. It's the people who think they know the answers you need to be wary of."

His eyes were so wickedly blue and deep she could lose herself. "You mean like I used to be?" Gen joked. "I used to be so sure of myself."

"So did I."

Something fierce and primal shook through her. Electricity pulsed between them, and suddenly Gen wanted his mouth over hers, all lips and tongue and teeth, until he possessed and claimed every part of her. She ached to open her thighs and take him deep. Dig her nails into his skin. Mark him. Surrender. Fuck. What was happening to her? Her heart hammered. "Wolfe."

His name broke from her lips just as the drummer onstage went into a loud solo. People cheered him on and whistled, and the spell was broken. The tension eased, and she let out a shaky breath. Their relationship was changing, and she didn't know what to do. A strange sexual chemistry buzzed and grew stronger. Maybe sharing intimate space was messing up her head. After all, seeing someone every day for meals, for TV, and in their sleepwear forced a certain closeness. Add a life crisis and general sexual frustration and—*boom!*—a cocktail of a mess.

Gen swore she'd keep it together. No way was she going to ruin her friendship because her body was weak.

No. Way.

Her upcoming date couldn't come fast enough.

* * *

HE NEEDED TO GET laid.

Bad.

Wolfe dropped her hand and eased away. Her body was so soft and womanly. She'd finally put weight back on and lost the sharp edges stress had lent her. Those killer curves were back, and his fingers itched to grab and stroke and pleasure.

The shocks were coming faster and more frequently now. Moments when their eyes met and heat surged between them, leaving him weak. What was happening between them? Every night he lay on the couch, battling sleep and imagining her in bed. Cotton nightgown twisted around her thighs. Lips parted and moist as she breathed. Those beautiful corkscrew curls falling wildly over the pillow.

He was beginning to wonder if he'd sleep better in the car.

Wolfe used to be able to put his hands on her without fuss. He'd grab her around the hips and tickle her ribs, which she despised. He'd ruffle and tug on her hair. Wrap his arms around her for a big bear hug. Sure, they'd always had a connection, but the tiny simmer had exploded into a wildfire, and he didn't know what the hell to do. What had changed? And why did he suddenly want so much more?

She must've reached the same conclusion, because she forced a smile and spoke with fake cheer. "Thanks for the defense, friend." She subtly emphasized the word as if reminding both of them their true relationship. For his sake? Or hers?

He smiled back. "Anytime. *Friend*."

They both turned and listened to the music. The band was pretty good, able to crank out a variety of alternative and some recognizable pop songs without sounding like karaoke. Gen swayed her hips and mouthed the words. She'd always been a great dancer, able to throw herself into the music and the moment without caring how she looked. A strange ache fluttered from his gut. What would it feel like to claim her, man to woman, rather than friend to friend? Would she explode in bed like she did in the daylight, full of energy and joy and determination to wring the most out of the moment?

The man who held her heart for keeps needed to be extraordinary. Needed to match the same inner lightness she exhibited in her soul. The memories flashed hard and painful. Wolfe scratched absently at his leather wristband, accepting he'd never be that man, never be good enough for her.

At least he'd protect her.

Even from himself.

A fierce possession reared up. Gen belonged to the world of the living; of beautiful things; of a future filled with happiness and babies and domestic bliss. This time, he'd make sure she chose correctly.

The music slowed to a moody ballad, and the pink-haired singer launched into some classic pop song he vaguely remembered from the radio. His voice held a rich baritone, lending an air of smoky nightclub atmosphere. Night folded around them, battling the blinding lights from the stage. Stars exploded in the sky. The air was heavy with the scent of popcorn, cotton candy, and damp grass. Couples began to dance near picnic blankets, bodies entwining and moving slowly together.

He blinked when she held out her hand. Her eyes yearned for something big, something he desperately wanted to give her but knew he didn't have. Wolfe fought the lump in his throat and opened his mouth to make some excuse to bolt.

"Dance with me."

Her voice echoed the singer's. Low. Raspy. Seductive. He meant to say no.

Instead, he took her hand and pulled her into his arms.

Home.

The warm comfort of familiarity mingled with the spark of sex. She didn't just fit into him, she completely consumed his space, stealing his breath and cells and heart. Wolfe held himself back, battling for distance her presence wouldn't allow. Full breasts pressed against his chest. Thigh brushed thigh. The scent of peach shampoo drifted up, reminding him of sweet juices and the first delicious bite into flesh. An animal moan rose up from his chest, ready to escape his lips in an agony of need.

Words of unfulfilled longing filled the air in the seductive tone of the singer. The low beat of drums and guitar in the background added to the scene. Back from the crowd, trapped in darkness, they were alone in the world. With a sorceress's skill, Gen wove her feminine essence around him simply by surrendering to his embrace.

He gave up the fight. Just this once.

Burying his face in her curls, he grabbed her waist and pulled her tight, his growing erection trapped between their bodies. She gasped. Wolfe wondered if she'd move away, stop the dangerous game they flirted with, but once again she surprised him. Wrapping her arms tight around his back, she arched into him full power.

He gritted his teeth against the sweet ache of need. His feet moved in a faint parody of dancing, allowing each body part to touch, tease, and slide against one another. Fingers dug into him, urging him on. Wolfe ached to slide his hand under her shorts, under her panties, and dive in. Could he scent her musky arousal or was that just his mind fantasizing? She shuddered. Oh yeah, she was wet, and needy, and wanting . . . him.

His lips had a mind of their own. He dipped his head and tasted the soft crease where her shoulder met her neck. Like powdered sugar, he craved more. His teeth nibbled on her collarbone, and she made a low, hungry noise.

"Wolfe? Oh, God, what are we doing? That feels so good."

His brain exploded. He swiped his tongue to the vulnerable curve under her cheek, opened his mouth, and bit.

Her body shuddered. She grabbed his face with shaking hands, forcing him to meet her gaze. Drugged blue eyes stared back at him. Her breath came out in uneven pants from her plump lips. She was so damn honest in her responses, so willing to give him whatever he needed. "Why am I feeling like this?" she whispered, clinging with a feminine strength he found sexy as hell. "What are you doing to me?"

"Don't know. Same thing you're doing to me." He stared at her mouth, so close, so moist. "I want to kiss you."

"Oh yes. Just this once. Yes."

He didn't wait a second longer. Just lowered his head and captured her lips. Slid over and into the slick, sweet cave, thrusting his tongue with slow, languid motions, deflowering her completely. He leaned against the tree trunk and hitched her higher, until her legs wrapped around his hips. Her taste swamped him, driving him to capture the very essence of her mouth, refusing to let her keep anything back.

She didn't. Hanging tight, she melted in his arms and surrendered completely. Her body heat engulfed him, licking flames of fire that drove him mad for more. He couldn't remember when a kiss had stolen his breath and sanity, but nothing mattered except the need to rip her clothes off, taste her everywhere, give her pleasure. Using his teeth to scrape against her bottom lip, he captured her needy moan and worked his hips in a slow, grinding thrust. She ripped her mouth off his and panted, digging her nails deep into his shoulders. She tilted her head back so he saw the wetness on her swollen lips.

"Feels too good," she panted. "Give me more."

Oh yeah.

He moved quickly, turning her so her back pressed against the rough bark of the tree. Losing his head completely, he forgot he was in a public park, forgot she was his best friend and sex wasn't an option, forgot everything except getting closer and deeper into her until he faded away.

He took her mouth again, bruising, but she kissed him back with such raw hunger and need, Wolfe shook. He gripped her head and pulled her hair, notched into the center of her thighs, and gave it all to her with everything he got.

She was wild in his arms, biting and licking back, arching up for more, until the simple kiss burned barriers and exploded out of control. Wolfe dimly heard the song ending and the smattering of applause. Low chatter and movement finally cut through the fog.

He lifted his head. Froze. Dragging in a breath, chest tight, dick so hard and swollen it could be registered as a deadly weapon, he fought for sanity.

She opened her eyes. Her pupils were dilated. When she spoke, her words came out slurred. "Wh—what happened?"

Holy shit, he did it again. The awful Britney Spears pop song clanged loudly in his head. He couldn't blame anyone but himself this time. What type of friend was he? She was vulnerable right now. Needy. He had to suck it up, get himself under control, and be the supportive buddy she deserved.

But how would he ever look at her again without wanting to kiss her?

"Wolfe?" She blinked. "What's wrong?"

He forced a smile and slowly lowered her back to the ground. Her breasts dragged over his chest and almost caused him to weep. "Song's over." His voice came out a bit rough, so he softened the words by running a finger down her cheek. She seemed to catch his unease, and an awkward silence descended as the lead singer spoke her gratitude. Everyone clapped and began to gather their stuff, trudging out of the park. He was left with a hard-on and a cloud of confusion as he tried to decide the best route to take.

"Ready to go?" he asked.

"Sure." This time he didn't take her hand. They didn't speak. The shops were closed, the stars twinkled overhead, and their shoes clopped on the pavement. Halfway home, she finally broke. "I'd like to say I'm sorry but I'm not."

He bit back a laugh. She was always so . . . unexpected. Honest. Once again, he vowed not to destroy the most precious relationship he had. "I'm not either, sweetheart. I am sorry if we blurred the line though. Our friendship means more to me than some raging hormones. Maybe the lead singer did it. She kinda reminds me of Pink."

The joke fell flat and her smile seemed forced. "Right. We got caught up in a moment."

"This weekend will be good for us. We'll both start dating again, and release some of the pressure."

Why did her shoulders suddenly slump? He thought mentioning her date would ease her mind. He had no right to screw with her head and get her to want more.

Even if he did.

Hell, yes, he wanted more than that kiss. If he was honest, he'd confess he wanted Gen in his bed, naked, open, and ready to do his bidding. He wanted her heat and passion and sweetness. He also realized if he ever slept with her, besides wrecking their friendship, he'd never be satisfied with anyone else.

But Gen could never know or suspect. She needed to have an open mind and heart for her date. Even though the thought of another man touching her made Wolfe want to wreck his face. He'd manage not to screw it up for her sake.

Her soft sigh echoed into the night. "Guess so. I always did have a thing for Pink."

He relaxed slightly. She was playing the game. Leaving it behind them. Helping him pretend it meant nothing.

Much better this way.

They walked the rest of the way home in silence.

GEN MADE UP THE couch and tried not to mope.

She needed to get over this. They had kissed. She had liked it. Hell, she'd loved it. She'd never been so turned on in her entire life. They had touched and traded bodily fluids and now it was over. Done.

The echo of the shower running rose to her ears. The image of Wolfe naked and wet made her belly lurch and her thighs tingle. She'd been wondering if that kiss they shared on the dock in Saratoga was a freak occurrence. After all, that type of heat between friends was impossible. Right?

Instead, tonight confirmed the worst. She wanted her best friend in bed. Bad. She wanted to do all sorts of dirty things with him, and was super close to suggesting the whole friends-with-benefits package for a moment, and then he had to go mention their dates. Talk about a buzz-kill.

Gen changed the pillowcase on his memory foam pillow and sighed. Wolfe was probably hot for every girl he kissed. She couldn't think of herself as special. Hell, he practically told her he was hard up from not sleeping with someone and needed sex. Definitely an oversurge of testosterone. Add in some moody music, her body pressing into his, a seductive night with the stars, and wham. A crazy, hot kiss against a tree. Now over.

She shook her head. Time to be a big girl and not get all moody over the whole thing. Especially with him staying here. Maybe Wolfe was right. Maybe her upcoming date would work out well and take away these crazy emotions she was starting to feel. Maybe—

"Holy shit!"

She froze. The roar from the bathroom shook the tiny house on its foundation. Heart pounding, she stumbled forward, terrified he'd slipped in the tub, or cut something important, or saw a ghost with bloody teeth and eyes ready to rip him apart. Stupid Syfy channel.

Gen called out his name and reached the door. It was flung open and she caught a blur of nakedness rush past her. A puddle of water soaked the floor and steam drifted out lazily. Trying to keep calm, she stuck her head inside and looked around, but nothing seemed wrong. The water ran in the tub, the curtain was pulled back, and the mirrors were fogged. A pile of clothes lay in a heap on the floor. Towels were strewn around. Other than a mess, there was nothing in there.

"Dammit, Wolfe, you scared me. What's going on?"

"There's a fucking tarantula in there! I've never seen anything like that—don't you clean?"

She opened her mouth to tell him exactly what she thought of his chauvinistic remark, then stopped. Gen recognized the tone well. He was terrified, and as much as she loved to tease him, she respected this one weakness regarding crawly, hairy bugs. She shook her head and marched back into the bathroom, grabbing a handful of tissues. "Where is it?" she called out.

"By the towels. I saw it drop down from the ceiling. Nasty motherfucker."

She smothered a laugh and began searching for it. "Why can't you hang the towels up on the hook? They get wet and moldy on the floor."

"Can we talk about that after you kill the spider?"

She picked up the towel and shook it out. Nothing. "And what's that crack about my cleaning? I sweep the cobwebs, buddy, but I haven't seen you get out the vacuum yet. Maybe you should help more if you don't want creepy crawlies around here."

"Will you just get the spider, Gen?"

She bit her lip at the high tone of his voice and narrowed her gaze. If it was so big, why didn't she see it? She lifted the bath mat and jerked back as the bug skittered over the white tile. What the hell?

Tarantula, huh? The thing was dark and fat, but overall pretty small to make him scream like a girl. Ah, the blackmail could be incredible. She grinned with evil purpose and crushed the bug in the tissue. Sorry, Arilyn. In this case, she was in the camp of killing bugs and did not classify them in the animal kingdom.

"Got it."

A sigh of relief reached her ears. "Thanks. Are you okay?"

She held back a snort. "It was a close call but I made it. You're right. He's huge. Wanna see?"

His voice cut like a whiplash. "Don't screw with me, Gen. Flush it in the toilet or I swear to God—"

"Aww, whatcha gonna do? Come on, maybe it'll help your arachnophobia. I'll show you." Grinning, she walked out of the bathroom, holding out the tissue ball in her hand like a present.

"Get that thing away from me!" Gen opened her mouth to tease him, but he looked so freaked out she started to feel bad.

Then she realized she shouldn't be focused on his face right now.

Because he was naked.

Holy hotness, Batman.

Gen knew he had a great body. The world saw it in billboard color when he modeled boxers, with his badass leather wristbands and nothing else. But seeing him fully exposed in all ways almost made her hit the floor from the sheer weakness in her knees.

Wolfe was amazing.

Rivulets of water slid down a mass of hard muscle. Not an ounce of softness showed on his body. From the eight-pack abs, powerful biceps, and bulky thighs, he was lean, mean, and toned. Deep olive skin. Dark hair sprinkled his chest and narrowed to the mouthwatering line going lower. His tattoo crawled over his body like a gorgeous painting. Her gaze dropped to the nest of dark curls between his thighs.

Oh. My. God.

He was pierced.

She almost gasped at the silver barbell that pierced his cock, which was impressive and steadily rising as she kept her gaze locked on target. Heat twisted through her body, and her mouth grew dry as she imagined her fingers playing with him, watching him grow hard under her ministrations. Imagined her tongue flicking the barbell, making him groan. Imagined what he'd feel like buried deep inside her. Would the metal hit her G-spot? Tickle her clit as he thrust back and forth? The room blurred and her fingers clenched with the need to touch.

"Gen."

Her name rasped in the air. She watched him grow bigger, longer, surge forward in a massive erection under her hot gaze. "Yeah?" she murmured, fascinated with the male beauty and strength before her.

"Gotta stop looking at me like that, sweetheart. I'm dying here. I need a towel."

She blinked. "Oh. Right. A towel." Her tongue snuck out to wet her bottom lip. He groaned as if he was in agony. "Sorry."

Gen didn't move. He was so hard. She ached to stroke the tip and know what he felt like. Clasp her hand around the root and pull up and down slowly. Drop to her knees and open her mouth and take him deep inside. Would he taste as clean and delicious as he smelled? Or would he have an earthy, musky flavor with his arousal?

She jerked as he said her name again, more forcefully. "Yeah?"

"If you don't get me a towel now, I'm gonna lose it."

Oh, she was so tempted. Stroll over, grasp his cock, and make him forget for a while. Make them both forget. But when she finally lifted her gaze, there was more than lust and need in his eyes.

There was desperation.

With numb motions, she walked into the bathroom, grabbed the towel, and brought it over. He wrapped it around his hips and held it with one fist, as if afraid she'd try to yank it off him. Color flooded her cheeks. How humiliating. She must've been staring like some horny teenager looking to get rid of her virginity.

"Sorry." Gen forced a smile. "Got carried away."

His hand shot out. Grasped her chin and tilted her head up so she was forced to look at him. Blue eyes caught and held hers in a grip so tight and so fierce, the breath was forced out of her lungs. Raw hunger vibrated from his gaze.

"Don't ever apologize to me again for anything we do together."

She stared back at him, helpless. Waiting for him to make the decision for both of them, since she was too far gone to say no. If he reached for her, there'd be no turning back. One kiss, one touch, and they'd be in bed. Naked. Together.

Gen trembled. Waited.

He dropped his hand.

"Thanks for killing the spider."

She couldn't answer. He walked past her and shut the bathroom door. With shaking knees, she collapsed onto the sofa and wondered what the hell she was going to do.

eighteen

WOLFE SMILED AT the woman across the table. This was their official third date. The one that tipped the scales into sex . . . or not sex. So far, Brit was screaming *yes*, and he was glad.

Yep. Real glad.

Gen's date was tomorrow night. They'd already discussed the mechanics of disappearing for the night, so he was set to bring Brit to his apartment in Manhattan and get his groove on. The cheap cliché sounded garish in his head. Maybe he should stop thinking so loud to himself and concentrate on his date.

She was gorgeous. Not too made up. Long, dark hair sleek and straight. High, full breasts. A tiny waist. A bit slim, but most women he dated now were. Everyone was terrified of having some hips and ass on display, but it was the frickin' magazines' fault. In Europe, a full-figured woman was coveted. He wished it would come back to the U.S.

She smiled back and he noted her gleaming white teeth. Oh yeah, definitely bleached. No one's teeth were that naturally bright. "I'm so glad you finally called, Wolfe. I had a great time at lunch and was looking forward to getting to know you better."

Her gaze dropped a bit lower. It was well rehearsed. Very different from Gen's shocked and fascinated look when she got a peek at his intimate piercing. He didn't think he'd ever get over the way her eyes widened and sheer want transformed her features. Had he ever viewed such a naked hunger from another woman? Someone who knew who he was and wasn't categorizing his body as a separate entity?

He forced his thoughts away from Gen and concentrated on his date. "I had a good time. Was looking forward to seeing more of you."

"How much more?" She tilted her head in flirtation.

"A lot." His words were automatic, but he figured his body would follow. He needed an outlet desperately, and though he'd hoped there could be a bit more with Brit, something was telling him one night would be enough.

"That could be arranged," she drawled.

He never missed a beat. "Then maybe we should get the check."

She didn't argue. Just raised a perfectly arched brow and smiled wider. He got the bill from the waiter, paid, and escorted her out of the restaurant. She chattered about work, about Purity, about her father and the expectations people had of a woman in a male-dominated industry. Another time and place, he might have enjoyed her sharp intellect and polished demeanor. In a way, they were both the same, cut from the same cloth. They'd worked hard for their success, enjoyed physical intimacy and good dialogue, and were open for what happened next.

Too bad everything seemed flat lately.

But it didn't matter. As long as Brit knew the deal, he was not going to feel guilty. He'd been without sex for over three months and was reaching the breaking point. "I'm heading back to my place." Wolfe paused. "That okay with you?"

Brit turned and winked. "Yes. I just have to get up early for a presentation tomorrow."

Dread curdled in his stomach. He'd been hoping to avoid a sleepover. Things got . . . intense in the morning. Either it was too forced, in the hopes of a casual, breezy good-bye, or the awkward silence slowly killed him, knowing it was over for him but not for her. Hell. He respected Brit and she deserved more than a quick lay and a push out the door. When had he gotten so cold? So good at staying distant from everyone, whether or not he gave his body?

A chill enveloped him but he refused to think about it. How many times since that fateful night did he give his physical body but never any part of him inside? He was broken. Nothing would fix him, there was no magic formula of love or healing, but he could give pleasure, give honesty, and be kind.

Maybe that was all he had left.

He pulled into his assigned space and opened the car door. Led her upstairs, past security, up the elevator, and down the hallway. She kept talking, oblivious to his growing tension and confusion. He'd done this a thousand times before. Just because he was living with Gen didn't mean he couldn't do what he needed, give in to the raw urges of his physical body to finally sleep without dreams. He had to have the release.

Wolfe eased into automatic host. Got her a glass of wine and sat down on the couch. He made appropriate noises for her comments, looked into her eyes, and engaged in conversation. But his mind drifted, away from his condo and back to Verily.

Back to Gen.

Brit finally set down her wineglass and moved in. Her hands stroked his hair, tilting her head in a flirtatious manner that made her hair slide over her cheek and cover one eye.

Gen's curls did it naturally, without any pretense, but he wasn't thinking about that right now.

"I've wanted you for a long time," she murmured, leaning in.

"Me, too. Brit, you know I don't do long-term, right?"

He hoped for a shocked look, pure indignation, maybe a slap. Instead, she laughed softly. "Baby, I don't have time for long-term. Don't get ahead of yourself. But tonight I'm all yours."

"That's all I want."

He kissed her. Waited for the snap of desire, or at least a stirring from below to let him know it was going to be fine. He got . . . nothing. Of course, it was only a kiss, and maybe he needed to up the game in order to get his anatomy interested.

His tongue moved inside her mouth. She tasted like rum, and had a sharp, tangy scent that overwhelmed him. Her body was extremely thin and sharp, so her bones hit his muscles when he moved closer. Wolfe concentrated on letting his instincts lead, determined to wring as much pleasure from this night as possible.

Brit moaned and jiggled her breasts. "Oh yeah, baby, give it to me."

He frowned. *Give it to me*? A bit practiced, maybe, but usually it would turn him on. Why wasn't he turned on? Wolfe worked harder, sliding his hands over her body and pulling her closer. All the components worked well separately, but once he put them all together there was no heat.

Just an empty buzzing.

Cursing under his breath, he broke the kiss. Her lips were ruby red and parted. Her eyes darkened and she stood up, pulling him with her. "Let's go into your bedroom. I want you to fuck me hard. Take me however you want. I'm yours."

The words would usually thrill. He needed to lose himself in sex and the moment. But Wolfe realized nothing was going to help tonight. He could fake it, and force an orgasm, but it would make him feel dirty. And he'd promised years ago he'd never make himself feel that way again.

The choice gave him pause for only a moment. No. He refused to wake up the morning steeped in shame because he lied. He lied enough without heaping more on his soul. Wolfe teetered between faking a sudden stomach bug or dealing with feminine wrath. Once again, honesty won out.

"Brit, I'm so sorry. I can't do this right now. My head's not on right."

She never paused, just strode over and gripped his soft dick between her hands. "Not your little head I want right now, babe," she drawled. He winced at her roughness. "I'm more interested in your other one."

Awkward.

He slowly and deliberately removed her hands. "That one isn't working well tonight. Listen, I'm sorry I led you on." Ah hell, a little lie wouldn't hurt. "I'm not feeling too well."

She frowned. "Need to use the bathroom? I can wait."

Ugh. Wolfe shook his head and grabbed his phone. He tapped out a text for his Purity driver to pick her up and take her home. "No, I think this is gonna be a long night. I really need to be alone. I'll have my driver meet you out front."

She cocked her head and considered. Probably realizing the combination of rejection and bullshit lies. Finally, God smiled upon him and she nodded, grabbing her purse. "Sure. I don't want our first time to be memorable that way. I'll catch you next time?"

"Absolutely." Okay, so he had chickened out, but he couldn't deal with the whole talk thing right now. He'd tackle the dialogue next time they saw each other. She didn't kiss him good-bye. Just winked and strode out of the condo with a practiced swing of her hips.

Wolfe let out a groan of relief.

Blessed silence settled in. He brought the glasses to the sink, glancing around his place. Why did the space feel so empty? Usually he liked the simplicity and no-nonsense decor. He thought of his apartment as a good location to decompress, spend time alone, and refuel for work. But it never felt like home.

Gen's place did.

Was it the bungalow? Charming decor, bright colors, crooked pavement, and stuck windows lent an aura of charm. Or was it Gen? The way she exploded from room to room in a rush of activity, scattering her belongings and scent in a trail? The way she liked the television and music loud? The OCD habit of alphabetizing her books by author's last name?

He rubbed his forehead. Things were getting too complicated. He might not be bedding Brit tonight, but Wolfe needed to make sure Gen believed he had. They needed the distance and reminder they weren't lovers. He'd sleep here tonight, say nothing about his date, and let natural conclusions do the speaking for him. Technically, it wouldn't be a lie.

The image of Gen standing before him in soft cotton, damp skin, and no panties slammed through his mind. His dick rose to full attention, and Wolfe groaned. He needed release, and there was only one way to do it.

He closed his eyes, unbuckled his pants, and stroked himself to a shuddering orgasm with Gen's name hovering on his lips.

"IT'S GONNA HURT."

Gen lay down on a padded bench, her rear up in the air and her pants resting on the lower part of her hips. A bit intimate but not much she could do. Gen looked into her friend's worried face and patted her hand. "I'm used to needles. I got this."

Kate bit her lip and averted her gaze from the whirring instrument inches away from Gen's skin. "Do you need alcohol?"

"No drinking in my shop," the artist interjected. He wore leather pants and a black T-shirt, and had long, braided dark hair. His ink was all black and detailed the stations of the cross on both arms. Fascinating. Verily's only tattoo parlor sat at the edge of town. The owner was the nephew of Tattoo Tony from a small shop in Marlboro whose claim to fame was once having detailed Cher's famous ink on her rear. "No refund on tats, so sober customers only."

Gen laughed at her friend's withering stare. "Fine. Just make sure you're not looking at her naked ass," Kate whipped back.

The artist rolled his eyes. "Lady, you wouldn't believe some of the places I put tats. There's nothing I haven't seen."

Gen spoke up. "Sorry, just ignore her." She lowered her voice to a whisper. "Not you, too? You should've seen Arilyn with Officer Petty. She turned into a raging bitch."

"Our Arilyn?" Kate asked in amazement. "Impossible."

"I swear! She accused him of not doing his job and got all mouthy. I think he was hot for her. There was something almost electric in the air. Oh, and he smokes."

Kate gasped. "That'll never work. I'm worried about her yoga teacher. She seems a bit mopey lately. Think he's cheating again?"

"Probably. He screwed around on her twice, hiding it in a bunch of bullshit about men not being naturally monogamous and embracing their innate tendencies. He's a player."

"Should we talk to her again?"

"No. She needs to come to the conclusion on her own. Same way I did with David."

"Yeah, I guess you're right."

The artist leaned over her ass and spoke brusquely. "Ready? I'm gonna be a while."

"Ready." Excitement slithered through her. Maybe this was what it felt like being a bad girl. Izzy would be proud of her. The thought of her twin sent a pang of regret through her, and Gen wondered if she should try to reach out again. Maybe since her screwup with David, Izzy would be more apt to have a conversation.

Kate shrieked as the needle hit the small of her back. Tiny pinpricks of pain shot through her, but it was bearable. "Kate, you're freaking me out. Breathe."

"Sorry. Why are you doing this again? Are surgeons allowed to have ink?"

An image of Wolfe flashed in her mind. Strolling out the door, looking hot as hell, ready to bed some gorgeous, confident, sexual female who'd make him feel good, touch him all over, and take him deep in her body.

Bitch.

She wanted to scream. Instead, she'd given him a thumbs-up like she was his buddy who didn't care how many women he screwed. And she used to be. Usually, she'd laugh, call him a man whore, and be done with the episode. Now the game had changed. Jealousy coursed through her and she didn't know how to handle it.

She focused on Kate's question. "Yeah, you're thinking military. As for why? Let's just say I need to shake things up a bit. I feel like doing something a bit crazy. Outside my comfort zone. Know what I mean?"

"Totally. Of course, you could've come with me to visit my mom and she would've gotten you high."

Gen grinned. Kate's mother was a posthippie, pot-smoking sex therapist with a big heart. "How is your mom?"

Kate nibbled on a few Skittles. Sugar helped balance her fear of needles. "Fine. She got all excited about this new client who was experiencing erectile dysfunction. She aims to cure him."

"Your mom is a badass."

"Slade loves her. She's been pretty chill about the wedding, so we're thrilled she's leaving most of it to us."

"I can't believe you're getting married soon. I'm so excited."

Kate smiled. "Me, too. Maybe Kennedy will be next if Nate has his way. Speaking of men and living together, how's it going with you and Wolfe shacking up?"

The memory hit her like a left hook. Wolfe standing naked in her living room. Wet. Hunger flashing in those blue eyes. She swallowed. "Uh, okay."

Kate swiveled her head around. Her gaze reeked of suspicion. "You don't sound *okay*. You sound involved."

She tried for a casual air. "Just doing the roommate thing. Sharing meals, a TV, et cetera."

"Sharing a bed?"

Gen flinched. The artist cursed and slapped her upper thigh. "Don't move."

"Hey, you're not her dom!" Kate yelled.

The guy raised a needle. "Quiet, girl, or your friend's gonna get a very different tattoo."

Gen sent her a pleading look. "Kate! Let him do his job, please."

"Fine. Are you sleeping with Wolfe?"

"No. We're friends. I told you a billion and one times. In fact, he's out tonight screwing some woman who probably means nothing to him."

"Interesting. Why do you sound jealous?"

Gen glared but it wasn't too intimidating with her pants down. "I'm not. I want him to get past these brief sexual affairs and experience a real relationship. He refuses to join Kinnections and keeps insisting he's unable to commit."

"Maybe he is."

"Bullshit. He's scared of letting someone in. It's frustrating. Hell, he hasn't even told me about his past, and I've known him for years."

"That's his journey, Gen, not yours," Kate said gently. "He's gotta be ready for more and you can't force him. Why don't you concentrate on your upcoming date? Are *you* ready?"

Was she? Since Wolfe began wrecking her peace and once-stable libido, she forgot what she wanted from the date. A hopeful beginning? A confirmation there was love out there for her? A leap into the unknown to remind herself sex didn't have to be a battlefield? Or love. Or whatever that Pat Benatar eighties song said.

"Yes. I'm excited. It was a good match per the computer system, right?"

Kate nodded. "You really complemented each other. He's divorced, but completely ready to date and fall in love again. He's a pharmacist, so he'll appreciate your medical background. He likes to have fun, and he's not stodgy at all."

"Kate?"

"Yeah?"

"If all goes according to plan, I'd like to sleep with him."

The low chuckle of the tattoo artist was nothing compared to the gasp her friend gave. "No! It's against the rules of Kinnections. Well, the implied rules. No sex on the first date. You're not out to get laid but to build a healthy, satisfying relationship."

"Will you throw me out if we have sex?" she asked curiously.

Kate moaned and covered her face. "No, don't be silly. But I don't think Charles is that type of guy. If you just wanted to get laid, you should've told me!"

Gen tamped down a giggle. "Why? Do you have a separate list of men who want a one-nighter versus a long-term relationship?"

Another laugh emanated from behind her. Kate glared.

"No. But I may have chosen differently. He's relationship material. Not hot sex."

Her shoulders slumped. Of course. Why was she surprised? None of her friends thought she was built for short-term. Especially not Wolfe. Was it so wrong to want to buck the system now and then? Was it so wrong to want a night of passion and impulse before worrying about china patterns and white picket fences?"

"Ah damn. I said something wrong. What'd I say?"

Gen avoided her gaze. "Nothing, don't be silly. You're probably right. I was just thinking since I broke off my engagement, diving into another relationship wouldn't be a good thing. Maybe I need to have a bit of fun and frolic. Does that sound terrible?"

Kate reached out and squeezed her hand. "Not terrible at all. I'm sorry I didn't ask more questions about what you want." She tapped her finger against her lip. "Maybe Charlie will surprise you. If you have heat, he may want to go a bit crazy and sleep with you."

Gen couldn't help it. She laughed. Kate had expressed the thought as if it was a complete novelty. Who was she kidding? She'd never had a one-night stand and never been interested in one. She liked connection, dialogue, and emotion. But Wolfe didn't have to know.

The thought morphed into a plan. She'd go on her respectable date with Charles, but she'd keep her mouth shut about the ending. Wolfe might assume she slept with him, and maybe that would put a barrier between the weirdness that was sprouting up all the time. If she experienced a spark with Charles, she would let her gut instinct lead the way. A voice growled behind her back.

"You can always get him in the mood by showing him this beauty," the tattoo artist said. "Sure you don't want baby's breath sprouting from the rose instead? Ladies seem to go for that one."

No. She may have picked a rose, but this was her own little secret. A bit of darkness within the beauty. Pain within the pleasure. She may not want to live in that world, but it existed, and she would never try and shut it out again. It was now a tiny part of who she was.

"No," she said aloud. "I want the thorns with the drops of blood."

"You got it."

Kate winced and looked away, but with each prick of the needle, Gen edged closer to satisfaction. Maybe it was time she accepted that she didn't always have to walk in the light. Do the right thing. Make good choices. Maybe there was more to her than she ever thought possible, and getting this tattoo was her first step.

Gen smiled and gave herself up to the experience.

"HOW WAS YOUR DATE?"

It killed her to be casual, but Gen decided she'd die before showing her real emotions. Jealousy. Rage. Confusion. Jealousy.

He hadn't come home last night. Of course, Wolfe warned her, but still she'd stayed up until dawn, listening for the door to open. He waltzed in at 8 a.m. doing the whole walk-of-shame thing. Except he wasn't in the same clothes. Freshly showered, dressed in faded Levi's and a black tank that showed off sculpted arms and his ink, he looked like sin on a stick. Relaxed, too. Like he'd wrung out all his previous tension having wild monkey sex with the slut. Umm, date. Whatever.

She needed to stop talking to herself.

"Good. You got extra bacon?"

She fumed but forced a sunny smile. "Sure. Did you have fun?"

"Yep. Are you making eggs, too?"

Her eye twitched. "Worked up an appetite, huh?"

He pulled back at that remark and studied her. She

turned away and fiddled with the skillet, cursing her inability to be cool. The silence behind her spoke volumes. Wolfe finally cleared his throat. "How was your night?" he asked.

Her back tingled in rebellion. If he thought she'd been lying around with the remote, he was sorely mistaken. "Really good." The bacon sizzled in the pan and spurt out fragments of grease. She maneuvered the spatula around the eggs. "It was actually kick-ass."

She sensed his frown but refused to turn around. "Oh. That's good. Your date is tonight though, right?"

"Yep."

"You went to Mugs with the girls, then?"

She scooped up the eggs and bacon and slid them over. Picked up her coffee and sipped. "Nope. I got a tattoo and a Brazilian wax."

His expression was well worth the shock factor. Those blue eyes widened and his lower lip hung down a bit. His gaze scoured her from top to bottom, settling on the apex between her thighs before quickly being dragged back up. Sweat popped up on his brow.

Gen grinned and dug into her eggs.

"What the hell are you talking about? What tattoo? Where? Why?"

She shrugged. "Felt like it. I think the Brazilian hurt more."

An intense light gleamed in his eyes. Her body reacted by saluting to attention. Her nipples stiffened. She grew wet between her legs. She hated it. Having him cross over from the camp of friend to man she desperately wanted to sleep with was brutal. Should she try to get back some of the ribbing and teasing associated with their friendship? After all, if Wolfe was sleeping around, she couldn't be included in the troop of women he desperately wanted to sleep with. So if it was just *her* panting after *him*, she better get back on equal footing.

"Why do you need it?" he asked roughly.

"The Brazilian?"

His fingers clenched the fork in a death grip. "No. The tattoo."

"Told you. It was impulse. Kate came with me. She was pretty freaked out by the needles and my nakedness."

The fork clattered to the floor. Wolfe breathed heavily. "Who saw you naked?" he asked in a high voice. "Where did you get it?"

She arched a brow. "Calm down, dude. You got a piercing in your dick. Had to hurt like a bitch. Why'd you do that?"

Ah, he flushed again in that kind of adorable, masculine way. Ducking his head to pick up the fork, he tossed it across the counter. She got him a replacement, waiting for his answer. "Because I was pretty screwed up at the time. I pushed limits, didn't mind pain, and wanted to torture myself for a bunch of messed-up things."

She leaned forward. Her voice was whisper soft. "Like what?"

"Never mind. I really don't want to talk about the piercing, Gen. Where's the tat?"

Disappointed, she turned back to her breakfast. Of course. After all, they didn't share dark and lonely stories. An emptiness pulsed in her gut, with the need to know more of him. It had never mattered before—she was always grateful for whatever he chose to give. Now?

Not so much.

She patted her lower back. "Tramp stamp."

He sucked in his breath but she ignored him. Cleaned up her plates and stacked them in the dishwasher. "Can I see it?" he asked.

"It's covered. I'll show you another time." No way did she feel like revealing it to him right now, when she felt so vulnerable. If he tried to touch her, she might lose it. Best to keep the tone light and let him know the expectations for tonight. "I need you to sleep at your apartment tonight."

Darkness crossed his face. "Not a good idea. I think David's watching and I don't want you to be alone two nights in a row."

"I won't be. If everything goes according to plan, Charles will be staying the night. I'd rather not get into any awkwardness."

"You don't even know the guy! What if you're not attracted to him? Why can't you have a nice dinner and come home? We can go over his assets and liabilities together over a beer and TV."

Her temper surged. She made sure not to bang his plate around when she cleaned it up. "Maybe I'm looking for more than friendship tonight, Wolfe. Maybe it's time I prove to myself there are other men who'll want me."

"Sweetheart, don't talk like that. A man would be nuts not to be hot for you. I don't want you to rush or make a bigger mistake if he's not the right one. You need time. I'm telling you this stuff because I'm your friend."

"Yes, you are." He flinched. She wiped the counter and began stacking the dishwasher. "As my friend, you'll make yourself scarce. I'd rather bring him here than go to his place. This date means a lot to me. I have a good feeling about it, and I miss sex. Connection. I need to know there's something more than what I had. Is that so wrong?"

He pushed his fingers through his already tousled hair. Frustration beat in waves around his figure. "Does Kate know your intentions?"

"Yes."

He frowned. "And she's okay with this?"

Gen dragged in a breath and grabbed for patience. How could he have slept with a woman last night and have the nerve to ask her questions? Judge? Why were the rules different for her? "Kate encouraged the encounter." The lie came easily. Was it the first one she'd really told him? Or did all the denial about being unhappy with David count, too?

"Can I meet him first?"

She gasped. "No! Did I meet your so-called date last night before you screwed her? Look, this topic is now closed for discussion. The house is off-limits tonight. And I'll share as many details about my date as you did yours."

Gen stalked out of the breakfast nook with those fighting words, but he grabbed her arm and spun her around. Wolfe never lost his temper. Gen knew he was ruthless in business. Sexual around women. But with her, he was consistently easygoing and relaxed.

Fascinated, she stared into his eyes and noticed the tick in his jaw. The way he ground his teeth. The raw sexual en-

ergy pouring from his body in waves. Those blue eyes filled
with a swirling array of emotions she couldn't name. What
did he want from her? And why did this anger feel so different? Almost as if it was combined with lust and want
and sexual frustration?

"You really want to know what happened last night?"
he growled. His fingers burned into her skin. She wanted to
cry out with satisfaction for receiving his mark.

"No thanks," she shot back. "Don't need to know how
many orgasms you gave her. I already know you're a cham-
pion in that department."

"Don't push me. You may get more than you bargained
for." His breath rushed over her mouth. Coffee and pep-
permint. She stiffened so she wouldn't lean closer for a
taste. Gen meant to step back, cool down, and let it go. The
song from *Frozen* screamed out at her. Begged her. *Let it
go. Let it go.*

"Maybe not." She tilted her head all the way back and
challenged him. "Maybe it's you who'll be surprised if you
push me."

His breath came out choppy. "What are you doing,
Gen? Or do you even know?"

The cryptic conversation seethed with boatloads of
meaning. Her body shook with the force of holding her
emotions back. "Ready to tell me about your hot date
now?" she taunted. "Bet she was a skinny-ass model. You
like those. Bet she had moves that put you to shame. Did
she stay the night or did you kick her out at the 3 a.m.
mark? That's when you usually get itchy."

He muttered a vicious curse. A sense of danger settled

over her, and she pushed harder to make him lose his patience, sensing she'd finally get to the real stuff.

"Did you have the talk beforehand, letting her know it's just fun and games and you don't do relationships? At least after she screams your name a number of times, you can make yourself feel better by saying you were honest. Walk away with a clear conscience and a smile on your face. How many orgasms erase your guilt?"

His other arm shot out. He dragged her against his chest, fury pumping from his pores. "One more word," he warned, "and I'll show you clearly what she got last night."

Excitement curled in her belly. "I'll give you two."

"Don't you dare."

"Fuck. You."

His mouth slammed down and claimed her.

Gen pushed herself up on tiptoe, dug her nails into his shoulders, and met his tongue halfway. They drank, twisting their bodies against each other in a desperate, vicious craving for contact, for skin and lips and teeth, for his dick thrusting between her thighs again and again and again.

Feasting, drowning, he cupped her ass and lifted her high up, grinding against her while his tongue never stopped diving in and out of her mouth. Gen burned up in his arms, shaking with a desperation and need to have him completely, and she moaned low and needy while he captured the sound and drank deeper, until . . .

The doorbell rang.

They stumbled back from each other like they were caught in a White House sex scandal. A knock followed the bell.

"Gen? It's Arilyn. Kate's running late so she'll meet us at the dog park. You ready?"

Their gazes caught and locked. Her lips throbbed and she wanted to press her fingers to her mouth and confirm that the kiss had really happened. The floor seemed unstable under her feet. The clean scent of his soap and lemon lingered. Her body pulsed with need to finally put an end to the torture, but she pummeled it back at the sight of his expression.

Reserved. All emotion was wiped away and there was only . . . distance. A polite distance. A friendly distance.

Her gut clenched. Fighting off the sickness, she turned and opened the door to Arilyn.

Her friend floated in with two leashes in hand and squirming, happy puppies. "Hi, Wolfe. Hope I didn't interrupt breakfast." She must've caught the odd aura in the air because she trailed off, glancing back and forth. "Or something."

Gen forced a smile. "Nope, we just finished. Didn't we?"

Wolfe gave her a moody look. She held her breath, but he slowly nodded. "Yeah. We did."

Gen dropped to her knees and buried her face in comforting fur. She refused to let him see how much he'd hurt her. "I'm ready for the park," she said brightly. The black-and-white mottled puppies jumped up and down, swiping her cheeks with wet tongues and nibbling on her fingers with sharp baby teeth. Maybe she'd get a dog. They always made her feel happy. "Are you going to the office, Wolfe?"

"Not today."

His curt words made Arilyn stare at him. Gen stood up, grabbed her purse, and headed for the door. "See ya later."

She felt his gaze boring into her back as she stumbled in the need for escape. Gen grabbed one of the leashes and ignored Arilyn's raised brow. Screw it. She'd have a nice day with her friends and dogs and eat ice cream, and then she'd go home early and get ready for her date. Much better if he didn't return until tomorrow. Tomorrow, the balance might be back in order.

Maybe.

Hopefully.

"Gonna tell me what's going on?" Arilyn asked.

"No."

Her friend gave a soft laugh. "Didn't think so. I'm here if you need me though."

"I know. And I'm here if you ever want to talk about Yoga Man."

They shared a knowing look, then burst into laughter.

nineteen

HE WAS LOSING his mind.

Wolfe paced the small kitchen and waited for Gen to come out of the bedroom. He'd already texted her this afternoon to apologize for being an asshole. She quickly forgave him via a smiley face on the phone, but he sensed there was something much bigger and more complicated seething under the surface.

He'd kissed her.

Again.

A groan spilled from his lips, and he pulled a beer from the fridge. Her taste would haunt him forever. So sweet. Better than juicy fruit and sticky honey. The way her body molded to his, responding as if she had no choice, swept up in a hurricane or tornado or some type of God-driven event. Silky skin and wild hair.

He'd been two seconds from taking her against the wall. Or the floor. Or the counter. If Arilyn hadn't walked in, who knows what would've happened. The possibility haunted him all day until he felt halfway insane.

He shouldn't be here. Most of the morning was spent at the gym. Her announcement shattered any rational thought and splintered his brain with two of the sexiest words on the planet.

Tattoo.

Brazilian.

He wouldn't be seeing either of them. Maybe her date would. Hell, Wolfe knew he should stay put in his apartment and ride out the storm. Tomorrow, things might be better between them. Back to good old friendship.

Wolfe cracked open the top and guzzled. The icy liquid soothed his throat but did nothing to quench the thirst in his soul. Odds were good nothing physical would happen tonight. Gen might talk a good game, and her body might want sex, but her head and heart usually got in the way. She wasn't built for one-night stands. Not like him.

He figured he owed her an apology in person. He'd square things up, then leave her alone.

The bedroom door burst open.

Wolfe sucked in his breath. She was gorgeous. Her hair fell in neat ringlets that his fingers itched to mess up. She'd lined her eyes with some type of black that made the navy blue depths jump right out and grip tight. The smattering of freckles across her nose made his lips want to follow the trail, ending at her plump pink mouth.

But the dress killed him.

He knew about the little black dress. This one was little, all right. With her curves, the hemline rode up a bit higher than normal, showcasing her muscled calves and generous hips. The material was some weblike lace substance or crochet, knit together in a delicate pattern that stretched over her breasts and plunged dangerously to a V like a thrill-seeking ride plummeting down a dangerous hill.

Glittery, jangly silver jewelry draped her body. Chains

around her ankles and wrists, with earrings swishing in her hair. The shoes crisscrossed in the front, zippered in the back, and screamed edgy sex.

His spit dried up. Under the little black dress, she sported a Brazilian wax that left her completely bare, open, and accessible. Her usual fresh scent had been replaced by a musky sandalwood perfume, exotic and slutty at the same time. He fucking loved it.

He fucking hated it.

"Can you finish zipping me up?"

His ears registered the request but his feet were frozen to the floor. He probably looked like Forrest Gump, looking confused and spouting about chocolate.

"Wolfe?"

"Yeah, sure," he muttered. He dropped the beer onto the counter and forced himself closer. She fisted her hair in one hand and lifted the strands off her neck to give him easy access. The dress gaped open and flashed the vulnerable line of her spine, the silky soft skin at her nape. His hands shook as he grasped the tab and pulled up.

The hiss cut through the sudden, explosive silence. He caught her quick, indrawn breath. Awareness crackled between them.

"Thanks."

He kept his hands on her back for a brief moment. Fought the urge to zip it back down, strip her naked, and take her right there, no more questions or asinine excuses or polite conversation.

Instead, he stepped back.

"Sure."

She glanced at her silver watch and clicked over to the coffee table. "What are you still doing here? I told you everything's forgiven." Her smile flashed in the dim light. Her breasts rose and fell with each breath. Was she wearing one of those tight corset things to make everything look smooth and even beneath the black fabric? She didn't need it. He imagined how his hand would sweep over the familiar curves. Funny, he didn't know what color her nipples were. Ruby red and tart like cherries? Or like her mouth, a soft blush of pink that turned dusky with arousal?

The room tipped drunkenly and flames engulfed his blood, churning thick and sluggish in his veins. Maybe he had the flu. Or he was having a heart attack. He'd never experienced arousal this intense before. He didn't even think it was possible.

"Wolfe? Are you listening?"

He shook his head and fought for clarity. "Just wanted to see you off. Make sure you're safe. Does Kate have this guy's number?"

An amused smile touched her lips. "Of course. He's a client. I have money, too, Dad."

"Let me stay." Her eyes widened but he rushed on. "I swear, if I hear a guy's voice outside I'll jump out the window. I want to be sure David doesn't come poking around."

She straightened her spine and grabbed her ridiculously small beaded purse. "No. You promised and I'm holding you to it. David hasn't bothered me in weeks and I think he's gotten the message. I need my privacy for tonight. It's important to me."

"Don't sleep with him, Gen."

The plea spit from his lips before he could wrestle the words back. She gasped and teetered on her high heels. For one minute, he swore she'd agree. She'd walk over, put her arms around his shoulders, and tell him she didn't want to sleep with anyone but him.

"I can't promise anything." Her gaze challenged him to stop her or try to change her mind. "I want what you have."

Emotion drained from him in a rush that left him empty. If it was up to him, he'd fight the demons of hell to make sure she didn't have a life like his. Sex that ended with emptiness. A heart that was numb at the center. The last month of being around her had changed him. Brought a steady peace and vibrancy he had only experienced in spurts before. But it couldn't last, and eventually if he took her to bed he'd lose the last great woman who made all the pain worth it.

He managed a nod. She turned her head, but not before he caught the flash of disappointment on her face. So typical. He hated himself for not being man enough to let her go with open arms for the happiness she deserved. But he'd always been a jerk.

"I'll see you in the morning," she said politely.

"Enjoy your date."

He couldn't look. He heard the door close and reached for his beer, knowing this was for the best. He'd head to his apartment and get trashed. He wouldn't think of her, or dream of her, or pretend they had anything else to aspire to other than a perfect friendship.

Wolfe lifted the bottle and chugged it down.

* * *

COSMOS WAS A BALANCE of good food, lively conversation, and a comfortable atmosphere. The scents of garlic, tomato, and basil filled the air, and roomy tables and booths scattered throughout the dining room allowed for private conversations. The oak bar was large and busy, with groups sipping cocktails and nibbling at famous brick-oven pizzas. Kinnections held many of its mixers at the popular restaurant, so she was happy they had agreed to meet here.

Gen spoke briefly to the hostess, who led her to the table. She dragged in a breath and pushed all thoughts of Wolfe aside. Not tonight. For the first time in a while, she felt sexy, confident, and daring. The ink still stung on her lower back like a naughty reminder. Visions of falling in lust with her date, scrambling back to her place to have a satisfying bout of sex, and sharing her space with another male who was neither friend nor enemy teased her like a mirage.

No wonder women bombed so many times on dates. Talk about high expectations for a first meeting.

Gen stopped and smiled at the attractive man before her. Whoa. Very hot. He stood up quickly, smiling back, and shook her hand with a warm, firm grip she enjoyed. Light brown hair matched his eyes, which seemed open and inviting. Lean, angular features, a proud Roman nose, and actual dimples screamed out one awesome word.

Score.

She took her seat. "It's quite lovely to meet you, Gen," he said, a gorgeous accent curling like smoke around her. Yum. She couldn't seem to place the geographic location, but she wasn't surprised. She'd almost flunked history. Twice.

"Me, too. I've been looking forward to it." They settled on drinks and food, and launched into casual conversation. "Forgive me, I can't seem to place your accent."

He laughed and clasped his hands together on the table. "I'm originally from France but have been in the States for a while now. I studied pharmacology here, settled down, and never looked back. I enjoy visiting, but I consider New York home."

A pleasant glow buzzed around her. How long had it been since she'd been interested in another man? Even before David she barely dated, too busy with medical school, grades, and general achievement. His attention buffed her skin to a healthy shine better than any expensive exfoliator. "I've always wanted to visit France. I haven't traveled much."

He sipped his wine, his long, tapered fingers wrapped around the glass. "Understandable if you're a surgeon."

"Still a resident," she corrected.

"Do you love what you do?"

The question threw her. Did she? Funny, Wolfe had asked her the same thing on the dock that night. She never stopped to analyze her emotions or happiness regarding her career choice. It had always been something she was committed to and never looked back on. But lately, now that she'd stepped away for a while, a dull ache rested low in her gut, reminding her of what she had left behind. She longed for patients, and the surge of energy when faced with a case, and the calmness within the storm at the first cut of the scalpel. The world fell away, and she was reminded of who she was. Her destiny.

"Yes," she said softly, staring into his eyes. "For a while

I've been a bit lost, looking for confirmation I made the right choice."

He leaned forward. "I think we all do at one point. If we didn't question, would our final choices be worth it?"

She smiled. "You speak like a philosopher rather than a scientist."

Charles laughed. "I guess I do. I've always been what you would term an old soul. I made mistakes along the way but I can't regret them."

"Agreed."

Their food arrived, and they fell into easy conversation. Besides emanating a delicious sexual energy, Charles was sharp, polite, and funny. By the end of the dinner, her heart pounded with a mad glee. She might have been out of the game for a while, but she'd bet her life they had electricity. As they walked out of the restaurant, he held her elbow in a firm grip, steering her down the sidewalk toward her car. Anticipation flowed through her veins, as sweet as the sauvignon blanc she'd drunk. Oh, how badly she wanted to take a wild leap and do something crazy. To allow her body to finally release all the constraints of her mind and past time with David. To stop questioning her ability to attract men, surrender to sex, and please her mate.

"I've had a wonderful time meeting you, Gen," he drawled. They stopped near her Ford Fusion. "It's quite rare I have such an in-depth, interesting conversation on an initial meeting."

She loved the way he spoke, a combination of scholarly and lilting syllables, like music paired with the perfect lyrics. Gen turned and tilted her head up. His brown eyes were soft, and twin dimples winked at her in the moonlight. Ignoring her pounding heart, she leaped into the unknown and swore to enjoy the fall.

"I feel the same. Perhaps we should continue this fascinating conversation at my place?" Her voice trembled so slightly, Gen prayed he wouldn't notice. She pursed her lips just a bit to give him a bit of temptation. Hopefully. Her palms sweat. This was scary. But she wasn't far off, there were vibes coming from him that told her he was attracted.

He gave a soft, sexy laugh and took her hands. She tried not to wince at the evidence of her nervousness when he squeezed gently. "You are a delight. May I be completely honest?"

"Absolutely."

He leaned in. Her gaze settled on his full mouth. Wolfe flashed in her memory, but she shoved the image hard and fast, refusing to lose this opportunity.

"You are the total package. But after my divorce, I made myself a promise. I married the first time because I thought it was the obvious next step. She was smart, kind, and funny. But I loved her as a friend, not a passionate partner." He lifted her hands and pressed a soft kiss to her sweaty palms. "You remind me of her. We would have fun, be companionable, but there would never be the spark I need in a relationship. The raw passion I'm looking for. But of course, you feel the same way. You must also realize we don't have that type of fiery connection that makes us crazy, ache to drop into bed, and make love until we both fall apart. We just have . . . friendship."

Gen blinked. Her heart stopped pounding and paused. The wild leap into the unknown had turned into a free fall that ended in a tangle of broken limbs splashed over hard, cold concrete. Numb, she managed an enthusiastic nod. "Yes, yes, of course. I completely agree, I was just enjoying our friendly discussion."

He smiled back. "As was I. I will tell Kate we are not meant for another date, but I do hope to see you again, Genevieve. You were wonderful company for a lonely soul."

She plastered on a fake smile, managed to suffer through a peck on the cheek, and waved as he headed toward his own car. Crowds spilled onto the streets, enjoying the warm night air. White lights twinkled amid the row of trees lining the sidewalk. Her gaze caught on a younger couple wrapped up in each other, their hands stroking over each other as if unable to tear themselves away from breaking contact, laughs low and intimate, creating a bubble no onlooker or stranger could break.

Gen slid into her seat and turned on the ignition. She drove carefully back home to her bungalow, focused on the road in front. She parked at the curb, noting Wolfe's car was gone. Good. He had done as she requested. Grabbing her purse, she let herself into the silent house and flicked on a few lights. Looked around. And wondered why she couldn't seem to feel a thing.

She stood by the door for a long time. An empty beer bottle lay on the counter. Wolfe had a terrible habit of forgetting to clean up after himself. He'd make an awful husband, probably driving his wife insane, nagging him to put his clothes in the hamper, the wet towels on the rack, and his dirty dishes in the sink. Shaking her head, she went into the kitchen, rinsing out the bottle and putting it into the recycling bin. She wiped down the counters and loaded a few stray dishes in the washer. Maybe she'd have a nice glass of wine and relax. There was a lot on her DVR to watch.

Gen pulled out a wineglass, filled it with the leftover white she had in the fridge, and sipped it. Maybe a book. She had a huge stack and tons on her Kindle, just waiting to be read. She stood in the silence, wondering again why her mind felt so empty. Odd. Usually she had a train of thoughts mingling in chaos, except when she was in the OR. Maybe that's why being a doctor was such a turn-on. To finally turn off all those thoughts was such a relief.

David had told her many times she was too impulsive and needed to approach the world with more rational, logical thoughts. She'd tried many times to tell him when she surrendered to her gut the voices stopped and everything slid into place, but he disagreed. She'd tried so very hard to change. She had loved David, respected him, and wanted to be worthy. Never got there though.

How long were they together before they lost their way? How had he turned so cold and vicious? She did remember hours spent in the bedroom in the beginning, but had he been faking it even then? Was he intrigued by her, but not attracted in that primitive, masculine way men needed to be truly in love? Maybe she couldn't inspire that type of lust.

Gen set the glass down carefully on the counter. Her heels clicked as she walked into the bedroom and sat on the edge of the bed. She stared at the wall for a while. Such a pretty soft blue. But Mrs. Blackfire was right. Lots of work to do on the house. It really needed a painting and some handiwork. She had time now. Wasn't a doctor. Didn't have a relationship. And no crazy one-night stands for her. She just wasn't the type, whether or not she got a Brazilian wax or a tattoo or spent hours in the bathroom trying to inspire men and their sexual hunger.

A yawning despair yanked her down hard, into the pit of depression she'd fought on and off over the past year. The realization she might never find what she longed for—a love that was whole and beautiful. A passion that transcended reality and grasped the physical body in a merciless grip of abandon. Kate had. Kennedy, too. Alexa. Lance. It was out there.

Not for her though.

Gen looked down at her sexy dress, and fuck-me heels. The generous curves that exploded out of the fabric. She touched her curls, which were already springing crazily around her head. Funny, she hadn't realized she was crying until her fingers came away wet. There went the eye makeup. She imagined streaks of mascara, giving her a raccoonlike appearance.

She battled the raging storm, but it was too much. The emotions swept over her like a tsunami, pulling her under, pieces of debris poking and shredding flesh, and then the sobs broke from her chest and she let herself go.

Gen ducked her head and cried. She cried for the loss of David. For the constant doubts that had plagued her ever since she'd given her heart to another for care, and limped away halfway broken. For her confusion, her weakness, her doubts.

For the awful, real feelings she had for her best friend.

She didn't know how much time passed, but slowly the tears stopped and the tiny piece of calm grew. Gulping in deep breaths, she allowed the last of her grief and anger and sadness to spill out of her body.

Gen never heard him.

Like the knight he was, Wolfe appeared. He sat down next to her on the bed and wrapped her in his strong, familiar arms. His blistering body heat melted Gen's ice and stiffness, and she relaxed into him, still sniffling, burying her face into soft, fragrant cotton. His lips pressed the top of her head, and his voice murmured sweet, soothing words until her gulping sobs finally calmed. For a little while, she surrendered, giving it all over to him, and in doing so, was able to let it go completely.

The lightness returned. Peace. He hugged her against his rock-hard chest, his arms bands of steel refusing to soften. She'd never felt so protected and cherished, and she fell quiet, completely drained.

"Sweetheart, are you hurt? Please tell me."

She shook her head against him, refusing to look up.

"Did he do something to you? Touch you? Hurt you?" She shook her head hard again.

"I'm trying not to lose it and go completely apeshit, sweetheart." His body began to shake, and Gen finally realized he was barely holding on to his control. "Just tell me who did this and I'll take care of it. Give me a name."

She sniffed. "No one. I'm not hurt. Why are you here? You promised."

He let out a strangled laugh. "I tried. I got halfway

home, then turned back around. Figured I'd park down the street and sleep in the car. I needed to be sure you were okay."

Her heart tore. He was so good to her, so sweet and kind, and all she wanted was for him to crave her in a crazy, primal way, to strip her, fuck her, bite her, claim her.

Gen slowly pushed him away and looked up. She probably looked scary. Ugly. Broken. Hot anger chopped through her in ragged waves. Screw this. Screw him. Screw them all.

She shut down and spoke coolly. "Thank you yet again for trying to save me, but I'm okay. No need for your armor tonight. Sorry for the drama."

His gaze narrowed. His eyes shot streams of sapphire fire. "Don't play games with me, Gen. What happened tonight on your date? Why did I come home to find you crying your heart out?"

If she stayed close to him, she'd only humiliate herself. Beg him to want her, and then there'd be no going back. She swiped at her eyes and got up from the bed, needing the distance. "Just let it go. I'm a girl, dammit. Sometimes I cry, and I like to do it in private without an audience." She turned from him so he couldn't see her face. "I don't want you here tonight."

"Tough shit."

She spun back around and gasped. The rage was good and clean and sweet, pushing away her silly tears and the pity party she despised. "You have no right to interfere," she snarled. "I gave you space when you wanted to go fuck your date! I didn't ask you a million questions or invade your privacy."

"You didn't find me crying either. I know you, Gen. I've watched you cry over hurt animals, abused children, and those awful chick flicks I hate. This was different. This was a cry from your soul, and I'm gonna find the motherfucker who did it and kill him."

Her eyes widened at his casual statement. Possession and determination carved out the lines of his face. He still sat on the edge of the mattress, staring at her, refusing to cower or give in to her demands. What a good . . . friend.

She took a step forward and practically spat in disgust. "I told you, nothing happened. It wasn't David or Charles or anyone, and I'm not talking about this anymore. Get out."

"No."

"Get out!"

"No. Did he try to make a move on you? Did you freak? I knew this wasn't a good idea. You're not ready for sex without commitment, and if he couldn't handle it I'll teach him a lesson for the next time."

She snapped. Somewhere the thread had gotten plucked so thin there was nothing left holding her to sanity. A sheen of pure red hazed her vision as she teetered on heels too tall and cool for her and gave him the humiliating truth.

"*I* was the one who wanted *him*!" she screamed. "You want to hear the whole story? He was perfect. Charming. Sexy. I felt more powerful and energized than I have in a while, so I invited him to my house to sleep with me. And you know what he said? Wanna guess?"

Wolfe remained silent, his gaze trapping her and refusing to let go.

"He said no thanks! He said he married the first time and ended up divorced because he didn't feel a wild passion for his wife. Said she was nice, and a good conversationalist, and funny. Everything I was. But not sexy. Not enough to tempt a man to lose his mind and heart to her. So there's that. I failed again. I'm good as a companion, and a colleague, and a friend, and that will have to be good enough." She let out a wild laugh and pushed her curls back, not caring anymore that she was a mess. "So David was right, and nothing's going to change it. Not a stupid tattoo, or a matchmaking service, or a wax."

He made a move to get up, but she lost it, knowing once she spotted the pity in his eyes she might never be the same. "Don't you dare feel sorry for me! I need you to leave. I'm begging you to go out the door and give me time. Tomorrow I'll put myself back together and everything will be fine." Her voice broke but she pushed on. "I just need some time alone. To process. Please, Wolfe, please just go."

She had nothing left, so she turned and walked toward the window. He didn't move from the edge of the bed. Didn't breathe. She pressed her forehead to the cool pane of glass and prayed to finish this awful night in isolation. Tomorrow she'd get her shit together and it would be okay. But tonight all bets were off, and she felt dangerously out of control . . . on the pinnacle of something so fierce she didn't know how to handle it.

The mattress creaked. Shoes hit the floor. She held her breath and waited for the blessed silence, but instead of heading out, he stopped right behind her. His body heat roped her in and pulled tight, like a helpless calf at the rodeo. She held the windowsill in a deathlike grip, sensing him closing the distance inch by precious inch, until his chest pressed against her back.

"Look at me."

The rough growl was full of danger, command, heat. She was helpless to disobey, leaving the safety of the window to turn and face him full-on. He reached out and tipped her chin up.

Blistering, raw lust shot from his eyes. As if they were glowing from under the sea in the Caribbean, she tumbled into the depths of a gaze that promised everything with a Warning: Danger label attached. His grip tightened, refusing to allow her to retreat, and he crowded her space by taking another step between her thighs. The sill dug into her lower back. His scent drowned out everything but the need to touch him, feast, taste—the delicious mix of lemon and soap and cotton surrounding her.

"I need you to listen closely, because I'm only going to say it once. Understood?"

Her lips parted. This was no friend. This was a deadly man with an agenda. Transfixed, she nodded, unable to form words, mere prey beneath the command of a dangerous predator.

"I'm done with excuses and conversation and politeness. I'm over this bullshit of you questioning the power you have to grip me in a vise so tight I can't even breathe without wanting you with my last breath. I'm tired of walking around with a dick that won't go down when I catch your scent, or look at your sweet curves, or imagine being buried deep within you. Are you still listening, Gen?"

Her body flamed so hot and bright she was surprised burn marks didn't appear on her skin. She began to shake, and her belly uncurled so a river of warmth coursed between her thighs, tightening her muscles, gripping her with a need she'd never experienced or believed could be real. "Yes," she whispered.

"Good. Because tonight I'm going to fuck you. All night. If I was a true friend, I'd walk out that door and give you the space to rebuild your walls. You deserve that. But I'm a selfish prick who needs you in my bed so bad I'll trade my soul to the devil for one taste of you. Still listening?"

"Y-y-yes."

"I'll give you three seconds to run. It's the smart thing to do. Just walk away from me and we'll never mention this again. We'll go back to being friends, push this whole episode aside, and go on pretending. But if you're still standing here after that, you're mine. Every part of you. And I promise you'll never question your ability to cast a sexual spell on a man so deep and encompassing he'll spend the rest of his life comparing you to every other woman he touches."

Her head spun, the room tilted, and she grasped his arm to keep her balance. "Wolfe."

"One."

Her stomach dropped to her toes. His mouth moved closer.

"Oh, God."

"Two."

She swallowed, one foot poised for flight, knowing it would wreck everything, change their relationship forever, open a door that could never be shut and locked again.

"I don't—"

"Three. Too late. You belong to me for tonight."

"I think—"

"Don't think. Just give me everything you got."

He cupped her cheeks, dropped his head, and took her mouth.

*H*ELL WAS SO very worth the trip.

From the moment Wolfe began driving to his apartment, his gut screamed foul. He'd finally turned around, cursing the whole way, and figured he'd stake out the place to make sure no one bothered her. The idea of meeting her one-night lover screwed with his head and his stomach, but he'd honor his promise.

When he spotted her car, he only meant to peek through a window and make sure she was safe. That's all. Nothing else. Until he heard the sobs. Sheer panic hit him, and the adrenaline rush was wickedly high. He'd been ready to kick ass and throw his fists, but she'd been alone on the bed, weeping her heart out until he felt as awful as after a three-night binge in Vegas. Gathering her in his arms was so natural, he never thought about anything but getting her to calm down, and taking away the pain. Then he'd kick the shit out of someone.

She was so damn beautiful—makeup smeared, lips swollen, hair messy and sexy over her shoulders. When she confessed what had happened, it took him a while to recover his powers of thought and speech. To think a man out there couldn't want her was beyond him. He lived with the knowledge and torture every minute, every day, a priceless treasure within reach that he was unable to touch. The self-disgust within her eyes tipped the scales. He was done. There was no way he was walking away without proving how gorgeous and hot and desirable she was.

Yeah, it was a real sacrifice.

Wolfe played fair and gave her the opportunity to run. When she still stood before him, the victory that she'd be completely his almost brought him to his knees.

Until his mouth took hers.

And he realized he'd belong to her just as completely.

She owned him. He expected softness and surrender and a complete relinquishment of control. He intended to dominate, pleasure, possess. But she was so much more. Her tongue battled his when he parted the seam of her lips to plunder and invade. When his fingers gripped her hips to lift her up, she wrapped her legs around him, tangling her fingers in his hair and holding on tight. Her dress hiked above her thighs, and his erection pushed against the fragile barrier of her panties, demanding entry. She made a low, whimpering sound in the back of her throat and he went wild, walking her forward so her back slammed against the wall and he was able to get more leverage. He bit and sucked her lower lip, diving back deep to relish her taste — that combination of fruit and honey he couldn't seem to get enough of. She twisted against him, just as wild and hot to get at him, and the damn dress cock blocked him until he wrestled one hand to rip at the back.

Their mouths broke apart and she panted, "Get it off."

"Trying. Zipper's stuck. Do you love the dress?"

"Kind of."

"I'll buy you another." Holding her braced tight against the wall, he grasped the top of the delicate lace crochet thing and roughly pulled.

The tearing sound cut through the air with total satisfaction. He removed the ripped fabric and came in contact with warm, soft skin, bare and fragrant and delicious. Her full breasts were restrained in a black bra, and tiny lace panties covered the juncture of her thighs. Her thighs squeezed and one of her spiked heels dug into his ass. He grunted in heaven and a bit of pain.

"Oh, sorry."

"Don't be. It's gonna get a hell of a lot worse. Jesus, you're more gorgeous than I imagined. Look at you."

He cupped her breast, flicked the tip with his finger through the lace, and watched in satisfaction as her nipple tightened to a hard point. Her chest moved up and down for gulps of air, and her pulse beat wildly at the base of her neck. A rosy glow flushed her white skin. "I dreamed of this for so damn long, but the reality of you is so much better." He lowered his head and sucked on her nipple, nibbling with his teeth and getting her all wet. His fingers flexed to dive deep into her pussy to find the same, but he was afraid he'd come in his jeans like a horny teen if he took too much of her too soon.

In typical Gen fashion, she went after what she wanted, arching up for more and bumping her pussy against the hard ridge bulging from his jeans. She scratched at the back of his neck and wiggled, trying to get the bra off. "Stop teasing, and take this thing off me."

"Might as well buy you a new bra."

"Huh?"

He tore the front in half and her bare breasts sprung into his palms. Her nipples were tight and stiff, pushing against him in demand, and he plumped them up and feasted, sucking hard and circling his tongue until she grabbed at his back, trying to inch up his shirt.

"Get naked. Now."

He ignored her demand, twisting her nipples the same time he dove back into her mouth, needing to get drunk on her essence. She cried out in pleasure, and he swallowed the heavenly sound. "So sweet." He kissed her again and again. "So fucking sweet. But I need more." He wanted her crazed, until she didn't care about hurting him or doing anything but getting satisfied by orgasm after orgasm. He scented the musk of her arousal and knew he'd find her dripping wet, ready for him. The knowledge she wanted him as badly shook his center, and he fought for control as she pulled him into the tide of raw emotion and want he'd never experienced before.

"If you don't get those damn jeans off I'm gonna lose it." She panted out the threat as her body melted and writhed against his fingers and tongue and teeth. Her fingers weakly pulled at his clothes, fumbling to unsnap and free him, stroking the hard bulge of his dick, and that's when he decided he couldn't take it any longer.

He needed her to come.

Now.

"After." His hands left her breasts, slid down her trembling belly, and tucked under the elastic. "Designer panties?"

"Yes, they cost more than the dress—oh, God!"

He tore them quickly, tossed them aside, and drove two fingers into hot, sweet heaven.

"Wolfe! Ahhh, that feels so good . . ." she moaned long and low, her pussy clenching around his fingers and refusing to let go. His thumb swirled gently around her clit, teasing, using hardly any pressure while he pumped inside of her with slow, deep strokes. He captured the pretty little sounds emanating from her throat, swiping his tongue over her plump bottom lip, and watched her face tighten as she neared her climax. Her pupils dilated and every muscle in her body stiffened, arching harder against his palm, reaching for something only he could give her with one final stroke of his finger.

"So close. Can't take anymore, oh please—"

He circled her clit one last time, slow and lazy. "Come for me, Gen. Now."

He rubbed hard at the same time he thrust upward.

She broke apart, shaking uncontrollably as the orgasm hit her. Her nails dug hard into his shoulders, and she clung with a superhuman strength to his body, her flesh wrapped around every part of him. He helped her ride out the spasms, soaking in every flutter of her expression: the way her teeth dragged at her lip, the misty look in her eyes, the dampness to her skin, the wet heat clamped around him, refusing to let go.

"You're so fucking sexy," he muttered darkly in her ear, biting hard on her lobe and absorbing the shudders that wracked her. "I gotta do that again."

"No." Her word sounded slurred. "First naked. Off with the clothes."

"You're not the boss in this bedroom, baby." He kept her legs apart, not wanting to slide his fingers out of her pussy until the last possible moment. His tongue plunged back into her mouth to shut her up, and he wondered if he'd ever get tired of watching her orgasm. It was the sexiest thing on the planet, and already he wanted to do it again. And again.

She uttered her next words like a drunk desperate to communicate. "Give me some equal time on my knees and I'll have to disagree with you."

He laughed, adoring her smart mouth and humor and passion. How could such basic lust be entwined with playfulness? He'd never laughed before during sex or foreplay. But already she was trying to drag his shirt off again with shaking fingers, refusing to give him an inch.

He loved it.

"I intend for you to spend a long time on your knees," he said, picking her up in one swoop and carrying her to the bed. "But I only started. Now let me look at you."

Her hands hovered in midair, ready to cover herself in an innate modesty he intended to strip her of immediately. "I'm not like the models you date. Or sleep with."

He swore right then and there he'd never date a skinny-assed woman again. Hell, after seeing Gen's killer curves, unblemished skin, and ripe breasts, he'd never look at another female anyway. He worshipped her petite shape, so easy to pick up and cuddle. Loved the map of her body, each rise and fall of her anatomy. But nothing compared to the sight of her wet pussy, swollen and bared before him. Plump lips just begging for his mouth and tongue, knowing her taste made him intoxicated.

Time for truth. "I never slept with her, sweetheart. I thought of you the whole night and couldn't do it. But I needed a barrier between us."

"Why?"

"Because I wanted to jump you bad."

She smiled, but her hands still stayed by her breasts, as if worried he wouldn't like what he saw. As if that were possible.

His voice lashed like a whip. "Don't you dare cover yourself. I love your body and always did. Remember what I said before?"

She rested her hands back on the mattress and shook her head.

"We don't apologize to each other. Not for what we do together or feel. We own it all, Gen. And I intend to do every filthy, dirty thing I've imagined without fucking apologizing. Part your legs."

Her thighs slid open and he feasted on all that pretty pink flesh laid out for him. While he looked, he jerked off his clothes, finally standing naked before her. She leaned up to look at him, but Wolfe knew there was plenty of time later. Right now, he needed to taste her, push her to come all over his tongue and lose herself again in his arms.

"That Brazilian is the sexiest gift a man can ask for, sweetheart." He knelt between her thighs and blew hot breath over the swollen folds. She jerked and moaned, her fingers clutching the sheets. Yeah, she was beyond primed. Once she lost her ability to yell at him or demand, she was caught in her body's grip. Just like he wanted. Her clit was so tight and hard, one good flick of his tongue would make her come again, but he wanted her crazed first, the sound of his name breaking from her lips.

Wolfe bent his head.

Swiping her slit slow and easy, he tasted, teased, sipped like she was fine champagne and he intended to make the drink last. His arms pinned her flailing body down with an iron strength, never rushing his pace, her cries filling the air with a desperate hunger that would haunt his dreams. Wolfe inhaled her musky scent, licking the hard nub, and pushed his thumb in and out of her soaking channel. Her pussy clamped down hard and tried to suck him deeper, but he teased until she was a thrashing, senseless being held on the edge.

"No more," she gasped, her blue eyes fierce and past sanity. "Damn you, Wolfe, make me come before I kill you."

With a low chuckle, he took her clit between his lips and sucked. Hard. Harder. Pinned three fingers together and plunged in deep.

She came again, and he drank it all, never stopping the suction motions so she fell into another orgasm so beautifully he wondered if he'd ever allow her out of bed again. She clung to him with a sweet desperation he couldn't refuse. Sliding up her body, kissing every inch of her skin, he paused again at her mouth, nibbling at her lips, cradling her face in his hands as he adored her.

"Son of a bitch," she said, her voice a thin whisper of sound. "You're killing me. Still need more."

"Me, too." He kissed her long and deep. "See how good you taste on me? I can't get enough. I'll never get enough."

"Inside. I need you inside me." She arched up, her honesty and openness humbling him until he wanted to drop to his knees and worship her all over again. "Please."

"Jesus, sweetheart, I forgot a condom. Have any?"

"Top drawer. Hurry."

He retrieved the box quickly, fit himself with a condom, and settled her deep into the mattress. Lifting her ankles up and pushing them forward, he opened her fully to his gaze and paused at her threshold. Her body shook slightly underneath.

"Are you ready?"

Half-lidded eyes stared back up at him. He fell into her gaze as easily as he'd fallen for her the very first time they met. Skin slick with sweat, curls framing her face, swollen lips bitten and bruised, she invited him in, hands clinging to his shoulders as if he were the only steady thing in her world.

"Take me, Wolfe. Take it all."

He cursed viciously and surged forward.

Deeper, deeper, he pushed until he slid home, buried inside her raging, wet heat, desperate to hold on and not come immediately. He watched her face, each expression more delicious as she adjusted to his length and never backed off. Her nails cut, and her thighs squeezed tight, refusing to let him go.

Wolfe tried to breathe, tried to go slow, but there were too many sensations breaking over him to know anything but the driving need to claim her.

He groaned. "I'm gonna lose it. It's too good."

"Don't stop," she panted. "Please, I need—"

He didn't wait. Just pulled all the way out, then slammed back inside. Again. Again.

He kept the ride slow and steady, building with intensity as she neared climax again. He gritted his teeth against the explosion ready to detonate, his balls tightening, each slide in and out better than the last. He worked one hand on her clit, rubbing, watching her hover on the edge, eyes mad with lust and need. Shifting his hips a bit, he drove back in, making sure the edge of his piercing rubbed against the sensitive wall of her channel. Her surprised cry told him he'd succeeded, so he did it again, and again. Rubbed her clit harder. And then—

She screamed his name and shuddered beneath him. Fierce satisfaction caused an animal howl to escape his lips, and he finally let himself go, pumping frantically as he emptied his seed and light exploded in his head. The orgasm went on so long and so hard, he didn't think he'd ever be able to pull out. A wall trembled around the most private part of him no one had ever been able to touch. And as they collapsed onto each other, wrecked, Wolfe realized something else.

He'd never be able to make love to another woman again without wishing for Genevieve Mackenzie.

"DO YOU REMEMBER YOUR date's last name?" Wolfe murmured against her shoulder.

Her ass was cushioned against his thighs. His rapidly rising fiftieth erection nudged securely between her legs, and his arm banded her tight to him so she was open to any nibble, lick, or caress he bestowed on various body parts. Deep satisfaction loosened her muscles, and Gen felt like she'd swallowed an aphrodisiac. Her body was primed to want everything and anything he gave her, upping the ante like the slut she'd always craved to be.

She loved it.

He plucked playfully at her nipple.

"Why would you need his name?"

"I want to send him flowers. You know, as a thank-you."

A laugh bubbled from her lips, then turned into a low moan as her nipple hardened and begged for more. "You're beastly."

"You're gorgeous." He chuckled as he pinched her nipple, making streams of heat shoot to her pussy. "And hungry. And so fucking responsive I can't stop."

Gen stretched, offering up her naked body, feeling like a goddess under his hungry, lust-filled gaze. "Who says you have to?"

He growled low and flipped her over onto her tummy. "You're right. But first I want to see the tat. Who else saw it?"

The thread of possessiveness thrilled her, even though she knew it was just for the night. "Just Kate. And the artist."

"Good. Now lie still like a good girl."

Her heart pounded madly. He was beyond an amazing lover. He played her body like a musician, but was able to switch from loving and sweet to dirty talker, dom, and rocker bad boy. She loved every aspect of him, hard and soft, and knew she could spend the rest of her life relishing each part he wanted to show her. Gen thought he'd give his body to her, but it was so much more than she imagined. In only a few hours, he had shared parts of his heart, and she'd treasure that for the rest of her life.

The rational voice tried to chime in with warnings. She realized it was only about one night. One night to satisfy their sexual urges, be together as man and woman instead of friends, and that he'd never allow himself to move further into a relationship with her. By dawn, he'd be freaked out, terrified, and begin to retreat.

But it was okay. Would have to be. Because she still had hours before the sun came up and she intended to enjoy every second to the fullest.

She turned her head to the side and relished the large, hard hands that rubbed the soreness from her shoulders and back in a delicious massage. A moan spilled from her lips, and she melted into the mattress. He muttered something dirty as he moved lower, kneading her breasts, down her ribs and to the flare of her hips. With each slow decline, she grew wetter, her pussy throbbing for contact. She wiggled a bit to put pressure on her clit, but he surprised her with a slap on her ass.

"Hey!"

"Don't think I know what you're trying to do. I refuse to let you climax without my help."

"Fine. Keep it moving, then."

A sharp nip on her spine, and a long slide of tongue ending at the curve of her rear shut her up real quick. She was trapped in a sensual spell, both misty and sharp, until nothing mattered except his voice and touch and commands. She'd never had that with any of her previous partners. She'd enjoyed sex, loved David enough to give herself over until he began to hurt her more with every sexual encounter. But with Wolfe? She was completely possessed by him. A twinge of fear shot through her. She had an instinct that if she spent more intimate time with him, he'd end up owning her completely.

The rest of her thoughts scattered as his fingers traced the outline of her tat, gently stroking the sensitive skin. "So beautiful." She imagined the scarlet rose petals, the curve of the stem stopping right above her buttocks, and the drops of blood dripping down each wickedly sharp thorn. "Blood. No baby's breath." He paused but his fingers never stopped caressing her. "Why?"

"Pain with pleasure. Hurt with love. Betrayal with trust. I'm learning it's not about one thing but a mix. And I never want to forget it again."

She heard his sharply indrawn breath, but his fingers remained so gentle on her skin. "I wish you never had to know that," he murmured.

Gen gripped the pillowcase and spoke fiercely. "I'm glad I know. Don't wish for me to be sheltered or protected from things that are real. I'm strong enough to face them, survive, thrive. Just like you."

This time, he dug into her skin, but she relished the brief pain, even arching into him. "What am I going to do with you?" he whispered. "I've known you for years, yet tonight I feel like I'm meeting you for the first time. It's too much. It's too—"

"I know." The hunger hit hard again and she was helpless to fight. Hell, she didn't even want to. Her body shook with a crazed need. "It's too fierce, too good, but I don't care. I want to burn in it for a little while. Take me again, Wolfe." Her voice broke. "I can't seem to stop the wanting."

He bit her hard, and she relished the pain, crying out in sheer pleasure. Wanting his mark on her, she pushed back in for more, and his rough hands grabbed her ass, kneading, stroking, pleasuring, slipping between her legs to gather the wetness there and spread it over her clit. He worked his fingers in and out while his tongue stabbed inside, and she rubbed her nipples against the covers and wept for him, modesty and shame and civility long gone in the heat of the darkness of night.

He pulled her legs apart, dragged her upward so she braced herself on the bed, and took her hard. The scrape of his piercing massaged her clit, making her wild, and she grabbed the bedposts to have something to cling to as she built toward another earth-shattering orgasm. His cock pulsed, taking up every inch of her body until there was nothing left but him. Her muscles screamed in protest, her belly clenched, and his fingers took her higher, roughly, his cock working her and their wet bodies slapping against each other in carnal bliss until she came so hard tears streaked down her face. Light shimmered within and shoved her into a tunnel of such sharp pleasure it mingled with pain, providing a stimulation she never thought existed. Her muscles gave way and she fell back into the pillows, even as Wolfe held her hips, bruising, welcoming, and came inside her with a guttural moan that touched her soul and beyond.

She knew then it was too late. Had always been too late.

She was madly, irrevocably, soul-deep in love with her best friend.

"THIRSTY."

He chuckled and the bed moved. She tried to lift her head but it was stuck to the pillow in exhaustion. When she realized she'd miss him naked though, she managed to lift herself halfway with a grunt.

Oh yeah. Definitely worth the pain of moving. His ass should be bronzed. All tight muscle and a yummy line separating the lighter skin from his olive tan. His thighs bunched as he walked, disappearing briefly and returning with a large glass of water. The ice tinkled but her gaze locked on the heavy weight of his cock and the intriguing barbell piercing near the tip. Like before, she licked her lips and watched him grow hard, but this time she intended to take advantage.

"You're doing it again," he warned, handing her the glass.

She drank with greed, water running down her chin and onto her breasts. He leaned down and licked it off. "Doing what?" she gasped.

"Looking like you want to devour me." He sucked on her nipple and watched the tip elongate. Was it possible to die of orgasms? How could her body be ready again to take him? The scent of musk and arousal clung to the sheets and their skin, drifting in the air like a perfume. "Keep it up and I'll give you something to devour."

Oh, the dare was too much. She managed a scowl, flicking a stray curl out of her eyes and handing him the glass. He sipped, looking so confident and at ease with his sizzling sexuality Gen decided to make him pay. When he turned to put the glass down, she stopped him by grasping his wrist.

"Hold the glass, Wolfe."

He looked at her in surprise, then seemed to gauge her intent. Sucking in his breath, he watched as she climbed off the bed with careful motions and knelt on the floor in front of him. A heady power and need gripped her, making her so wet she wondered if she could orgasm right there just looking at him. Slowly, ever so slowly, she ran her hands up his calves, over his thighs, and cupped his hard cock.

He hissed, and his fingers clenched around the glass. "What are you doing?"

"If you're wondering, then I'm not doing my job." She leaned over and blew her hot breath over his erection. He jerked, every muscle straining with tension. His cock grew bigger, throbbing with demand in front of her. Her tongue slid over her lower lip as she learned each hard ridge and valley by touch. The crisp nest of hair, the hot skin, the gorgeous metal barbell piercing his flesh. As he grew, she stroked more boldly, flicking the ends of the metal until he jerked again and let out a groan. Oh yeah, that was sensitive.

"Not sure I can take it, sweetheart. Maybe you should come up here before I lose it."

"Maybe you've been a big bully and it's time to pay the piper." He went to reach for her, but she pulled back and wagged her finger. "Stay put. And don't spill any water. This may take a while."

"Gen—"

She opened her mouth, grasped his cock, and took him deep.

He tasted so good. Salty. Musky. Male. She didn't worry about doing it right, or using technique like she had with David. Her instincts to pleasure him, to explore every last inch of his gorgeous body and make him weep for her in pure need, drove her forward, her tongue flicking his piercing, her mouth sucking hard, while her hands fisted and stroked up and down the base, squeezing his balls lightly until her name broke from his lips in a litany of music. David had forced her to do things in the name of love she hadn't enjoyed. Tonight, with Wolfe, she needed him on such a basic level there were no barriers or rules or holding back.

"I'm going to—"

She sucked harder, dragging her tongue across the slit, and took him to the back of her throat.

He came, shuddering and cursing, and she swallowed every drop without thought. Her knees ached, her mouth was swollen, but her spirit soared so high and so fast even God couldn't catch her. Kissing him, caressing gently, she rose back up and took the glass back, resting it on the side table. His face was carved out in blissful lines, the gorgeous scruff of his beard bracketing full lips, the piercing sapphire heat of his eyes, the relaxed muscles of his cheeks and jaw.

His voice was a husky growl. "I didn't spill."

Gen laughed, wrapping her arms around him and holding him tight. They held each other for a long while, caught in time, as the sun chased the dark and dawn grew close.

WOLFE RAN THE DAMP washcloth over her sweat-beaded brow, slowly cleaning her with gentle strokes. When he pressed the cloth between her legs, over her inner thighs, Gen whimpered in pleasure and relaxed her thighs. Open. Vulnerable. Loving.

His throat tightened, and suddenly his chest felt funny. Emotions surged in a rocking mess until he didn't know which were the safe ones to separate from the pack. He continued tending to her, looking at her various bruises and feeling like shit that he was glad he'd marked her.

At least, for a little while.

He'd need to deal with their actions in the morning. Talk. Decide what was best to salvage the most important relationship he'd ever had. And he would, but right now he wanted to enjoy being her lover, tend to her, care, fuck, bruise, own, until every inch of her skin was forever claimed as his.

Yeah, he was screwed up.

"Why a serpent?"

Her beautiful blue eyes probed his, asking for something he'd never given her before. An answer to the mysteries of his past. A glimmer of who he'd been and was. He couldn't deny her anything now, but he was surprised how easily he responded.

"It embodies everything I want to express," he said simply. He paused, trying to make sense and explain fighting through the horror to get to the other side. He'd never tell the whole truth. Couldn't, not even to her. But she deserved to hear more and understand why he was too broken to ever be involved in a healthy relationship. "The serpent is a symbol of light and dark. I was fighting for my sanity back then. I stumbled on an old library book someone had thrown in a Dumpster that detailed the history of snakes and various legends. Fascinating. Snakes shed their skin and become new. They're also full of deceit, marked by a forked tongue that mingles truth with lies. It represents fury such as poison and vengefulness when it strikes, never warning the victims beforehand." The past battled to breach the wall he'd carefully built, but most of his defenses held tight. He continued talking in an academic tone. "The serpent is also a symbol of guardianship. Even when threatened, it holds its ground and defends. When I found myself in the tattoo parlor, I didn't think twice. I wanted to remember every time I looked at my body."

She studied him in silence, both assessing and delving deeper than any woman before. Why did he suddenly crave to spill his guts? His belly clenched. No. Some secrets were meant to be buried in the ground forever.

As usual, she surprised him by both her acceptance of his speech and her question.

"What is it whispering to you?"

His hand rubbed the side of his neck where the forked tongue stopped, curling around his ear. The skin beneath his leather wristbands itched and burned. How did she know? Wolfe swallowed and kept his voice steady. "Live."

She never jerked back or reached for him. Her gaze flicked to his covered wrists as if she knew that was the key to his secrets but then she just nodded. That quiet understanding and acceptance of his one-word answer soothed him in a way nothing ever had. His body lit, and the hungry need to bury himself back in her sweetness shook him to the core. Without hesitation, she reached for him again, welcoming and opening her thighs.

He barely choked out the words. "No. You're too sore."

"Don't care." Her smile lit up her face with light and joy, transfixing him. "I feel alive when you're inside me."

Wolfe groaned, humbled by her generosity and ability to love so well. And because he was selfish, he took what she offered, fitting himself with a condom and pushing her slowly back into the mattress. Her wetness welcomed him as much as her arms wrapped around his neck, urging him on. With one slow slide he buried himself, shaking at the tightness and slick heat that gripped him mercilessly.

"Easy this time," he whispered. "Tell me if I'm hurting you."

Her hips bowed, and he began rocking himself in and out of her in tiny increments, easing himself into the ride. He pulled completely out to make sure the end of the barbell hit her clit, and she shuddered and groaned beneath him, surrendering.

Fierce possession streaked through him. There wasn't a part of her that didn't belong to him; every inch of her skin was marked by his tongue or teeth or hands, and his name broke on her lips like a prayer, a litany, a melody. He pushed her higher, climbing along, not wanting the moment to ever end. Memorizing every pant, drop of sweat, and cry, he angled his hips and hit her G-spot, diving so deep and slow they became one. Her fingers clenched and her body opened fully, allowing him to do anything. With a low growl, he bit her neck and surged forward one last time, feeling her break around him in spasms that shook him to the core.

His own orgasm threatened sanity, clutching every muscle with a pleasure that scorched, and as his seed spilled inside her, Wolfe knew it was already too late for him, and he'd never be the same man again.

Instead of crying, he buried his face in her hair and let go.

twenty-one

SHE HATED MORNINGS.

Genevieve rolled over and stared at the sun streaming through the windows. The scent of sex and man hit her hard, but the bed was empty. The impression of his head on the pillow and her sore body was the only evidence he'd left behind. She listened to the quiet. Probably snuck off at dawn when she was in a coma. Simpler that way. Time to recover, gain distance, and approach a rational conversation about a completely irrational, sex-driven night.

Crap.

Sadness hovered but she pushed it away. No. She'd promised herself not to mope over something he couldn't give. Last night had shown her the depths of the man she'd always loved as a friend. Not his fault she now loved him in all ways. He believed he wasn't enough for a full relationship, and she could take up the sacrifice and beat herself bloody by trying to convince him, but it wouldn't work. Not in the end. After all, she'd learned love was also a choice.

Wolfe didn't want to choose her. He was safer with his scars and his past buried, giving her a true friendship and everything he could possibly offer. But not his full heart.

The quicker she understood the facts, accepted them, and tried to move on, the better.

But it wouldn't be easy.

She rolled out of bed, wincing at the use of muscles rarely worked, but a deep satisfaction and pride coursed through her. He'd shown her what it was like to be wanted on a bone-deep level, wanted so badly nothing else mattered. It was a priceless gift and she wouldn't forget it. She'd never accept anything less.

The shower felt like heaven, the hot spray loosening the tightness and washing away his scent. When she looked in the mirror, she gasped. Discolored marks on her neck. Bruises on her hips and thighs. Her nipples were sore, and every time she walked the spot between her legs ached. She'd been well used and loved. Damn, how cool.

Gen dressed in yoga pants and a white T-shirt, and twisted her hair up to dry naturally. Thank goodness it was Sunday. She'd recover, think, and lie low. She'd been hoping to meet with Izzy today, but didn't feel up to it now. Izzy had seemed to soften since her wedding disaster, but still kept her distance. No, she'd reschedule when she felt a bit stronger and ready to fight to get back a relationship with her twin. Right now, she was too damn tired.

Gen reached the kitchen and began setting up the coffeepot.

The door opened.

She twisted around in surprise and met his gaze. He held two paper bags and juggled a cup holder. Wearing faded Levi's and a black linen button-down, he looked fresh and comfortable. Only the lines around his eyes hinted at a lack of sleep. He hadn't shaved. Stubble hugged his lips and jaw, giving him that sexy morning-after look that made her body wake up and beg for more play. Rich chocolate curls fell in disarray over his brow.

Oh, this was bad. Real bad. Because now she knew how soft his lips were. The delicious bite of his strong, white teeth. The intoxicating taste of his tongue against hers. A thousand memories of last night flashed before her, and her nipples tightened painfully while her thighs squeezed together in an effort to relieve the pressure.

He kicked the door closed. Dropped the bags onto the counter. Stared.

The same memories were in those piercing baby blues, growing darker with desire as he kept studying her, his gaze lingering on all the sensitive parts he had touched and bit and licked. She tried to talk, failed, and tried again.

"Thought you had left." She cleared her throat and forced out more words. "Thought you went home."

His brows lowered. "You think I'd just take off after the night we had?"

She swallowed and tried not to cling to the wild hope they could make this work. Whatever this was. "Didn't know."

He set the large coffee in front of her. "Now you do. I may be a jerk sometimes, but I'd never hurt you like that."

Gen stiffened her spine. "If you stayed just because you're afraid I'll freak out, don't worry. I'm fine. You can take off your armor."

His lips tipped in a smile. "You are always cranky before your coffee. Drink up." She glared but managed a few sips, closing her eyes in ecstasy at the first hit of caffeine. "I brought pastry, too. Apple turnover. Just out of the oven."

She slid onto the stool while he opened the bag, removed the wrapping, and put it on a plate. The sticky phyllo dough combined with fresh apples sent a sugar rush into her blood. "So good," she moaned. "Thanks."

She glanced up and froze.

His gaze devoured her alive, heavy with need and a hint of primitive maleness that made her want to strip off her clothes and tempt the beast. The image hit her hard. Knees spread, his mouth on her pussy, writhing and moaning her pleasure while he brought her to orgasm. The pastry dropped from her fingers.

He seemed to fight his decision to close the distance between them. Take her in his arms and kiss her. But then he turned away, and the spell was broken. Gen sipped more coffee, her appetite suddenly gone.

Screw this. She'd never been afraid to speak her mind with him before. Sex wasn't about to take away her honesty.

"Guess this gives *awkward* a whole new meaning," she offered. "You look like you'd rather have a battle with a tarantula."

A strangled laugh echoed in the air, but he still didn't meet her gaze. "We're definitely on unfamiliar ground. I've never done this before."

"Had wild sex with a woman?"

"Had wild sex with my best friend."

"I'm still your friend," she said quietly.

He sighed. "I know. But I wonder now if I'll always want more."

She sucked in her breath. He turned. Gen ached to touch him, smooth the worried frown from his brow, but they needed the distance. "What if you could have more?" Her heart pounded as she threw the words out. An invitation to her heart and soul. No RSVP needed. Just show up and claim. She was so stupid. She so didn't care.

Slowly, the hope and life drained from his expression, and a bone-numbing grief took hold. "I can't, Gen," he said. His arms lifted in supplication and surrender. "I can't give you what you need."

"How do you know? Maybe all I need is for you to try."

"And ruin our friendship? Turn something good into pain and resentment? Because that's what I do well. I can't get close, tell you who I am. I never will. I'm only half a man, and how can that be good enough for you? One day you'll hate me, and we won't be able to go back. If we stop now, we can salvage the good stuff."

She hated his rationality and the excuses he made without trying. She hated him not wanting to fight for her, for them, for himself. Something terrible had happened to him, and he seemed to accept he'd never get past it. And since he refused to share, it was like fighting a ghost. Loss slumped her shoulders. No. She wouldn't beg anymore for something he didn't want to give her. Never again.

"How?" she asked. "How do we move forward?"

He took a step closer. "Let me stay a little longer. Give me a chance to get back to friendship."

A humorless laugh escaped. "Are you kidding? Living

together is what made this whole friendship thing change between us. You have to move out."

He shook his head stubbornly. "No. I don't trust David not to pull something else. With a restraining order against me, it means he can't get near you while I'm here. I'll give you space, Gen. I'll prove we're meant to be better as friends. I swear."

She groaned and buried her face in her palms. Ridiculous. All he had to do was walk in the room and she wanted him. Did he really think she could forget the most amazing sex of her life and get back to beer, darts, and being buddies?

The voice inside her gut screamed, *But it's what he needs*. Losing her would damage him. Damage her. She couldn't walk away. If they both tried, maybe they could exorcise that one night and change it into something good. A bonding experience. She heard Kate's high-pitched voice yelling in her ear that she was batshit crazy, but what else could she do? If it didn't work out, she'd make him go back to his apartment.

You want him here. You'd use any excuse to keep him close.

So what? She'd get over it. Now that she knew there was no way for anything more between them, maybe she'd be able to let it go.

Lie.

Leave me alone.

"And if it doesn't work?"

His face reflected pure stubborn lines and an implacable determination. "It will. I'll never forget last night. You showed me things that were—" He broke off, but she needed him to finish.

"Were what?"

"Special." His lips tightened. "Beautiful."

Tears clogged her throat. She swallowed past the burn. "But you don't want to try?"

"No."

His word exploded like gunfire. She wanted to yell and scream and cry. Shake him, beg him, hit him. Instead, she accepted because she had no other options left.

"We'll try for another week. Eventually, you need to go home to your real life." Gen ignored his wince, reminding herself he'd been the one to choose the course. "If I'm uncomfortable, you have to promise to leave."

"I will. I swear I'll make it right."

She nodded, but he knew she didn't believe him. Not anymore.

Gen went back to her pastry, but this time she didn't make a sound.

GEN KNOCKED AND OPENED the door. Kate was muttering to herself, surrounded by files, and her dog, Robert, lay quietly on a worn doggy bed in the corner, sleeping in the sun. At the sight of her, the dog lifted his head and wagged his tail, canine joy vibrating his body as he rose and scrambled over to her for a greeting. His hind legs were paralyzed, but that didn't slow him as he dragged his rear over the floor and threw himself into her arms. She'd seen him fifteen minutes ago, but each time was like the first joyous encounter.

Gen laughed, bent down, and caught him. Pressing kisses to his head, she allowed his presence to reach deep inside and soothe her. Kate had rescued Robert years ago when she found him on the side of the road, run over twice by a car. His back legs had been smashed. With Kate's usual stubbornness and all-encompassing love for creatures big and small, she'd committed to his operation and healing, and now had a companion for life.

Besides Slade, of course.

Gen had seen Slade with the dog, and a tight bond had been formed between them. The path might have been rocky, but now it was as if they were an adopted family. Seeing Kate settled and happy made everything worth it.

"Do you want me to take him for a walk? You have his scooter here, right?" Gen asked, rubbing the sweet spot between his ears. He gave a doggy moan of ecstasy.

Kate sighed. "Thanks, but he's good for a while. My sitter couldn't come today so I figured I'd give him a treat and take him with me. Slade has court so he won't be home till late."

"Sounds good. You look stressed. Anything I can help with?"

"You've already been saving my ass. Thank God for brilliant surgeons who turn to matchmaking. Hey, you want to shadow Kennedy tonight at the Purple Haze? There's a mixer and you can learn the ropes."

"Sure. I have nothing else going on." The thought of Wolfe trying to reinforce their friendship when she only craved to jump his bones was a bit complicated. Better to get home late.

Gen rose to her feet, wincing at the soreness lingering between her thighs, and turned.

"Holy. Shit."

She whirled back around. "What's the matter?"

Kate's gaze sharpened, sweeping past her figure. "Why are you wearing a scarf today, Gen?"

Her mouth fell open. The bright pink silk was light, fun, and covered the array of hickeys on her neck. Her heart pounded wildly but she tried to be cool. "Thought it looked good with the outfit. Why? You have a rule against scarves?"

The joke fell flat. "Take it off. I want to see something."

She forced a laugh. "No. It's hard to tie it correctly."

"You had sex! Why didn't you tell me the truth? I know you decided not to see Charles anymore, but I had no idea it was because you slept with him. How was it? Bad? Good? Medium? Do you regret it? Are you happy? Did you have an orgasm?"

The questions peppered her faster than a machine gun. Crap. She'd been so close to escape. After dodging Kate's texts on Sunday, she marched into her office this morning to tell her all about the date. Gen stuck to the main truth, saying the date had been good but they both decided not to pursue a relationship. Her friend took the news good-naturedly, telling her over and over that finding the right match took patience, time, and effort.

Now she thought they'd screwed each other.

"Umm, Charles and I didn't have sex."

Kate blinked. Studied her hard. "Wait a minute. I know you're hiding evidence under that scarf. You've been walking funny all day, but I thought it was the shoes. Even your lips have that pouty look that says you've been sucking on something for a long time. I know you had sex, I feel it!"

Why did Kate have to be so damn perceptive? Should she lie? She played the privacy card as a last resort. "Kate, please don't ask me any questions. I'm not ready to discuss my personal business, and I'd appreciate it if you give me some time and space and I'll give you more information when I'm ready."

Perfect. Textbook. Even Kate couldn't deny her.

Her friend picked up the phone and punched out numbers. "Kennedy? Get in here pronto. And get Arilyn. I'm with Gen and she had sex and she won't tell me details. Yes, of course we need the Baileys!"

Kate crossed her arms in front of her chest, leaned back in the leather chair, and glared. "Why don't you try repeating that bullshit again?"

Gen closed her eyes in defeat.

The door flew open. Kennedy held four bottles of miniature Baileys in her manicured hands. Her high heels clicked confidently over the floor, and her Donna Karan chocolate-colored suit screamed professional elegance. Arilyn trailed behind her in yoga pants, a soft cream tunic, and her long strawberry hair pulled back in a braid. She looked about twelve.

Robert claimed his affection by both women, then slid back over to his bed to nap.

Kennedy handed everyone a bottle, slid into the purple cushioned chair to Kate's right, crossed her legs, and twisted open the cap.

"Who'd you have sex with, Gen?"

Arilyn shook her head and sighed. "Kennedy, give her some time to feel comfortable and open up. You're scaring her."

Kennedy snorted. "She's a doctor. She doesn't scare easy. She's also lying to us, which is a big no-no."

"*You* lied to us," Arilyn pointed out. "Remember when you were dating Nate and refused to admit your feelings for him?"

Kennedy waved her hand in the air. "Doesn't count. I was lying to myself, not you guys. Who'd you have sex with, Gen?"

It was over. Might as well admit defeat.

Gen opened the bottle, took a long drink of Baileys, and embraced the stinging heat as it hit her belly.

"I slept with Wolfe."

Kate sputtered into a coughing fit. Kennedy's eyes widened with admiration. Arilyn gasped.

Silence settled over the room. The three of them took big slugs from their bottles, then settled.

"I didn't see that coming," Kate admitted. "I mean, I suspected you guys were hot for each other for a while, but I thought you were doing the friend thing."

"Is that why you're wearing the scarf?" Kennedy asked. "To hide the evidence?"

"Yep."

"Damn, girl. Was it amazing?"

Gen collapsed into the last empty chair and slumped down. "Yes. More amazing then you can ever imagine."

"I always knew you two would burn up the bedroom,"

Kennedy commented. "My main problem is your face. Why do you look miserable?"

Arilyn reached out and took her hand. "Honey, what happened? You should be giddy and over the moon."

"It was a night I'll never forget," she murmured. "I felt as if we were one. Completely bonded, and so deep inside each other we'd never be whole without the other."

Kate sighed. "I know that feeling."

"Best feeling in the world," Kennedy agreed.

Arilyn remained silent.

"But then morning came."

"Fucking dawn screws up everything," Kennedy growled, taking another sip of liquor. "Did he get spooked?"

"Majorly. Explained he didn't want to ruin our friendship and that he could never be in a committed relationship. Said he was broken and he'd end up hurting me."

Kate shook her head. "Sounds like Kennedy when she fell for Nate."

"Shut up, Kate. I came to my senses. Sounds to me like Slade and all his crap about divorce and oxytocin."

Kate stuck out her tongue.

Gen laughed, loving the way serious talk was always mixed with the wretched humor life threw at them. "He'll never tell me about his past. I know it's bad. How can I force him into a relationship he doesn't want? And what about our friendship? I don't want to lose him either. The whole thing is a mess. Stupid sex. Stupid fifteen orgasms."

Arilyn gasped. "Fifteen?"

"Holy shit," Kennedy whispered.

"No wonder you're walking funny," Kate said. "These men keep upping the ante, don't they?"

"Why does sex have to complicate everything?" Gen groaned.

"Because it feels too good not to have to pay," Kennedy said. "Do we have a plan of action? What do you want?"

Frustration and helplessness warred. Both won. "Doesn't matter. I need to deal with reality. I told Wolfe to move out, but he refused, swearing he'll get us back on the ground of friendship."

Arilyn murmured in sympathy. Kate told the truth. "Men are brain-dead, sometimes. Each time you look at each other you'll be thinking of sex. Slade and I tried to ignore our attraction for a long time, but eventually we broke."

"Yep. It's *When Harry Met Sally* all over again. Once you do the dirty deed, friendship takes a backseat," Kennedy quipped.

Gen glared. "Not making me feel better about this, guys."

Arilyn smiled and patted her hand. "Maybe he needs some time. I've found confronting men and demanding certain things make them defensive. But if you just continue as is, living with each other, dealing with the sexual tension, eventually he'll break. Drag you into bed. The body is weak, especially a man's penis. After enough times of sleeping together, you'll just fall into a relationship without needing to speak of it or define it."

They all stared at Arilyn. Since she refused to talk about her on-again, off-again relationship with her yoga teacher, refusing to even name him, any nugget of information was gold.

"Like Yoga Dude?" Kate asked.

Arilyn shut down. "Just a general observation," she muttered, lapsing back into silence.

Kate and Kennedy sighed in defeat.

"He's using David as an excuse to stay close, but I don't think I'm in any danger. David has probably moved on, and there's been no contact since the night at the station."

"He never pressed charges against Wolfe?" Arilyn asked.

"No. The restraining order is still valid but he dropped assault charges. Probably knew the truth would come out in court."

"Asshole," Kennedy said. "I still don't trust him. Abusers retreat only when they have a plan in place, and if he still wants you, he's coming back."

Gen shivered. She knew Kennedy didn't mean to scare her, and it was a fair warning, but another reason she could never go back to the hospital was David. Just seeing his face brought the past roaring back. The way she'd become weaker and slipped away day by day. The control and abuse he finely wielded like a weapon, hiding it from everyone. She hated the woman she'd been during their relationship, but finally recognized she'd been strong enough to run when she could. How much better she understood now women who stayed. She remembered how badly David wanted to begin having children quickly. She would've been trapped in a nightmare, like so many others out there. Goose bumps broke out on her arms and her heart ached for strangers she didn't know but finally understood. Strong women. Independent women. Smart women.

"I'm still being careful," she said. "I just don't like Wolfe using it as an excuse."

"Hmm. Well, you have a few options. You can insist he leave and then deal with the fallout. You can allow him to stay and see how your relationship evolves. Or you can greet him when he gets home bare-assed naked with a smile. He wouldn't last three seconds."

Gen laughed at Kate's speech and finished up her Baileys. "All good options. I'll have to think. Maybe see where the week leads."

"Has your family come around? I know David manipulated them big-time."

Gen nodded. "I've been spending more time with them. Being honest is hard. I was so embarrassed and hid so much it was easy for David to spin his own tales. But Alexa and Mom support my decision, and even Dad is slowly coming around. Izzy said I did the right thing. Actually called me brave."

"You are. We're all here for you," Kate said. "You'll never be alone again. And when there's man trouble, best friends are the key."

Emotion clogged her throat. The other girls nodded, and Gen felt embraced by bonds as strong as family, because of the choice they made to be together. Sometimes choice was stronger than blood.

"Thanks. Love you guys."

Kennedy rolled her eyes. "Let's get the group hug over with so we can get back to work."

Robert barked.

Laughing, they all hugged in a circle, and for the first time, Gen felt hopeful. She'd keep an open mind and heart and see how things went. She'd never stop loving Wolfe, but if it was possible to sustain a friendship, she'd try anything.

twenty-two

WOLFE GLANCED AROUND and double-checked the setup. A case of Sam Adams. Bacon cheeseburgers and fries from Mugs. A carton of mint chocolate chip ice cream. Stack of DVDs on the table, ready to fire up. Scrabble board.

Yes. He was covered. Everything screamed all of their favorite things to do together as friends. Best buds. He wouldn't have any sexual thoughts, even if she wore something ridiculously skimpy. He already had the photo of pregnant nuns paused in his brain, ready to fire at the first sign of arousal.

He could do this. He had to convince her they could be friends again or he'd lose her completely.

Wasn't an option.

She came through the door looking tired. Her hair was pinned back and loose waves escaped and framed her cheeks. The sun made her freckles stand out more, a cute smattering over her nose. Her lipstick had worn off, showing the natural pink of her lips. Her petite, lush frame was wrapped in a short denim dress that flirted above her knees and flattered her hourglass body. She kicked off her beaded flats, threw her purse down, and tore the clip from her hair.

"I'm tired and cranky and you'd better not ask what's for dinner."

She was magnificent.

He grinned and got to work grabbing the plates and serving an ice-cold beer. "Got takeout so we didn't have to worry. Why don't you put on some sweats and I'll have this ready?"

She grunted her approval, taking a deep sniff of the burgers, and trudged into the bedroom.

He had everything ready when she popped back out in yoga pants and a purple tank top with the Kinnections logo on it. Her feet were bare and he caught the flash of bubble gum toenails. Remembered how her toes would curl under when he hit one of her sensitive areas, especially when his mouth was—

No. Focus. Nuns.

He breathed and motioned her to sit. "All ready. Shit day?"

She took a big bite of the burger and whimpered. "So good. Nah, just tired. I didn't get much sleep."

The words flew from her mouth like a cannon shot. Their gazes crashed together, remembering the reason they hadn't slept, and Wolfe cleared his throat, breaking the connection. "Uh, yeah. Anything new and exciting going on with Kinnections?" That should be a safe subject.

Gen shrugged. "Not really. Another engagement. Kennedy was ecstatic about the growing statistics. Helped Kate a bit with her wedding plans. Saw Robert today. You?"

He searched for something interesting while he ate. "Booked another big convention with the IT geeks. I think golfing helped. Those Wednesday outings with Nate opened up a whole new clientele. He's a smart son of a bitch."

Gen smiled. "Rocket scientists usually are."

"Aerospace engineer."

"Right." She munched on a few fries. "How are Sawyer and Julietta doing? And the baby? How old is she now?"

"Four months." A pang hit him. He missed his family. Since opening Purity, he hadn't been able to visit as much. He'd made it over for a long weekend for the birth of the baby, but Sawyer said she changed so much every day. He needed to schedule another visit. "They're good. Seem happy. Gabby has her days and nights mixed up so it's a bit tough, but Sawyer is crazed over her. God help the girl if she ever believes she can date."

Gen laughed. "With your Italian family? It'll be a miracle. You should see Nick with Lily and Maria. Lily came home spouting about having a boyfriend in second grade. The man sat down and explained that hanging out with boys would make her less smart. Alexa found her crying in the morning, saying she was afraid to talk to boys and lose brainpower. Of course, Nick was in the doghouse for a long time with Old Yeller and Simba."

Wolfe shook his head and laughed with her. This was perfect. Sharing funny stories about their families was one of their favorite things to do. She reached for more ketchup and the tank gaped open, giving him a glimpse of purple lace. She had a matching bra? What about the panties? Could it be a thong? No, she'd always said they were uncomfortable, but now his gaze would be glued to her ass to see if he caught any lines and—

"Wolfe?"

"Huh?"

"I asked if there was any Diet Coke left?"

"Oh yeah, here." He slid over the soda and got himself back together. "I got us some movies to watch tonight. Figured we both needed a lazy evening."

"I'm not watching *Fast & Furious* sequel one million."

"No, I got stuff you like. *Shall We Dance. The Notebook. Steel Daffodils.*"

"*Magnolias.*"

"Right."

She glared at him suspiciously. Her full lips wrapped around the straw and sucked. The room misted for a few seconds, and Wolfe remembered the exact heat and pressure of those lips around his cock. How sweet and erotic the sight of Gen on her knees was, giving so much pleasure until—

He jumped from the table, turned on the faucet, and began splashing cold water over his face. "What's wrong with you?" she asked.

"Hot flash."

"You're not even menopausal yet."

"Ha-ha. Men get them, too." He shook off the clinging droplets, switched to puppies in shelters as his go-to image, and sat back at the table. He would do this or die.

"I don't feel like watching weepy chick flicks," she said. "Can we channel surf?"

"Sure. Or we could play Scrabble."

"Too brain-dead." She switched from soda to beer, taking a long sip and sighing in pleasure. "I did my first mixer at the Purple Haze. It was fun. Lots of work to make sure things go smoothly, but there's nothing like watching that first meeting. The hope each one has to find love. Gets me every time."

He shifted in his seat. "Yep."

"I'm thinking of telling Kate to try again. Find me another date. I think I had the wrong approach with Charles. I was looking to confirm my sexuality, but no man can do that for me. I need to do that for myself." Her blue eyes glittered with memories that matched his. "You helped me see that."

His skin burned and his heart pounded and his palms sweat. "G-glad you finally realized it. You think you're ready to get back out there?"

Her gaze hit him like an arrow. "I think I'm ready to try."

His mouth went dry, so he took a long slug of beer. "Right. Yeah, probably a good idea. To get back out there." The words fell flat and a bitter taste stuck in his mouth. What did he expect? He'd been the one to say they had no relationship other than friendship. It would be good for him to finally let her go and stop trying to protect her. Forget the jealousy and possession. That was only for lovers. Boyfriend and girlfriend. Shit like that.

He directed the rest of the conversation toward neutral subjects, cleaned everything up, and waited while she showered and changed. Her pj's were almost the same, comfy flannel shorts and a tank top. No bra. Her nipples pushed against the soft fabric, tempting and inviting his lips to suck and lick and bite.

But he didn't. Friends didn't do that.

They took their beers to the couch and stretched their legs out on the table, and he gave her the remote. He kept his gaze off her bare legs and pinned to the screen. They settled on *House Hunters*. He groaned enough to give the impression of surrendering, but damned if that stupid show hadn't hooked him good. He usually couldn't fall asleep until he knew which house the couple picked.

Gen scoffed at house number two. "Did you see that? The guy doesn't care what his wife wants. The kitchen is a mess, and he's only focused on having a man cave. Selfish jerk."

"Give me a break. She's all crazed about having a billion people over for parties. Wanna bet how many parties they have? A handful. Not with three kids—they have no time to entertain."

"Maybe if he helped her more in the kitchen instead of relaxing in the man cave, they'd have more people over."

"Maybe if she'd give him some alone time without nagging constantly, he'd help enough to throw the parties."

She scoffed. He snorted.

Wolfe relaxed. They settled into their usual playful banter, and hope gleamed bright over the horizon. They could do this. Once they retrained their bodies not to respond, he was sure their strong friendship would triumph.

The couple picked the house with the good kitchen. Gen whooped, while he tried to look cranky and fight a smile.

The channel clicked.

The couple flashed over the screen. The girl was in a

man's button-down, bare legs, hair messed. The guy held her tight, lifted her up, and suddenly they were in the bed. No. No. Why did this movie look so familiar? He prayed she'd change it, but the remote rested in her lap, her shorts hiked up enough to show off miles of thigh, leading to the center. All roads leading to sweet heaven.

"Remember this movie?" she asked a bit breathlessly. "I love Timberlake!"

No. Way.

Friends with Benefits.

The plot was a nightmare. Best friends who decide to sleep together without getting involved in a real relationship. His muscles tightened. "Kind of lame, huh?"

"I liked it." They watched in silence as the couple kissed passionately and began ripping off each other's clothes. The air grew hot, his skin itched, and he wondered if he was going to lose his mind. He slugged down more beer.

One glance over told him the worst. Gen was aroused. Her nipples were tight and hard, pressed against her tank. Her pulse pounded at the base of her neck. If he looked into her eyes, he was positive her pupils would be dilated. Her lips would be moist. And if he slid a hand under those shorts, under her panties, he'd find her drenched, tight, and throbbing. For him.

Wolfe gripped the neck of the bottle. Prayed. His erection pushed painfully against his jeans, fighting to escape, and the room tilted as he struggled to fight the raw, bone-deep need to tumble her back and fuck her long and hard and well.

The sexual tension twisted a notch tighter. His skin broke out in a sweat. Still her gaze stayed glued to the screen, but he caught her thighs squeezing together as if trying to ease an ache. Her teeth sunk into her lower lip.

The dialogue in the movie slapped him in the face.

"I miss sex."

"I miss sex, too."

"I mean sometimes you just need it."

"Why does it always have to come with complications?"

Nuns. Puppies. Babies crying. He dove for any type of images that would allow him a clean breath; a thought that wouldn't strangle his dick with painful, wretched heat. Slowly, ever so slowly, her head turned. Those blue eyes caught and held his.

And it was done.

They both moved so fast, barely a second passed before she was on his lap, her mouth fused to his, her fingers tugging at his hair. His tongue plunged into her mouth, drinking in the sweetness he missed and craved, and her ass ground against his thighs in a frantic effort to get closer. His hands yanked down her tank, baring her breasts, cupping the heavy weight and rubbing her tight nipples. She groaned deep in her throat and he swallowed the sound, his tongue tangling with hers while she began pulling at the snap of his jeans, tugging the zipper down.

"Off," she growled like a sexy tigress. "Now."

"Trying. You feel so good, taste so good." His hands were everywhere, greedy to touch her pale, silky skin, gorging on the scent of peaches and honey as his tongue continued its push and pull from her mouth. "Lift up." She raised herself a few inches and he managed to get her pants off, taking her flimsy underwear with them. He hissed as the scent of her arousal hit his nostrils. "Can't wait. Need you now."

"Yes, yes," she chanted, her legs parting wide. He helped her get the jeans over his hips and kicked to the ground. Her fingers wrapped around his cock, and he almost wept with gratitude that he'd gone commando today. She scratched at his shoulders, bit his neck, and wiggled madly to get closer. Her skin burned under his hands, and lust glazed his sight as he tried to drink her in, enjoy her open sexuality, the way she challenged and fought him at every step for more.

He gripped her thighs, lifted, and got ready to plunge.

Shit.

"Condom," he croaked. She stroked him roughly from base to tip and a shudder wracked his body. "Where?"

Her curls spilled around her face and she blinked from a daze. "Don't have any. Got mad at you so I threw them all out."

"You didn't."

"I did. You have any?"

A strangled laugh escaped. "Threw them away so I wouldn't be tempted." She kissed his mouth over and over, and his chest broke open, oozing out a rough mess of emotion. So loving and sweet and whole. "Sweetheart, gotta slow down. Gonna lose it."

"Don't need the condom. I'm on the pill for my period. I'm clean."

He kissed her long and hard. "I just got tested, so I'm good. Are you sure?"

She squeezed his cock hard. "Does it look like I'm sure?"

"Yes. Hold on tight. You're going on a ride."

This time he didn't pause as he lifted her high and pulled her down hard and fast onto his cock.

She cried out, closing her eyes, gritting her teeth. He panted for breath, the extraordinary feeling of being buried so deeply within her tight heat so good he wanted to weep. She pulsed and milked him with tiny grips, urging him for more. Leveraging his back against the cushions, he began to lift her up and down, each time slamming a bit harder, sliding an inch deeper. The barbell hit her clit with each slow drag, and he twisted his hips to hit her special spot that made her body clench and shiver all over. Oh yeah. So fucking good.

Her voice broke. "Gonna come. Oh, God, can't wait."

"Not yet. I'm not done with you."

She arched for more, ready to get to climax, but he slowed the pace and the angle, refusing her. She groaned, bent over, and bit his shoulder. Hard.

"That's right, baby. Give me all you got."

"Bastard." She dug her nails into his chest, rubbing her nipples against him, and clenched her thighs tight in an effort to get him to move faster. He punished her by pinching her nipples, then grabbing her ass to control her better.

She surrendered, whimpering, shuddering, and suddenly he was done with play.

Wolfe surged one last time.

She came hard, crying out his name as her body convulsed. He kept the intense pace until the last of her pleasure was wrung from her body. Rubbed her clit side to side with fast motions, spilling her into another hard orgasm. Then let go.

He came inside her, loving the feel of her on his bare skin, loving the feeling of being completely connected and part of her sweet little body without any barriers between them. She collapsed onto his lap, her arms tight around his shoulders, his dick buried deep in her cunt.

Wolfe closed his eyes and held her like the precious gift she was. Knowing he couldn't fight it any longer. Not knowing what the answer was.

She opened one eye. "Still friends?"

He laughed, kissing her shoulder. "Definitely. Friends with benefits?"

"Yes. I don't want to fight it. How about this? We take it day by day. If we want to have sex, we do. No questions asked."

"I don't want us to date or sleep with anyone else."

She smiled and kissed him gently. "That's a requirement. Let's see how it goes. When you move out, maybe that will be a signal for us to go back to being platonic. But why deny ourselves this?"

His fingers caressed her buttocks, catching her shiver. "You're right. Because this is extraordinary."

"We don't have to end up like a stupid movie. We can play this on our terms."

"You're right. Our friendship is strong enough to handle great, mind-blowing sex. It will be good for us."

"Definitely. Now take me to bed," she demanded.

He lifted her up and stalked into the bedroom. Amazing how clear everything suddenly seemed. Maybe seeing that movie was a sign. A good sign. They'd handle it together. In the meantime, they wouldn't have to fight their attraction. Taking it day by day was sheer genius.

What could possibly go wrong?

He ignored the warning voice and concentrated on the woman in his arms.

VINCENT SOLDANO STEPPED INTO the makeshift bedroom, pushed away the cheap Harry Potter poster he'd gotten when he was young, and put the rest of the money into the hole in the wall. He felt like the prisoner from the Shawshank *movie, hiding his escape route behind some lame-assed wall hanging. But it worked. None of the men or his mom had found it since he'd needed to move his stash.*

He was getting the hell out.

He had money. The knife. Clothes. Backpack. A few personal items. Food and water. He'd grown larger over the last year, and held more of a presence. He was less of a scrawny kid, on the verge of being a man, and he figured it gave him a better shot in the world. No foster care or crap for him. Just him, his wits, and his survival.

The shouts grew louder and he cursed under his breath. Wished he'd left yesterday, but he wanted one more day to make sure his escape was well planned. Better to have his mother completely drugged up and wasted so she didn't think to look for him awhile. The more distractions the better, and last night had been way too quiet. But now it seemed a full-fledged party was going on. After the sex and the drugs, he'd be able to stroll out the door without a glance back.

It was finally done.

He spent the next hour distracting himself, listening to the night grow more rowdy. The knock on the door surprised him. He tensed.

"Yeah?"

"Hey, kid, come on out here. Your mom needs you."

He rarely listened, but something about this being the last time seeing his mom made him a bit soft. His knife was in his pocket, but this time he'd gotten much more adept at using it. He was pretty deadly, practicing constantly and giving himself drills in order to protect himself. Next time, he'd be ready.

He stepped out with a scowl. "What?"

His mother leaned against the wall, eyes bloodshot, mouth half open with ecstasy. Seeing things that weren't there or didn't exist. He hoped they were good things rather than bad. "Hey, baby!" A thin trickle of saliva ran from her lips and dripped on her torn tank. One bare breast hung out and he deftly avoided looking at her body, concentrating on her face. The paraphernalia was laid out carefully. Weed. Crack. Empty bottles of whiskey and vodka. Beer cans. Someone was screwing in the back room, but the asshole who had knocked had a funny look in his eyes. Like he was excited about something.

"Your mom is toasted," the squat, muscular pimp announced. "She's not gonna be much help for me tonight. So we need you."

His gut twisted. Adrenaline began to pump through his

veins, a reaction to the dangerous aura in the air. The dealer called himself Scott. Been around awhile, taking care of his mother when she was strung out, pushing her to work harder being a whore. Vincent didn't get the same creepy kind of vibe he got from the last few, and Scott seemed to leave him alone. Didn't seem like he was into males.

And that's where Vincent realized he'd made his major mistake.

"Yeah, well, can't help you out." He acted casual, sneering, the knife comfortable in his pocket. He headed toward the door, but the dealer blocked him. A tiny smirk came across his lips.

"I think you can," he drawled. Vincent tensed. Knew he had a good shot at taking him. "See, your mom ran out of money. Ran out of favors. So tonight, she called in her last chip."

His mother smiled so sickly and sweetly he thought he'd vomit. "Sorry, baby. Gotta help me. Gotta help."

He clenched his fists and fought for breath. He might have to run without his stash. Fuck. "If you think I'm some kinda whore like her, you're wrong. You touch me and I'll kill you."

Scott grinned. "Ever try it? Maybe it's not so bad. Tell you what, do it this one time for me and we'll call it even. I won't bother you or your mother again."

He took a step back but refused to glance at the door. Too close. He'd have to run. His hand slid behind his back, slipped out the knife, and clenched it in his hand. He couldn't miss. There was too much at stake. "Didn't know you were a homo, pimp," he sneered, trying to distract him. "Whatsa matter? Your dick not big enough for a woman?"

Scott kept grinning and began walking toward him. "We can do this hard or real easy. I've given you time. Space. Let you steal money from me when you thought I wasn't looking. But now it's time to pay up."

Vincent swallowed past the nausea and fear overtaking him, lifted the knife, and with a perfect arc threw it in the air.

The blade hit its target, piercing the man's upper chest.

Vincent didn't wait to see the damage. He turned and raced for the only exit, knowing if he didn't get there he wouldn't have another chance.

Scott's howl reached his ears. Scrambling feet. The knob turned, slid, twisted. Clean air rushed over him. One sneaker hit the ground, found purchase, and he began to run.

Rough hands dragged him back. Light exploded as something smashed against his head, and he fought for consciousness, the swirl and mix of male voices and shouts mingling in the air. His mind screamed one word the entire time he desperately tried to break away, the one word that would be repeated in his nightmares for years after the horrid night.

No no no no no no . . .

Two men tossed him into his room onto the bed. He groaned and twisted, but they were much bigger than Scott, and one guarded the door while the first dragged him off the mattress and threw him to his knees. He gagged, ready to vomit, his palms plastered to the battered wooden floor.

"Gonna teach you some manners. Also gonna teach you how to make some money."

Scott walked over, jerking his head up by his hair. He

*grinned with an evil purpose, blood dripping from the shal-
low wound near his shoulder. "You'll pay for that one. I'm
gonna enjoy you working off your mama's debt."*

No. No no no no no . . .

The first man laughed and began unbuckling his pants.

No no no no no no . . .

And then the nightmare began.

twenty-three

GEN WALKED OUT of Cafe Xpressions with a bag of biscotti and big plans for that night. She planned to make scampi with pasta, and then work off the calories by engaging in her new fave sport.

Sex. With Wolfe.

She hummed under her breath, swinging the bag and soaking in the sun.

"Genevieve?"

The familiar voice popped her bubble, and she felt her happiness slowly leak away as she stared at David. A tiny shiver of fear trickled down her spine, though they were in broad daylight. Pressing her lips together, she turned to walk away but he said her name again with an odd urgency.

"Please give me a minute. I know I don't deserve it. We can talk right out here in front of witnesses. Please."

She stiffened but turned around. He must have come straight from his shift, since he still wore his scrubs. His burnished hair looked mussed, but glinted like a halo in the sun. Tiny lines bracketed his mouth and eyes, giving him an exhausted look she knew too well. A pang deep inside exploded through her. She missed the hospital. Missed the work. Missed feeling a part of the bigger picture, sacrificing her time to save lives. She fought to keep the longing off her face in case he misread her emotion.

"What do you want?"

"First? To apologize. My actions make me sick. I lost it, was so crazed with jealousy I wanted to hurt you."

"Sorry. I can't forgive you. You took away anything good we once had when you laid your hands on me with violence."

He nodded, his jaw clenched with tension. "Understood. I still had to say it out loud. I made arrangements for your stuff to be delivered this weekend, if that's okay."

She raised an eyebrow. Max had been working on it, but things stalled when David's lawyer threatened to drag her to court, declaring that her affair with Wolfe entitled her to nothing. "I don't want any personal deliveries."

"No, I won't be there. You win, Gen. It's over. I'm going to stay away from you. I've gone over every piece of our relationship and think I know how I went wrong, but if you won't give me another chance, I can't fight you."

"We can never go back," she whispered.

"I know." For a brief moment, those first few months drifted past her vision and sadness leaked through. Once, she loved him. Wanted to marry him. Now he was just a stranger. Life was both odd and bittersweet. When Wolfe took her in his arms, all the pieces clicked into place. She'd never before felt such a bone-deep rightness in her soul.

"But there's one thing I need to ask you," he said.

Here we go. She narrowed her gaze.

"You need to come back to the hospital."

Her muscles tightened. It took a few moments to catch her breath and speak calmly. "I can't. You know why."

David shook his head, intensity radiating around him. "You belong in medicine, Genevieve. You have a gift. I saw it from the very first, and to see you wasting away in some cheap matchmaking company is a crime."

"Kinnections is a successful business that helps people find love. How dare you judge me."

His lips pressed together. "You're hiding there. I also know I'm the reason. Look, the idea of you working beside me, seeing you every day but not being able to claim you as mine, almost destroyed me. I did everything in my power to force you out. Another apology owed. So I'm transferring."

Her mouth dropped open. "You're the backbone of the surgical unit. And I don't believe you. It's just a trick to get me back."

"No, Genevieve. I've been offered an opportunity at Boston Children's Hospital. It's time to make a move. I can do a lot more, especially in the teaching and surgical fields. I've been stifled for a while, but I didn't want to admit it. Especially with you finishing up your residency and wanting to stay in New York."

Shock hit her in waves. The opportunity of returning to the career she had lived and breathed for so long suddenly shimmered before her again. "Why are you telling me this? Am I supposed to believe you're suddenly ready to accept our breakup? After you got a restraining order against Wolfe? And convinced my parents I was having emotional problems? Forced me from the hospital in the first place?"

He never flinched. Just gazed at her with the same intensity he used on the residents. "It's the truth. I felt you slipping away and did everything in my power to keep you. I never trusted that asshole anyway—he was gunning for you the whole time. But I'm not about to waste the rest of my life begging you to come back to me. I wanted to tell you in person about my decision. Contact the residency director, Brian, and he'll get you back into the program. I've already cleared it."

Her heart thundered, roaring in her ears. "It may be too late."

"It's never too late. Don't waste yourself on a career unworthy of you. You're better than that." His gaze flicked over her. "You're better than Wolfe, too."

She opened her mouth to protest but he'd already turned on his heel and walked away.

Gen stared at the empty pavement. So many decisions. She enjoyed Kinnections. It was more challenging than she originally thought, and working with her best friends was a dream come true.

But she was a doctor. A surgeon. The medical field was in her DNA, and though she'd tried to run and forget it, hoping she could have a fuller, more balanced life than before, Gen realized all roads led back to the hospital.

She had a lot to think about.

Gen headed toward her house, thoughts spinning.

WOLFE STARED AT THE large-screen monitor in front of him. He'd just closed a big account that would be book-ing all its future conferences at Purity. *Screw you, Plaza. We have arrived.*

He looked forward to telling Sawyer about his recent coup. Every win was another opportunity to give back to the man who'd offered him a chance and dragged him out of the gutter.

As usual, his blood heated at the idea of using his brain and skills to get what he wanted. Especially in business. His personal life had been a flat, unending desert plain with nothing in sight he craved. Made things so much easier. Empty, but easy.

Until Gen, of course. Now he bounced through his workday like a kid looking forward to Christmas.

He shook his head in self-mockery and looked around his office. He'd furnished it in a replica of Sawyer's office in Italy. Mahogany wood. Burgundy carpet. Interesting sculptures and knickknacks that appealed to him. A floor-to-ceiling bookcase filled with rare editions and popular fiction. And a private entrance to a gym where he pounded out his frustrations on a punching bag to eighties heavy metal.

How many times had he slept here without thought? Now the minute 5 p.m. arrived, he headed out the door. His personal assistant almost fainted when he announced his refusal to stay late and chair a meeting. Wolfe knew he wasn't needed. He just liked being involved in all stages. Until a sexy brunette cast a spell on him.

He pushed back the worried thoughts ready to spring loose. Couldn't last. He didn't care. One full week had already passed and things were perfect. He decided to wring out every last ounce of pleasure until what they had slowly dissolved. Who would've thought this friends-with-benefits thing could work? But so far, it did. They spent their time together, engaged in mind-blowing sex most of the night, and enjoyed each other's company. No questions, restrictions, or contracts. No promises. Just the moment, and a boatload of pleasure.

His cell buzzed and he quickly scooped it up. A smile curved his mouth immediately. "Hey, Sawyer. How the hell are you?"

A low laugh echoed over the receiver. "Was gonna ask you the same. Heard you beat out the Plaza in the Conway contract. Nice work."

Wolfe shook his head in disbelief. "Who do you have planted here? The ink's still wet and I planned to call you later to give you the good news."

"I couldn't wait. Listen, I wanted to ask you a favor."

He clenched the phone. "Anything."

"Think you can fly out here next week? Spend a few days with us?"

"Is everything okay? Julietta? Gabby? You?"

Another laugh. "Calm down, we're all great. We just wanted to share something. Plus, Julietta misses you. So do I."

The emotion surged hot and strong, enveloping him in the only comfort he'd ever had in his life. "I miss you, too. Yeah, I'll wrap up in a few days and get out there."

"Good. I want to catch up on things. Texting and Skype just aren't the same. And Gabby needs to torture her big brother."

Sawyer grinned. "Give me a break. You guys just want a sitter."

"Busted. I already bought the tickets to La Scala, so don't think you're backing out now."

"Looking forward to it."

"The plane will take you when you're ready. Just text me."

"Done. See ya soon. Give the girls a kiss."

"I will."

The phone clicked.

Home. Funny, New York was the place he decided to settle and grow with his career, but Milan would always hold his heart. The first time he'd learned about family, and love, and respect. The first time he'd been given an opportunity to be more than a piece of garbage. He couldn't wait.

The thought of leaving Gen even for a few days dimmed the joy, but he pushed it aside, refusing to deal with the hornet's nest of emotion ready to sting.

His cell rang again. He picked it up. "Everything okay?"

Her soft sigh spilled into his ear. Instantly, he grew hard. Damn, she was a sorceress. "I forgot the Italian bread. Can you pick some up on the way home?"

"Of course. What's for dinner?"

"Scampi with pasta."

His stomach rumbled. He was getting spoiled by her cooking, and had begun making up for his lack of culinary skills by cleaning and fixing up her house. He'd sealed the cracks in the tub, fixed the broken front step, and painted the bathroom. The pleasure on her face made every drop of sweat worth it, and he enjoyed using his hands to make their home nice.

Her home.

He ignored the mental slip.

"Sounds great. I'll snag a bottle of red to go with it. Hey, did you DVR *Love It or List It* last night?"

"Yep. Why?"

"No reason. Just figured you wanted to see if they ended up selling it. I thought she did great with the renovations, but the guy was kind of a jerk. I mean, how was she supposed to know once they ripped up the basement there'd be mold?"

"Oh, *I* wanted to see it, huh? Why can't you admit I got you hooked?"

He snorted. "As if."

"You're sounding more like Nate. If you're not interested, I can always watch it early and delete it before you get home."

Damn. How was he gonna get out of this one? "Whatever," he said. "Won't bother me in the least." He made a mental note to check the computer and see if they had the new episodes uploaded yet.

Her delighted laugh made him want to reach through the phone and touch her. Smooth back her hair. Trace the luscious curve of her lip. Kiss the freckles sprinkled across her nose.

"I won't delete it. And I won't tell either. Drive safe."

"I will. See you in a bit."

He clicked off and grinned. A great meal. A little TV. Intriguing conversation. And a lot of nakedness.

For the first time in his existence, life was perfect.

*   *   *

WOLFE DROPPED THE SHRIMP and stared. "You actually spoke to him? After what that asshole did to you?"

He recognized her sigh of impatience as a good friend. Fortunately, or unfortunately, the lover card had been pulled, and he wanted to howl in protest at any other man getting near her. Especially her ex. "You're overreacting," she said, sipping her Pinot Noir. "It was in broad daylight on the street. He seemed apologetic, and for the first time, sincere."

Yeah. Forget the howling. He was going baboon crazy on her, thumping his chest and pounding on her *sincere* ex-fiancé. The jealousy burned like whiskey but didn't settle into a nice afterglow. It just made him sick. He pushed away his plate, suddenly not hungry. "I don't trust anything he says, Gen. He's an abuser, an egotist, and a control freak. Why didn't you call me?"

Her brows snapped with temper. Yep. The spark in those blue eyes was her first warning. "Because, contrary to popular belief, I can handle myself. Sometimes I do quite well without a knight in armor."

Yeah, she was pissed. The knight crack again. He'd never felt close to being a rescuer. He was just playing catch-up for not recognizing her deep unhappiness earlier. "What if he's lying to get you back to the hospital so he has more control? And I don't believe he'll return your stuff without an excuse to see you again. I told you we should've filed the restraining order!"

Her lips pursed. Second sign of impending temper. "It was my decision to wait. I told Slade to hold off until things settled. I didn't want him to target you."

"Me? You were worried about me? I can take care of myself."

"And I can take care of myself," she growled. "David dropped all the assault charges and the lawsuit, didn't he? He's out of our lives and now he's transferring to Boston. No reason getting all upset."

"I'm not upset."

"Then everything's great."

Silence descended. They glared at each other, not sure why the other was mad and not sure what to do about it. He tried to sound calm and reasonable. "I don't like the idea of him getting you excited about going back to the hospital. Like a carrot he wants to dangle in front of you, then yank away."

"I know. If I decide to go back, I'll be dealing with a lot of emotional backlash. Resentful employees who believe I forced him out. Nothing wrong with taking a step back before making any decisions. Brian already called me and confirmed David's new position in Boston."

Why did he feel like she'd snuck behind his back? What was wrong with him? This crippling possessiveness was way out of his comfort zone. He figured she'd talk to him first, go over her options, tell him where her head was. But it seemed she didn't really need him and went ahead with making her own plans.

Isn't this what he wanted though? They didn't have a permanent relationship. And friends weren't expected to confess details about their decisions. Right?

"Do you miss the hospital?" he asked.

She stilled. Tangled her fingers together. Yes, she did. It

was all over her face, and suddenly his heart ached for the life she had turned her back on. She was born to serve, and though Kinnections was a good break for her to take a breath, she needed to go back.

"Yeah. I do."

He nodded. And damned if the next screwed-up question didn't tumble out of his mouth. "Do you miss him?"

She jerked. Her eyes widened, and she suddenly simmered with emotion. Clenching her fists, she leaned forward over the table like she wanted to strangle him. What had just happened?

"Why? Are you afraid I'm thinking of him when I'm fucking you?"

Wolfe jumped from the chair, his own anger lighting up and pumping through his veins. She never talked like that. Never challenged or pushed in such a primitive way. "That's a crappy thing to say," he snarled. "Why are you trying to pick a fight? I just wanted to watch TV!"

She jumped up from her chair and shook her finger at him. "So did I! But I hate when you treat me like some ridiculous child who needs constant protecting. And if I was still missing David, I would never have gone to bed with you!"

"Fine. Good. Whatever."

"You're acting like such a mitch."

He turned back, shock in his eyes. She did not just say that to him. "What did you call me?"

"A mitch. You know. A male bitch."

"Yeah, I know. Nate uses that word for his hairdresser, but if you call me that again there will be consequences."

She threw her head back and fake laughed. "Is that how you handle things in your world? Big-bully threats to your one-night-stand girlfriends? How about a little communication? How about admitting that maybe you're just as confused as I am about what we're doing together, that you may be jealous of David, and that we both have no clue what to do next?"

She was right. But the line between friendship and girlfriend was too terrifying to step over. He didn't know how to play that role. He'd been alone far too long and knew he'd fail. He narrowed his gaze, took in her defensive stance, and relied on the only asset that always worked.

Sex.

"Maybe you like the sort of threats I give you," he drawled. "Like ripping off your clothes and tossing you on that bed, till your smart mouth doesn't know how to say anything else but my name?"

Oh yeah. Her eyes blazed and he caught the tightening of her nipples under her shirt. For a second, he thought she'd surrender. Would've cashed in all his chips on the bet and let it ride. But then she stiffened her spine, straightening to her mighty five-foot stance, tilted her chin, and stomped past him.

The bedroom door slammed behind her.

Wolfe groaned. He'd screwed up again. How had the whole conversation gotten redirected into an argument? What if he hadn't come in and David had raped her? Wolfe shuddered at the memory. He'd use his dying breath to make sure that never happened. He didn't want to shield her from the world, or lock her in a bubble like the asshole had. He just hated watching her get hurt. And now he was the one who'd hurt her.

He rubbed his fingers over his forehead and began cleaning up. He'd apologize. Give her a few moments to calm down. Maybe explain where his head was at, and how watching the attack affected him. Wolfe concentrated on stacking dishes, putting away the leftovers, and refreshing the wine. He'd knock and give her a peace offering. Try to communicate. He'd sleep on the couch tonight, give her some time, and—

The door opened.

Gen strode out in black lace boy shorts, matching push-up bra, and black leather stilettos.

Holy. Crap.

His gaze devoured the sway of her hips, the luscious curve of her ass, the mouthwatering cleavage on display. Her legs flexed with each step, pushing her breasts out. Her nipples pressed against the lace. Without a glance over, she clicked over toward the kitchen, completely ignoring his instant erection, hanging tongue, and lust-filled eyes.

"Oh good, you cleaned up for me. And poured more wine. Perfect."

He tried to speak but only made some caveman noises.

She turned, and Wolfe caught the gorgeous ink hovering above the lacy band of her panties. The thorns wept blood, trickling down into the covered spaces of her bare ass.

"Wh-wh-what are you doing?" His voice sounded like a girly, high-pitched squeal.

She grabbed her glass, took a sip, and cocked her hip.

Her belly quivered. Miles of pale, bare skin burned in his vision. "What do you think I'm doing?" she drawled. "Using sex to close out an argument."

He blinked. "B-but you said that wasn't a good way to communicate."

She smiled at him with such dazzling sexual charm he became dumbstruck. "That's true when a man uses sex as a weapon. But a woman? Well, that's completely allowed. Can we make up now and watch *Love It or List It*?"

"Yes."

He was on her in two seconds. Lifting her up and pressing her down onto the clean wood table. Knowing he'd never make it into the bedroom, Wolfe took what he wanted and swore he'd cherish for the rest of his life.

His woman.

She never had a chance. His mouth devoured hers, delving deep while he ripped off the tiny shorts and spread her legs. The moment his fingers slipped inside, her wetness coated him, but he couldn't wait. This was no foreplay or slow, sweet teasing. This was pure sex and taking and hunger, so he maneuvered his belt open, took his dick in hand, dragged her to the end of the table, and paused at her entrance.

Ripping his mouth from hers, he gave the command. "Grip the edges of the table and don't let go."

She did.

One deep thrust and he was buried inside.

She moaned. Arched. Held on to the table like it was the only thing in the world to save her. And it was.

Wolfe held nothing back, pounding inside her drenched,

silken pussy over and over, refusing to let up the pace or give her time to recover. She cried his name, bit down on her lower lip, and came.

He didn't stop. Raising her higher so his piercing scraped her clit, he refused to slow, forcing her into another orgasm, while she begged and yelled and wept with pleasure.

Then he did it again.

Her body slumped helplessly underneath him. Her fingers gentled and she surrendered into the biting pleasure/pain, giving herself over completely.

Wolfe let go, burying himself deep and spilling his seed. His hips jerked as the stinging satisfaction rolled over him in waves, dragging him under.

Spent, he kissed her belly, her lips, stroked her damp hair back. Looked into her eyes, the gorgeous navy blue that beckoned him to give in, give over, and love her completely.

"Have I told you how much I adore your communication skills?"

She smiled, wrapped her arms around him, and kissed him.

twenty-four

GENEVIEVE SKIPPED UP the steps like she had so many times as a child. "Hurry up, we're late."

Wolfe trailed behind her, shaking his head in amusement. "Whose fault is that? I was dressed and ready. You're the one who came out of the shower all wet and naked and inviting."

Heat burned her cheeks. Unbelievable she could still blush. He'd stripped away all modesty and barriers with his voracious sexual appetite and adoring appreciation for her body. Gen had never felt so gorgeous, even with her full curves. Even knowing he'd dated skinny models. It was if she was finally coming into her body in her late twenties, enjoying her own unique assets and not looking to be someone else.

"Shush, someone may hear you."

She ignored his low, sexy laugh and flung open the door. Now that things with David were a bit more settled, Gen was looking forward to spending quality time with her family without the crippling guilt. She'd moved on. David had moved on. Maybe her father would finally stop calling her with concerned questions and hopeful suggestions to contact David to try and work things out. Maybe he'd finally soften toward Wolfe, though she intended to keep their new relationship a secret.

Jim MacKenzie lit up and gathered her in a big bear hug. "About time. I was about to eat all the antipasto by myself."

"Mom has my back. Bet she hid some pepperoni just for me."

"I did!" came the yell from the kitchen.

Jim's smile slid off his face when he caught Wolfe standing behind her. He stiffened and gave him a polite nod. "Wolfe."

"Jim. How are you? Thanks for inviting me."

"Fine, thank you. Maria was the one who extended the invite."

Gen winced. Ouch. Her father was one of the kindest people she knew. His job as an alcoholism counselor put him in touch with varying types and he rarely held judgment. But something about Wolfe turned him into a stranger. She deliberately caught Wolfe's hand and led him inside. A show of unity. A silent *back off* to her dad.

Jim frowned.

"The whole crew here?" she asked, walking into the living room, where appetizers were already laid out and bottles of red and white wine were breathing. Her twelve-year-old niece, Taylor, was texting on her phone at the same time she bopped to music on her player.

Gen walked over and waved a hand in front of her. The blond-haired angel grinned, tore off her earbuds, and gave her a hug. "Hi, Aunt Gen! Hi, Wolfe. Aunt Gen, you are not going to believe it. I swear you will absolutely hit-the-floor die right now when you hear."

She assumed her serious face. "Tell me."

Taylor's bright blue eyes gleamed with a secret. Oh boy. She knew that look well. She and Izzy had perfected the art. "I'm going to Paris."

Whoa. "Are you kidding me? Your mother's letting you travel overseas? For what?"

"There's a special foreign-language transfer student program I want to sign up for. I spend the month in Paris, learning French and the customs, and stay with a family. Do you believe this?"

Gen looked around for intervention from her insane brother and sister-in-law. This could not be possible. "When are you going?"

"When I'm sixteen."

Relief sagged her shoulders. Wow, that was a close call. "So, you're telling me in only four years you're going to live in Paris, learning French and being generally fabulous?"

"Yes!"

"I can't believe it! I'm so excited!" She jumped up and down with Taylor, squealing and holding hands, while Wolfe laughed behind them. "I'm so coming to visit you."

"Totally."

Lance and Gina came in from the backyard, and they launched into a discussion about traveling and how Maria never allowed them to go farther than the next-door neighbor's.

"I don't understand these children today." Her mother sighed, setting down a tray of bruschetta in front of them. Wolfe dove at the same time as her father, and Wolfe jerked back, allowing him the win. "What's wrong with staying home? Plenty of time to do traveling later in life. You all turned out fine."

Lance kicked back in the chair, feet propped up on the worn ottoman. "Gina may disagree with you, Mom. Says I have issues."

Gina and her mother both swatted him on opposite sides. Taylor giggled.

"Where's Alexa and Nick?" Gen asked.

"Lily has a virus, so they're both staying home tonight. I'll bring her chicken soup tomorrow."

Gen smiled. She loved how her mom's chicken soup cured illness and general malaise. They plunged into general conversation, with teasing, jibes, and lots of wine. Her mother had just declared dinner ready. Everyone got up and began filing into the dining room, when a loud bang echoed through the house.

Izzy walked in.

Gen stared. Her sister had stopped coming to family dinners a long time ago. She remembered that fateful dinner when Izzy had barged in hopped up on drugs, sneering at their so-called happy family and launching personal attacks on everyone. Gen shuddered at the memory.

So much hurt and betrayal, as if they were living through their father's alcoholic spiral all over again. When her father finally threw her out, yanking all privileges to visit in a symbol of tough love, Izzy swore never to return.

She'd been clean for a while now, but something was different. Usually her razor-sharp wit, sarcasm, and raw energy shimmered around her. Today, she looked . . . reserved. Troubled. Her pitch-black hair with purple streaks was pinned up from her face. She'd gone easy on the makeup, allowing the same freckles Gen sported to pop through. Navy blue eyes that matched her own were clear but held a weariness she hadn't seen before.

The rest of the family seemed frozen, caught between surprise and worry that her good behavior was a mirage.

Wolfe broke the silence and stepped forward. "Izzy, it's good to see you. Hope you didn't want any antipasti. We pretty much annihilated it."

Was that relief that flickered across her face? A half smile curved her lips, which were a natural pink rather than bloodred. She wore jeans and a simple black T-shirt, baring two of her tats. Sneakers instead of spiked metal heels were on her feet. "Gen always hoarded the pepperoni anyway."

Joy surged through her, and not caring how uncool or how much her twin hated it, she launched herself for a tackle hug. "I'm so happy you're here!"

Izzy laughed and hugged her back. Red tinged her cheeks. "Me, too."

They both turned at Maria's voice, slightly husky from emotion. "My beautiful girls are here to dine with us. Today is a gift."

Jim cleared his throat. "Perfect timing, sweetheart. Let's go dig in."

Dinner was idyllic. Izzy was quiet, but smiled more often. Her usual snarky comebacks were nonexistent. Gen noted her gaze consistently darted around the table, as if studying everyone's mood. Did she have some type of announcement to make? Better to play it cool and let her sister open up when she felt comfortable. The idea of having a real relationship with her again made her heart ache with need. All those late nights giggling and sharing secrets. The way Izzy protected her from the bullies at school who made fun of them for looking alike. Crying together over the loss of their father, and holding hands under the table during the bitter fights between their parents. So many memories tumbling past her vision, and an ache she'd never been able to get over. As if a piece of her was always missing.

So she enjoyed her sister's presence, drinking her in, and let the warm glow of family wash over her. Wolfe was comfortable with everyone but her father, so he got involved in the playful banter without hesitation.

God, she loved him.

Gen ducked her head and concentrated on her plate. How easy the admission was. No fanfare or drama. Just a quiet knowledge that all roads had led to Wolfe. All the pain, and growth, regrets of the past meant nothing now. In fact, the present was even sweeter for having found him on her own. Their timing had never been right before.

Until now. She had a chance. The plan was simple. Let him lead, follow Arilyn's advice, and let the moment rule. One day he might just look up and realize he loved her, too. Realize it wasn't that scary, and that he could finally trust her with his past.

"You look really happy."

Gen tilted her head and gazed at her mother. The quiet words and knowing look gave her an approval she couldn't have asked for but received anyway. "I am," she said.

"Is David bothering you anymore?" Gina asked with concern. "That whole restraining order was really scary."

Gen's father mumbled something under his breath. Wolfe glared at her.

"He delivered all my stuff back," she said. "He's decided to take a position in Boston, so he'll be moving soon."

"Does that mean you're going back to the hospital?" Lance asked.

Her gaze slid past Wolfe, who watched her with a burning intensity. "Maybe."

"Why is it even a question?" Lance demanded. "You're too far into your residency to quit. If seeing David was the main reason, you shouldn't hesitate."

Her family stared, waiting for an answer. She didn't have one yet. She wanted to go back, but this time she refused to let anything or anyone stand in her way. Was she ready to recommit to endless work shifts, a sparse personal life, and the all-consuming resentment of everyone at the hospital? Was she looking at things differently because of her feelings for Wolfe? Gen finally spoke. "I need a little more time, Lance. If I go back, I know what's waiting for me. I love medicine, but it's a grueling schedule and takes everything out of me."

Lance shook his head. "The longer you wait, the harder it will be. I say dive back in. Start on Monday. It's not like you have a personal life or a fiancé anymore."

Gina and Maria gasped. "Lancelot, you do not talk like that to your sister!"

"I didn't mean it like that, Mom. I just wanted to point out she has no barriers any longer. I'm sorry, Gen."

Gen waved her hand in the air. "I know what you meant. I'll make my decision soon. I'd appreciate the support without pushing me about it."

Lance tightened his lips but remained silent. Jim glared at Wolfe as if the entire dialogue was completely his fault. And Izzy ducked her head, concentrating on her plate like it held all the answers in the world.

What on earth was going on?

No announcements came at dinner, so Gen decided to take the leap. "Izzy, will you come upstairs with me? To talk?"

Her family took the lead and shooed them away, telling her they'd clean up. They climbed the spiral staircase and went to their old room. As they opened the door, a slight mustiness rolled over them, but much of the room was still the same. Pink walls. Shelves and knickknacks and the same scrolled white furniture. Same mirror with postcards, stickers, and old pictures. The beds had been replaced with one queen-size mattress for guests, but as they sat on the bed, all the years growing up together came surging back.

Izzy sat next to her. "Our room seems like it's been locked in a time capsule. I wonder if that old *Playgirl* magazine is still in the closet," she commented. "Mr. September."

Gen laughed. "I was such a wreck Mom would find it! Should we check?"

The old wicked grin curved her sister's lips. "Definitely." She dragged a chair over, opened the closet, and reached up high to move one of the ceiling tiles. When they discovered one had broken, they'd kept the hiding spot as the go-to place that Maria would never find. Izzy jumped off the chair, waving a worn, tattered magazine in the air. "Got it!"

"No way. Bring it over."

They squeezed together on the bed, flipping through the pages. Giggles broke through as they commented on their old favorites, groaned over some obscene positions, and reminisced about the good old days. "Every time Mom made us go to church, I'd think about this magazine to get even," Izzy said. "Talk about Catholic guilt."

Gen tugged at her sister's ponytail. "I used to try and come up with good sins for Father Jonas. But when Tim and I fooled around in his car and he got to second base, I refused to share. I remember confessing to God at night in secret, hoping it would be good enough."

Izzy laughed. "I never confessed anything I wasn't truly sorry about," she quipped. "Maybe that's why I never went to confession."

Their gazes met and they burst into laughter. Her throat tightened with emotion. "I missed you," she said softly.

Izzy nodded. Her hand slowly reached out to snag hers. Gen almost held her breath, hoping it was real. "I missed you, too. I—I don't want to talk about the past now. Or how screwed up everything got. I came over tonight because I realized that as bad as things were between us, I wasn't there when you really needed me. After David. I thought you had a picture-perfect relationship, like the rest of your life. I never suspected he was trying to control or hurt you."

"Yeah, I didn't realize it at first either. And by the time I did, I was also keeping the secret. It happened so gradually. And then it felt too late. We were engaged, and everyone loved him, and I didn't want to disappoint anyone."

Izzy stared at their linked hands. "Funny, huh. You lived your life not wanting to disappoint anyone. I lived mine trying to do it first, so I'd never have expectations to fail. Guess we both made mistakes."

Gen smiled, blinking back the sting of tears. "Yeah, guess so."

"You're sleeping with Wolfe."

Gen jerked back. "H-how did you know?"

Izzy smiled. "I can just tell. He's a good guy. He tried to help me many times but I hated him, too. I was in a bad place for a long time, Gen. I don't want to go back there anymore."

"Then don't."

Her twin squeezed her hand. "I won't. Does Wolfe make you happy?"

"We're just friends with benefits. At least, that's what he thinks."

"You love him."

Gen closed her eyes and surrendered to the beauty of admitting it aloud to one person in the world. "Yeah. I do. Not sure what's going to happen, but that's how I feel."

Izzy gave a long sigh. "Complicated, huh? It's obvious he's crazy about you. Always was. Just be careful. He has a lot of stuff going on inside, and you already got your heart broken once."

Sadness threatened but she beat it back. "I know. I'm not gonna push. Maybe we'll just find our way."

"Maybe."

"Why did you hate him?"

Izzy smiled faintly. Raw pain reflected on her face, but Gen didn't ask questions. Just held her hand. "I didn't really. I think I recognized he got to the other side. I did stuff I'm not proud of. Got a way to go to climb from underneath. Seems I'm always searching for disaster."

"I'm here if you want to talk. I won't judge. Not anymore."

Her sister gazed at her directly. A flash of understanding passed between them. "Thanks. I want us to—" She stopped, dragged in a breath, and tried again. "I want us to have a relationship again. I'm so tired of being angry. Tired of hurting you and everyone I love. I want my sister back."

This time she didn't bother to blink back the tears. She just let them flow. "Me, too."

Gen reached for her, hugging tight, and for the first time in many long years, Izzy hugged back just as tight.

WOLFE SIPPED HIS SAMBUCA, enjoying the burning hot flavor of licorice coating his throat. The chatter of voices in the kitchen rose, but Maria had kicked him out, so he prowled the outside deck, enjoying the fall evening. The lawn spread out before him, bright green and cheery. A weeping willow tree stood by an old swing set, a bit battered and rusted. He imagined Gen growing up here, surrounded by friends and family who cared. Even with the troubles with her father and Izzy, they had battled through and triumphed.

The box bolted and locked deep within his soul shuddered. Then grew silent again.

"Wolfe."

He turned his head. Jim MacKenzie slid the glass doors closed with a decisive click. Uh-oh. The older man's face was set in a serious expression that didn't bode well for him. Why did he have a bad feeling about this?

"Jim. Great night, huh?"

He didn't answer. Just studied him with a narrowed gaze. What had he done to inspire such distrust? The entire family fully accepted him into the fold except Gen's father.

"Or maybe not," Wolfe muttered. He took another sip, wondering if he should just go back inside.

"I want to talk to you about Genevieve."

Yep. It was gonna be bad. Wolfe squared his shoulders, met his gaze, and nodded. "I figured something like this was coming. I'm not sure if I ever offended you, or did something out of turn. If so, I apologize."

His eyes softened a tad. "Actually, you didn't. You've always been polite in my home. Nice to my family. In a way, I'm sorry I've treated you with distance. I was actually hoping I'd never have to engage in this conversation, but now I realize I have no choice. I'm concerned that Gen is getting too close to you. I know you've been friends for a long time, and I kept a careful eye on it, but I never sensed a problem. Until she broke up with David."

Wolfe tightened his grip on the glass. "David hurt her. I hope you see that. I know you always defend him, but he's dangerous for your daughter, and I swear I'll never let him hurt her again."

Jim pointed his finger. "See? That type of protectiveness is growing. Do you know how many times you looked at each other during dinner? My daughter is glowing, yet she just broke up with her fiancé. She's seeing you in a new light, and I can't let that happen."

Shame filled him. Was he so bad that her father hated the idea of him being in her life? Inside, a dangerous battle raged, but he swallowed the emotions back and kept his face impassive. "Is it the piercings? The tat? What has you so worried?"

Jim shook his head. "Of course I don't like them, but that's not it. You see, Wolfe, you're just like me. One man recognizes the other. And I can't allow Gen to fall in love with someone who's eventually going to destroy her."

Wolfe jerked back. He respected Jim MacKenzie. He'd failed his family, followed the lure of alcohol, but managed to battle through and help others. Managed to heal his family. "I don't understand. You're a good husband. Father. You made amends for your mistakes."

Jim's eyes burned with purpose. "I'm an alcoholic. I grew up with demons chasing my every step. I thought Maria could save me, and she did for a while, but they found me and dragged me into the pit. I destroyed everything good. My wife. My kids. I brought pain and heartache, and I always knew it was there, waiting on the edges for the time when I was weak. Yes, I finally won. I got counseling, went to AA, dedicated my life to helping others and making sure my family never suffered again. I got lucky. They forgave me. But I look at you, and I see the same demons in your eyes. You run, you fight, but they'll get you, and you'll take Genevieve with you. I won't allow that. Not again. She's been through too much, and she deserves a good life. A career in medicine, and not a partner who's damaged."

The words floated, fell, and buried deep into his soul. Like a cigarette burn, it seared, then became dull. Lifeless. But Wolfe knew there would be a scar forever. *Damaged*. Jim knew it whenever he looked at him. As if he knew what happened on that night so long ago.

The years spent building himself back up and surrounding himself with the support of Sawyer and Julietta blew away in a cloud of smoke. Suddenly he was back where he had started. Penniless, empty, living on the streets with nothing. Wanting to die but being sentenced to live.

Her father was right.

Gen deserved more.

Amazingly, his voice sounded steady. "You're right, of course. And I understand."

Jim looked startled, peering at him with suspicion. He studied him for a long time before slowly nodding.

The door opened.

Izzy and Gen came out, arms linked. "What are you guys doing out here?" Gen asked.

Jim laughed. "Just guy talk. Is dessert ready?"

"Almost." Gen smiled at him, her eyes lit with a hidden joy from being with her sister. It was also part of her nature. She was light, happiness, life. She was . . . everything.

He forced himself to smile back. "Sounds good. The mosquitoes are biting tonight. I'll meet you inside."

He turned and went inside, knowing once again everything had changed.

twenty-five

I'M GOING TO Italy. I'll be gone for a while."

Gen studied his profile. Something had happened. His usual ease and humor was gone. In its place was a stiff, reserved man who spoke to her politely, smiled in the right places, and was completely numb.

"Oh. To see Sawyer and Julietta?"

"Yes. He wants me to come out for a while. I forgot to tell you about it. I'll be leaving in a day or two."

She backtracked and tried to keep up. Why did he sound funny? As if he was reciting a speech? Gen flipped through the past twenty-four hours. Nope, the sex had been amazing. The drive and dinner at her parents' tonight were fine. He'd joked, relaxed, and treated her normally. Then she'd found him on the deck with her father and—

Her father.

Yes. During dessert he refused to participate in conversation. Acted like a robot. Something had transpired between them and it wasn't good. Uneasiness skittered through her. She was going to murder her father for getting involved.

Gen kept calm. "Sounds wonderful. I know you've missed them."

"Yes."

"What did you and my father talk about?"

His fingers tightened around the steering wheel in a death grip. Bingo.

"Nothing."

"Bullshit."

His brows snapped together. They pulled into Verily and crawled down Main Street. "It was nothing. Football."

"He doesn't talk about football."

"Baseball, then. The Mets, of course."

"It was bad, wasn't it?"

He didn't answer. She dragged in a breath and got ready to dig her heels in and attack the problem head-on.

Until she saw her house.

Wolfe eased to the curb. The bright yellow bungalow with white shutters suddenly seemed menacing and evil. In bloodred spray paint, the word *whore* was scrawled across the front of the house.

Wolfe cut the engine and muttered a curse. He flew out of the car, immediately scanning the scene for lingering intruders. She climbed out, mouth gaping at the dirty, hateful word destroying her safe haven. Why? Why would someone do this?

David.

He'd brought her stuff back. Was leaving the hospital. Or so he said. Was this just another angle to control and break her mentally?

"Stay here. I'm gonna check the house."

She watched him walk around the property and disappear inside. After a while he came back out, flipping open his phone and hitting three numbers. "I don't see anyone around. I'm calling the police. It's going to be all right."

A combination of horror and outrage flooded her. Wolfe spoke quickly into the phone while she stared at the vandalism. How dare he try to steal her sense of safety? This type of humiliation had his signature all over it. Cowardly. Manipulative. Her fists clenched with the urge for retaliation.

In minutes a siren screamed, the familiar red and blue lights flashing madly and interrupting the serenity of the small town.

The car pulled up next to them and Officer Stone Petty climbed out. His uniform was slightly wrinkled, but he radiated a dominant, brutal energy that reminded everyone he was in charge and things were on his terms. His sharp eyes took in the scene as he slowly walked forward. His leather shoes squeaked on the concrete. "Ms. MacKenzie. Wolfe. You call this in?"

She tilted her head way, way back to meet his gaze. "Yes."

"You just get back home?" He jerked his head toward the house.

"We went to dinner at Gen's parents' house. Just pulled up and saw this. I looked quickly around the property and in the house but didn't find anything. Then I called 911."

Disapproval tightened those brutal lips. "Never go inside the house. Always call it in—you never know what you'll find."

Another car door slammed. Officer Devine joined them. His caramel hair looked slightly tousled, and his uniform was sharply pressed. He greeted them with a friendly, open look, and exchanged words with Petty.

"The ex?"

"Maybe." Petty turned to them. "Have you heard from Dr. Riscetti lately?"

Gen nodded. "He came to see me over on Main Street. Asked to talk. We spoke briefly, and he said he's moving to Boston and that I should go back to the hospital. He apologized for his behavior, but I told him I'd never forgive him. He seemed apologetic. He returned my stuff this weekend."

Petty nodded, making some notes. "Did he say anything about Wolfe at the time? Threaten you again? Insult you?"

"He said Wolfe was an asshole and I was above him."

Wolfe shook his head. "Called me an asshole, huh? Well, he's the real asshole. And if you guys don't get your shit together, I'm going to do things my way."

Officer Petty raised a brow. "I hope I didn't hear that. Stay here, please. We're going to look over the house and grounds, and then take some more information."

Wolfe simmered with impatience but managed a quick nod. Officer Devine shot them a sympathetic smile and the cops began doing their thing. The ugly red word made her gut twist. *Whore.* What would the neighbors think? She wanted it off now. Scrubbed clean.

"We'll fix it," Wolfe said, as if knowing her thoughts. "He's not getting near you, Gen. Not with me here."

She thought of him leaving for Italy and being alone in her once-safe house. No panicking. She'd be fine. If she got spooked, she'd stay with Kate. Or Arilyn. Or at her parents'. David wasn't going to run her life any longer, and it was time she dealt with this.

Gen squinted at the sight of a slender, ethereal figure floating down the sidewalk. A ghost?

"Are you okay? What happened? I heard the sirens and saw the lights, but I wasn't sure it was for you. Gen, why aren't you talking?"

She almost laughed at the sight of Arilyn hauling ass in a long white cotton nightgown. Bare feet, hair loose, she looked like she belonged in another century, the moonlight bathing her in mist. She was no image though. Strong hands pulled her in for a hug, as if she needed to make sure her body was intact.

"What are you doing here? I'm fine. We just got back from dinner at my parents' and found this."

Fierce heat glowed in her friend's green eyes. "I'm babysitting Robert tonight for Kate. They're in the city for a business dinner. I heard the sirens." Her gaze studied the ugly word and she pressed her lips together. "Now I'm done. Your ex has officially pushed me too far. I'm gonna get him."

It was so rare to find Arilyn in any type of temper. Gen actually laughed, her mood lifting at the mama bear protectiveness of her friend.

"Get in line," Wolfe muttered. "He's a dead man."

"Are the cops here? Did they take forever again when you called? I hope it's somebody more qualified than that Stone Petty. I don't think he knows what he's doing."

"Ms. Meadows. What a pleasure to meet you again. Or not."

Arilyn spun around and glared. The cop towered over her, even with Arilyn's impressive height. But her friend didn't seem to care, stepping forward and bristling with outrage, even in her white gown and bare feet. "Is this finally enough evidence to lock that psycho up?" she challenged. "Or do you need CSI to do some forensics?"

"A spray-painted insult doesn't warrant a CSI investigation, Ms. Meadows," the officer drawled. "It's ugly, juvenile, and a call for attention. But not a death threat."

Arilyn's lips twisted. "Great. So David has to verbally threaten her with murder for you to do your job? Do you plan to do any work at all or sit back until she's in real danger?"

Officer Petty practically snarled, lowering his face closer to hers. "Maybe if I didn't get interrupted constantly by snooping neighbors who believe they have all the answers, I could actually use my time to investigate instead of defend my job."

"I don't snoop," she challenged. "And perhaps we need a different officer here to confirm the investigation is done properly."

Gen made a squeak. Wolfe didn't say a word. Devine looked fascinated.

A muscle ticked in Petty's jaw. "Perhaps you need someone to keep you in line and out of trouble. And since no one else will volunteer for the job, perhaps it's gonna be me. How about a night in jail for police interference?"

"You wouldn't dare. First I'll report you. Then I'll sue you."

He gave a mean laugh. "Go ahead. I'll look forward to it."

She gasped. "I don't like you!"

"I don't like you either." His voice dropped to a growl. "Now, be a good girl and get out of my way so I can finish up here and get some donuts."

Arilyn stepped back. And fell silent.

Yep. Round two went to Officer Petty.

The sound of a walker slapped against concrete and the blazing light from her next-door neighbor's house gave fair warning. The evening was about to get much worse.

Mrs. Blackfire reached them, her beady eyes peering over her thick glasses. She wore house slippers, a hairnet, and a faded pink housedress. She took in the bloodred scrawled word on Gen's once happy house, the flashing lights, the policemen, and Arilyn's ghostly half nakedness.

"What's going on around here?" she snapped out. "This is my neighborhood and I'm a taxpayer. I demand to know who did this."

"More taxpayers," Petty muttered under his breath. "Why'd I ever come to Verily?"

"Is this a sex thing?" Mrs. Blackfire asked. "I saw this on *20/20*. Is this woman running a brothel?"

Gen's eyes widened. "No! I'm the victim here and I did nothing wrong. Someone vandalized my property."

Officer Devine stepped in. "Ma'am, you live next door to Ms. MacKenzie? Did you see or hear anything?"

Mrs. Blackfire snorted. "No, I fell asleep early tonight with the TV on. I woke up when I heard the sirens."

Devine scribbled something down. "Name, please."

"Mrs. Joan Blackfire. Who would do such a thing?" Her gaze narrowed on Wolfe. "You! Snake! Do you have any Jet friends who want to cause trouble?"

Gen waited for Wolfe to lose his temper, but his eyes flickered with a touch of amusement. "It's Wolfe. And no, my friends would never do this. It's her crazy ex."

"We don't know that," Petty said.

"Maybe if you investigated we'd find out who really did it," Arilyn said.

Petty smothered a curse. Arilyn glared. Officer Devine cleared his throat. "No evidence of intrusion, so it was kept to the outside. Other than Dr. Riscetti, is there anyone else who would make you suspicious? Girlfriends you fought with? Women after Dr. Riscetti?"

"No," Gen said. "There are many people at the hospital who were angry with me, but we've had no contact for weeks. I haven't fought with anyone. The only person that makes sense is David."

Officer Devine nodded and took out a business card. "Here's a company that can do discreet and quick cleanup for the house. Your insurance should pay for it minus the deductible."

Her fingers trembled as she took the card. "Thanks. Will you let us know after you speak with him?"

"Yes. We'll get his whereabouts, delve a bit deeper, and see what we come up with. I'll also be asking your other neighbors if they saw anyone. Unfortunately, if there's no witnesses, we may not get the person."

Arilyn snorted.

Petty glared.

"Thanks for your help," Wolfe said. "You have our cell phones?"

"We're set."

Mrs. Blackfire raised her voice. "Officers, while I have

you both here, can you please look at that tree?" Her bony finger stabbed the air toward the large, graceful pine tree bending slightly over. "It's diseased and ready to fall on my property. I'd like you to advise her to cut it down."

Gen closed her eyes. The violence of the night faded under the ridiculousness of the whole situation. A chuckle almost escaped her lips. Leave it to her crazy neighbor to put things in perspective. The Tree of Spite rustled slightly in the wind as if it, too, were laughing at her.

Officer Petty let out an impatient breath. "You need to call your insurance company, Mrs. Blackfire. Or a tree service. We can't help you with this issue."

Her eyes narrowed. "You don't do much for the taxpayers, do you?"

Stone Petty tightened his lips and turned his back, stomping to the police car. Devine grinned and followed.

Mrs. Blackfire finally went home. Arilyn squeezed Gen's hand. "You'll stay with me tonight, Gen."

"No. I'll take her to my place," Wolfe announced.

Arilyn's mouth dropped open. The vocal claim went beyond friendship and into intimate lover territory. Gen's first instinct was to agree, but she wasn't about to allow David to chase her from her home again. "I'm staying here. I'll be fine."

Wolfe's jaw clenched. "I don't think—"

"He's not going to win." She practically spit the words in fury. "He's a coward and I refuse to leave my house."

Wolfe muttered a curse, then nodded. "Fine. We'll stay here."

Arilyn took in the conversation with interest. "Let me know if you need anything," she finally said.

"I will."

They hugged good-bye and Arilyn went back to Kate's house. Gen grasped the doorknob and stepped inside her bungalow. Wolfe followed.

They gazed at each other in silence for a while. "I'm not running anymore," she finally said.

"Yeah. I know. I just don't trust him."

She set down the card Officer Devine had handed her and rubbed her temples. "I don't want you to worry about me when you're in Italy. I'll have Arilyn come stay with me, or my sister."

"I was thinking I had a better idea."

"What?"

"Come with me to Italy."

Gen blinked. Was he nuts? She couldn't go to Italy. She was too busy with stuff. Work. Family. Friends. Work. "I can't just leave everything and bop off to Italy. People don't do that. I have responsibilities here."

"You work for your best friends. I think they'll agree you need a vacation and give you the time off."

Gen shook her head. "No. I refuse to be treated like a child you constantly worry about leaving behind. I'm not going to Italy."

His slow smile heated her blood, curled her toes, and scared her silly. "I'll just have to change your mind, won't I?"

She crossed her arms in front of her chest. "You can't make me do anything. You may think this hot-blooded caveman behavior is sexy, but you're dead wrong."

The corner of his lip lifted. "Better call Kate and tell her you leave Tuesday."

"I'm not going to Italy. And I'm not sleeping with you tonight."

He kept silent, but his knowing grin did bad things to her tummy and other places. Gen promised herself she'd stand strong on both counts.

"We'll see."

She stuck out her tongue and swore on a stack of mental Bibles she'd never weaken.

Never.

This was one standoff she was going to win.

GENEVIEVE COULDN'T BELIEVE IT.

She was in Italy.

The last two days had passed in a blur. Her friends took her off the work schedule without pause, pushing her when she resisted with lame excuses, and even helped her pack. She had to hand it to Wolfe.

He never even said I told you so.

The car crawled through the busy streets of Milan toward the house she'd been dying to see. Pedestrians clogged the sidewalks, mopeds roared in and out of traffic, and a heavy, smoglike mist settled over the city. Wolfe laughed as she twisted madly around, trying to soak in all the sights, sniffing the delicious scents of bread and coffee and exhaust that mixed together in a bouquet to the senses.

The crumbling three-story building looked a bit worn when they finally stopped. Huh. She'd imagined Julietta and Sawyer lived in a mansion, but the place did emanate a quaint character she loved. Lots of terra-cotta, brick, plants, and flowers surrounded her. The driver took their bags, but before her feet hit the ground, Wolfe's family rushed out, screaming and yelling in Italian, and smothered him whole.

Gen stared. Wolfe had never liked being touched by too many people. When they made love, there was no barrier between them, but in daylight, distance always radiated around him. He was always polite to people, shook hands, but seemed to scream hands off. He'd slowly opened up more with her own family, but he seemed to allow it rather than steeping himself in affection.

Her heart clenched as he threw himself into their arms with open enthusiasm, accepting the bond of affection that was even stronger than blood, because it was pure love by choice. Gen blinked back tears, enjoying the scene, until he managed to break away and reach his hand out to her. Slowly, she took, it, and he pulled her against him.

"I finally brought Genevieve," he said in a gruff voice. "Convinced her take a vacay and spend some time with us."

"Finally!" Julietta squealed, tugging her in for a family hug that rivaled her mother's. Julietta was more beautiful than ever, her long dark hair flowing over her shoulders, and almond-shaped eyes filled with a joyous light and mischief. Dressed in tailored black pants, a sleeveless ivory blouse, and ballet flats, she exhibited pure elegance and grace.

Gen laughed and hugged back. "Wolfe didn't give me much of a choice. Thank you so much for letting me stay with you."

Sawyer grinned and pressed a kiss to the top of her head. "We've been dying to get you over here. You work too hard." His golden eyes gleamed with affection, a complete contradiction to the wicked scar that gouged his cheek and hooked under his chin. His lips curved in an easy smile, and the lean, angular features of his face seemed softer than normal. Probably because of baby Gabriella. Wolfe said Sawyer was baby crazy and sometimes babbled in meetings now, forgetting when he was around adults. She loved imagining such a strong, dominant male softening under a baby's coo.

Julietta linked her arms with Gen's and led her upstairs. "We'll eat, settle in, and plan our itinerary. I know you'll want to do some sightseeing."

"And babysitting," Sawyer added with a wink. "Gabby's napping now, but she'll be up soon."

Wolfe groaned. "I knew there was a reason you needed me."

Sawyer's next words took away her breath. "I don't need a reason to want you here, Wolfe. I missed the hell out of you."

He clapped Wolfe on the shoulder and Gen could swear the light glinted off some moisture in her lover's eyes, but it was gone so quickly she figured it was her imagination.

WOLFE GRINNED AT THE expression on Gen's face when she saw the inside of the home. He knew the outside was deceiving, but once the arched door opened, the space dazzled the eye. Shiny parquet floors, old gleaming wood that smelled of lemon polish, vaulted ceilings with heavy chandeliers, and an array of antiques and paintings that reminded one of another time. He'd normally find such decorations cold, but not with Julietta and Sawyer. It was all home, from the touches of magazines and books, various crocheted blankets in bright colors, baby gates guarding the elaborate steps, to the rush of garlic, tomato, and bread simmering in the air.

He was home.

Julietta took Gen for a tour while he walked to the kitchen with Sawyer. "You look good."

Wolfe turned with a grin. "Thanks. Bet you miss all the piercings and crazy hair though."

Sawyer laughed and handed him a bottle of water. "Nah, I like the man you've become. But I always gave you credit. I still remember picking you up that first day. Within a few days, you managed to kill your hair and get a tattoo and more piercings than I can imagine. You gave me a big fuck you. Remember what you said?"

Like it was yesterday. "I said, 'What do you think now? I'm as fucked-up on the outside as I am on the inside. Still want me?'"

Sawyer nodded. "Swear to God, I think I loved you right then. You were such a pain in the ass."

Wolfe shook his head, taking a long swallow of water. "You needed a challenge."

"I did. I'm glad you brought Gen. Surprised, but glad."

"Why?"

Sawyer frowned, as if thinking about the question.

"You never cared about anybody enough to want to bring them home. I know you've been friends for a long time, but this feels different. You're together now?"

Wolfe stiffened. He didn't want Sawyer or Julietta thinking it was permanent or long-term. It would only complicate matters and maybe embarrass Gen. Better to keep it to friendship and not admit they were sleeping together. He forced a smile. "Nope, still just great friends. Since she broke up with her fiancé, I thought a trip would be good for her."

Sawyer studied him for a while. Those razor-sharp eyes pierced and shredded through the lies, just like they had when he was young. But he accepted the declaration for now. "Sure. Either way, I'm glad you're both here."

"Looking forward to catching up. Besides babysitting, I have a feeling there's something else you want to talk about?"

"Yeah. But I'd like for all of us to sit down together. Tonight if that's okay? Over dinner?"

"Absolutely. You cooking?"

"Do I ever?"

Wolfe laughed. "Good. Some things never change."

They grinned at each other, then walked into the kitchen.

It was gonna be a hell of a week.

twenty-six

WOLFE SAT IN the library, which did double duty as Sawyer's office. Settling into the generous curved leather chair, he sipped cognac and let the quiet of the evening soak in. The low table held biscotti, some pastries from La Dolce Famiglia, and two other glasses filled with amber liquid. Julietta tucked her legs underneath her, leaning against the arm of the sofa, and Sawyer, who was sitting in the matching leather chair across from him, held a folder in his lap.

The scent of pipe tobacco permeated the air along with the aroma of liquor, musty paper, and leather. Wolfe took a deep breath and enjoyed the calm that spread over him. Gen had retired to her room early, and the window was open, letting in a soft breeze from the terrace.

"Thanks again for dinner," he said. "Between you and Gen cooking for me, I've been gaining some weight. Gotta kick Sawyer's ass in the gym this week and get myself back under control."

Sawyer snorted. "I may be old, but I can still take you any day. Wisdom beats age."

"Not in the gym."

Julietta laughed. "You're both winners. What do you mean Gen's cooking for you? I thought she lived in Verily."

He'd totally forgotten they didn't know he and Gen had been living together. Temporarily, of course. "Her ex was giving her problems, so I moved in for a while. Just to make sure she was okay."

Her shrewd gaze saw as much as Sawyer's, but she just nodded. "I see."

Wolfe steered the subject into safe territory. "How about you satisfy my curiosity on what's in the file? Something good? Did I inherit?" He waited for the laugh, but Sawyer's face tightened, as if he was stressed. A worried gleam lit his eyes. Wolfe leaned forward. "I'm just kidding. If it's a problem, I'll help you fix it."

Julietta gave a soft sigh. "Not a problem. Actually, it's something we've been waiting years for. Didn't know if it would happen. We just hope you're as happy as we are."

Okay, now he was getting freaked out. "Guys, you're killing me. Can you just tell me what's going on?"

Sawyer pulled out a document. His finger tapped steadily against the blue folder, his leg shaking just a bit. Yep. A definite sign of nervousness from his usually controlled guardian. Had he done something bad with Purity? Gotten them in trouble? Sickness clawed at his gut.

"Remember that conversation we had years ago? When you were about twenty-one?"

Wolfe let out an impatient breath. "We had a ton of conversations. Is there a specific one you're referring to?"

"Your adoption."

He stilled. His gaze flicked to the paper, then back up at Sawyer's face. He tried to gather his thoughts, unsure where the whole dialogue was going. "Yeah. You wanted to legally adopt me, and we went to court a few times, but there were issues. Made my name change look like a walk in the park."

Sawyer nodded. Julietta twisted her fingers, nodding as if to encourage Sawyer to keep talking. "We didn't know what happened to your mother at the time. I was more concentrated on keeping your life stress free. Didn't want to bring up the past. So I got my PI to get all the information, and we've been working on this for a number of years." Sweat gleamed from Sawyer's brow. Wolfe took another sip of cognac, knowing the next few minutes were about to be life changing.

"We found out about your mother, Wolfe."

He ducked his head, needing a minute. Knowing the answer. "She's dead."

Julietta reached over and squeezed his hand. He returned the pressure. "Yes, sweet boy. She died years ago. We found where she's buried. You can go see her if you want."

"Was it an overdose?"

Another slight pause. "Heart attack. Could've been the drugs, but there was no autopsy."

Wolfe wondered why he didn't feel . . . more. In a way, he'd grieved over his mother's death since he ran away that fateful night. She'd been dead to him, and he'd struggled with the fact for so long, the confirmation just cemented the knowledge that she was never coming back. "I'm okay," he said slowly. "I kind of expected it, and I dealt with this a while ago."

Sawyer nodded. "That's what we hoped, but hearing it aloud sometimes brings back nasty stuff."

"I appreciate you finding out for me."

"After we were able to confirm what happened to your mom, other items fell into place. We tracked down some necessary documents, and it's been in the legal system for a while. But we have our answer."

Wolfe cocked his head, still confused. "What answer?"

"Your adoption. We can legally adopt you as ours, Wolfe. And we want to, if you'll accept us."

The simple statement pierced through the shield of his heart and buried deep. Raw emotion exploded within him. He glanced back and forth, seeing the hope on Julietta's face, the tension in the way Sawyer clenched his jaw. They were nervous? Nervous he wouldn't want them? The shaking began, beginning with tiny goose bumps and breaking into shudders that began to wrack him from the inside. He'd been nothing before them. They'd done him a favor, taking in a smart-assed street kid with issues, and they were asking him if it was okay?

"We love you," Julietta whispered. "But if you don't want to go ahead with this, we understand. We won't be hurt. You'll always be ours, in every way that counts, but this would make it legal."

Sawyer put up his hands. "You can think about it as long as you want. If it's a no, we won't talk about it again, and there's no need to feel guilty. Understood? Whatever you want is what we want."

The word stumbled over his tongue and shot out into the world. "Yes."

His almost-legal parents stared at him. "Yes?" Julietta choked out. "You want to be ours?"

Wolfe let out a shaky laugh. "Hell, yeah, you think I'm crazy? I had no idea you were still pursuing it. I've always thought of myself as your son, but to finally have the papers to back it up? Hell, yes."

Sawyer grinned, joy lighting up his face. "Hell, yes!"

Julietta hugged him, and Sawyer just kept grinning like an idiot, too overwhelmed to try and hug it out, which Wolfe was grateful for. No way did he want to bawl like a pussy. But inside, he felt . . . different. More whole.

He really belonged to a family now. Legally. They belonged to him, just as much as he did to them.

Hell. Yes.

Sawyer pushed the folder over with a pen. "There's a ton of stuff to sign, but the lawyers already looked over everything. You'll have to get used to your new name though."

"Wolfe Wells." He repeated the name. "Umm, yeah. Not the best, but it's not like I have to get through middle school anymore."

They burst into laughter.

And he signed the papers.

GEN LAY ON TOP of the covers, staring at the gorgeous ceiling with the painting of the Madonna and Child overhead. Probably not cool if you wanted to have dirty hot sex, but since that wasn't happening tonight, maybe she should say a rosary instead. Her mother would be happy. Kind of.

Ugh.

She'd been exhausted from the trip, but also sensed

Wolfe needed some time alone with his family. After a nap, she was now wide awake and buzzing with energy. Didn't feel like reading. Her brain kept misfiring over the mixed signals Wolfe threw out. One minute he treated her like a buddy, bringing her on a trip to be nice and protect her from the big bad wolf. The next moment, he touched her and sexual electricity buzzed, and his eyes darkened with that hungry look as if he'd like to feast on her for hours in a really good way.

Unfortunately, he'd clearly set her up in a bedroom way down the hall from his. Like a sign he didn't intend to visit. Julietta and Sawyer obviously believed they were just platonic friends. Guess no benefits this week. Which was good. They'd decided to keep it open and flexible, even though she'd fallen in love with him.

A slight tapping echoed in the room.

She shot up from the bed and opened the door.

Wolfe stood in front of her, looking delicious in sweats, a tank top, and bare feet. His hair was mussed like he'd been dragging his fingers through the curls. He smelled like soap and a bit of liquor. "Did I wake you?"

"No. Can't sleep."

He shifted his feet. Those blue eyes flamed to life as his gaze raked over her, but he remained safely out in the hallway. "Wanna go for a walk?"

No. She wanted him to get naked, and get busy on her bed, but Gen nodded. "I'll change."

"You're fine."

She hesitated. Not expecting a late-night sex call, she'd sported flannel pants with pink flowers, and a matching pink V-necked T-shirt. Her hair was crazy from lying on the pillow, and she had no makeup on. Gen wrinkled her nose. "I'm a mess."

He reached over and linked his fingers with hers. The heat jumped like a live wire between them. She barely held back a hiss. "You're a beautiful mess," he said softly. "Just come walk with me."

She was such a sucker for this man. "Okay." She pulled on a pair of Keds and followed him down the stairs and into the night.

It was pitch-dark, apart from the occasional streetlight and the glow of the moon. Wolfe led her firmly down the path, keeping her hand securely locked in his. Their feet slapped against the cobblestones, and the ancient buildings thrust into the sky, surrounding and protecting them like beautiful old trees. Even late at night with the shops closed, pedestrians lingered, sipping espressos and clutching large bags from one of the most famous shopping streets in the world, Via della Spiga.

Wolfe seemed to have no direction. He swung her arm back and forth, lapsing into a comfortable silence, and she relaxed. When he finally spoke, he told her the earth-shattering news as if it was the most natural thing in the world to share. As if he'd been sharing intimate details with her forever.

"Sawyer and Julietta legally adopted me."

She stumbled and he quickly caught her. Gen gasped and gripped his hand. "What?"

His slow grin lit up his features. Lord, he was sexy. Gorgeous. Sexy. "Yeah. That was their big news and why they wanted me to come visit. We tried years ago, but they couldn't find my mother, and the paperwork was a mess. Went to court a few times but nothing really came of it. I assumed Sawyer quit, but he's been working on this the whole time."

"What did you find out about your mom?"

The grin slipped. "She died."

"I'm sorry."

He nodded. "I lost her a long time ago. I can't even be sad. She wasn't my mother anymore."

His simple words tore at her heart. To have a parent break you in half and destroy the innate love and trust of such a relationship haunted her. But Gen knew he didn't want her sympathy or tears or pity. He wouldn't have them either. She looked upon him as the victor. He got away, rebuilt, and found a family to love and cherish him. "I hate what you had to go through," she said softly. "I'd kill her myself with my bare hands for hurting you. But you got to the other side. And even though a piece of paper is important, Julietta and Sawyer were always your family anyway. I just love that we can celebrate it's legal."

He gazed off in the night, as if trying to express his thoughts. "I can't believe they wanted me," he finally said. "I was a pain in the ass. I mean, of course I wanted *them*, but the idea they never gave up trying to adopt me blows my mind."

She reached up on tiptoe, cupped his cheeks, and forced him to look at her. She memorized every beloved feature: the scruff around his jaw, the proud slanted nose, the strong dark brows, and those lightning-blue eyes that held secrets he'd never share. Gen choked on the words. "Because you give them just as much joy, Wolfe. You're special. They love you more than you can imagine, because you gave them precious gifts. Your trust. Your friendship. Your respect. Your heart. Everything you are."

"It'll never be enough."

She smiled at the ridiculous statement, and before she could slam down the barriers, her soul escaped and flew free.

"Don't you realize who you are? How you make people happy?"

The world tilted. Held its breath. And waited.

"Don't you realize how much I love you?"

He froze. She was reminded of a cartoon character with the balloon of words floating overhead, waiting for a response. Gen wanted to duck her head, laugh it off, and go back to their agreement. But it was too late. She couldn't take back the truth, or her real feelings. He might not like it, but dammit, he was going to have to begin dealing with it.

Seconds ticked by. A minute. He didn't move, refused to speak, just gazed at her with an all-consuming hunger that told her more than any answer could.

He pressed his forehead to hers, shaking his head back and forth, trying to deny the moment. "What are you doing to me?" he murmured. "This is going to lead to disaster."

A half laugh escaped. Her breath rushed over his lips. "Yeah. Probably."

"We should go back to the way things were. It'll be better."

"Don't want to."

"I can't give you what you want."

She closed her eyes and hung on tight. He could, but he didn't realize it. Didn't want to believe it. "I disagree."

"You're so stubborn. We shouldn't sleep together anymore. It's gotten too complicated."

"So deny me."

His lips hovered an inch from hers. "I can't. I'm wrecked. But I don't want to hurt you."

His mouth pressed, retreated, slid over her lips. She wrapped her arms around his shoulders. "So don't," she whispered back. Then kissed him.

Sweetness. Her knees weakened, and she slumped in his arms as his tongue slid between her lips and drank. He kissed her like she was precious treasure, fragile and worthy of the most exquisite tenderness. A whimper caught in her throat as he worshipped her with his mouth, and tongue, and lips, allowing his body to give her what his mind couldn't.

Everything.

"Take me to bed."

Her demand made a laugh escape his lips. He nibbled on her ear, bit her lobe, and caressed her back in long, sweeping strokes. "One last time."

"One last time," she repeated. The lie was easy to utter as he swept her up into his arms and carried her back to the house. She didn't care as he made love to her with such care and attention. She fought off her orgasm so she could revel in every touch and kiss he bestowed. When he finally surged inside her, she let herself go, shattering around him, telling herself another lie over and over as he claimed her throughout the night.

She loved him enough for both of them.

"I'M NERVOUS."

Wolfe looked down. She twisted her hands together, paused on the front step. Suddenly, the years whizzed past and the memory hit hard. Standing at Mama Conte's door for the first time, in his nice clothes and stiff shoes, waiting for a family dinner he didn't want or believe in. The resentment and misery of believing she'd mock him, or disapprove. The fear of going inside a real house with a real family and not being part of it.

He shook off the image. Julietta's mother, Mama Conte, was a legend, and though Gen had been dying to meet her, he understood the sudden anxiety. Besides raising four children and being the founder of the family bakery empire, La Dolce Famiglia, she seemed able to focus in on a person's secrets with a stunning ease. "She's going to love you. Trust me. When Alexa and Nick visited a while ago, Alexa learned how to make homemade pasta under her instruction, and it may be good for you to do the same."

That earned a grin and a punch in the shoulder. "Smart-ass. You just want to me to cook for you."

"Damn right."

He opened the door and they walked in. Gen drank in the scene before them, and Wolfe knew quite well what she was experiencing. He remembered it well, and the sights and sounds and smells always hit him hard every time he came to visit.

They'd taken the funicular up and walked to the large but intimate home situated on the hills in Bergamo. Wrought iron balconies held terra-cotta pots with bright geraniums and other flowers. The elaborate gardens twisted around the house and spilled into the backyard, leading to a patio where the family liked to sip wine and cappuccino, basking in the sun and the hills spread before them. The house itself held the Italian character he loved so much, from bare wood floors covered with braided rugs to photos lining the walls and cluttering the furniture, with all roads leading to the kitchen, the heart and soul of the Conte home.

Gen gasped. The solid pine table sat in the center. The stove and countertops were filled with fresh ingredients, from mozzarella and sliced tomatoes to bottles of olive oil and baskets of garlic. An herb garden lined the windowsill. Colorful towels were scattered about, and the table was already set with burgundy dishes and bowls in cheerful patterns laid upon a white lace cloth. The thick cutting board held fresh, crusty bread, and pots bubbled over, steam and an array of tantalizing scents fighting for dominance.

Nirvana.

There weren't many places he felt completely at peace, but Mama Conte's kitchen was one of them. The woman managing the dozens of pots at the stove turned, a welcoming smile curving her lips as she wiped her hands on her apron and moved forward.

"Oh, *mamma mia*, I didn't even hear the door! Darn hearing. Don't get old, my sweet boy. It is not good."

Wolfe gathered her in his arms and almost laughed at the fierce strength of her embrace. Those weathered hands had kneaded dough for so many years that she was stronger than some of the gym rats he worked out with. Her cane leaned against the counter, which she'd been relying on a bit more because of her arthritis. Her long gray hair was twisted up in her usual bun, and she wore a red housedress, apron, and comfortable shoes. Wolfe knew she'd been a knockout once, obvious from the graceful lines of her face, high cheekbones, and laughing inky eyes that reminded him so much of Julietta and her sister, Carina. She snapped the towel at him with expert ease when he finally pulled away.

"Where are your manners? You bring a girl with you and don't introduce her first?"

Heat flooded his cheeks. He cleared his throat and turned. "Genevieve MacKenzie, this is Mama Conte."

Gen smiled and opened her arms. Mama Conte hugged her just as tight, and studied her figure with a sharp assessment that was part of her charm. "You are just as beautiful as Alexa. I was able to meet your nieces when Alexa and Nick came to visit and stay with me. It still is one of my favorite memories."

"*Grazie*. It's also one of my sister's favorite memories. You made her feel welcome, and now she cooks homemade pasta for the family."

Mama Conte tilted her head back and laughed. "And so shall you. Not like my son Michael's wife. Margherita is always trying to duck out of the kitchen, but she does other stuff well so I shall forgive her."

Wolfe grinned. Maggie ranked cooking as one of her least favorite things to do. Mama Conte loved sparring with her daughter-in-law, and had fallen in love with her from the very first. She'd even been present for the birth of Maggie and Michael's twin boys.

"Come in and sit. Where are Julietta and Sawyer?"

"Right behind us. Gabby was napping so they decided to wait a bit."

Mama Conte shook her head. "Ah, once the *bambinos* come, it is a whole new world. It is exhausting, joyous, and the biggest adventure one can have, no?"

Wolfe grabbed a piece of bread, dipped it in olive oil and pepper, and handed it to Gen. Used to helping in the kitchen when he visited, he poured the Chianti and grabbed a slice for himself.

"Sit," Mama Conte said when he tried to help. "I want to hear everything from New York. Tell me about Purity and what you are up to."

He dove into brief chatter, keeping it light, and Gen joined in. He was surprised when she admitted she'd run out on her wedding, and that Wolfe had helped her. Even more startled when she shared her struggle to find her way back into medicine, questioning all of the decisions she used to swear she knew. He let her talk, loving the way she gave of herself so genuinely, not realizing it was a gift. Mama Conte listened, encouraged, and shared nuggets of wisdom that should one day be bound in a book and sold for profit.

By the time Julietta and Sawyer arrived with baby Gabby, they'd settled into a huge feast, with the sound of

Italian music drifting in the background from the speakers. A new gift from Michael, she admitted, and though she preferred a good thinking silence, she said she was starting to get into listening to music more often. The baby was passed around, and Wolfe nuzzled her gently, the sweet baby scent of powder and innocence drifting in his nostrils and soothing him.

"My turn," Gen demanded, holding out her arms. He completed the transfer, always the scariest part with infants, and watched her stare down at Gabby with complete adoration.

A wave of raw emotion slammed into him. His breath caught.

An image of Gen holding his baby—*their baby*—punched him in the gut. She kissed the top of her head, murmuring inane words that made Gabby coo, and the room spun around him like he was on a crazy bender.

What was going on? Yes, he'd enjoy watching his Gabby grow up. Loved being around big family gatherings with children running around. But children weren't in his future. Never bothered him before. Hell, he never even thought about it. But looking at Gen, and how she fit so perfectly in Mama Conte's kitchen with a baby in her arms, made his heart stutter a bit.

Why now? Why did he suddenly want, need, crave the idea of a future?

He pushed his plate away, no longer hungry. Touched the two leather wristbands that were now a part of his anatomy. And tried not to remember.

He was quiet for the rest of the meal. By the time the

grappa, fruit, cheese, and pastries appeared, Gen groaned. "I don't know if I can," she whined. "I'm so full."

Mama Conte shook her head in disapproval. "Why don't you get some air and walk a bit? It will help you digest; you cannot miss the apple cake."

Wolfe laughed as Gen rubbed her belly, trying to help it along. "Come on, I'll show you the terrace." They stood outside, overlooking the sloping hills and the endless blooming of green. The scent of earth and lemons drifted around them. He reached out to hold her, then suddenly realized he had no right. Not anymore. If he wanted to move the relationship back to friendship, he needed to stop touching her like a lover. Right now, it was too dangerous.

She stepped close, as if to wrap her arms around his waist, and he moved fast, heading toward the edge of the balcony. "Beautiful night." He refused to look back, his heart pounding. Would it always be this hard? Would he ever be able to look at her, tug on those curls, gaze into her face without wanting her with a hunger that was never satisfied?

"Yes."

"Are you having a good time so far?"

"How could I not? I'm in Italy, with you and your family. I've been fed, spoiled, and pampered. I adore Mama Conte and Gabby. I've shopped in some of the most exclusive shops in the world, ridden on a moped with you through the streets, and kissed you in the moonlight."

"Gen—"

"I love watching you here. You're different. More open. All this time, I thought I was part of that inner circle."

"You were. You are. We've been friends for a long time." The word spat from his tongue and sounded like a curse now. "I care about you."

"Not enough to share your past. Not enough to take me into your bed without lying about what we really are."

He flinched. She was going to kill him. Tear him into bloody pieces and scatter his ashes. Why did she have to demand so much now? He tried to keep things light. "I told you more than I have anyone else. You know about my druggie mother, the years spent on the streets, how Sawyer found me. What more do you want?"

"You know."

He refused to glance back. Kept his gaze trained on the scenery and prayed she wouldn't move close. She didn't. The distance between them yawned like an endless expanse of space growing bigger every moment he remained quiet. Birds screeched. The low hum of chatter and laughter from the kitchen drifted through the window. Finally, he spoke.

"It wouldn't make any difference."

Her sigh hurt his ears. Hurt his heart. So sad, yet here she still stood, fighting for something he could never give her. "How about this question: What do you want, Wolfe?"

Her body, soul, heart. To be enough of a whole man to give her everything. The courage to step forward and try.

Instead, he lied. "This. Us. Friends forever. We decided to include sex as long as it didn't affect our relationship. But let's admit things are getting complicated. Backing off may be a good idea now."

She never answered.

He never turned.

The doors opened and Mama Conte's voice rang out strong and true. "Come in, children. We're ready for the final course."

When Wolfe finally had the guts to turn around, Gen had already disappeared inside.

THE MEN LEFT.

Vincent Soldano lay on the floor in the fetal position, cradling his broken body. The horror of what they had done to him, made him do, flickered over and over in his mind like a broken record. He dug his nails into his temples and tried to rake out the images, the memory, but he was steeped in filth so deep, he knew he'd never climb out.

It was over.

If only he had run. If only he hadn't waited. Yesterday, he would've had a life to live. Today, there was nothing but shame and dirt and a nightmare so vivid he'd never sleep again.

He couldn't live like this. Wouldn't.

The low murmur of voices outside drifted through the thin walls. He turned his head, looking, his blurred gaze barely registering the items and familiarity of the room he'd grown up in. Vomit threatened when he caught the picture of his mother and him from years ago on the chipped mirror.

He didn't have a mother anymore.

He craved silence. Emptiness. Every muscle ached and burned, but he managed to crawl across the floor, looking for something, anything, looking for a sign.

The light glittered on the blade of the knife.

Slow, painful inches until he reached for it. His hand shook as he grasped it between his fingers. His head roared with agony, rage, pain so raw and encompassing that Vincent knew already his sanity had snapped, oozed out of him with the men and their rough hands and fingers and filthy bodies.

He would never be clean again.

He lifted the knife and turned his wrists over.

Began to cut. Over and over.

When the blood ran rich and red, peace finally came.

Vincent Soldano lay back on the floor and waited to die.

He was fourteen years old.

twenty-seven

WOLFE LEAPED OUT of bed, the scream trapped in his lungs. Sweat ran in rivulets down his body, and he quickly grasped his wrists, feeling the leather bands protecting, blocking out the memory. He dragged in a breath, used to the routine, and tried to calm his pounding heart.

Leaning over, he placed his hands on his knees and fought back the nausea. It had been a while since the scene had replayed so vividly in his head. Sure, the nightmares came regularly, but like a longtime enemy, they'd learned to live with each other. Sometimes he slept. Sometimes not. The deal and pact with the devil had been made years ago. When the devil came to visit, he went to the gym and pounded out the rest of the memories.

His head exploded with the images of years past. The knife. The men. The horror. The cowardice.

Out. He had to get out.

Shutting down to survival mode, Wolfe pulled on a pair of shorts, grabbed his sneakers, and left.

Down the stairs.

Through the hall.

More stairs.

Click on the light. The room lit up, a haven from the

night, a place Sawyer had built for both of them when the demons visited.

The workout room had soundproof walls, a kick-ass speaker system, and every piece of equipment imaginable. He donned his gloves and went straight to the punching bag. Free weights were scattered across the concrete floors, and mats hung haphazardly. A chin-up bar, rowing machine, and endless instruments of torture and healing lay before him, offering a glimpse back into the regular world.

He hit the button on the speaker and KISS came pounding out in waves of hard-ass metal.

Yep. Sawyer had been in here recently.

Wolfe got to work.

WHERE WAS HE GOING?

Gen lay awake in the dark and listened as someone walked down the stairs. Came from Wolfe's end of the hallway. She should lie here and try to go back to sleep. He'd been quite vocal in his determination to put her back in the friendship box, even after their incredible night of sex and orgasms and tenderness. He refused to even look at her now, choosing to engage in ridiculous conversation, duck his head, and keep far away from her in case she jumped him.

Which she had wanted to do. Plus beat him. But she kept her dignity and tried to remember Arilyn's advice. Live in the moment. Don't analyze or question. Let the day guide the relationship. Don't pressure.

Arilyn's advice really sucked.

Screw it. She'd follow him. Gen already knew he suffered from regular nightmares. Sometimes she'd wake to use the bathroom and find a tangle of empty sheets on the couch where he slept. She knew he liked to hit the gym or go running, but when she tried questioning him more about the nightmares, he shut back down again.

She padded on bare feet and tried to follow the trail. It took a few times and checking various rooms in the mansion before she finally found another door that led down a staircase. The knob turned easily in her fingers.

She stepped in.

The bold sounds of heavy-metal music, rough and angry, screamed through the speakers. The room was full of gym equipment, but there was only one focal point as she shut the door behind her.

Wolfe.

He stood in the center of the room. A large punching bag swung from a chain. He wore boxing gloves and the leather wristbands. Sneakers on his feet. Bare chested.

She sucked in her breath.

He was beautiful. Raw. His fists moved in a blur of pounding, attacking the bag over and over, sharp jabs, wicked lefts, feet planted as he beat the crap out of something imaginary, something that had broken him and changed him forever. His hips rotated with each punch, highlighting eight-pack abs. The serpent gleamed with sweat, twisting over his body like a friend and confidant.

Liquid dripped from his hair, brows, sliding down his chest. His eyes were dark slits, concentrated on another time, hate and fury whipping around him in waves. She stood completely still, not daring to breathe, her gaze clinging to the mass of rock-hard muscles, bulging biceps, powerful thighs. His body was like a well-trained beast, smooth and golden and strong, and the wanting slammed through her, causing a moan to vibrate from her chest. Heat spread in her veins and her pussy grew wet and ready.

Gen had no idea how long she watched him or when he finally realized she was in the room. With a vicious kick, the bag swung and surrendered to his brutality, and his head turned.

Their gazes clashed. Locked.

Time stopped.

His breath came out in short bursts. Never breaking the connection, a fierce hunger and rage gleamed in those blue eyes, and for the first time, Gen was afraid.

He was uncivilized. She'd entered a place he blocked others from visiting. Gen glimpsed the dark beast lurking behind the barriers, but Wolfe kept it chained, deep in the dungeon, not fit for human contact. Right now, as she looked at him, she realized she had just entered hell.

"You need to get out." His jaw clenched, and he practically hissed out the words. The serpent seemed to be whispering the commands in his ear. "Now."

She almost left. Knew it would be better. But she'd reached a turning point, and had one last shot at getting him to break. Open up to her. Give her a chance to let her love him. In this room, tonight, the demons needed to be sprung.

"No."

A growl rose from his throat. "Not fucking around, Gen. It's not safe here."

"I don't want to be safe from you." She glanced pointedly at the bag. "Nightmare?"

The pain carved in his face made her want to weep, wail, leave. But she stayed, swearing to see it out to the ugly end, no matter what the result. They owed each other this much. "Yeah. I get them now and then, so I prefer to work it out of my system. Alone."

"Maybe that's the problem. You've been alone too long."

"Not up for this now. Go back to bed and we'll talk in the morning."

"What if I don't want to talk?"

He muttered a vicious curse. She dropped her gaze and watched his iron-hard erection stretching his shorts. "I don't think you want to talk either."

"Don't. I'm not safe right now."

She took a step closer. "There's that word again. *Safe*. Do we need to be safe from each other? Safe from the world? Why don't you tell me what you really want and cut through all this exhausting bullshit?"

She shivered at the barely civilized gleam in his eyes. "I want you to get your ass upstairs and away from me. I'm hanging by a thread here, and if I snap, I'll hurt you."

Gen stretched out her open arms, palms up. "Every time you run from me, or lock me out, you hurt me. What was the nightmare about, Wolfe? I know it was bad. How bad?"

She heard his teeth grind. "Bad. Nothing you need to

hear. You wanna fuck? Fine, go wait for me upstairs and I'll give you what you want."

She didn't flinch. Heard the pain and desperation in his voice. Gen stood her ground and dug deep. "Tell me about the bad. The nightmares. Does it have to do with the bands over your wrists you wear day and night? The ones you touch constantly, as if reminding yourself you didn't die?"

The shock in his eyes destroyed her. He blinked, staring at her as if she was about to attack, so she softened her voice and took a tiny step closer, arms still reaching out. "Every time you refuse to share it with me, you give the memory more power. It gets darker, and more evil when you don't give it light. You're already a survivor. What's the nightmare about?"

A fragile thread snapped, and suddenly he turned into a wild thing, barely recognizable as human. Pupils dilated, he roared and attacked the bag, as if he wanted to attack her. He kicked and punched and hit in a rage, but Gen never moved, never blinked, letting him empty out the swirling mess until he was drained. "Get out."

"No. Tell me about the nightmare."

A keening sound broke from his lips. He ripped off the gloves and tossed them on the floor. She watched while he got dragged into the past, faced the memories in front of him, and finally talked.

"My mother ran out of drugs. Was so high for so long she couldn't function anymore. She wasn't even there; it was just some shell that used to pass for my mother. The men wanted more money for drugs. That night, I was going to run. I had everything planned, but they came in my room." He closed his eyes. Sweat dripped down his brow. "They raped me. Beat me. And when it was over, I knew I was already dead. Just like my mother."

She never paused, pushing him further, certain she'd die with him by the end of the story. "What did you do, Wolfe?"

His mouth opened and closed. He opened his eyes and gazed vacantly at the wall, his body shaking slightly. Then he slowly reached down, tugging the wristbands off. Horror washed over her. The scars were deep and dark, a crisscross of slashes with no obvious pattern marking the skin. "Took the knife. Needed to end it. Sawed at my wrists over and over. Waited to die."

Her cheeks felt wet but she ignored them, focused on forcing out the rest of the story, festering like a live infection that was slowly killing him. "But you didn't die. What happened?"

"Passed out. So happy. Thought I was free. But I woke up in the same bed. Wrists bandaged. Blood everywhere. Not sure how long I was out, or what happened. I got up, looked outside, but no one was there. My mother was gone. Rooms were empty. I left."

"Where did you go?"

"Walked. Walked forever. Slept in the woods. Waited to die. Don't remember much of those first few days. I found a diner and asked for food, and they gave it to me. I stole. I found places to sleep. I stayed low. Finally I met two other boys like me. They showed me how to survive. Beat up patsies for their stuff. Kept away from cops and shelters. See, it was all a game at first. I figured I'd die eventually, either in a knife fight or jail. I never did though. The days kept passing, and I got used to existing again. But when I looked at my wrists I remembered that night. So I started covering them up. Not seeing them. Pretending it didn't happen. Refusing to remember."

Every part of her body ached and burned to take him in her arms, cry, hold him. To finally know the truth, yet feel so distant from him ripped at her soul. He was slipping away from her, inch by inch, and in sheer desperation, she crossed the room and grasped his shoulders.

Those vacant eyes filled up with emotion. A wildness that made her dig her nails into his skin and shake him with the last ounce of her strength.

"But you did remember. It happened, and you survived. You're here now, with me."

"I'm not whole."

The simple words sliced like razors. She cupped his cheeks, holding his head still. "You are whole. They broke your body, not your soul. Your mother broke your heart, not your core. Every day you chose to live, to take a shot and let people back in, like Sawyer and Julietta and Gabby and me, you said a big fuck you. You are whole."

He shuddered, sliding his hands around her as if craving the warmth of her skin to melt the ice. "On the edge. Can't keep it together."

In a flash, she recognized the thin line between pain and pleasure, survival and death. The choppy emotions were too much and he needed an outlet, something to hang on to and fight for. He needed something good and pure and real to replace the horror. Frantic to pull him back from the place where the demons lived, she surrendered to instinct.

"You don't have to keep it together." She tangled her fingers in his hair and pulled. Pressed against him, feeling each muscle and the damp sweat glistening on his skin, she spoke fiercely against his lips. "I'm the one who loves you. Use me instead."

Lust flared to life. He tried to push her away, but she clung to him like a wild thing, sensing the wall between them ready to crumble. "No, I'll hurt you."

She sank her teeth into his lip and dug her nails into his scalp. "Good. Fuck me. Take me. I'm already yours. This is what's real, and good." A low groan escaped him, and he grabbed her, hitching her high up so her legs wrapped around his waist. His breath came out in choppy gasps.

"Gen—"

"Right here, right now, with us. This is beautiful. Use me and remember that." She took his mouth, pushing her tongue deep inside, drowning in the musky, heavenly taste of pure man. His whole body shook like he was held in the grip of a fever, and then he was kissing her back, chaining her to him with arms like iron bands.

They drank, feasted, writhed, the hunger driving them higher and faster. He staggered a few steps, placing her down on the weight bench, and ripped off her shirt. She grabbed his shoulders, arching, accepting the bite of his teeth on her nipples, the deep sucking of his mouth, the flick of his tongue. Ripping off her pajama bottoms, she lay naked and open on the bench. Tugging down his shorts, she wrapped her fingers around his erection and squeezed tight, wringing curses from his lips, scraping her nails over his balls until he pushed her back on the bench.

"Spread your legs. Hang on to the bar."

She obeyed, desperate to give him everything she had. He lined up so he towered over her naked body, his hands cupping her breasts, his dick paused at her entrance. She felt swollen and needy, as if the first thrust of him inside would make her come.

"You're mine."

He drove in deep. She cried out as his piercing hit the magical spot. "Oh, God."

He did it again. Grasped her knees and forced her up higher, so each slide in and out merged such intense pleasure it bordered on pain, and she tried to wriggle away. "Too much."

"Not enough."

Another thrust. Faster. Harder. Deeper. She shook her head but he refused her retreat, forcing her to accept all of him, the slap of their bodies and the frantic movements growing more urgent, sending her up so high she didn't think she could ever get back down.

"Wolfe!"

"Come. Come for me, Gen."

The orgasm milked every muscle in her body, squeezing mercilessly so her scream splintered the air and got smothered by his lips over hers. Her hips jerked helplessly as he spilled his seed inside, following her over, and the spasms kept going on and on and on . . .

She didn't even realize she was crying until the deep sobs spilled from her lips. He murmured soothing words and scooped her up into his arms, cradling her while she cried for the boy he was, and the pain he endured, and the devastating way she loved him more than anyone in the world.

She cried for him, and for her, and the fear that tonight still wouldn't be enough for him to love her the way she needed.

He held her for a long time. Finally, when she calmed, he led her back upstairs, tucked her into bed, and climbed in with her. Wrapping his arms around her waist, he pulled her tight against him. She lifted his battered, scarred wrists to her lips and gently kissed them.

They slept.

HE WAS GONE.

Gen rolled over and stared at the wall. The morning light crept in. He'd made love to her two more times last night, transcending the physical. They'd entwined tight into each other's souls, so close they were no longer individuals but burned together as one.

She'd never be the same. Never love someone the way she did Wolfe. Last night could've been the beginning of a new chapter. One where friendship was forged into love and a relationship to grow with.

Instead, Gen sensed last night was his final good-bye.

Slowly, she sat up. She winced at the slight bruises on her body, but no pain compared to the one in her broken heart. The scent of sex and musk rose to her nostrils. Some-how she had to find a way to reach him, or she would be forced to make the only decision left.

Give up on him.

Gen showered and dressed, making her way to the kitchen. Julietta juggled the baby on her hip, a spatula in her hand and the phone tucked beneath her ear. A rapid stream of Italian flew through the air: *"Sono sulla mia strada. Rimanere li."* She threw the phone down. *"Che idiota!* Why must I deal with stubborn men?"

Gen grabbed the platter of eggs and veggies, and took the baby. "I'm asking myself the same question."

Julietta shook her head, put together two plates, and settled Gabby in the bouncy seat. Two steaming cups of coffee were plunked on the table. "Drink. Caffeine makes things better. Is Wolfe being an *idiota*?"

She choked out a laugh. "Yes. Seems we reached an impasse." Gen remembered Julietta didn't know about their friends-with-benefits package. "I mean, with our friendship, of course."

The woman's lips curved in a knowing grin. "Ah, you think I am an *idiota*? I know you're sleeping together. I know you're in love with him, and he's in love with you, and he's probably tearing himself up inside with denial and the past and refuses to deal with the truth of the relationship. Am I close?"

Gen stared. "How did you know?"

Julietta shook her head and sipped more coffee. "It's all over his face and yours. Wolfe is my son. I knew one day he'd fall in love and struggle. He's a lot like Sawyer, and we had a hard road to follow. Is there something I can do?"

Gen sighed. "Don't think so. It's up to him to make a

choice. I just can't do this anymore. Play at a friendship that's changed. I can't go back."

"You shouldn't have to." She tapped a finger against her lips. "He's gone to therapy, but there's a part deep inside of him no one can touch. I've never seen him as open as when he looks at you. His heart is lighter, and he's more at peace. You make him happy."

Gen fought back tears. She hated being weepy and girly. Enough with the crying. "Thank you for that. It means a lot."

"Has he told you about his past?"

Her throat closed up, but she forced the words out. "Yes. He finally told me everything."

The woman nodded, lapsing into a thoughtful silence. "He gave you a gift. But other than Sawyer, and maybe his therapist, he's never told anyone. I think there will always be a dark place inside of him we'll never truly understand. But I taught Sawyer he doesn't have to live there anymore. They both deserve so much more." Her voice broke, and her eyes flickered with memories from her husband's past. Gen watched her, soothed that she understood and had battled the same obstacles. But now they had a family, and a future filled with promise. Wasn't it possible to have the same happiness with Wolfe?

"What do I do?" Gen whispered. "I love him."

Julietta reached over and squeezed her hand. "Fight. I fought for Sawyer, but it wasn't easy."

"And if he doesn't want to fight for me?"

Her hand slipped away and sadness flickered over her

facc. "Love is a choice, isn't it?" she said softly. "Sometimes we can only do so much."

Gen's cell vibrated, interrupting the conversation. She glanced at the ID. The Verily police. "I'm sorry, I need to take this."

"Go. I'm going to get Gabby ready for the day."

Gen clicked on the phone and walked into the library. "Hello?"

"Dr. Mackenzie. Officer Petty."

"Hi, Officer. Did you get ahold of David?"

"Matter of fact, we did. He was in Boston at the time. Witnesses corroborated."

Her spirits sank. "Any way he could've snuck away? Gotten someone else to do it? I just don't understand."

"We got 'em. Actually, we got her." His voice was laced with derision. "Do you know a Sally Winters from the hospital?"

The room spun. What? "Yes. We worked together. She's a friend of mine. Are you telling me she did this?"

"Yep. She was writing the words *liar* and *whore* on your house again last night when one of your neighbors confronted her in the act. We were called in and caught Sally with the paint can. She admitted the whole thing."

"Which neighbor?"

"Mrs. Blackfire."

Gen shook her head. She pictured her nosy neighbor with a telescope and fought off crazy laughter. Guess spying did come in handy sometimes. "How did she catch her?"

"She said she didn't like graffiti messing up the value of

the neighborhood, so she did a night watch for the past few nights." A touch of humor leaked out. "She's a bit of a spitfire. Tried to press charges against Sally Winters, but it's your property. Your call. Anyway, Sally admitted she'd slept with David after your breakup and thought it was permanent. She was afraid he wanted to get back together with you so she concocted a plan to scare you off."

Gen bit her lip. Something still wasn't right. Even if Sally was interested, the entire episode screamed manipulation. "Are you sure David didn't put her up to it?"

A short silence settled over the line. "She denies it, but I wouldn't be surprised. Still, I got it all on record in her deposition. Need you back here at the station though."

The knowledge her coworker and friend could stoop to such a level pained her. She also knew how David worked. Probably promised her a future without telling her about Boston. Sowed the seeds of what he wanted Sally to do. Relief loosened her muscles. David wouldn't be stalking her any longer, especially after Sally was caught. She was finally free.

Now it was time to take the last stand.

"Thank you, Officer. I'll be flying home tomorrow if that's acceptable."

"Of course. Contact me when you're home."

They said good-bye and she clicked off.

Funny, it was almost as if part of her life was also clicking into place, finding a new home in the scheme of her life. She wanted to be a doctor again. Go back to the hospital and finish what she started. She wanted to rebuild a relationship with her twin, and make more time and balance for her friends.

And she wanted Wolfe.

Gen found him outside on the balcony. Sipping his coffee, looking out over the city streets, deep in thought. She paused and studied him.

The millionaire model turned hotel magnate wore his usual getup of shorts and T-shirt. His bare feet were propped up on the coffee table. Chocolate-brown curls fell in disarray around his head, and the familiar scent of lemon, soap, and coffee clung to him. She imagined not waking up with him in the morning, or kissing him good night. She craved to be the one to kill the spiders for him, cook for him, yell at him, and make love to him every spare moment.

Last night, he'd given her the truth.

Now he needed to give her his heart.

"Wolfe."

He jerked, sloshing coffee over the rim. Setting his feet back on the ground, he mopped up the spill and set the cup on the table beside him. "Sorry. Didn't hear you."

They gazed at each other. Remembering. Her gaze flicked to his wrists, covered by the leather bands once more. He tugged at them, then stilled.

"How do you feel?" she asked softly.

"Good."

"The police called. They found who did it." His brows snapped in a frown. She quickly went over the scenario, and he seemed to accept the explanation. "I told them I'd be flying back tomorrow."

"We can do that. I'll help you repaint."

"I've decided to go back to the hospital."

He nodded, as if trying to keep up. "Good. You deserve to be there. It may be a bit rough at first, but you can handle it. I always knew that."

"Wolfe?"

"Yeah?"

"I love you."

He flinched. Turned pale. Her heart dropped, but she'd committed to her last stand and damned if she wasn't going all out. How many times had they mentioned love to each other? In friendship, and laughter, and fun? The words had spilled out so easily before, yet today they held a whole new meaning and were stuck deep inside where the memories had been trapped. Refusing to come out.

"Well, we're friends."

She stiffened her spine at the raw hurt. "Not like that. I'll always love you as a friend. But it's more now. I love you as a man. My lover. As my partner."

He jumped back, pressing his back against the balcony. "Why are you doing this now? Let's fly back, get our heads in the game, and see what happens." A nervous laugh escaped. "A lot of shit went down last night and I told you stuff no one knows."

"Do you love me?" His eyes widened. Gen swore he was already calculating the odds of jumping over the balcony rather than face her questions. She closed the distance, forcing him to deal with her. "Because last night meant something more to me. You shared a gift by telling me the truth. But it's more than that. I look into your eyes and see a man I want with my whole heart. I want you in my life as more than my friend. Do you want that, too?"

He swallowed. Stared. Pure fear shone from those bright blue eyes.

And he didn't answer.

Gen stopped inches before him. "I love you," she said again. "Right now. Right here, I need to know how you feel about me. The truth."

The sun beat down bright and hot. The roar of mopeds and heels clicking on the sidewalk rose in the air. He didn't move, didn't blink, standing as still as a statue. Or a victim watching his attacker move in.

Her fingers shook. Her gut clenched in terror. She was losing him, and she didn't know what to do to push him over the edge, make him fight for her, admit his true feelings.

"Please say something," she whispered. "Anything. I can't do this anymore. I'm fighting for both of us, but if you don't give me a sign, something to hope for, I'll—" She struggled to continue, battling the raw emotions that rocked her to the core. Gen grabbed his T-shirt, tugging him forward. The heat between them caught and surged.

"I don't care about your past. I care about your future—with me—but you have to say it. Dammit, Wolfe, say something!"

The silence was deafening.

Her grip loosened. He stared at her, refusing to speak. Gen took a step back, and another, until her back pressed against the door and there was a space between them as large and deep as the Grand Canyon.

It was over.

* * *

IT WAS OVER.

He knew it. Sensed what was going to happen when she stepped on the balcony with him. She was so beautiful. Even as he stood dumbstruck, she raised that stubborn chin and challenged him. *I love you.* Words that struck a chord inside and healed. Word that struck a chord inside and destroyed.

Julietta and Sawyer and Gabby and Mama Conte were different. It wasn't the kind of love that consumed you raw, devoured you whole, and made everything messy and terrifying and bloody. This type of love, this possession to be and give the world to one person, wasn't possible. He'd end up hurting her, because he was damaged. He'd done terrible things. The years of violence on the street. Beating up strangers and ripping away their innocence. Stealing. Being raped by monsters. He wasn't clean, or good enough for someone like her. He didn't trust himself to raise a family, be a healthy spouse and father. What if one day the demons rose again and gobbled him up? She deserved more, and if by not saying the words she needed to hear he could protect her, so be it.

Her own father knew it. Called out the truth right to his face.

Jim knew about the demons and said they'd always come back. He wouldn't let the bastards drag both of them into the pits of hell.

She moved away. Coldness seeped into his chest, familiar numbness wrapping around his organs and dragging him into nothingness.

Say something.

The plea and the tears gleaming in her eyes would haunt him forever.

He opened his mouth.

Her voice shattered and broke like a thousand pieces of fragile glass. "I can't do this anymore."

The door shut.

Wolfe turned away. She was gone. He'd done it. Severed the final ties between them. Maybe, with time, they could go back to friendship. He'd bury his emotions, wait the proper grieving time, and approach her. At least she was safe. Getting her life back on track. Coming into herself again.

He'd wait. For now, he'd tell Sawyer to let her fly home so she could have the time she needed to get over him. He'd return in a few days, lie low, and slowly introduce himself back into her life. With distance. Safely.

As a friend.

Say something.

Wolfe bowed his head and reminded himself he had done the only thing possible.

He'd saved her from himself.

twenty-eight

GENEVIEVE SLID INTO the booth and grinned. Her besties roared with approval and pushed over a margarita with just the right amount of salt rimming the edge. Today was her last day at Kinnections before officially going back to her residency. After a long conversation with Brian about options, a heart-to-heart with some key people at the hospital, and a discussion about Sally's vandalism on her house, Gen felt better prepared. She was a surgeon and it was time to claim her future. There would still be plenty of ghosts to fight, but she was finally ready to take them on.

"I'm gonna miss you guys," she said, lifting her glass. Kate, Arilyn, and Kennedy clinked their glasses together and drank. "I kinda got used to having you around all the time."

Kate lifted a brow. "That's not going to change. I know you're going to be crazy busy, Gen, but I don't want you to ever slip away from us like before. You need balance. You need us."

"Absolutely," Arilyn chimed in. "Life passes too quickly, and though your work is important, it's not everything."

"Hell, when you start getting weird or secretive, we'll just drag you out for a drinkfest," Kennedy informed her.

Gen laughed. "Thanks guys. It's good to be back at Mugs."

They launched into girly chatter about shoes, the latest matches at Kinnections, and wedding plans for Kate. She also noticed Kate's hesitation to discuss any details, and immediately grabbed her friend's hand. "Kate, listen to me. I know things have been uncomfortable with my wedding blowing up. But I'm so happy for you and Slade. Because you showed me the difference between a real love match versus what looks good on paper. Talking about dresses and favors and flowers is fun, and it doesn't make me sad. Understood?"

Kate nodded, and her face relaxed. "I just felt so bad. You're my maid of honor and I didn't want you to regret saying yes to me."

"Never. It's going to be an epic wedding, and standing by your side will make me happy. Now, no more bullshit."

Kate laughed. "Done. Now can someone help me talk my mother out of donating marijuana brownies for the favors?"

Kennedy lifted a brow. "I think I'm about to encourage it."

Arilyn kept oddly quiet throughout the next round of drinks. Finally, Gen leaned in and pitched her voice a bit higher to be heard. "A? What's up? You seem distracted. You okay?"

Kate and Kennedy shared a knowing look. Arilyn smiled, but it was weak compared to her megawatt genuine one that made people happy. "I was wrong," she finally said.

Gen cocked her head. "Wrong about what?"

Her green eyes flickered with a hint of regret. "I told you it's best to let the moment lead. Not discuss the terms of a relationship or the rules, or real feelings. I meant what I said at the time, but lately I've been thinking I'm very wrong."

Kate began to get that mean look. Gen figured she was about to beat the living crap out of Yoga Man. Kennedy actually curled her fingers into her fists as if getting ready to train. "Did something happen?" she asked gently. "Did he hurt you?"

Arilyn's shimmering golden red hair shook, then settled. "Not yet. But it's the coward's way. If you love someone, you need to be honest. Brave. Tell them straight out and blow up the fucking rules. Because I'm starting to believe there shouldn't be any rules when you love someone."

Gen almost doubled over with pain. The image of Wolfe flashed in her mind, and the hurt wasn't any better. It was blinding, breath-stealing pain that made her heart whimper. Since they arrived back home two weeks ago, he'd moved out of her house and kept his distance. A few texts, some calls. One night she could have sworn she caught sight of his car parked down the road by her house, but when she walked outside to investigate, the car was gone.

She sensed him everywhere, yet nowhere. Since that fateful day on the balcony, Gen realized she couldn't live her life in a constant state of need anymore. It might hurt, and she also worried she'd never truly get over him—that she'd wind up searching for a mate who would be only a pale imitation of the man who held her heart. But she was going to give it her best shot.

This time, there was no consolation prize of friendship. Those chick flicks had been right after all.

Sex between friends ruined everything.

The group sighed with sympathy. "I'm sorry, A," Gen

said. "When I finally told Wolfe the truth, he couldn't give me what I needed. But you're right. I think it may be better to find out sooner rather than later."

"Yeah."

They drank their alcohol while the music blared in the background. "Do you think Wolfe will come after you?" Arilyn asked.

Her stomach pitched. "If he's not ready to be all in, I don't want to hear it. And if he's biding his time, thinking this will all go away and we can be buddies, he's going to be sorely disappointed."

"He'd never be that stupid," Arilyn said. "Wolfe is a pretty smart guy."

Kennedy snorted. "He has a penis. Trust me, he may be stupid, especially since Gen's thrown him into a tailspin. No woman has ever demanded anything more than a quick lay and a good conversation. He doesn't know how to handle it, because he's never been in love before."

"I hate love," Arilyn said grumpily. Another shared look between Kate and Kennedy.

Gen sighed and drained her drink. "Me, too. Love sucks."

Kennedy raised her hand in the air and flagged down a waitress. "That, my darlings, is why they created alcohol. Another round, please."

They looked at each other and began to laugh.

WOLFE WAITED UNTIL HE spotted her coming up the sidewalk.

He sat in his car, in the dark, waiting for the woman who had replaced his nightmares and now haunted his dreams. Since that fateful night, things had been cold and stilted between them. He'd been ready to accept the blame and ride out the rocky path until she calmed down and realized they were better as friends.

But the last two weeks had almost killed him.

She was going back to the hospital. He was so proud of her. Sometimes, when he couldn't sleep, he drove up to Verily and parked on her street. Looking at her sunny yellow bungalow made him happy. Now that David was out of her life and safely in Boston, now that the culprit had been caught and punished, things were going back to normal.

And so should their relationship.

He caught his breath as the moon threw her in silhouette. She was gorgeous. Probably out with the girls at Mugs. She wore tight jeans, high-heeled sandals, and a shimmery gold top with lots of sparkle and lace. Her hair was curled in tight corkscrews and tumbled around her shoulders in a silky mess. Pouty red lips mouthed the words to a song he couldn't catch. Yeah, definitely Mugs. Her hips swung a bit as she bopped to the mental rhythm and skipped up the stairs. The porch light flickered on.

She disappeared inside.

His palms sweat. Wolfe cursed under his breath and got out of the car. He refused to be a pussy. Sure, he'd hurt her, but it was far better than watching her begin to hate him when she realized he was only half a man. The rape and attempted suicide had wiped out a part of who he was. He rebuilt himself, but there was so much violence in his past. She was clean. He was dirty.

She was better off without him.

He wiped his hands over his jeans and trudged up the walkway. He'd keep it light, friendly, and polite. Just check on her. Maybe share a beer. Surely she'd let him inside and begin to forgive him? Surely she'd understand why he had done it and realize things could be good again between them?

He knocked.

Her face froze when she saw him.

His heart stumbled, then dropped into free fall.

Her voice blasted out a spray of pure ice. "What do you want?"

Wolfe tried not to jerk back. This wasn't like her. Gen would never treat him like an unwelcome stranger. "T-to see you. Catch up. It's been too long." He waited like a dumbass on her porch while she studied him like a bug she considered squashing. His temper reared. For God's sake, this wasn't what was supposed to happen. "Are you gonna keep me out here or invite me in?" His half joke fell flat when he gazed into those blue eyes and saw . . . nothing.

A wall stood between them. If he reached out, Wolfe swore he'd be able to touch it. Somehow, he had to get them back on track and fix this.

"Gen, please. Let me in. For one beer?"

Finally, she opened the door and let him in.

Trying not to breathe out in pure relief, he remained casual. Walked over to the refrigerator and grabbed two beers, flipping off the caps and handing one over. Like a familiar dance, he expected her smile of welcome or some smart-ass remark that made him laugh. Instead, she just took the bottle and held it in her hand as if afraid to drink.

Irritation cut through him. "So, you went to Mugs with the girls?"

"Yeah."

"Have fun?"

"Sure."

He nodded, sipped his beer, and tried to keep calm. Her one-word answers were pissing him off, but if he lost his temper, she'd throw him the hell out. And why was he so mad? He'd been the one to push her away, so he couldn't expect this to be easy. Maybe it was best to launch right into the topic they were both avoiding.

"I wanted to talk to you." More silence. "I'm sorry about what happened that day on the balcony." No expression. "You can jump in anytime, you know."

"What exactly are you sorry for?"

So cold. Controlled. He pulled himself to full height and swore he'd make her understand. "I'm sorry I hurt you. I did the only thing I could. A relationship like that could never work with us, sweetheart. I'm fucked-up in the head, and can't stand the idea of messing us up. We're better off as friends, don't you agree? I wanted to give you some time so you could come to the same conclusion."

She just stared at him. Analyzing his words as if he was a stranger. He'd buried himself deep into her body and made her scream his name in orgasm. He'd rescued her from the wedding. He'd told her the truth about his past. And yet there was not even a flicker of emotion revealed on her face.

"Anything else you wanted to say?"

"Why are you doing this? I don't understand why you'd want to throw away our friendship. Do you need more time? Tell me what to do to make this right and I'll fix it."

She slowly put the beer down. The only sign she was affected by him was the way she wrapped her arms around her chest, hugging tight, as if she was trying to protect herself. Regret flowed and the numbness inside melted away to explode back into a fiery pain that hurt every part of his body. She was killing him. All he craved to do was take her in his arms, make her happy, make her laugh. But this was different from when she left David.

Now she looked at him like he was her very worst nightmare.

"You can't fix this," she finally said. Those blue eyes remained calm. "I don't think you really understand, Wolfe. We're not children anymore. I can't just flick a magic wand and make myself not love you anymore. I can't share a beer and a burger and not want to take you into my bed and give you everything I am."

"Sweetheart, we'll work it out. With time, things will get better, like they were. I swear."

She let out a humorless laugh. "No, it won't. Not if I keep seeing you and reminding myself of what I can never have. It's over between us. All of it. The friendship, the casual get-togethers, the texts and the calls and the emails. I need you to go away and stay away. I don't want to be your friend anymore."

Panic clutched at his chest, making it difficult to breathe. "You don't mean that. You're still pissed off and hurt, and I get it, but I'm not going anywhere. How can you walk away from what we have together? Don't you want to fight for it?"

"I could ask the same of you."

They stared at each other in a standoff. He slammed the beer down and shoved his fingers through his hair. "This is different," he gritted out. "Fuck, I told you why I didn't want to do this! You're punishing both of us for something I have no control over. I'm trying to protect you!"

A sad smile curved her lips. "No. You're trying to protect yourself. For a man so brave and strong and pure of heart, you're taking the coward's way out. You've hurt me by not fighting for us. Hiding behind a lie won't make it go away. I'm sorry if you can't get everything you want, but I'm not a consolation prize. I played all my cards and I lost, and now I'm done. With you. With us. You'll have to find someone else to hang with. Someone else to drink with and play darts with and pretend you're something you're not with. Because I'm out."

She walked away and opened the door. His mouth dropped open. She was throwing him out? She didn't want to see him anymore? The floor tilted up and a fierce roaring beat in his ears like a flurry of birds' wings, making everything fuzzy and disorienting. He couldn't lose her.

He'd die without her.

"Go home, Wolfe. Please don't try to contact me. I need the time to heal and learn to live without you."

"Don't do this—" His voice broke, so he tried again. "Please."

"This isn't a punishment. It's just what I have to do."

He didn't know how long he stood there. She waited

him out, refusing to meet his gaze, until he managed to walk across the floor and stop beside her. "Gen."

She said nothing.

Wolfe left.

When the door shut behind him, he realized maybe there was something even worse than what had happened in his past.

"HONEY, WHAT'S WRONG? YOUR mother and I are worried."

Gen forced a smile at her parents. She dragged a fork through her pasta, but her appetite had been sorely lacking since Wolfe left a few nights ago. A bone-deep sense of loss haunted her, and she struggled to get to the other side. Funny, she'd felt nothing like this when she left David. As if half of her heart had been cut out and given to someone who didn't want it.

She'd come so close to breaking and taking whatever he wanted to give her. But Gen knew it would destroy her slowly. Much better to rip off the Band-Aid and suffer intense but shorter pain. At least, it seemed like a good idea at the time.

"Just working some stuff out."

"You're happy being back at the hospital though, right?" her father asked.

"Yes." Returning to her medical career was the first step. Now she focused on what she wanted but refused to put herself back in an unhealthy place where work ruled every second and thought. She could be successful but still have a life. Without David, she relished restoring her own power, making decisions and choices on her own. She'd finally come full circle.

"It's Wolfe, isn't it?"

She stared at her mother. Maria clasped her hands on the table, meeting her gaze directly. Her father gasped. "That boy is only a friend. She just got over David! It has nothing to do with Wolfe."

"Yes, it does."

Her admission cut through her father's outburst like a bullet. Maria nodded slowly. "I suspected. The way you kept sneaking glances at one another. The joy on your faces." She smiled. "I remember when your father and I fell hard for each other it was the same way. Hard to keep that type of love hidden from the world."

"Love? Have I stepped into the twilight zone?" her father said. "When did you and Wolfe become more than friends? Is he the reason you broke off with David? Did he hurt you in some way? I'll kill him—I swear, I'll go find him right now."

"Jim, calm down."

Gen sighed. Her father was stable and a rock when it came to interventions, health issues, and financial disasters. But when one of his children got their heart broken, he turned into a raging lunatic. "Dad, listen to me for a second. Wolfe had nothing to do with David and me. David was too controlling, and we weren't good for each other. But I realized I had deeper feelings for Wolfe as we spent more time together. I fell in love with him."

Jim groaned and jumped from the chair. "I knew this would happen. He's not good for you. What did he do?"

"Do you need one of your heart pills, dear?" Maria asked.

"No, I'll be fine if my daughter just answers my question."

"Dad, please calm down. I know he didn't mean to hurt me. I wanted more than friendship, and he couldn't handle it. He's had some issues in his past, and he doesn't believe he's worthy. He doesn't want to take a chance on me."

Her father lapsed into silence. For a while, he studied her face, and then finally ducked his head. Maria took her hand, her soft brown eyes gleaming with understanding. "I'm so sorry. I know you're in pain right now. Do you think he'll come around with some time?"

Damn tears again. It was like permanent PMS. She blinked rapidly. "No. I know he loves me, but he's stuck on the idea he'll hurt me in the future. I can't make him try."

"No, you can't." Maria came over and tucked her into her arms. Pressing kisses to her head, she rocked her back and forth like she was little. "You'll be okay. Not for a while; it will hurt deeply. But you did the right thing by trying."

"Maybe it's for the best," her father said gruffly. "Maybe he would've hurt you."

Genevieve sniffed. "There are never guarantees, Dad. All I wanted was him to be brave enough to take the leap with me. What hurts the most is he doesn't see how special he is. How gentle, loving, and protective. He makes me . . . better."

Maria let her cry, and when she finally lifted her head, she felt calmer.

Her father was gone.

twenty-nine

WOLFE COMPLETED THE third set of pull-ups and dropped.

Mötley Crüe blared loud and badassed behind him. He guzzled water, donned the boxing gloves, and set himself up for another round of punishing, brutal punches.

He'd do anything to stop the pain.

He was into the first round for a good five minutes before the music shut off. Catching his breath, he wiped his face with a towel and faced Sawyer. "Come to get a good thrashing?" he asked with a grin.

Sawyer didn't smile back. Instead, he got that worried, pinched look on his face. Uh-oh. Wolfe remembered that expression when he was nineteen, twenty, and yeah, maybe even twenty-one. He wanted to have a *talk*.

"Maybe later. Got a minute?"

He wasn't up for it now. Having a heart-to-heart with the one man who understood him might let loose some shit he wanted locked up for good. "Can I catch you later?"

Sawyer sighed and sat down on the bench. "Won't take long. How come you came back to Italy?"

Wolfe stiffened, avoiding his gaze. "Told you. I'd planned on staying a few weeks, but needed to fly Gen home. I just decided to come right back. Hell, man, if I'm messing up your mojo I'll get the hell out. All you had to do was say so."

"Don't."

The quiet word made him pause. He was being a dick and he knew it. "Sorry. I'm dealing with some shit. Trying to get my head together."

"Now that I understand. Look, I'm glad you're here. Hell, I'm stoked and want you to stay as long as possible. But you've been different, and I think it has to do with Gen. I don't want to get in your business, but you can talk to me. I've been there."

Wolfe dragged in a breath and faced his stepfather. "I know. I just need some time. I'll be okay."

Sawyer gave a curt nod, but his face was plainly disbelieving. "I can respect that. I'm here if you need me. I will tell you this, though. When Julietta and I first got together, I wanted it to be about sex. Only sex."

Wolfe made a face. "TMI, dude."

"Sorry. Trying to make a point. It turned into more, but I fought it because I didn't think I was good enough. Believed I was damaged, from the stuff I did in the past. She convinced me otherwise, but it took time. You see, Wolfe, when a woman loves you, she doesn't see the past or the mistakes or the crap. She just sees the future."

Wolfe remained quiet. Sawyer stood and squeezed his shoulder. "That's all I got. But you better shower soon because you need to go on an appointment."

"With who?"

Sawyer turned back to look at him. "Mama Conte expects you for dinner at six."

"You coming?"

His stepfather shot him a look. "Not this time. She requested only you. Good luck."

He disappeared, leaving him with his thoughts and regret and sweat.

"Ah, fuck."

WOLFE BEGAN TO RELAX.

The dinner was perfect. They'd feasted on only four courses instead of six, and having Mama Conte on a one-to-one basis was enjoyable. He'd learned stories about Julietta growing up, the launch of her bakery, and got a glimpse of the powerful man Mama Conte had loved, married, and lost. She never mentioned anything personal, and Wolfe caught no judgment or worry in her gaze. He finished grinding the coffee beans, and prepared them two cups of espresso to go with the buttery amaretti she'd just baked.

"Did you ever think you'd fail when you first started La Dolce Famiglia?" he asked, settling back into the pine chair.

Mama Conte smiled and sat next to him. "Of course. But I had a partner at my side, and knew if I failed, at least I tried. There is no shame in dreams or hard work or failure. Only not trying."

He nibbled on a cookie. "Like Sawyer's dreams for Purity."

"*Sì*. And the way Michael began his own dream with La Dolce Maggie. He wanted to be a race car driver when he was younger."

"No way." He couldn't imagine Michael as a young, brash race car driver. The tall, elegant Italian man ruled with a booming voice and incredible charm, and was one of the sharpest businessmen in the country. "I can't picture it."

"Ah, it was hard to give that part of himself up. When my husband passed, Michael took it upon himself to run the business and never looked back. I am sure he had regrets, but his path has led him to Maggie and a new life. We never realize at the moment what our futures hold. Sometimes we must go on a leap of faith."

He sifted through her words, his brain clutching the theory like a Bible to the heart. How wonderful to think each moment, good and bad, has purpose. He never really thought of his life like that before. And after losing Genevieve, there was a gaping hole he couldn't fill, a haunting emptiness that no food or water could ever satisfy.

"Do you remember what I told you that Sunday years ago? When you first visited me?"

Wolfe blinked. The afternoon of their initial meeting was carved in his brain as one of the turning points in his life. He'd dined with Sawyer and Julietta, and she'd asked to speak with him in private for a few moments after dessert. "Yes, of course. You said I was always welcome in your home, that I was part of your family. You said I had worth, and one day I'd see it."

She smiled faintly. "Good. Do you remember the last thing I said?"

He played back the conversation in his memory. "You said I was searching for something, and that one day I'd find it. But I'd need to be brave enough to think I deserved it."

"Yes, my sweet boy. I've watched you grow up into a man I'm proud of. You've become a son to Julietta and Sawyer, and a grandson to me. You are the heart and soul of Purity, and you have a wisdom and gentleness that humbles me. The last time you visited, I knew you'd changed. I didn't know who it would be, but once I met Genevieve, everything made sense."

He shifted in his chair while his defenses rose. "Gen and I are friends." The words stuck in his throat and the lie burned his tongue.

She threw her head back and cackled. "Started as friends, yes. But you are soul mates. Meant to balance each other."

"Mama Conte, I don't want to talk about this right now. It's not going to work between us. It's for the best."

She kept talking as if he wasn't even there. "If only there was a way I could make you marry each other. But alas, it won't work this time."

"What?"

"Nothing. Have you figured out what you're searching for?"

The change of topic was hurting his head. "Nothing. I have everything I want." Another lie.

"Wolfe Wells. This is important. Don't be flip—tell me the truth."

The demand came like a whiplash. He stared at the elderly woman gazing at him with eyes of steel, and the answer surged from within, poised on his lips, and spilled from his very soul. "Beautiful. I'm searching for something beautiful out there." The emotions snuck from under the wall, took root, and began to bloom. He was used to chopping off the flowers with the weeds, but this time, he stopped himself.

Her smile was pure joy and comfort and goodness. She reached out, wrapped strong fingers around his wrists, and lifted them up. "Yes. And you have finally found it, my sweet boy. It's love. Genevieve is your answer, but sometimes the hardest, bravest thing in the world is to let someone love you." She slowly slipped off the wrist guards, releasing his scarred skin to the light. "Allow yourself to be happy. This boy who tried to take his life, the one with all the hurt and loss, is part of you. But he does not have to take over. Not anymore. You must go to her and give her the truth. Do you understand?"

Wolfe stared. Her voice echoed to a place inside his soul, back to the dirty bedroom where the men had used him and he'd tried to escape. But then another image took hold, one of Gen's face, open and laughing, her eyes full of love as she kissed him, held him, and showed him something that was possible.

Something beautiful.

An odd stinging hurt his eyes. "What if I fail?"

She squeezed harder and stroked his cheek with tenderness. "It doesn't matter. When you try, you win."

He began to shake. When he was little, and he desperately craved someone to hug him, tell him it was okay, soothe the tears away, there was no one. But right now, in Mama Conte's kitchen, he felt safe.

He felt loved.

She took him into her arms and held him tight.

* * *

"I NEED A PLAN."

Nate remained quiet as he set up his shot on the golf course. The air hung thick and heavy for the October afternoon, and a slight dampness still clung to the grass from the morning drizzle. It hadn't stopped either of them from their normal Wednesday morning golf game. Wolfe's swing was clean, with a perfect arc and trajectory. "Nice, dude."

"Thanks. Good to know I haven't lost my edge. You canceled twice this past month. Losing interest in me? Or is jetting off to Italy on a whim more important than the game of champions?"

He rolled his eyes and grabbed the club. "Hanging out with Benny the hairdresser a bit much? The drama is catching."

"Mitch."

"Metrosexual."

"Ouch."

Wolfe laughed, got prepped, and made his shot. His smirk when the ball landed close to the green made Nate shake his head. "Maybe a vacation in Italy is exactly what you need to help your game. Want a handicap?"

"Asshole." Wolfe grinned and they began walking.

"Back to your comment. What type of plan we talking about?"

Wolfe figured it was time to push himself to be more open with everyone close in his life. Not easy, but time to try. "Let me give you the short version. Gen and I started

sleeping together, fell in love, she asked for more, I freaked
and said no, she left, I'm trying to get her back."

"Why'd you freak?"

"I got issues."

Nate barked out a laugh. "No shit. Who doesn't? Okay,
so she's pissed off and doesn't want to see you."

"Correct."

"Sounds like what happened with Kennedy and me."

"Yeah, but a big declaration with a billboard on a golf
course isn't gonna help me. I need epic."

Nate wrinkled his nose. "The billboard was epic. I
heard Kate got recliners from Slade."

"That's lame."

"Yeah, I told him that. How about a poem? You can
name Purity after her?"

Wolfe glowered. "Dude, these suck. I come to you with
my heart open and this is what you give me?"

"I'm a guy. I don't know what women want. Can you
create a song and serenade outside her door?"

"Forget it."

They went back to the game, but Wolfe was no closer
to figuring out how to confess his love, apologize, and beg
her to take another shot on his sorry ass. Somehow he felt
as if his silence hurt her the deepest. How could he blame
her? He'd hurt the one person in the world he treasured.

Ever since coming home from Italy, he'd begun to look
at things differently. With less fear. He even started therapy
again, wanting to do everything to keep working on himself. He pulled at his wristbands, the skin sweating underneath, and suddenly stopped.

Gen was a straight shooter. No frills. Fierce and brave and honest.

He would keep things simple. No billboards, poems, or Goodyear Blimp signs.

Just the truth.

"I got it."

Nate nodded. "Good. Now, can we finish the game before you go off to claim your woman?"

"Yes. Let's play."

His heart lighter, Wolfe concentrated on golf, grateful for good friends.

GEN LAUGHED AS LILY and Maria climbed over her, trying to get in more hugs than the other. She grabbed them and tickled them mercilessly, the shrill giggles reminding her that life had its beautiful moments even within the pain. She slumped onto the carpet, exhausted, while Alexa shook her head.

"Let your aunt rest, girls. She's not as young as she used to be."

Gen stuck her tongue out. "Speak for yourself, sis. I just did a double shift or I'd kick your butt in the Just Dance Wii marathon."

Lily jumped up and down. "Yes! I want to be your partner, Aunt Gen!"

"No, me!" Maria yelled.

Alexa pulled a sad face. "What about your mother? I can dance!"

The girls fell silent, looking guilty but not offering.

Nick laughed, snagging Alexa around the waist. "My money's on you, babe. I just think the girls enjoy a more modern dance than *Thriller*."

"What's wrong with Michael Jackson?" she demanded. "They need to know the classics."

The doorbell rang. Gen rolled to her feet. "Stay, I'll get it. Probably Lance and Gina, they're running late. We must've locked the door by mistake."

Maria shouted from the kitchen, "Can someone answer that?"

"I'm going!" She raced down the hall and flung open the door. "Forgot your key? What did—" She broke off and stared.

Wolfe.

A low whimper escaped her lips. He looked gorgeous. Sexy as hell. The navy crewneck with the Purity logo stretched over his lean muscles and highlighted the piercing blue of his eyes. Worn jeans rode low on his hips. The familiar lines of his face looked a bit weary, but her gaze greedily drank in the full line of his mouth, the slant of his brows, the sharp angle of his cheekbones. His jaw was clean, and the subtle scent of aftershave and soap drifted to her nostrils.

She gripped the knob, trying desperately to hang on to her sanity. "W-what are you doing here?" she whispered.

"I came to talk to you."

"My family's here. I told you not to do this to me." She clamped down hard on her bottom lip to keep it from trembling. To keep her from saying she still loved him, wanted him, dreamed about him. "You have to go."

"Not until I say my piece."

Footsteps echoed behind her. "Is that Lance and Gina—oh! Wolfe, darling, come in, come in."

"Thanks."

Her mother overran her denials and allowed the man who had broken her daughter's heart inside her home. He stood awkwardly in the foyer, shoulders a bit slumped, sheer nervousness flickering over his face. What did he want? What could he possibly have to say to her after weeks of silence?

"Come in."

"No, I better stay here. I wanted to say a few things to Gen."

Uh-oh. She sensed a crowd gathering behind her, and when she glanced back, the scene confirmed her worst fears. Nick and Alexa peeked around the corner. Her father stood behind the group, a frown on his face. Her mother remained stock-still in the middle of them, as if waiting for something. Thank goodness Lily and Maria had gone to the basement to play Wii.

"I'll get out of your way," her mother said, turning.

"No. Stay." Gen's gaze flew to his. Determination and fear glimmered in blue depths. "There's some things I've needed to say to her for a long time. And since you're her family, and part of her life, I should say them to you, too."

Silence descended. The faint music from downstairs drifted up. No one seemed able to breathe, waiting for him to speak.

Gen's heart began to pound so hard she hovered on the edge of a panic attack. Sweat ran down her back. Why was he here? For another apology? Or for something else? Something she could only dream about?

When his eyes focused on her, everything else melted away.

"When you asked me to tell you my real feelings, I was too afraid. We'd been friends for so long, and it was safe, but over the past few months it became so much more. I fell in love with you. Every part. But I never felt worthy of you because of the things I've done in my past. So much shame. I convinced myself I was doing what was best for you, saving you from me and a future of hurt. But I was wrong, Gen. Finally, I know the truth."

He took a step toward her. She remained frozen, in the grip of his words, on the edge of a summit of so much beauty it took her breath away.

"I love you. I've always loved you. And I don't have to let the past define me or our future together. I may screw up and hurt you, but I have to try. If you'll have me. If you can forgive me for not being brave like you, and not taking the leap you deserve, I swear, I'll spend the rest of my life making it up to you."

Her mother sucked in her breath. Gen heard her sister sniffle in the distance.

Gen stood in front of the man she loved and opened her mouth to say yes.

And then he quietly pressed his wristbands into her hand.

The scarred, bruised flesh was naked to her gaze.

"No more hiding. I used to look at myself and wonder why I didn't die. But now I know. I was meant to find you, and Sawyer and Julietta. Mama Conte. All of you." He tilted his chin proudly. "And I want to be a part of this family, if you'll have me."

He'd given her the ultimate gift, one so precious and fragile she was afraid to move and break the spell.

Gen lifted her hands, reached out, and went into his arms.

Home.

His warmth and strength closed around her. She stood on tiptoe, kissing him, running her fingers over his cheeks while she whispered over and over, "I love you."

In minutes, her family was around him, offering him the support and openness that was part of their core. Alexa was already crying, and her mother hugged him, and Nick slapped him on the shoulder. When she finally managed to pull him inside, her father walked over.

"Dad," she warned, wrapping her arms around Wolfe's waist. "I love him."

Wolfe looked her father in the eye. "Jim, I—"

"No." Her father put out his hand. "I have something to say first. I was wrong." They waited while he seemed to gather his thoughts. "I told you to stay away because you'd hurt her. I said you were just like me." He shook his head. "I was only trying to protect her from something I have no right to keep her from. I may have made stupid mistakes, but if someone had taken Maria from me on that basis, I'd never have my family. I wouldn't have something worth fighting for, worth living for. So I was wrong. We all deserve a chance, and I hope you forgive me."

Wolfe reached out and shook his hand. "Already forgiven."

Gen's family drifted away, and it was just her and Wolfe. She couldn't stop touching him, leaning against his strength, and realizing he finally belonged to her.

"What changed your mind?" she asked softly.

Wolfe smiled. "Some very smart people who love me."

She laughed and kissed him. "I'm glad."

He kissed her back and wrapped her in his arms. "So am I."

epilogue

GEN LOOKED AROUND at the mess and sighed. She hated moving and packing, but it would be worth it. Haphazard piles of papers, boxes, and clothes lay everywhere. How did she have so much stuff in a bungalow?

"Gen? You here?"

"In the bedroom!" she shouted. Kate trudged through the door with a cup of coffee and Arilyn trailing behind. Gen jumped over the mattress and scrambled over. "Coffee! Oh, thank you, thank you!"

Kate laughed. Arilyn frowned. "I think you're addicted to caffeine. Tea has antioxidants and numerous health benefits. Maybe you should switch."

"I'll start tomorrow," she muttered, sinking her nose into the heavenly scent and breathing deep. "I need some sort of vice to get through packing."

"Well, we're here to help," Arilyn said briskly. Already her ruthlessly organized brain took in the mess with a positive energy. "I hope you're not rushing this on my account. Letting me rent your place is lifesaving. They actually found mold when they ripped out the pipes of my house." She shuddered. "Imagine what I've been breathing in with my poor animals?"

Gen squeezed her hand. "I'm so happy you can move

in. Wolfe and I need to be closer to the city for work, and this place is a bit tight, but I refuse to sell. It's too special."

Arilyn looked around and smiled. "Yes, it is. And you're sure it's okay to bring all the dogs?"

Gen laughed and scooped up a box. "Bring as many as you can fit. I lived with my sister Alexa, remember? She was always sneaking in hordes of animals from the shelter. According to Nick, she still does."

"I love your sister," Kate said. "Your whole family's coming to the wedding. We'll have a blast." She began stripping sheets off the bed and throwing them into the box in messy Kate style, when she paused, pulling something from underneath the mattress. "Hey, what's this?"

Gen turned. Kate held a piece of white ledger paper.

The love spell.

The memory of that night surged up. A little tipsy on margaritas, and feeling sad over her growing doubts about David, she'd urged Arilyn and Kennedy to complete a love spell from the little purple book Kate had given her. Where was that book? And what had she written?

"It's the spell," she whispered, snatching it from her friend's fingers. "I can't believe I forgot about this!"

"From the *Book of Spells*?" Kate screeched. "Arilyn, didn't you do one, too?"

Arilyn flushed. "Yeah, but I was really tipsy that night. I don't know where I put mine."

"Read it, Gen! Do the traits you listed match Wolfe?"

"That would be impossible." She skimmed the contents, remembering that the instructions clearly said to write a list of all the traits wanted in a man, make a copy, burn one in the fire, and put the other under the mattress. Mother Earth

or the universe was supposed to bring you the man you requested. Kate had sworn it worked for her and Slade. Also
with Kennedy and Nate. "I did the spell when I was engaged
to David, so the qualities probably . . ." She trailed off.

A chill crept down her spine. How odd. None of the
qualities listed were part of David's makeup, yet she clearly
remembered jotting down everything she dreamed of having in a soul mate.

She read the list aloud:

> *A deep friendship.*
> *Respect.*
> *A wicked sense of humor.*
> *Mind-blowing sex.*
> *A man with character.*
> *A man who believes in me no matter what my*
>   *choices are.*
> *Nonjudgmental.*
> *Not a perfectionist.*
> *A bit of a badass.*
> *One with faults just like me.*
> *A man willing to take risks.*

This list was about Wolfe.

"Oh my God, it worked, didn't it?" Kate asked.

Her fingers shook around the page. Impossible. Gen
looked up. Her friends stared. "This list is Wolfe. Not
David."

Arilyn shivered. "A coincidence? Right?"

Kate chewed on her lip. "Maybe. But we have one
more person to confirm the validity of the spell." Her gaze

shot to Arilyn. "You need to check if Yoga Man matches the traits you wrote down."

Arilyn's laugh seemed forced. "I'm not even sure where I put it. Look, this is silly. Let's stop talking about love spells and voodoo and get back to packing. I'll start out in the living room." She grabbed a box and disappeared through the door.

Kate and Gen exchanged a look. "She so has that list under her bed."

"Absolutely," Gen said. "We'll work on her later. Do you still have the book?"

Did she? Gen scoured her bookshelf and pulled out the violet book: *The Book of Spells*. No author was listed. "Here."

Kate put up her hands. "I don't want to touch it. Last time I got a shock. Just keep it here and we'll see what happens with A."

"Deal."

"Can I join in on this deal?" She looked up. Wolfe held out a cup of coffee and a bag from Swan Pastry, and grinned. "Caffeine anyone?"

Gen flew into his arms, jumping up and holding tight. Their mouths fused together, and her heart swelled so big and full she felt like her chest would burst. Slowly, he slid her back down to the ground. "I missed you."

"Me, too."

He winked. "Hi, Kate."

Kate's grin was big and infectious. "Hi, Wolfe."

"Thanks for helping us out."

"No problem. I'm so happy for you guys." She stepped close and threw her arms around both of them for a quick hug. "You're the bes—holy shit!"

Kate jerked back, her mouth open in a shocked little O,

and stumbled back, falling on her ass. She blinked up from the bedroom floor and glanced at her outstretched hands.

"Are you okay?" Gen jumped to help, but Wolfe had already scooped her back up. "What happened?"

"Don't come near me!"

Gen froze at her friend's command. Terror struck her, but then Kate burst into laughter so deep and joyous a frown came over her face. "If you don't tell me what's going on right now, I'm gonna freak."

Kate shook her head, still keeping her distance. "I'm sorry, didn't mean to scare you. I just s-s-saw a s-spider."

"Where?" Wolfe looked frantically back and forth. Gen gazed at her friend suspiciously.

"Oh, it's gone, don't worry about it." Kate waved her hand in the air as if dismissing the whole episode. "I gotta go. I'll be r-r-right back." They watched her climb over the bed in order to avoid walking past them and then pause at the doorway. "I'm s-s-so happy!"

She disappeared.

"What was that about?" Wolfe asked. "Do you see any spiders?"

"No, babe. And if I do, I'll kill them for you. It'll be in our marriage vows." She stared thoughtfully at the empty doorway where Kate had disappeared. Hmm. When Kate touched a couple meant to be together, she usually received an electrical shock. Was it possible she'd experienced the touch with her and Wolfe? Gen shook off the idea and swore she'd ask later.

He tugged on her curls and grinned. "Smart-ass." He looked around the bedroom. "Tell me the truth. Are you going to miss this place?"

She smiled. "Of course. It's the place where we fell in love. But Arilyn will take good care of it, and we'll make a new home. Our home."

"Yeah, our home." A frown marred his brow. "Speaking of homes, did you DVR *House Hunters*?"

She rolled her eyes. "We missed last night because it was already set up to tape *The Bachelor* at the same time. We can catch it on a rerun."

"That's it. We're getting two DVRs in the new place. And two remotes."

"Fine."

"And no more of those creepy twins. Property cousins or something? They're weird."

"*Property Brothers*. And they're hot! They'd be able to fix up this bungalow and make it a knockout."

"They're creepy and I'd never hire them. Besides, I love the bungalow just the way it is." He gestured to the crumbled paper in her hand. "What's that? Another to-do list?"

She looked down at the evidence of her love spell. If only he knew. She chucked it into the garbage and swore not to get spooked. Love spells didn't work. Anyway, who cared how things happened? All she knew was the love of her life was all hers, and they were building a future together.

"The best kind of list. I love you."

"Love you, too, sweetheart."

He bent down and kissed her again, and everything was . . . beautiful.

acknowledgments

SO MANY PEOPLE to thank . . . so little space!

A big hug and thank-you to my fave editor, Lauren McKenna. You were right about delaying Wolfe's book. The wait was so worth it!

Thanks to my agent, Kevan Lyon, for all her hard work.

Thanks to my dad for reminding me to write what I know, and telling me to change the setting to Saratoga Racetrack, one of the best places on earth. Our annual gambling outing is one of my favorite memories, and I hope it continues for a long time. Love you.

Cyber hugs to all my writing friends and conference buddies. A special shout-out to my Belles on Wheels Gallery bus sisters: Christina Lauren, Kristen Proby, Kresley Cole, S. C. Stephens, Alice Clayton, Kyra Davis, Emma Chase, Katy Evans, and our wonderful publicists, Kristin and Jules. Simply put, I made friends for life and had a hell of a good time doing it!

For my Probst Posse—the most rocking street team of all. Thanks for brainstorming and sharing this journey. I adore all of you.

To my family who puts up with me and the endless deadlines—I promise to cook next week! Really!

Finally, to my readers. You are the reason I do this. Thank you for reading my books.

Keep reading for an exclusive sneak peek of the fourth sizzling installment in the Searching For series,

searching for always

Coming summer 2015
from Gallery and Pocket Books!

prologue

OFFICER STONE PETTY was having a shit day.

It started with some type of brownout that killed his alarm and made him late. He despised tardiness in all forms and enjoyed a morning routine that set him up for the day. Hot, black coffee. Toast with butter, and real bacon. None of that turkey junk. Reading the paper, a quick shower, and taking his damn time.

Instead, he raced to get cleaned up and dressed, forced to skip everything and stuck with the horror that was called coffee in the station. Not even officially on duty, he'd been forced to stop a teenager speeding, dealing with his general mouthiness and hormonal idiocy that hadn't taught him yet not to talk back to people in authority.

After a few hours on his beat, a foul smell in his squad car drove him crazy. He finally pulled over, trying not to gag, and discovered a pile of dog crap buried in a paper bag in the trunk. Sons of bitches. It must've been a boring night at the station, since one of his coworkers had decided to liven things up by pulling the literal tiger's tail. He loved his job, but sometimes he wanted to beat the hell out of them all. Boredom was the worst crime in the police station, and drove the guys to entertain themselves. On a slow fall night in Verily, guess he'd been the victim.

Plotting his revenge, he got rid of the poop, decided to skip lunch, and proceeded to roll over a busted glass bottle and pierce his tire.

Stone realized the fates were against him today. He was desperately trying to quit smoking, but the thought of the sweet smoke filling his lungs killed him. He dragged in a breath and tried to concentrate on the nicotine patch on his arm, working overtime. He didn't need it. He was strong. He could beat the nasty habit, even though he loved it so hard, he'd pick smoking over anything else.

Finally, the awful craving eased. Good. His best bet was to just clock in enough time to get the day done, lie low, and try again tomorrow. He changed the tire, tearing a small hole in the knee of his uniform, and sweating profusely. It was one of those weird Indian summer days in October, and he'd worn his long sleeves today. Sweat trickled down his brow and under his arms, making him crave a shower. His temper frayed, but he held tight and swore to have patience. Anger got him in trouble every time. Like some kind of downhill roller coaster ride, it descended him into disaster. He was on a tight leash to begin with and needed to chill and ride out the rest of the day.

Calmly.

His partner had taken the morning off and should be hooking up with him within the hour. Devine always settled him with his easy humor. They worked well together, and long enough to call him his friend.

When he got back in the squad car, his speaker beeped.

"Car forty-three. Possible domestic abuse on Two Sycamore Street."

Stone reached for the radio. "Car forty-three en route."

"Backup is needed. Officer Devine on the way."

"Copy."

He eased onto the road and headed toward the house. Any type of domestic abuse required two officers on the scene, which he respected. Hell, it had always been his hot spot anyway, and they did very well with bad cop/good cop. With Devine's movie star looks, and his own rough appearance, everything balanced.

He drove past Main Street in Verily, enjoying the small town charm and sprawling river views. A bit eclectic and weird for him, with the crazy artists, cafés, and mass of organic food, clothing, and wellness centers, but Verily called to him in some strange way. He always wondered what it would feel like to be one of those people. Centered. Calm. Happy.

He dealt with such intense emotions, and a dark brooding anger inside of him, that living in Verily was like stepping near the light.

Stone frowned at his sudden poetic thoughts and refocused. He'd reached Sycamore.

He pulled to the curb a few feet away and studied the scene. No nosy neighbors out, but it didn't mean people weren't watching from their windows. He checked his watch. Devine should arrive in a minute. Climbing out of the car, he strolled around the house, scanning for clues and straining his ears to catch any type of noise.

The white Victorian seemed a bit shambled. Peeling paint. Broken step. Sagging porch. The windows were dirty, but he noted a small vegetable garden on the side that was neat and weed-free. Someone had cared and maintained it well. A pink tricycle with streamers that had seen better days lay abandoned in the driveway. Was that crying? His muscles tensed.

"No!"

The female scream turned his blood cold. A crash echoed through one of the half-open windows, and a child joined in with the screaming.

"Bitch!"

Stone shot to the door. Knocked. "Police, open up."

Another crash. Stone grabbed his radio. "Officer entering premises at Two Sycamore. Still awaiting backup." No time to wait for Devine. Enough suspicion of bodily harm to break in.

He did.

The door was open so he shot through.

The scene before him was out of his worst nightmare.

A big, meaty guy dressed in jeans and bare chested beating the crap out of the woman, probably his wife. She was trapped in the corner, hands over her face to protect it while he punched her. Her screams punctured the air, but that wasn't what made him lose it.

It was the child.

A pretty girl, probably around five, sobbed and clutched her father's leg, begging him to stop hurting Mommy. Stone had almost reached him, ready to scoop up the girl so she was safe and get the asshole off his wife, but he was too late.

The guy paused in bashing his wife's face, turned, and picked up the child.

Then threw her across the room.

The girl hit the wall with a bang. Slumped to the floor in a crumpled pile of delicate bones. Her soft blond hair covered her face. She didn't move.

Things happened in slow motion. Stone had been through enough shit to know he needed to keep calm, get the medics, handle the situation, protect the unprotected. His training usually kicked in with no pause.

Instead, he was ripped to another time and place, and the haze of red swarmed his vision and his logic.

Stone grabbed the man in one fast motion. He got an impression of surprised bloodshot eyes, fingers clawing and trying to pry him off, and shrieks peppering the air.

He hit. And hit. And hit.

The man slumped to the ground, but Stone didn't stop. He punched with all his might, all his emotion and locked-up rage that came through to punish a monster who hurt defenseless women and liked it.

He didn't know how much time had passed before he was dragged off the guy. Ambulance alarms sounded in the air, and Devine was shaking him by the shoulders, saying his name over and over, trying to get him to focus and get back to the light. Medics rushed in, cries rang out, and when Stone Petty came to, he realized it was too late.

The damage had already been done.

Yeah. All in all, it was a shit day.

one

MARILYN MEADOWS LOOKED around the cheery bungalow that was now her new home. Boxes lay half-opened, clothes were stacked in piles, and her foster dogs, Lenny and Mike, were battling over her only pair of expensive shoes. Scarlet red. High heels. Strappy. She'd bought them last month to surprise her lover.

He'd been surprised all right. So had she when she caught him banging one of his yoga students.

The black-and-white rat terrier mixes tumbled over the floor in a challenge to see who'd make the first bite. With their floppy ears and white stripes dividing their faces, her new fosters were a bit too cute to live. They also got away with way too much because of their looks. She opened her mouth to discipline them, then shut it. Yes, it was bad for the puppies' training, but it felt kind of good to see them tear those heels apart. She'd never wear them again without that memory clocking her like a sucker punch. At least Lenny and Mike could have some rebellious fun.

The low hum of anger buzzing inside surprised her. She'd spent most of her days searching for peace, kindness, and harmony within the world. Last week, she would've announced to anyone she'd found that quiet place inside and had never been happier.

Not this week.

Arilyn held back a sigh and began hanging her clothes up. Organic cottons and linens wrinkled too easily, especially with no dryer. She smoothed her hand down the soft fabrics and lined them up neatly in the closet. At least her new place was sound. After discovering mold at her last rental, and weeks of dealing with bad electric and burst pipes, her friend Genevieve MacKenzie offered to let her rent the quirky bungalow. Thank goodness, Gen had found the love of her life and was now moving in with her soul mate, Wolfe. Even better, she had left an empty cottage to rent. It was situated close to Arilyn's job, and two doors down from her other friend Kate, who she worked with at Kinnections matchmaking agency.

She tried to concentrate on the positive spin of finding a great place, especially one that allowed her to take in foster dogs on a regular basis, but her usual attitude had taken a hit. Besides anger, depression threatened like a nasty rumble of thunder before a storm. Dammit, she was supposed to be in Cape May on a romantic getaway. She was supposed to be making love and finally working through the kinks in their relationship. She was supposed to be hearing those magic words after five years of an on-again, off-again affair.

You're the one.

Marriage. Maybe a family. Both of them teaching yoga together in his studio, on a quest for higher peace and satisfaction while they loved each other with open hearts and souls.

Her fingers clenched around her gauzy cream blouse.

Instead, she'd walked into that studio and watched her life crumble before her.

The woman bent over, hands on the floor, naked ass in the air. Her lover pounded her from behind, his long gorgeous dark hair streaming down his back, fingers gripped around her hips, driving in and out of her while she moaned and groaned, and he gave tiny grunts of satisfaction.

The woman screamed. He laughed darkly, lifted his hand, and smacked her naked ass. She yelped. Then he did it again, and again, until her rear turned red and she was coming and screaming . . .

Arilyn turned from the closet and pushed her clenched fists against her eyes. The image burned like acid.

He'd never made love to her that way, with a violent, dirty need combined with lust. With her, he practiced tantric sex, a slow-moving, spiritual, gentle swell of need that climbed gradually. Their lovemaking took place in many locations, but it was always completely controlled, quiet, deeply satisfying. He worshipped her body with his. Never bent it to his will or ripped crazy orgasms from her.

She'd never forget his face. So deeply satisfied, like he was surrendering in a way he never could with her. Was this what he'd wanted the whole time? Had he believed she couldn't handle his sexual desires? The almost violent, possessive, hungry primal instincts inside him?

Fighting a shudder, she began to unpack her crystals and meditation supplies. How long had she made excuses for his inability to truly commit to her? Yes, he revered his privacy and followed a spiritual path without conventions, societal role plays, and sexual expectations. That was what she'd loved about him. They viewed the world similarly and wanted to make a difference. He was a workaholic, but in a good way. Always driven to help others in their journey. Another reason he was afraid to commit to a long-term relationship. He feared she'd become demanding and force him to quit his beloved career.

But after years of being hidden in the background, while he refused to meet her friends or family, and conducted their affair after hours and in secret like a torrid affair, she'd finally given him the ultimatum. The idea that no one ever uttered his first name faded from being a thrilling secret to a quiet humiliation.

Thirty approached. She craved permanence and a chance to have a family. Was that too much to ask? She didn't want to pigeonhole him, only to grow and change by his side. After his first indiscretion, she forced herself to trust him again. After all, he apologized, confessing his fear that love would overpower his spiritual path. He promised never to cheat again. As the in-house counselor at Kinnections matchmaking agency, Arilyn advised clients many times that a relationship couldn't work halfway, so she forgave.

Things finally changed. They'd been happy for a few months, and he even agreed to meet her family.

Humiliation cut through her. The fire crystal shook in her hands. She breathed deep and tried to absorb the healing powers meant to relieve sharp anxiety and induce calm. Stupid. His face when she opened the door haunted her.

Those gorgeous dark eyes widened with shock. Her gaze swept over his beloved face, taking in the high brow bone, long, sharp nose, square jaw. He stared at her, not moving, not speaking, while the silence beat around them in angry waves of energy.

"Arilyn."

Her name on his lips made her shudder. The musical, lilting quality of his timbre usually hypnotized her, whether in yoga class or the bedroom. The hurt rolled over her in waves, and she longed to curl up in a ball in her bed and try to make sense of it. Instead, she just stood there like an idiot, waiting for him to say something.

"I'm sorry, Arilyn." His voice deepened with grief and regret. His eyes filled with sadness. "I broke my promise. My body is weak, but my heart still beats for you. It always will. You must find a way to forgive me."

No. For the rest of her life, she'd remember him grunting and coming in another woman's body. And for the first time in five years, the box deep inside of her finally locked. She'd never let him back into her heart or life again. She'd closed the box many, many times before, but never locked it.

A tiny click echoed in her ears like a gunshot.

It was finally over.

Her heart withered in her chest, drying up any tears that she might have shed. All that was left was a shell and a burning emptiness she'd never get over.

Arilyn studied the man she'd loved for the last time. Her voice came out like a winter's storm. Cold. Brutal.

Dead.

"It's over. Don't call, text, or contact me ever again."

Arilyn placed an amethyst stone next to the fire and began setting up her meditation corner. Lenny and Mike collapsed on the wooden floor, temporarily exhausted and exhilarated. Pieces of red straps and a chewed heel lay around them in destructive glory. She envied them. Her emotions bubbled beneath the surface worse than a witches' brew. Maybe a grueling session of ashtanga yoga would help her sweat out some of the mess. Arilyn studied the crystals before her and plucked the dark red stone from its perch. Definitely garnet. Used for balancing over-emotional states and stuck anger.

She twisted it onto the cord and slipped it over her neck. Maybe work was the key. Keep busy. Two weeks had passed for a solid grieving period, and now it was time to focus. She needed to get the cottage in order, plant her herb garden, run the dog shelter fund-raiser, and work on the new computer program for Kinnections. Since she quit her ex-lover's yoga studio, students had been asking her when she'd be teaching on her own. Maybe she'd rent the firehouse and give classes there. No reason for her own students to suffer just because she refused to set foot in the Chakras yoga studio.

She placed the fat purple cushion in the center of the woven mat and set up the variety of candles around her spot. Two wide bamboo screens kept it private from on-lookers and the pups. The incense sticks went up on the cir-cular table, since Lenny seemed to like them better than the organic treats she regularly purchased. Nothing like pooping out incense. That had been a fun vet visit.

Finally, her sacred spot was complete. Her stack of meditation CDs lay next to her ancient stereo, but she dis-liked wearing pods or headphones when she meditated. Arilyn rolled to her feet and grabbed some matches and the bunch of dried sage she'd brought with her. Final task before making dinner. Each time she set up residence in a new place, she cleared all the old energy to start fresh.

God knows she needed a new slate.

Her throat tightened as she began to light the sage. All of her best friends were now in strong, healthy relationships leading to marriage. As the final single of the bunch, her heart squeezed with envy. When was it her turn? She'd worked so hard in all aspects of her life to be a good person, to open herself to love, to become spiritually sound, to engage in a relationship that would bring her joy. Dammit, while others squandered their time partying, being selfish, and giving in to their ids, she did the hard work trying to transform herself. She did everything . . . right.

Right?

Guess not. She'd wasted the best years of her life stuck with a man who consistently lied and manipulated in the name of soul-searching. How could she have been so far off with her instincts? Was she just a chump after all? Was she even worthy of the kind of love she dreamed of, the kind that her friends had found?

She blinked furiously to clear her vision. Stop. She was being whiny and ridiculous. She had a great, satisfying life filled with goals and surrounded by plenty of people who loved her. Arilyn lifted the bunch of sage in the air, closed her eyes, and envisioned a home filled with love, peace, and light. The smoke trickled in thin wisps as she moved from room to room, including the closet and bathroom, paying particular attention to the bedroom and kitchen where most intense emotions were expressed.

Finally, the cottage was properly cleansed. She blew out the flame, moved the small pots containing her herbs to the windowsill for proper light, and grabbed the bottle of celebratory wine in the refrigerator. She deserved alcohol tonight. It would go nicely with her veggie burger and steamed edamame. First, she'd complete her asanas, do some pranayama, and then eat. Tomorrow, things would look better and she'd feel stronger. Peaceful. Back in control.

Arilyn was sure of it.

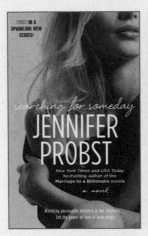
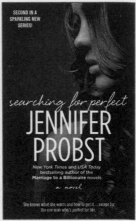
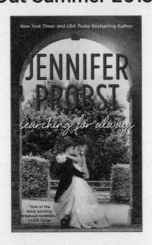